S★NG
— FOR A —
COWBOY

SASHA
SUMMERS

sourcebooks
casablanca

Published by Sourcebooks Casablanca, an imprint of Sourcebooks
P.O. Box 4410, Naperville, Illinois 60567-4410
(630) 961-3900
sourcebooks.com

Printed and bound in Canada.
MBP 10 9 8 7 6 5 4 3 2 1

Dedicated to my sister, Samantha!
From her unwavering faith, generous heart, and absolute support
to her ability to make me laugh—no matter what.
You are a blessing! I love you, Sissy!

Chapter 1

"OPEN, DAMMIT!" EMMY LOU PUSHED THE BUTTON AGAIN, smacking the pink-and-white polka-dot umbrella against her thigh. It still wouldn't open. The sky rumbled overhead.

"Ooh, language, Emmy." Her twin sister, Krystal, laughed. "Next you'll be saying shit or ass or fu—"

"No, I won't." Emmy spoke into the mic on the earbuds she had plugged into her left ear, her sister still laughing. "But this might be a little easier if I wasn't FaceTiming you right now." Umbrella in one hand, phone in the other, she started walking.

Krystal held her phone closer, flipping her lower lip for a full-on pout. "But I miss you."

"I miss you, too," Emmy said, blinking raindrops from her lashes. "Enough to walk through a parking lot, in the rain, with an umbrella that won't open, *and* keep talking to you." She kept pressing the button on the handle, but it didn't help. Of course, the rain was falling faster now, big, pelting drops.

"Where is Sawyer? Why isn't our bulky, scowling bodyguard carrying a massive bulletproof umbrella over your head?" There was a hint of accusation in her sister's voice.

"Be nice to Sawyer." Emmy wiped the rain from her eyes. "He is picking up Travis down the road—because our brother ran out of gas." She sighed, clicking the button on her umbrella again. "And I'm getting soaked because this thing is broken. I should hang up." Emmy laughed, peering at the stadium through the rain. Rain that was getting heavier and faster.

"But you won't." Krystal leaned forward. "Then again…you are starting to look like a wet rat. Walk faster."

Emmy stuck her tongue out at her sister, her steps quickening. She was sort of jogging now, weaving around the parked cars.

The squeal of brakes had her jumping a good ten feet in the air. A truck, going way too fast in a parking lot—in a torrential downpour—skidded to a stop mere inches from where she stood. It happened too fast for her to move. Too fast to do anything but curl in on herself, dropping her umbrella and holding her other hand, and phone, out to protect herself. Which, considering the vehicle was massive and she was not, didn't make any sense but… it was instinctual. She braced herself on the truck hood, her knees knocking so hard there was a high likelihood she'd collapse onto the slick concrete at any moment.

"Holy shit," Krystal was saying, the phone now facedown on the hood. "Emmy! Emmy? Can you hear me? Are you okay? Answer me."

She could have been hit… Almost was. *But wasn't.* Emmy flipped the phone over. "Here." But she was gasping for breath. Her heart pumped madly, reaching what had to be the maximum beats per minute. "Fine."

She was vaguely aware of the truck's driver's-side door opening wide, followed by rapid footsteps splashing in newly formed puddles. But she was still grappling with the whole near-death experience and couldn't process the arrival of her almost assailant.

"Where is the driver? Are they getting out? Hold your phone up," Krystal growled. "I want to see what this asshole has to say about nearly running you over."

"Are you okay?" said the mountain of a man heading her way.

"I'm fine," she answered, rubbing water from her eyes. Her hand shook. Her voice shook. But she *was* okay.

"You didn't see me coming?" he asked, stepping closer. "My truck?"

"Seriously, Emmy Lou, hold up the phone," Krystal snapped. "You couldn't see *her*? In her bright-yellow-and-pink, daisy-covered raincoat. Because, honestly, she might as well be wrapped, head-to-toe, in reflective tape. Asshole."

"Krystal," Emmy whispered into the mic hanging from her earpiece.

"Hold up the phone. You might need a witness." Krystal sighed. "Emmy Lou, I'm serious."

Emmy held up the phone, unable to stop trembling.

The man came around the hood of the truck and stopped. His eyes widened and his mouth opened, but he didn't say anything. Shock probably. Complete and total shock. Not just because he'd almost turned her into a smudge in the stadium parking lot, but because he was who he was and she was who she was and they were standing face-to-face...staring, at each other, in the rain...

"Brock?" Krystal sounded just as stunned. "Is that Brock? Is that you?"

No, there was no way that was possible. Emmy was not equipped for this. Not right now. Not in the least. She should be; it had been years. *Years.* This shouldn't be a big deal. Seeing him, that is. Being almost run over by him—by anyone—*was* sort of a big deal.

"Hey." Brock nodded, barely glancing at Emmy's phone and Krystal. His gaze was pinned on her.

"I'm..." Her voice broke. She was what? "I..." No better. *Just stop. Pull it together.* This was silly. "Hi." She forced a smile. "So..." She could do this. Talk. Breathe. *In and out.* Easier said than done.

His mouth opened, then closed and the muscle in his jaw clenched tight. The staring continued. He just stood there, rigid, wearing an odd expression on his face. A face that, all weirdness and near-death experiences aside, she knew well. *All too well.*

Adrenaline was kicking in now. Enough to get her moving, anyway. And that's exactly what she was going to do. Move. Away. The sooner the better. "Okay." She hung up her phone, shoved it into her pocket, and started walking—*do not run*—toward the stadium door. No looking back. Just moving forward.

Did she almost slip? Yes. Did she go down? No. Had she managed to save a shred of dignity? Probably not. She pulled the door
wide, stopping just inside to scan the signs and arrows for the
bathroom. Her phone started ringing. She didn't have to look at
it to know it was Krystal. She waited until she'd closed and locked
the door on the family restroom before she answered.

"Emmy?" Krystal asked. "Are you okay?"

"I didn't get hit—"

"I know, I know but…it was Brock."

Yes. Brock. She shrugged out of her raincoat and sat in the chair
placed next to the diaper-changing station. Her pulse was still
way too fast, and her stomach was all twisted up. "I know." Sitting
wasn't good. She stood, smoothing her pale blue blouse and staring down at her jeans. Her raincoat had left a perfect line midthigh.
Above the line, slightly damp. Below the line, saturated. She wig-
gled her toes in her rainboots, water squishing.

"This sucks." Krystal cleared her throat. "I wish I were there."

"I do, too." She stared at her reflection. "But I know what you'd
do if you were here."

"I'm not so sure."

"You'd remind me that I already spent too many years and too
many tears on him." Which was true. Their breakup—rather, his
sudden and complete disappearance from her life—had almost
broken her. She'd cried until she was sick, and Krystal knew it,
too. Krystal was the one who pushed her to get up, to keep going,
every day. Krystal was the one who told her it was okay to be angry
with him for deserting her without a word. And when Emmy Lou
was more herself, Krystal had turned all the tears and sadness and
anger into their double-platinum single "Your Loss." "And you'd
be right."

"True." Krystal paused. "But after I was done telling you all
that, I'd get up in his face and chew him out for almost running
you over. And that's just to start."

Emmy smiled, using toilet paper to dab away the smeared makeup from her eyes. "I'm sure you would."

"Then I'd tell him to stay the hell away from you," she snapped. "Like *away* away from you. And I'd tell Sawyer to punch him in the face. Or the gut. Or wherever it would hurt the most. I'd leave it up to Sawyer to decide—he'd probably know."

Brock had made a habit of staying away from her, so that wouldn't be a problem. Starting six years ago—when she'd still been sending letters to him, begging him to tell her why he was suddenly cutting her so completely out of his life. She covered her face with her hands, her stomach knotted and aching. *Humiliating, pathetic letters.* They should have been burned, not mailed.

"Emmy Lou. Is there anything I can do?" Krystal sighed. "I mean, besides booking a flight home—which I will do as soon as we get off the phone—"

"You will not." She sighed. "You and Jace are coming home in a week, right? I'll be more upset about you two cutting your vacation short than running into Brock." Which was mostly true. "I'm not going to fall apart. I'm not. Okay, he's here. Now I know. The chances of us running into each other again are slim. Promise me you won't come home. Finish your vacation."

Krystal sighed. "Where is Daddy, anyway? Why isn't he with you?"

"He and Momma had a therapy session this morning—I didn't want to get in the way of that. Besides, I had Sawyer. Well, until Travis called. I'm fine." She tugged the band from her hair and twisted, wringing out the water. "You're right. I do look like a drowned rat."

"Whatever. You're you, Emmy. All you have to do is walk into a room and the clouds part and angels sing."

Emmy laughed. "I can't believe you just said that."

"But you're smiling now," Krystal said. "And it's true." Krystal whispered something but the words were muffled. "Jace is here." There was smile in her voice.

"I'll let you go, then." Emmy put her bag on the counter. "Tell Jace I said hi, okay?"

"He says hi. And he will so kick Brock's ass if he needs to." There was a pause. "No, you don't know him… Yes, the football player… *That* Brock." Another pause. "He said he would totally kick his ass."

Emmy shook her head, but she was smiling. "I'm pretty sure that won't be necessary. But I appreciate the offer. Love you."

"You, too, sissy." Krystal made a kiss sound. "Talk later."

"Okay." She dug through her bag, pulling out her brush and makeup bag. Her momma would have a fit if she saw the state of her daughter. CiCi King was all about a woman looking her best—at all times. "Best might be pushing it." But that didn't stop her from attempting damage control.

Besides, she needed to remember why she was here. Her sweet daddy had found a way to work on a cause she believed in without interfering with the Three Kings' upcoming tour. She was the new face and voice of the American Football League. She'd sing their intro anthem, do some PR for the organization, and participate in a couple of the larger American Football League's Drug Free Like Me events. The charity program raised funds for drug addiction prevention, treatment, and recovery programs as well as outreach education in schools and sports camps. Between her millions of fans and followers and the several millions more football devotees, this was her chance to do something that mattered.

Little things like squishy socks, limp hair, or running into the boy—man—who'd crushed her hopes and dreams and heart didn't really matter.

———

"Don't you dare get water on my wood floors, Brock Nathaniel Watson." Aunt Mo's voice carried all the way down the hall from the kitchen.

Brock stepped back outside the front door, tugged off his worn-to-perfection leather boots, and left them on the ranch house's massive wraparound porch. His socks were just as saturated. With a sigh, he tugged them off and rolled up the cuffs of his jeans. The damn rain continued to pour down, thick sheets hammering the roof and ground with surprising force. A crack of thunder split the air and rolled across the grey-black sky.

A flash of Emmy Lou, wide-eyed and shaking, with rain dripping off her nose and chin, rushed in on him. Again. He couldn't shake it—shake her.

She'd been scared stiff. For good damn reason. If his brakes had locked up? His truck had skidded? The crushing pressure against his chest had him sucking in a deep breath, his eyes narrowing as he peered out into the storm. She was okay. Shaken, sure.

Hell, he was damn near in shock. She was the last person he'd expected to see. And this? Well, running her over wasn't exactly the sort of reunion he'd imagined.

Not that he'd spent much time thinking about her. That—she— was ancient history. Once the shock of losing her had worn off, anger had kicked in. He'd welcomed it—until it had all but consumed him. Then…that's when he'd hit rock bottom. Pulling himself together had meant shutting out destructive tendencies. Emmy, and the slew of emotions and thoughts she stirred up in him, had fallen into that category. After he'd learned his triggers and boxed them up tight, he'd closed that damn lid and never opened it again.

Until now… Well, this morning had been a surprise. More like a shock. A one-time fluke. Nothing more.

Her band, Three Kings, was probably doing some concert or something. Football wasn't the only thing that happened at the stadium, he knew that. But in the six years he'd been playing for the Houston Roughnecks, he'd never run into a single performer.

Of course, it would have to be Emmy,

Then again, he was normally in Houston. But their stadium was in the middle of some multimillion-dollar renovation, so the team would be spending most of the season here in Austin. His hometown. Emmy Lou King's hometown.

"You coming in?" Aunt Mo's voice jolted him back to the present. He stepped inside, pulling the door shut behind him.

"Your shoes out front?" Aunt Mo called out, the steady beat of her footsteps coming down the hall. The moment she saw him, she shook her head. "Look at you, Brock. Did you swim here? Go on, find something dry to wear before you catch pneumonia."

"Not just worried about your floors after all?" He grinned.

She rolled her eyes and offered up her cheek. "Don't you give me any sass, young man. You give me a kiss and get yourself changed for lunch."

"Yes, ma'am." He kissed her cheek, headed down the hall to his old room, and closed the door behind him.

"I made you some brisket to take home. And some meatloaf." She was on the other side of his door. "I remember you said the boys liked my oatmeal cookies, so I made five dozen for you to share."

He tugged off his wet clothes, shaking his head. "I'll take them to training, Aunt Mo." She was always baking things for the team; it was her way of "making sure those boys had some old-fashioned cooking to remind them of home." That was Aunt Mo. As soon as training, preseason, and games dates were posted, she knew. Her large print calendar was marked up with a rainbow of permanent marker ink. Aunt Mo never missed one of his games. She was a die-hard football fan. No, she was his fan, and it meant the world to him.

"Good." She paused. "And if there's any left over, you can share with them Connie."

He didn't have the heart to tell Aunt Mo his agent was a vegan. And a health fanatic. He'd only ever seen Connie eat salad. Without dressing.

"Connie could use a cookie or two. She's all skin and bones. You tell her to send Trish over here so I can teach her partner how to cook."

"I'll tell her." He chuckled, tugging on some jeans, socks, and boots, and pulling on one of the starched button-up shirts hanging in his closet. He ran a hand through his hair and pulled the door open. "Better?"

"It is." She hooked her arm through his. "Come on and eat. I'm guessing you didn't have a proper breakfast?"

He'd told her most of his meals were prepared for him by his trainer—something she'd clicked her tongue over. But it took a hell of a lot of effort, and about nine thousand calories a day, to stay in peak shape. Being six five and almost three hundred pounds of muscle wasn't easy. "I ate." At six a.m., he'd consumed five eggs, oatmeal, wheat toast with peanut butter and honey, an apple, and a banana. At eight a.m., he'd eaten near as much. Six meals a day, every day. All a necessary part of his fitness regimen.

"Not enough, I'm sure." Aunt Mo patted his forearm. "Sit yourself down and tell me what's what."

This was his Wednesday routine. Most Wednesdays, he'd fly his Cessna 350 from wherever he was to Austin, then make the drive to the family ranch. At eleven thirty sharp, Aunt Mo had lunch waiting. Some days, he brought some teammates along—and Aunt Mo loved that. She'd cluck over them all, remind them of their manners, make them clean their plates, and send them all off with a hug and invitation to come back anytime they liked. And since the team was in Austin for the time being, he suspected his teammates would be looking for an invitation sooner than later. That was Aunt Mo. When his mother had left them, it was Aunt Mo who had stepped up to take care of him and his father. She saw a need and she filled it, no questions asked.

"Anything new and exciting happening?" She started pulling serving dishes from the top oven and putting them on the hot pads placed all over her nice linen tablecloth. "I could use some excitement. Any word from the doctor?"

He shook his head. "No, ma'am." The likelihood of him starting the season on the bench was pretty high. And it frustrated the hell out of him. But a torn ACL could be a career-ending injury so, as hard as it was, he'd follow the doctor's orders.

"Well, now, that's fine." She was just as disappointed as he was—not that she'd let on.

"Things running smoothly out here?" After he'd signed his first contract, he'd spent a substantial portion on buying up the land surrounding his family's three-hundred-acre ranch—adding another nine hundred acres. Aunt Mo considered it wasteful. Brock considered it a smart investment.

"Why wouldn't they be?" she asked, frowning at him.

He grinned, shaking his head. Fair question, considering the crew he'd hired to manage the livestock and property knew what they were doing. Not to mention the two full-time security guards at the gate who also monitored the house and grounds at all times. Something else Aunt Mo didn't approve of. He shrugged. "Making small talk."

"When you should be eating." She sighed.

He peered into one cast-iron skillet. "Roasted sweet potatoes."

"Of course." She nodded. "You said you liked them."

"I do." He stood up and hugged her. "Thank you." Her hug had the instant grounding effect he needed. This morning, Emmy... Well, he was a fan of routines. The more predictable the better. You could set a clock by Aunt Mo. Predictable. And reliable. "Thank you." *Not just for the food.*

She wasn't the most affectionate person, but she gave him a quick, hard squeeze back before patting him and telling him, "Sit and eat now."

He took his time loading up his plate, waiting for her to make hers before picking up his fork. He scooped up some roasted sweet potatoes. "I almost ran over Emmy Lou King in the parking lot today."

Aunt Mo's eyes went round and she set her fork down. "What now?"

He swallowed and took a sip of tea. "She was there today. At the stadium. I was heading here."

"Brock." She placed her hand on his. "Land sakes, boy. What happened?" Her well-lined face creased with concern.

"Nothing." He shook his head. "I slammed on the brakes and stopped close enough for her to put her hands on the hood of the truck. I...I didn't see who it was."

Aunt Mo pressed both hands to her chest. "Oh my. Goodness."

"I got out and...it was Emmy." He cleared his throat, cut a large piece off the grilled chicken breast on his plate, and started chewing. It gave him time to get the lump out of his throat and the image of Emmy, wide-eyed and startled, out of his head.

"What did you do? She must have been in shock. Of course she was. What did you say?" Aunt Mo was watching him. "After you were done apologizing, I mean."

Had he apologized? Had he said a thing? Once he'd known it was her, he'd sort of blanked out. A damn fool, standing in the rain, staring at her like he'd just suffered a blow to the head.

"Brock?" Aunt Mo patted the back of his hand, the crease between her brows deepening.

"I'm not sure," he confessed. "We both stood there, getting soaked, and then she ran off." He shrugged, wondering why he'd decided to share this with Mo. The whole damn thing had a dream-like quality to it. But it was no dream. If it was, he wouldn't have her bright-pink-and-white polka-dot umbrella on his passenger seat.

"No wonder you're so out of sorts." Aunt Mo heaped more green bean casserole on his plate. "I can always tell when something's gnawing on your insides."

"You can?"

Her brows shot up. "Yes, I *can*."

"Better share, Aunt Mo. Don't want to be giving anything away to an opposing team."

With a nod of her head, she said, "You don't do it on the field. You couldn't—not and still catch the ball." She shook her head, cutting her chicken into tiny bites. "It's getting cold." She pointed at his plate with her fork.

Now he *was* curious. And she knew it. "Aunt Mo?" There was no hiding the exasperation in his voice.

She chuckled. "This." She held her hand up, rubbing the pad of her thumb back and forth along the tip of each finger. "You do that, over and over, when something is weighing on you."

He stared at his hands. Did he? If so, he never realized it.

"Only your left hand," she added. "Now eat. I figured you'd be seeing her now that she's signed on with the AFL. Time that little songbird had some good news. Especially with everything her family has been through the last year, poor little dear."

Aunt Mo had a huge soft spot for Emmy Lou. And since she was an avid reader of tabloid and entertainment magazines, she stayed on top of the King family drama. He'd tried to explain that most of what was said or written was probably twisted or straight-out fiction, but Mo tended to hold on to things that she determined were truthful.

Unfortunately, a lot of what happened the last year had been real. And horrible. A few years ago, he would have been there to support the Kings. He'd been pissed as hell when the media tried to dismiss Krystal King's sexual abuse allegations against a music industry legend as an attention-seeking ploy or out-and-out lie. The truth came out, of course. And other women came forward with similar claims, ensuring this asshole, Tig Whitman, would face real legal consequences for what he'd done. It was something—but not enough to heal the wounds he'd caused these women. Even Brock knew that.

"Emmy always was a football fan." Aunt Mo glanced his way. "Once you'd explained it to her."

He didn't want to think about that. But if Aunt Mo was right… *No. Probably just some gossip magazine headline.* "I thought that was just a rumor." He'd hoped like hell it was a rumor.

"What now?" Aunt Mo asked, a fork full of salad paused halfway to her mouth.

"Emmy Lou. Signing on to sing the AFL theme."

"It was." She nodded. "Until yesterday. There was a nice blurb on the news, showed her shaking hands with the league commissioner. All that. It's a done deal now." She smiled. "Now I'll get to see two of my favorite people doing what they love on the same night."

He gulped down his tea. *Not a problem.* Over the last few years, each AFL theme performer only attended a handful of games to sing live. What were the odds she'd be at one of his games? Slim, he hoped.

"Maybe you'll be in the opening song video? You know how they always film one of those fancy music bits to open the games? Make it all exciting, get folks pumped up." Aunt Mo put another chicken breast on his plate.

They normally only picked top players for the game lead-in video—the players who brought in the fans and the dollars. And while he was hell-bent and determined to get back on top, training harder than ever, he doubted he'd be on the short list this time.

Never waver. Never give up. Fight. With everything you have. Fight. How many times had his father kept him focused in high school? In college? He'd been right; his dad usually was. Brock could do this, show them; he was still the best damn defensive end in the league. He might be twenty-seven, but he had a couple more seasons in him.

Besides, he owed it to his team to give it his all. Even when he'd let them down, they'd stuck by him. First with his careless injury, then his damn pain med addiction and accident, and his mess of a divorce from Vanessa. Still, they'd been there for him. Believed in him. Now it was his turn to show them they'd made the right decision.

"You're doing it again," Aunt Mo said, nodding at his left hand.

He flexed his left hand. "I think you're seeing things."

"I see *you*, not eating what's on your plate." She was all feisty now. "You know the rules at my table—"

"You eat what's on your plate." He nodded. "Might be easier if you didn't keep sneaking things onto my plate." Once his plate was empty, he sat back and smiled. "Better?"

"I'll make up a quick plate, and we'll go." She nodded. "Anything left will be going home with you."

He started pulling out plastic containers and storing the leftovers away while Aunt Mo dished up small servings into a partitioned plate. She snapped a lid on and surveyed the less-than-clean kitchen. "Well, this will give me something to do when we get back."

"I'll help." He always did.

She nodded, collecting her house key and locking up behind him. "Spoke to the nurse earlier and she said he's having a good day today. Working on a puzzle and talking."

Brock didn't say anything. He never knew who he'd meet when they reached Green Gardens Alzheimer's clinic. Sometimes it was his father, David Watson. Other times, it wasn't. Some days were better than others. Some, he'd like to forget ever happened. But every Wednesday, he and Aunt Mo went and stayed until visiting hours were over. Or his father wasn't fit for a visit. Mo always called ahead, to "test the waters." That way, they could prepare a bit. If that was possible.

"Still raining? I'll be." Aunt Mo clicked her tongue as she peered out the front door again. "Umbrella's in the closet there."

Once it was retrieved and the house was locked up, Brock

carried the umbrella high. He helped his aunt into his truck before hurrying around to the driver's door and climbing in.

"Is this yours?" Aunt Mo asked, holding up the pink-and-white umbrella.

He shook his head. "Emmy."

"I see." She smiled. "It looks like something she'd own. All bright and sunny. That girl is a walking ray of sunshine."

There was no denying that. Emmy Lou King had been the brightest part of his life. She'd believed in his dreams and loved him completely. Until she hadn't. And when she hadn't, when she was gone, he'd learned how dark life could get. His hands tightened on the steering wheel.

"I know things went upside down for you two, but if you do see her again, will you give her my best?" Aunt Mo turned the umbrella in her hand.

"I doubt I will, Aunt Mo." He cleared his throat. If anything, he'd go out of his way to make certain there wasn't the slightest chance of that happening. "But *if* I do, I will."

Chapter 2

"YOU'RE STRESSING ME OUT." EMMY'S BIG BROTHER, TRAVIS, peered over his sunglasses at her. "I don't get it."

"I'm not doing anything." She pressed her hands against her pink rhinestone daisy-detailed and custom-frayed designer jeans trying to still the tapping of her foot.

"Exactly. You're sitting there, not posting on Instagram or Twitter or wherever else you have nine hundred million people following your every move." He frowned. "You're all...out of it."

"Maybe *you're* stressing *me* out? Being all judgy and staring at me. I don't get why you're coming with me," she said. "I have Sawyer. He'll protect me." She waved at her bodyguard in the rear-view mirror. His slight nod was his only acknowledgment.

Sawyer was pretty stoic. A nice guy when he let his guard down. But he rarely let his guard down—he was the job.

"You could use a massage, Emmy Lou." Melanie, her personal assistant, sounded off from the front passenger seat. "You haven't had one in a while."

"Sign me up, too. See? I'm here for moral support. Also, you know, to get away from Momma." Travis's over-the-top pained expression almost made her laugh. Almost. When she didn't react, he leaned back against the seat and smothered a yawn with the back of his hand. "And, you know, to heckle you."

"Travis." She frowned at her brother.

"Kidding. Kidding." He pulled off his sunglasses and looked at her. "I know I'm not the most sensitive guy in the world."

Melanie turned around in her seat to stare at Travis.

Sawyer cleared his throat. Was he laughing? Sawyer? That

never happened. Okay, it happened. But not often enough. Emmy couldn't hold back her smile.

"Hey, man, I can hear you." Travis glared at the back of Sawyer's head, then scowled at Melanie. "Not cool. Either one of you."

Melanie—she and Sawyer seemed to have some sort of ongoing poker-face championship—turned around, resuming the constant clicking on her tablet.

"Talk about tense. Maybe you do need a massage." Emmy teased. "You were saying?"

"I'm saying you are my little sister. You haven't dated since you and Brock broke up. Meaning you haven't dated anyone else. Ever." He looked confused, running his fingers through his tousled, dirty-blond hair and blinking several times before he moved on. "Putting aside how bizarre that statement was, I don't want you to face this alone."

Emmy Lou took her brother's hand. "Thanks, Travis." She smiled. "Plus, I know Krystal probably threatened you. Big time."

"Oh yeah." He nodded. "Totally said she'll kick my ass if I don't go." His hand squeezed hers. "But she's in Australia, probably exploring Jace's land down under so—"

"Travis. Oh. Please." She pulled her hand away. "What is *wrong* with you?"

"Me?" He turned to stare at her. "Okay, Miss Self-Inflicted Abstinence for No Reason. You realize half the world wants to meet you? The other half wants to…*sleep* with you. By that I don't mean actual *sleep*. And you're asking me what's wrong with me? You live like…like a nun. My sister, the nun of country music. What's wrong with *me*?"

"Why does it always boil down to sex?" She crossed her arms and stared out the window.

"Because. Sex." Travis sighed. "Maybe if you'd had more of it, you'd get it."

She didn't say a word. There was no way, *no way*, she was going to discuss her sex life with her brother. Travis lived to tease and if he found out she hadn't ever actually had sex, she would never *ever* hear the end of it.

"Is there some sort of privacy window or partition we can roll up?" Melanie asked Sawyer, clearly frazzled by Travis's oversharing.

"Nope." Sawyer shook his head, his sigh saying oh so much.

"Whatever." Travis waved off their comments. "Here's a thought, Em: maybe it's been so long you've forgotten?" He added. "I mean you guys broke up, what, six years ago?" He shuddered. "Six *years*?"

"I should have brought my earbuds," Melanie muttered.

In the rearview mirror, Sawyer glanced into the back seat, expressionless.

"We're having a private conversation here. Between siblings. Siblings who share everything." Travis winked at her. "And I thought *you* were a prude," he added, his whisper loud enough for all to hear.

Prude was one way of putting it. Sad was more like it. Maybe there was something wrong with her. But no one else had ever held her interest like Brock. No one else had made her ache for him, feel so out of control and safe at the same time. The idea of casual sex made her nauseous. Something else her brother would probably give her grief over. Since it was clear the entire vehicle wanted this line of conversation to come to an end, she attempted a not-so-subtle diversion. "Travis…Dad said something about you singing with Becca Sinclair? At the International Music Billboard Awards?"

"Yeah, yeah…" He slid his sunglasses back on, his jaw tightening.

"I'm sensing you're less than excited?" Which was a surprise. Becca Sinclair was an up-and-coming performer who could only help Travis's career outside of the Three Kings. She and Krystal had both had the opportunity to sing outside their band—she assumed Travis would want that opportunity. But apparently, she'd assumed wrong. Or had she? "What's up?"

"There's no way I'm the first choice for that." He shrugged. "I feel...*weird* about it."

"Why would you say that?" She took his hand again, tugging until he was looking at her. "What, you're not talented enough? You have too many platinum albums to say differently. You're definitely not lacking in charisma. And—"

"I'm hot." He grinned.

"You are very *modest*." She smacked his arm. "Stop being negative. If they didn't want you, they wouldn't have asked."

"They would if Daddy asked." His grin tightened.

That was it. Not knowing if he was wanted or if they were just doing Hank King a favor. Her heart ached for him. She removed his sunglasses. "I think you should do it, Trav. You deserve some time in the spotlight. I want that for you."

Travis tried to hold his long-suffering expression in place. But it didn't work. He tugged her into a monster bear hug. "You're a good sister, you know that?"

She hugged him back. "Because I love you and believe in you?"

"Yeah, yeah." He let her go. "I know that can't be easy."

"Loving you and believing you?" She laughed. "It is so easy. You're my brother. And even though I worry that you're going to wind up with some horrible disease that will make your man parts rot off or you'll drink until your liver explodes, I love you dearly."

The horror on her brother's face had her laughing all over again.

Sawyer tried to cover his laugh with a fake cough.

Melanie didn't even try to hide it. Her high-pitched wheezing giggle wound up making them all laugh.

"Who said Krystal was the wordsmith in the family?" Travis leaned back against his seat, laughing—but still horrified.

"Hold it." Emmy Lou held her phone up and snapped a picture of her brother. "I will post that."

"Of course you will." He put his arm around her, pulled her close, and held her phone up for another picture. He was tickling her and trying to take it, so the picture was at an odd angle, but they were both smiling. "Post that."

"Fine." She did, adding hashtags like #siblinglove, #bigbrothers, #hedrivesmecrazy, and #boundaryissues. "Better?" she asked.

He grinned. "Now your fans won't worry something happened to you."

She shook her head and went back to staring out the window, her foot resuming its restless tapping against the floorboard of the black suburban.

She'd been so excited about this. Drug Free Like Me was such a great program for so many kids in need. She was still excited for the most part. But now that she knew who she'd be working with, there was also an element of…anxiety. Yes, today was only a photo shoot—something she'd done more times than she could remember—but this was a photo shoot with Brock. Brock, who was one of the main DFLM ambassadors. She was a professional. She could do this. *I got this.* But she was having a hard time convincing herself.

"Who else is doing this?" Travis asked. "This ambassadorship thing."

She pulled the folder from her bag and handed it to him.

"Or you could tell me." He took the folder.

"Leon Greene." She ticked off. "Linebacker for—"

"I know who Leon Greene is." Travis opened the folder. "He's sort of a legend. And…" He started flipping through the pages of the glossy folder the Drug Free Like Me marketing team had provided.

Emmy had made sure to do a little research on the players she'd be working with. Clay Reese was a wide receiver for the Green Bay Bears. He was ranked third in number of yards last season and, from online sound bites, a healthy dose of self-confidence.

"Aw man, Demetrius Mansfield? Tree-Man? No shit? He's the best. Untouchable. Still pisses me off he was traded to the Miami

Raiders." Travis shook his head. "Good guy. And Brock, too, huh? That's it? There aren't more of you?"

"The AFL supports a lot of different charities, but these are the players I'll be working with." Too bad she'd picked the one charity Brock was involved in.

"Momma's got to be thrilled." He snorted, flipping through the pages.

Emmy glanced at her brother, unwilling to voice her suspicions.

"Oh." Travis's eyes met hers and widened. "She doesn't know. If she did, she'd be here."

Emmy chewed her thumbnail, her stomach churning.

"My lips are sealed. I'm not opening that can of worms. But, you know, let me know when that little nugget will be shared so I can get a front-row seat." He hugged her again. "If it comes up, I mean."

"If you're trying to make me laugh, it's not working." She frowned.

"Right. Well, we're here." He shrugged. "So you can stop worrying about Momma and go back to worrying about Brock." He patted her knee, closed the DFLM folder, and slid it back into her black-and-white-striped bag.

Sawyer pulled into the parking lot outside of a large warehouse. He parked, opened their doors, and trailed behind them across the parking lot.

"Vitamin water." Melanie held out Emmy's bright-pink insulated thermos.

"Where's mine?" Travis asked.

Melanie didn't acknowledge the question.

Emmy grinned, peeking over her shoulder at Sawyer. He was scanning the parking lot, on alert. Since the whole nightmare of an attack on her sister, her father insisted Sawyer never leave her side. They'd always had security, but this was different. Before, their security guards— the Kings Guard—hung back and blended in.

Now, they were front and center and unmistakable. A warning to anyone who felt the need to come after a King.

If anyone needs a massage, it's Sawyer. But the idea of Sawyer relaxing on a table while a stranger touched him was ridiculous. She smiled at him as he held the door to the warehouse open for them. "Thanks, Sawyer."

His nod was slight, his blue-green gaze sweeping over the parking lot before following them inside. She'd always considered Sawyer a monster of a man...until she walked into a room with four professional football players. A wall of lights was set up, a large step-and-repeat hung—the Drug Free Like Me logo stamped at regular intervals—and a photographer was already snapping pictures.

Instead of scanning the room for Brock, she focused on the photo shoot in progress. Demetrius Mansfield posed, arms crossed and scowling at the camera. Encased in his uniform, it was impossible to miss just how massive the man was.

"Like a statue," Melanie whispered, her mouth hanging open. "I'll get some pics and video to post later."

Emmy nodded, the familiar chaos of the photo shoot oddly comforting.

"This is going to be a serious ding to my ego," Travis whispered in her ear.

Emmy laughed, tempted to point out that these men were professional athletes—their bodies were their business.

"You, too, man. Next to him, you're a slacker," Travis said to Sawyer. "Maybe we need to hit the gym?"

Sawyer glanced between the athletes and Travis. "How much time are you willing to put in?" A flicker of a smile, then it was gone.

"Harsh, man." Travis shook his head.

"Miss King. I'm Shalene Fowler." A woman in a Drug Free Like Me T-shirt and jeans hurried across the room, dodging the maze of cords and plugs as she went. "It's so nice to meet you. Really. I'm the marketing and event manager for the DFLM Foundation. I can't tell you how excited we are that you've decided to help with this year."

Emmy shook the woman's hand. "Thanks for having me, since I'm not a player and all."

"Well, you're the new voice for AFL, so that's pretty close. And if you're agreeable to it, we'd like to make you an honorary player. I know you're on a schedule, so we'll do this as quickly as possible." She smiled. "We have hair and makeup this way."

Emmy Lou followed Shalene to the mobile vanity in the back corner of the room.

"We have a jersey for each of the teams." She pointed at the clothing rack. "We tried to get the players to agree on one but, as you can see, that didn't go over well."

"Team loyalty, I guess." Emmy Lou smiled.

Once she'd donned the blue-and-grey jersey of the Miami Raiders and her hair and makeup was camera ready, she was ushered to the Drug Free Like Me step and repeat and Demetrius Mansfield.

"Miss King." Demetrius held out his hand. "Nice to meet you in person."

"Emmy, please." She stared up at him, shaking a hand that was bigger than her head. "Great to meet you. I'm a big fan. I—we—" She broke off, pointing at Travis. "We were all sad to lose you to Miami."

"Roughnecks fans?" he asked.

"Always." She smiled.

"Can't fault you there. Good team." He nodded. "Number three, huh?" He eyed her jersey.

"You know, Three Kings?" She glanced down at the large three on her jersey. "I guess you could say it's my lucky number."

He chuckled.

"Emmy, can you hold the football?" the photographer asked. "Can you hold it between your palms, like this? And scowl, like Demetrius?"

She glanced over her shoulder at Demetrius. "I don't think anyone can scowl like him."

Demetrius smiled, instantly changing everything about the man.

After the initial awkwardness faded, she started to enjoy herself. Demetrius was a gentleman. Leon was all business. Clay Reese was way too full of himself, but she had more than her fair share of dealing with self-inflated egos, so it was easy enough.

After…well, that left Brock.

Once she'd changed into the red-and-blue Roughnecks jersey and had her hair and makeup touched up, she stared into the mirror and gave herself a mental talk-down. This wasn't about her. This wasn't about Brock. Whatever past they had was ancient history. This was an important cause *now*. One she was proud to be part of. *You're a King. A professional.* Not a pathetic, lovesick teenager who got weak in the knees over Brock Watson. Head held high, she headed back to the step-and-repeat.

Brock was waiting.

Brock and his all-American poster-boy looks. Dimples. Blue eyes. Light brown, close-cropped hair. And, of course, that body. Which, according to *Men's Fitness Today*, included twenty-one-inch biceps. He stood, spinning the football in his hand, without a care in the world.

If Krystal were here right now, she'd be giving her the don't-let-them-see-they-got-to-you look. But Emmy had never learned the whole *whatever*, disinterest thing Krystal had mastered early on. Hopefully she wouldn't act flustered—and no one would hear the wild thump of her heart.

"Water?" Melanie asked, holding out the water bottle. "Emmy Lou?"

Emmy Lou faced her assistant. "Wishing Krystal were here."

"Right. Well, um, she sent me this." She held up her phone, cleared her throat, and read, "Ignore him, and remember he's a total dick. An asshat. And no one would blame you if you kicked him in the balls." Melanie's cheeks were dark red. "That's it."

"Sounds like Krystal." She was laughing; she couldn't help it. "Sorry about the language."

"She's right." Melanie leaned closer. "He's just some guy now."

Emmy Lou smiled and took a long sip of her vitamin water.

"Ready?" the photographer asked.

No. She nodded. *Smile.* "Totally." She'd smiled through much worse situations than this. *This* was nothing. So why did it feel like *something*?

———

He focused on the ball in his hands, turning it over and over. Not Emmy Lou...in a Roughnecks jersey, with her long, blond hair fluffed out, and her pink lips glossy. The ball stopped moving, his grip tightening until his fingers ached. Staring up into the lights overhead made it easier to ignore the increasing tension building at the base of his head. *Get it together.* He rolled his neck, shook out his arms, and glanced at the photographer—then beyond.

Demetrius was shaking hands with Travis, the two of them sharing a laugh before they both turned to look between him and Emmy Lou.

Brock frowned. The two of them together? Could be trouble.

In another life, Travis King had been one of his best friends. Travis had been a talker. When he wasn't talking, he was listening. A trait he'd likely picked up from his mother, the infamous CiCi King. Travis had had front-row seats to his and Emmy Lou's relationship. Hell, he'd probably known they were doomed from the start. Which was more than he could say for himself.

Demetrius had been his teammate for years. More importantly, they were friends. If he remembered correctly, he might have overshared some of his and Emmy Lou's history with Demetrius. Unintentionally. He still had gaps in his memory… He'd lost too much to the damn pills. Luckily, his friendship with Demetrius wasn't one of them.

The two of them, swapping stories? Not good. One more reason to hurry this whole thing up.

Travis King's gaze met his, narrowing slightly as he gave Brock a head-to-toe once-over. While it wasn't exactly friendly, he did give Brock a nod. Brock nodded in return. Demetrius only shook his head, pointing. At…Emmy Lou. Standing right beside him. Smiling. Ready for pictures.

"When all eyes are on her, she is in her element." CiCi King's words were just as clear today as they'd been all those years ago. "Emmy Lou King is a star. It's her whole life, who she is." The pure disdain, almost sympathy, on her face had said enough. "There's *nothing* she loves more than her fans—making them happy." She hadn't needed to tell him he was lumped into that *nothing*. "She always comes back to that—always puts that first. Keeping that spotlight zeroed in on her. No distractions." That's all he'd been. A distraction. Nothing more. That was what he needed to remember.

Remembering the electric current they'd had, the constant need to touch each other, the way she'd seemed to light up when he'd walked into a room… None of that was real. That was the shit he needed to forget. Yeah, for a blip of time, he'd been a shiny, new toy. But once she'd been done playing, he'd been discarded—without a word from her. That was the shit he needed to remember. That had been real. So were the wounds she'd left.

The minute her gaze met his, the pressure on his chest intensified, forcing the air from his lungs. He'd forgotten how green her eyes were. "Emmy Lou." He cleared his throat, looking for something else to say. "I brought your umbrella."

"Oh." Her voice high, breathy. "Thanks." She paused, her gaze falling from his. "It's broken."

He found himself staring down at the top of her head. She was smaller than he remembered, thinner. Maybe, if he forced himself to look at her, *really* look at her, he'd see she wasn't what he remembered. How could she be? There was a time she'd been near perfect to him. He'd made a damn fool of himself over her and lost her anyway. Lesson learned.

"Let's get you two back to back." The photographer made a spinning motion with his hand. "Can we get them both a ball?"

He tore his gaze from the top of her head and turned away from her, waiting.

"Move in." The photographer waved them closer. "You know, *back* to *back*?"

Condescending son of a bitch.

"I don't think we'll be back to back." Emmy spoke up. "He's a good foot taller than me. More like his shoulder to my, what, head?"

There was laughter from those watching.

The photographer did not. "Fine. That. Do that." A few clicks and he stood. "Good. Give me a minute."

"Someone needs more coffee." She said it under her breath, but he heard her.

He hadn't meant to react. But he did. He tried covering his chuckle with a forceful throat clearing. It didn't work. If it had, she wouldn't be staring up at him in surprise.

Her smile hadn't changed. She was still beautiful. On the outside, maybe. The inside? He shook his head, forcing his attention elsewhere. Anywhere else.

"How about we do something different?" The photographer was smiling now. "We found a few pictures from your homecoming game and dance. We want to re-create those. It's the sort of thing fans will go crazy over."

Not just no—hell no.

But he could hear Connie, his agent, in his head then: *Never pass up a chance to make your fans love you. They want to—so give them a reason.* He was pretty sure this was one of those times. Connie would eat this up. If he said no? Walked out? That wouldn't go over well.

If he'd learned one thing from the clusterfuck that had been the last couple of years of his life, it was to listen to Connie. More of his fall from grace had been public knowledge than he'd liked. But she had been there, putting out fires and shutting down stories before they made it to print. Without her, things could have been ten times worse. *Maybe more.*

The big endorsements he was up for? She'd busted her ass to get them for him. After all he'd put her through, he owed her. A hell of a lot. He owed her everything—including this. Was reliving high school memories with Emmy Lou a damn hard pill to swallow? Yes. Would he force the damn pill down? Yes, he would. Even if it choked him.

"Fine." The word erupted, hard and loud and making sure everyone in the room knew he wasn't happy about any of this.

"Great." Was it his imagination or did the asshole photographer look like he was enjoying himself? "Let's start with the traditional pose. You know, the *prom* pose? Brock, stand behind her. Emmy, back to his front. Brock, arms around her. And both of you facing me. You two can hold the football."

"Not to question the creative direction you're going with, but what does this have to do with football?" Travis King asked. "Or being drug free?"

Brock couldn't agree more, but his jaw was locked tight—to prevent him from saying a damn thing.

"We're trying to reach as many kids as possible, Mr. King." Shalene Fowler was all calm diplomacy. "Not all of the students we interact with are football fans. Some are Three Kings fans.

Even more are Emmy Lou King fans. Your sister is recognizable to ninety percent of the under eighteen crowd. Homecoming, school dances—they're part of the teenage experience. And teenagers are a large part of the at-risk population."

Which immediately made Brock feel like an ass. His childhood had been pretty golden. Even after his mother had left, he'd had his father and aunt and their unwavering support and love. He'd had every opportunity.

"We feel strongly that these *playful* pictures will gain a larger audience—and provide a more personal connection. Especially since they did go to homecoming together." Shalene paused, turning her focus to him and Emmy Lou. "Of course, if you two would rather not, we can skip them."

Skipping them would be his first choice. But after Shalene's explanation, he kept his jaw clenched and his lips pressed shut.

"That's why we're here." Emmy Lou didn't look at him. "Right?" She didn't wait for an answer. "Bring on the cheesy homecoming pose." And just like that, the tension in the room dissipated and they assumed their pose.

For the next five minutes, Brock ran plays in his head. Better to imagine tackling some self-righteous quarterback than acknowledging Emmy Lou in his arms, pressed against him. If he was reviewing runs and blocks, maybe he'd be less aware of her head—just below his chin—and the scent of her hair. Citrus? Grapefruit? Something like that. Light and fresh and all too familiar. Distracting as hell.

The camera kept clicking away.

He changed tactics, trying to remember the calendar updates he'd received from Connie this morning. A late-night television spot. An endorsement deal meeting with Alpha Menswear. Something about a date change for the DFLM kickoff event. Not that he could remember either date—the original or the new one. Especially now that the photographer's assistant had stepped up and rearranged their hands. Now Emmy's hands were covering his, which were holding the football.

More clicks and flashes and the slight pressure of her hands against his.

He smothered a sigh, his fingers digging into the roughened surface of the ball. The slight movement caused her fingers to slide between his, threading them together, and snapping some sort of mental tripwire. Flashes of memory assaulted him, rapid-fire and bittersweet. He and Emmy, the feel of her in his arms, the press of her hands on his bare back, the cling of her lips on his, the soft hitch in her breath when things got carried away between the two of them... She tossed her head, one of her long curls sliding slowly across his forearm and reminding him of all the things wrong with this whole damn photo shoot. His jaw was so tight it ached.

"I think that's good," the photographer said, staring at the screen next to him.

Brock dropped the ball and stepped back, needing space to breathe. Enough was enough. He really needed them to be done. Hands on hips, he stared at the photographer, doing his best to rein in his tension.

"One more shot, and I think we should have everything." The photographer nodded. "If you didn't like that one, you definitely won't like this one."

His attempt to control his expression must not have been very successful. Travis and Demetrius were laughing. The big guy in the black "King's Guard" shirt seemed ready to stiff-arm him out of the way. And the girl with the giant glasses and tablet was all owl-eyed and frozen. Not to mention the rest of the room. And then Travis was taking pictures on his phone, whispering something to Demetrius.

He didn't bother looking at Emmy. Chances are she'd seen how unhappy this whole setup was making him, too. No reason to apologize for it. He was a football player—not a celebrity. Since his "comeback," he'd gone out of his way to keep his personal life out of the media. Now, exploiting a memory he still treasured this way left a bitter taste in his mouth. Did he understand having Emmy Lou King involved was good for DFLM? Hell yes. *But* that didn't make this okay. And it sure didn't make the whole smile and proximity easy. *Hell no.*

"Maybe that's good." Shalene forced a smile. "As is."

"The label sent this one." The photographer straightened, staring at Shalene in disbelief. "And the DFLM director specifically requested it."

Brock ran a hand over his face. "Let's just do it." He ground out the words.

"You heard him." Emmy sounded legitimately fired up and ready to go. If she hadn't glanced his way, he'd have believed her. But she did and, for a split second, he felt like a bastard. "Let's do this."

He nodded, doing his best not to snap. "Yep," he managed. Time to step up his game.

The photographer was smiling from ear to ear, setting off all sorts of internal warning bells. "Sure. Good." He nodded. "You need to carry her, draped over your shoulder." He paused. "I'm sure you're both familiar with the original picture."

He knew *exactly* which photo. Aunt Mo had a whole photo collage dedicated to that game. Senior year. State playoffs. The win had been hard-won, and he'd been on an adrenaline high. When Emmy came barreling across the field to him, he'd lifted her up—a little too high. He hadn't intended to drape her over his shoulder, but he'd been laughing, and she'd been laughing, and he'd wound up carrying her off the field that way. Once they'd reached the tunnel leading to the locker rooms, he'd put her down and kissed her. Long enough to have left them both panting. Hard enough that she'd known how bad he wanted her. And sweet enough that she'd never doubt she was his whole world. He remembered it, all of it, like yesterday.

The photographer held up one finger. "We need a minute to adjust lighting."

He risked a glance her way.

She was rolling up onto her toes, tapping her fingers on her thighs—like she was playing an imaginary keyboard—nibbling on the inside of her lower lip. Which meant she was anxious. Her gaze shifted his way and she whispered, "You won't drop me?"

Damn her and her green eyes. His voice was low, gruff. "I won't drop you."

She stopped chewing on the inside of her lower lip and stared up at him. "That's a relief. If you did, I'm not sure I'd survive the fall." A slight smile grew. "You're like fifteen feet tall now."

Up close, it was hard to miss... She hadn't changed much. "Almost." The word was thick.

"Might need a ladder? I'm not sure I'll be able to get up there otherwise." Head cocked to one side, she seemed to be calculating her odds. All cute and perky and...familiar.

He sighed, running a hand along the back of his neck. "Pretty sure I bench more than double what you weigh." No, she hadn't changed. *Dammit.*

Her brows rose. "I guess that makes sense. You're like a human mountain." She pointed at the guy in the black "King's Guard" T-shirt. "Sawyer, my security guard, looks teeny-tiny next to you guys."

Sawyer continued to stare him down. Big or not, the man looked capable of handling himself in a jam. The question was, why did she need this Sawyer guy? "You always have security with you?" *Why do I care?*

She nodded, chewing on the inside of her lip again.

"We're ready." The photographer already had his camera up.

Emmy was staring up at him again. "So...how do we do *this*?" She rolled onto her tiptoes again.

He closed his eyes. "I'm picking you up..."

"Okay." She went rigid.

Was she breathing? He wrapped his hands around her waist and lifted her. She weighed next to nothing, even resting on his shoulder. Since she was draped over his shoulder, he was basically eye level with her butt. Not that he was complaining. It was a nice-looking butt. Always had been. Especially now, showcased in tight jeans—a pink glitter flower embroidered on the back, right pocket. Pink and glitter—something else that hadn't changed about Emmy Lou. He took a deep breath. "Let's both pretend that this isn't weird as shit."

"What's weird?" Emmy's laughter was nervous. "I mean, this is my preferred way of travel. I get carried around like this all the time."

Maybe it was his nerves, but he had to laugh then.

"Look this way." The photographer was snapping like crazy. "Good. Nice smiles."

He wasn't smiling—he was laughing. *Dammit.*

"I'm pretty sure this is one giant step back for the female empowerment movement," Travis King said, his opposition voided by the fact that he was taking pics or recording this mess with his phone. "Way back. Like dinosaurs and cavemen."

"Cavemen and dinosaurs didn't live at the same time, Travis," Emmy said, her hand pressing against his back. "Your muscles have muscles." Her fingers pressed against his back once— then again. "His muscles have muscles."

Demetrius clapped his hands once and burst out laughing. "That's a new one."

"I'm serious," Emmy continued, poking his back, then his side.

Which was a mistake. He was ticklish. Very ticklish. "Emmy." But her poking continued. He shifted, trying to stop her. The more she poked, the more he arched away from the poking. The more he arched, the closer she was to the edge of his shoulder. When she slid off, the poking ended—and he caught her easily.

"I'm sorry." Her hand rested against his chest. "I forgot."

Because she knew he was ticklish. It was how she used to tease him. He set her on her feet and stepped back, removing her hand and easing the pressure on his lungs.

"I think we're good here," the photographer said.

About damn time.

Emmy Lou headed toward the young woman with the glasses and tablet, taking a long sip from the pink water bottle she was offered. *More pink.* Of course. She might not know he was watching her, but her brother did. So did Demetrius. And Sawyer.

He ignored them all and stooped to pick up the ball from the ground. *Get a grip. It's over.*

"Thank you all so much," Shalene was saying, all smiles. "We'll get the pictures and marketing material to your publicists this week. We're going to change lives."

That was why he was here. This program was important to him. He'd worked hard to be free of the drug-induced haze that had taken over his life. Staying on track, to center himself and remember what was important in life, was a daily struggle. Photo shoots, marathons, auctions, and telethons were all ways to raise money for these programs. The more, the better. He'd barely survived his addiction and he'd had every available resource available to him. Unlike the kids he was trying to help. They were what mattered. Not staged, phony prom pictures, the laughter of his teammates, or the scent of Emmy Lou's shampoo.

Chapter 3

EMMY SANG THE NEW LYRICS SOFTLY. "AND ALL I KNOW IS HERE we go. Ooh-hoo. Back to the start, straight to my heart. Ooh-hoo-hoo—"

"And then I was thinking of some sort of…zippy kind of chorus?" Krystal said, leaning toward the computer screen. "You know, toe-tappable?"

"Is that a word?" Emmy asked, scanning over the music. "I can only see half of your face."

Krystal turned her computer. "Better? Okay. Now, focus." She was sitting cross-legged on her rumpled bed.

"I am." And what Emmy saw made her happy: her sister, caught up in the throes of creativity and getting back to the things she loved. Krystal deserved nothing but love and happiness. "And I like it." She paused. "Is it for me?"

"Uh, yes." Krystal's brows rose. "I mean, if you like it. You know it won't hurt my feelings if you don't."

Emmy shot her sister a *seriously?* look. "When have I ever not liked one of your songs?"

Krystal grinned. "There's always a first time for everything." She flipped her long hair over her shoulder and leaned back on the stack of pillows. "You're looking a little skinny, Em." Krystal stared at her. "Like, too skinny…"

Emmy shrugged. "I know you're seeing things." Maybe she had lost a few pounds, but she couldn't help it. "Stress."

Stress. As much as she loved her family, and she did, her childhood home was filled with constant tension. Since she was the peacekeeper, she did her best to defuse things—but she could only do so much. And Momma…well Momma wasn't making things easy.

From the house renovations to the constant back and forth about the new tour costumes, Momma had her hand in everything. *Everything.* From Emmy's wardrobe to her schedule, Momma weighed in. Diet was a big part of that. Every bite Emmy took, or didn't take, was followed up with one of Momma's *concerned* reminders about the dangers of stress eating and ways to stay trim. She meant well but…

Krystal sighed. "You know, you have to take care of yourself. And when I say take care of yourself that means eat." She frowned. "Promise me you won't…"

"I'm eating." Emmy Lou interrupted. Yes, there'd been a time when she'd starved herself over every unflattering picture or "Is she pregnant or getting fat?" tabloid magazine article. But she knew better now.

"Emmy Lou." Krystal's eyes locked with hers.

There was no point arguing with her twin. She hadn't been eating. Intentional or not, it was the truth. "Fine. I'll eat a pie as soon as we're done."

"Right. Sure. And while you're feeding me lies to keep me happy—how was the photo shoot?" Krystal drew her legs up to her chest and rested her chin on her knees, staring at her. "Might as well spill—I'll keep asking."

Tell me something I don't know. Krystal was like a dog with a bone. Not just relentless in the pursuit of what she wanted but also in protecting the bone. Emmy, in this case, was the bone.

"It was a professional photo shoot." Aside from the breathing difficulties she'd had when they'd made initial eye contact. Or when they'd touched. Or when she was hanging over his shoulder. Not that anyone noticed. Rather, she hoped no one had noticed. "I think the shoot went well." One thing was certain, the years hadn't eased the more *visceral* connection between them. Not for her, anyway.

"I wasn't worried about the photos. You have *never* taken a bad picture, Em. There are about a million on the internet to prove my point, too." She paused. "Was it super...awkward with him there?" Her nose squinched up. "Without kicking him in the balls or something, I mean? Because he so deserves a good knee to the—"

"No." Emmy was laughing again. "Not really. I concentrated. You know, on the reason I was there? Raising awareness for youth and teen drug addiction. All that?"

Krystal blinked, her eyes narrowing and her lips pressing flat.

Emmy was just as adept at reading her sister as Krystal was... maybe it was the whole twin thing. But the shift in expressions was telling—in a not so good way. "What's happened?"

"Momma called." Krystal's tone was flat.

It was Emmy Lou's turn to blink. Their mother had reached out to Krystal? "Oh." Why? Momma had promised to leave Krystal alone. She'd promised to give her daughter space—space they both needed to heal. Then again, this was their mother. She wasn't always the most honest or forthcoming when it served her purposes—a fact Emmy was only beginning to fully grasp. "I thought... I hoped..."

Krystal shook her head. "I don't understand why she doesn't get that I...I can't deal with her. Not yet."

The rift between their mother and Krystal had always been a mystery to Emmy Lou. Had been. Past tense. Now? Emmy understood all too well. Learning the damage their mother's hidden drug addiction had inflicted—deliberate or not—had shaken the very foundation of their family. Recovering would take time. "Then don't. Not yet." The sheen in her sister's emerald eyes deflated Emmy's lungs.

"Maybe not *ever*." Krystal cleared her throat, sitting up, her spine stiff, and the defiant lift of her chin her standard defensive posture. "Maybe that makes me a coldhearted bitch, but...well, then I'm a coldhearted bitch."

"Whoa, whoa." Jace Black's voice came out of nowhere. Seconds later, he was crawling onto the bed and reaching for Krystal, grabbing her leg with a wide smile on his face. Krystal's laughter rang out, her attempts to get away halfhearted at best. Krystal wound up flat on the mattress, beneath Jace, breathless with laughter. "Negatory. Nothing cold about you." He was staring down at Krystal with the sort of heat that made Emmy Lou clear her throat loudly.

"Hey, Emmy. Didn't see you there." He chuckled and sat back, running his fingers through his floppy hair. "Guess we're talking about the photo shoot?" Jace frowned. "Travis said he was a dick."

"Tool," Krystal whispered, taking his hand.

There was a knock on Emmy's bedroom door. "Emmy?" Juliette Rousseau peered inside. "Am I early for our fitting?"

"No." She waved in her brilliant costume designer. "I'm just wrapping up with Krystal. Juliette is here." She turned the camera so Krystal could see the woman.

"Hi, Juliette." Krystal waved.

Juliette waved back. "I'll be back with the clothing. Set up in here?" Once Emmy nodded, she left.

Krystal twined her arms around Jace's neck. "I've been thinking. Now that you're hanging out with a bunch of manly men, maybe you'll find one worth taking a chance on?"

No way. "Maybe." Travis's nun-of-country-music comment resurfaced. She didn't want to be alone. But she couldn't remember the last time she'd felt a flicker of interest. *Not true.* Didn't want to remember was more like it. If she continued to hold on to Brock Watson and the idyllic time they'd had together, no other man stood a chance.

A lingering glance between Krystal and Jace left a hollow ache in the pit of her stomach. The love her sister and Jace had found in each other was impossible for her. They'd taken a leap of faith and it had paid off. Emmy would never take that leap again. Not that she was going to say as much to Krystal. Instead, she held up the sheet music. "While I'm considering all these new manly options, you can send me the rest—with the chorus."

Jace scooched up on the bed, sliding his legs around Krystal to peer over her shoulder at the sheet music. He hummed a few notes. "Chorus?"

Krystal nodded.

He hummed it through again. "No fighting this. No stopping fate. Third time's a charm. My heart can't wait?" Jace sang, his tone deep and husky.

"Really?" Krystal stared over her shoulder at him. "It's that easy?"

He shrugged. "Or something."

"Or something? It's pretty damn perfect. And you know it." Krystal shook her head. "Kiss me."

Jace looked all too willing to do that—and more.

"Okay. Okay. Wait." Emmy Lou laughed. "I'm disconnecting now so you can…whatever." She covered her eyes, smiling at their laughter, and ended the Skype connection. She penciled in Jace's contribution, singing through it softly, then laughed. Krystal was right. He'd made that look a little *too* easy. But there was no arguing the end results. It was a good song.

"I have some new things," Juliette said, holding the door open for her two assistants to push the large rolling clothes rack into Emmy's room. "Try this one." Juliette held out a long-sleeve minidress covered in reflective bangles. "It will make you sparkle."

"Like she needs help with that." Travis leaned in the door, a spoon hanging out of his mouth and a jar of peanut butter in one hand. "I feel like I need to put on sunglasses." He shielded his eyes from the assortment of shimmering garments on the rack.

"Hello, Travis. What do you think?" Juliette smiled.

"It looks like someone took apart a disco ball and glued it all over the dress." Travis flopped onto the foot of Emmy Lou's bed and scooped out another spoonful of peanut butter.

"That is exactly what I did." Juliette laughed and held the dress in front of Emmy Lou. "Try it?"

Travis shrugged. "Yeah, go on and blind all our fans, why don't you?" He turned to give her privacy.

Emmy Lou slipped out of her shorts and T-shirt, eyeing the disco ball dress. Krystal wore black and red and deep blues while Emmy Lou stuck with white and silver, champagne, and a variety of pinks. Were there times she'd like to add a little color? Sure— but Momma had taught her the importance of sticking to your brand from an early age.

While other kids were in scout troops or going to track meets, she and her siblings went to modeling academies, networked with the rich and famous, and learned how to succeed in the music industry. The two most important things: being recognizable and making an impact. Emmy Lou was the only one to perfect the art of making a *positive* impact. As a result, the record company and their publicist made sure to keep Emmy Lou front and center on all the Three Kings ads, CD covers, and videos.

She slipped the dress on, turned so Juliette could pull up the zipper, and caught sight of her brother—tapping out the beat to Krystal's new song on his knee, totally focused. "What do you think? She sent it this morning. But the chorus—that was all Jace." She took Juliette's hand and stepped onto the stool.

Juliette knelt, a few pins in her mouth. "Shorter?" Tape measure in hand, she folded the hem up, sat back, and nodded.

Emmy glanced at her reflection and shrugged. "Your call. You know I trust you."

"That's Emmy Lou. Miss Agreeable." Travis's gaze darted her way before returning to the sheet music. He leaned back on the bed, propped himself on one elbow, and read each page again. "I'd take this down an octave? For harmony." He stopped tapping, changed the rhythm, and tapped out the new beat. "And I'd make that beat longer at the end…"

It wasn't the first time she'd been struck by her brother's talent. Travis had a natural musical ability, like Krystal and their father. When it came to backup vocals, bass guitar, banjo, and the pedal steel guitar, there was no one better. He'd even taught himself to play the dobro because he said it added a homegrown, classic authenticity to their songs. But whenever she or Krystal suggested he take a turn and pen them a new tune, he'd roll his eyes and brush them off. Typical Travis.

"Then suggest the changes." She kept her tone light, knowing full well he'd shut down or blow her off if she made this into a *big deal*.

With a dismissive hiss, he turned the sheet music facedown on the pink-and-white comforter and ran a hand through his shaggy blond hair. "Nope. Krystal knows what she's doing. My input isn't needed." He pushed off the bed, sorting through the clothes rack with quick, jerky movements. "Pretty sure I know how that would go over."

"What do you mean?"

Eyes narrowed, jaw clenched, and posture rigid, he looked ready to give her an earful. Something big was eating at him. And since her brother tended to deflect with jokes or teasing or lots of alcohol and highly questionable choices, his serious expression had her complete and undivided attention. Just when she thought he'd say more, he went back to sorting through the shirts on the rack. "Nothing."

Which wasn't true. "Trav—"

"Forget it, Emmy." Meaning he didn't want to talk about it. He picked a shirt from the rack and held it in front of himself, his gaze meeting hers in the mirror. "Hey, disco-ball girl, stop looking at me like that."

But she wasn't ready to let it go—not yet. "I love you, Trav. And if you'll let me in, I'm here. Okay?"

"Yeah, yeah, stop getting all worked up." He nodded. "I love you, too. Even if you're a pain in the ass."

Typical Travis dodge maneuver. "Me? *I'm* the pain in *your*..."

"Come on, say it. You can do it. Ass. Ass." He drew out the *s*'s for added emphasis, then chuckled and pulled another shirt from the rack. "Sometimes a good curse word is appropriate. I thought for sure you were going to tell the photographer to fuck off when he had Brock swing you over his shoulder. Or at least, a *hell no*." Travis shook his head. "I'm thinking some people are going to be offended by that picture." He shrugged. "Brock caveman, you cavewoman. What the hell was that about?"

Emmy Lou shot him a look.

"What?" His wide-eyed innocent expression didn't fool her for a second.

"Are you really offended on my behalf? Or waiting for a chance to slip him into conversation?" It was a rhetorical question, really. The smile on his face was answer enough. "Real subtle, Trav."

"Good. You can change." Juliette pulled out a white, sequin-covered, long-sleeved jumpsuit.

With the help of Juliette, she changed without jabbing herself with pins. But once the jumpsuit was on, Emmy Lou had doubts.

"You look amazing." Juliette stood back, arms crossed over her waist. "This is a yes. After we shorten it." She gave Emmy a hand up onto the stool. "Travis?"

"Wow." Travis nodded. "That's new." He gave her reflection a thumbs-up, pulling on a faded, sleeveless chambray shirt. "This works. It makes my arms look good, don't you think?"

"Yes." Being surrounded by professional athletes had totally shaken her big brother's confidence.

"You have to admit, he's changed," Travis said, meeting her gaze in the mirror. "Barely cracked a smile. Brock, I mean. You probably didn't notice, though."

She had noticed. *It's for the best.* If he kept being a tool, as Travis put it, it would be a lot easier to pretend he wasn't the same person whose laugh and smile and kisses she'd loved most. Instead of taking the bait, she turned on the stool and avoided her brother's gaze altogether.

"Guess not, then." There was laughter in her brother's voice. "If it bothers you so much, I'll try not to bring him up—"

"It does not bother me—" But her quick denial was so loud and sharp that everyone in the room paused to look her way.

"Sure. Right. No more Brock Watson talk." He flexed for the mirror and sent her a cheeky wink. "Not from me anyway."

———

Brock ran a towel over his sweat-covered face. He had a break from training today but that didn't mean he was going to sit on his ass. The pressure was on. If he was going to get back in the game, be the peak contender he once was, he had to put in the work and time. Lucky for him, there was always something to do on the ranch.

It had been a pretty dry spring, so there was no choice but to supplement feed for the cattle. Between loading and unloading square hay bales, hefting fifty-pound bags of range cubes, checking on the water tank levels, and making a mental inventory of what they'd need to keep the herd fed through winter, he managed to keep busy.

Once he'd run through things with the foreman, he put in an old-school workout.

His trainer, Stan Jelinik, had taught him how to use what he had available to him. It was amazing how much use a person could get out of an old tractor tire. Dead lifts were always an option. So was a farmer walk—standing in the middle of a tire and carrying it, straight-armed, around one of the pins had led to many a wager among the ranch hands. Their support and competitive spirit were the added incentive he needed to push himself to the limits. If there was no cedar to cut down or wood to chop, he'd take a sledgehammer to the damn tire. One side, then the other—occasionally he'd alternate and work his arms, shoulders, and back to the max.

Aunt Mo was at her quilting circle, so Brock took a steaming hot shower, made himself a second breakfast, and sat on the wide wrap-around porch to enjoy the quiet. As much as he appreciated the housing the owners had provided, he'd rather stay here. This was home. Then again, it was a good thirty to forty-five minutes into town and another ten to twenty to the stadium. Not exactly convenient.

He set his empty plate on the wooden-plank porch and flexed his left heel, slowly stretching his calf muscle. Occasionally, his leg ached. The physical therapist he'd worked with during his rehabilitation said there was a chance it always would. Still, he had no complaints. The surgery he'd had four and a half years ago to repair his tibial plateau fracture had been a success. If it weren't for the occasional ache and the seven-inch scar on the outside of his knee, he could almost forget the injury had happened.

But then he'd get a call from his Narcotics Anonymous sponsor, Randy, or Green Gardens Alzheimer's clinic, and there was no denying how significantly his injury and the resulting fallout had changed his life.

And his struggle with addiction had made this last injury a son of a bitch to manage. A tear to his right ACL with minimum pain meds wasn't easy, but he'd done it. A week of meds, then on to acupuncture and electrotherapy. The last seven months he'd carefully followed every order from his doctors and physical therapists, his trainers and nutritionists. Once Dr. Provencher released him, he'd be ready to go. *The sooner the better.*

Don't let the fall break you were his father's words.

I'm doing my best. And he was. Nothing and no one would stop him from getting back on top. He didn't know how much longer he had on the field; no one ever did. But he wasn't giving up. No way he'd let his team, his father, or himself down again.

He stared out over the rolling fields, the distant low of one of his black-and-white Herefords and the coo of the occasional dove giving him the peace he needed before he faced the rest of the day. He downed the rest of his protein-powder, electrolyte-infused smoothie and pushed himself out of the sturdy wooden rocking chair.

He was washing his dishes in Aunt Mo's massive farm sink when his phone started ringing.

"Brock." Connie, his agent, was all business. "It's a go."

"You've got so many irons in the fire, I'm not sure which one we're talking about." Brock stacked the dish in the drying rack, dried his hands on a hand-stitched towel, and made sure the kitchen was up to Aunt Mo's standards.

"You are welcome." Connie laughed. "Alpha. Their offer came in and it's big."

"How big?" It was one thing to pitch sports drinks or athletic gear. That was his bread and butter, the tools he used daily. So in a sense, he was qualified to be their spokesman. A men's line? He wasn't so sure he was the right man for the job. But as Connie liked to tell him, she knew best.

"Big-big." And she was happy; he could hear it in her voice. "I'm emailing you what they've sent. Take a look at it and I'll call you this evening?"

"Sounds good." He nodded.

"How's your father?"

"He's hanging in there. You know he's tough." He smiled.

"That's why they called him Ox, isn't it? Give him my best." She paused. "But seriously, *read* the email."

He laughed. "Yeah, yeah." And hung up.

"Shit." He'd have to visit his dad after he stopped by the stadium. They were having special teams' meetings this afternoon and he wasn't about to be late. His father wouldn't want that, either—he was all about being the first one there, the go-to player, and the last one to leave. Brock was, too.

The drive into Austin took close to an hour, bumper-to-bumper and horns blaring. By the time he parked and headed inside, he was tense enough to run a few laps. Since his tension level was only likely to rise with his meetings, he might as well wait until the meetings were over to run.

"Brock." Russell Ewen, the defensive coordinator, headed his way. His once red hair had turned steely over the course of the last couple of years. "Before we get started, head down to Dale's office. It will only take a minute. Ames is here."

Ricky Ames. The new second-string defensive end and his new backup. The kid, barely twenty years old, had pro instincts, lightning-fast feet, and packed one hell of a punch. But all the talent came with a reputation. A big mouth and an even bigger ego. Brock wasn't exactly looking forward to meeting the kid. "Sure."

The Roughnecks' head coach, Dale McCoy, was a big believer in the older players mentoring the new additions. It was also highly motivational for the seasoned players. Nothing like seeing a younger, fresher player ready and willing to take their place on the field to remind them that trades and contract renegotiations were always options—no matter who you were.

Brock didn't take that for granted.

Ten minutes later, he'd showered, dressed, and was putting on his game face. He nodded his greeting at Dale's secretary, Michelle.

"You can go on in, Brock." She leaned forward, sliding her glasses down enough to peek over the rim. "Just between you and me, Ricky Ames is a little shit."

Brock chuckled. "Oh?" He'd always appreciated Michelle's candor—and her opinions. Over the years, he'd come to realize that she was pretty good at reading people. She'd been with the team longer than the head coach, so if she started a sentence with,

"Just between you and me," Brock tended to listen. Her straight-forward, no-nonsense conversation and unwavering devotion to the Roughnecks reminded him a lot of Aunt Mo. High praise indeed.

"He seems to think the *team* is lucky to have *him*. We know it's the other way around." She winked. "I figured I'd warn you."

Great. "I appreciate the heads-up." He took a deep breath and opened Coach McCoy's office door.

"Brock." Dale waved him in. "Wanted you to meet Ricky here. Ricky, I'm guessing you know who Brock Watson is."

"Who doesn't? I grew up watching you, man." Ricky nodded, crossing the room to take his hand. "You were, like, my hero. I've got a YouTube greatest clips of you forklifting half the damn league. Legendary."

"Reggie White did it best." Brock shook his hand. "Good to meet you."

"How's the leg? That hit." Ricky winced. "Man, it hurt like a son of a bitch watching. That's the sort of thing that can end a career."

"The leg is good." He shrugged.

"Glad to hear it." Ricky's cocky-ass smile grew. "I hear it's hard to give one hundred percent when you've been knocked down like that."

Brock chuckled. Ricky Ames was going to have to work a hell of a lot harder to get under his skin.

After a quick rundown of the daily schedule and another hand ful of awkward exchanges, Dale said, "Thanks for stopping in, Brock." Coach shot him an apologetic smile. "I'm sure Ricky will need some guidance once training starts."

Oh, he'd need it all right. But would the kid listen? Probably not. "Sure." Brock nodded, keeping it as noncommittal as possible. With a final round of handshakes, he left the office, closing the door behind him.

"See what I mean?" Michelle asked. "Little shit."

Brock shrugged. "Bet you felt the same way about me when I started."

"You? No, sir." She waved his comment aside with her bright-pink-tipped fingers. "You know my sister's husband's cousin works over at the DFLM Foundation?" She waited for him to nod. "Well, she might have sent me a proof sheet from that photo shoot—the one with Emmy Lou King. I just about died. I am a huge fan of Three Kings. That girl is about the prettiest thing I have ever seen. You never told me you two dated."

"Never came up, I guess." Because he went out of his way not to bring it up.

"You two look good together, Brock." She paused, but he didn't say anything, so she went on. "Is she as sweet as she seems? I mean, she comes across as the heart-of-gold type. Such a positive role model for young girls—a rare thing in this day and age."

At one time, he'd have said yes. But now? She was a King. CiCi King's devoted daughter. Which meant nothing was as it seemed. "I don't really know much about her anymore." Only that, for reasons beyond understanding, he still ached to touch her. "She's a celebrity, Michelle."

Chapter 4

EMMY CROSSED THE PARKING LOT OF THE CAPITAL CITY Events Center doing her best not to think about the last time she'd been here. It wasn't raining, she wasn't FaceTiming with Krystal, there was no truck barreling down on her, and no Brock. So far, so good.

She ran her hand over her ponytail and smoothed the neon-green Drug Free Like Me T-shirt she wore. Today was her inaugural DFLM event. Today would be all about singing to a couple hundred kids, throwing footballs, running relay races, and—maybe—climbing a rock wall. Today would not be about Brock, period. "You don't have to come in, Sawyer." Sawyer walked right behind her, silent and intimidating and way too intense.

"Yes, I do," Sawyer answered, holding open the stadium door.

Poor Sawyer. Considering the stress her family had caused him the last year, he probably had a medicine cabinet full of antacid. "I'm pretty sure there's no cause for alarm. And Daddy will be here in like…" She glanced at her watch. "Fifteen or twenty minutes."

"It's my job," Sawyer answered, following her inside.

"Fine. It's like talking to a brick wall anyway." She glanced at up him, hoping to draw him into conversation. He'd been part of her daily life for more than a year, but she still didn't know all that much about him. "Anyone who thinks our generation is entitled and lazy never met you." She used air quotes around *our generation*. "It takes a lot to impress my daddy, Sawyer. But I can tell, you've definitely impressed him." It might also have something to do with the fact that, when he was needed, Sawyer never failed to deliver. Over the course of the last year, Emmy Lou had come to think of her broody bodyguard more as family than an employee. "I do think you've earned a vacation by now. Don't you?"

Sawyer shrugged, barely acknowledging her question. He was assessing their new environment—jaw tight, posture braced, and gaze sweeping the mostly empty stadium hall. She peered around, trying to see things the way he saw them. But all she saw was a cleanup crew, a man in a hydraulic lift changing light bulbs, and a smiling teenager in a DFLM T-shirt. None of them screamed danger to her.

"Miss King?" The teenage girl sort of bounced toward them, her hands clasped in front of her. "Hi. I'm Lupe. You're here. In person. And I'm...I'm super nervous." She laughed, her cheeks deep red, and rubbed her palms against her jean-clad thigh. "I'm supposed to take you to the field."

"Hi, Lupe. It's so nice to meet you." Emmy Lou shook the girl's hand.

"Same. I mean—it's really *really* nice to meet you." Her gaze darted to Sawyer, her smile wavering.

"That's just Sawyer," Emmy said, pointing behind her, where Sawyer stood—stiff and silent. "He probably won't smile or say much, but he's totally a good guy even if he looks a little scary."

The corner of Sawyer's mouth twitched.

"Oh. Hey." Lupe nodded. "Okay, well, we're going this way." She turned and headed quickly toward one of the ramps that led onto the floor.

By the time they'd reached the ramp onto the field, Emmy had learned that Lupe wanted to be a high school guidance counselor. "Our counselor, Miss Lozano, is always there when we need her. At school, at home—she's even picked up one of my friends when things got really bad at home. I want to do that, you know? Be there to help so that no one is ever alone."

It wasn't the first time Emmy realized just how privileged she was. For all their flaws—and there were many—her family would always be there for her. "*You* are definitely amazing, Lupe."

Lupe's cheeks were bright red now. "Thanks."

The thump of music—with a heavy bass—drifted up the ramp. Shalene Fowler was there, a clipboard in one hand, a walkie-talkie in the other.

"Hey, Emmy Lou." She waved her forward. "You ready for this? We have a full house. And they are super excited! We've got the stage set up, per your assistant's direction, so we're ready to go."

"She wanted to be here, but she's got some nasty bug." If Emmy Lou hadn't put her foot down and demanded she stay home, Melanie would have been here anyway—green and nauseated. Not that being sick had stopped Melanie from running through the day's agenda, again, via FaceTime.

"Any questions?" Shalene smiled when Emmy shook her head. "Okay, we've got about five minutes."

Five minutes was all she needed. Emmy Lou glanced down at her custom-made, pink, sequin-covered Converse tennis shoes. Before the Three Kings had become a power player in country music, they'd been three awkward preteens singing their hearts out at every county fair and rodeo circuit. At one rodeo, a big one, Emmy had tripped on the laces of her cute ankle boots and fallen, face-first, in front of the entire crowd. It hadn't stopped her from getting up, smile in place, and singing, but it had left her insides twisted up and her confidence shaken. Her performance had suffered, badly.

She'd never let herself forget that day. Not the fall, accidents happened. But how it felt to disappoint her fans, family, and band. And herself. After that show, humiliated and nursing bruised knees, she'd promised herself she'd give each and every performance her best—no matter what. Ever since, she'd pause and check her shoes before every performance—whether she was wearing lace-up shoes or not—to renew that promise. She drew in a deep breath and nodded.

Minutes later, Shalene asked, "Ready?" At Emmy's nod, she held up the walkie-talkie and said, "Miss King is ready."

Emmy bounced up on the tips of her toes and rubbed her hands together. She was excited—really excited. The shouts and clapping and voices from inside the stadium triggered a surge of endorphins. There was nothing as exhilarating as the enthusiasm of a live audience. Normally Melanie or Krystal, Travis, or her daddy was there to give her a thumbs-up, a let's-do-this sort of thing. So she glanced at Lupe and gave her a thumbs-up. Lupe returned the gesture. She gave Sawyer a thumbs-up, too. For a split second, he smiled. Well, almost…sort of smiled. His eyebrow shot up, too. Then he was stony faced, his thick arms crossed.

For the most part, Emmy laughed off her sister's random Travis-Sawyer comparisons. They looked *nothing* alike. Sure, they were both tall, but Sawyer was big in a scary way. Travis, not so much. They had music in common, but that made sense. Why would Sawyer work for a musical family if he wasn't into music? Sawyer was good, too—he and Travis had numerous spontaneous jam sessions during their last tour. If Sawyer was picking up on some of Travis's poses and expressions, it was because the poor guy had spent so much time with them. So much so that, right now, Sawyer looked *way* too much like her big brother. *Poor Sawyer really does need a vacation.*

"Okay," Shalene said. "Let's go. The players will come out on the opposite side of the stage."

"Great." She stopped staring at her now-wary-looking bodyguard and followed Shalene down the ramp and up the metal stairs to the stage.

"Who's excited?" a voice overhead asked.

A chorus of shrieks and whistles rose.

Emmy Lou smiled.

"Let's give it up for Emmy Lou King."

Emmy took the microphone from one of the stagehands and jogged onto the stage, waving. An ocean of young faces, all wearing the neon-green DFLM shirt, stared her way. The music was already playing. It was prerecorded, but the kids didn't seem to mind. The familiar strum of a guitar, the quick beat of the drum, and she was singing a classic Three Kings tune. Best of all, the kids sang the chorus, too.

It's my promise, always given—when this world gets out of whack.
If there's one thing you can count on, it's that I've got your back.

She held the mic out for the kids to sing the chorus.

It's my promise, always given—when this world gets out of whack.
If there's one thing you can count on, it's that I've got your back.

She sang through the second verse, getting the kids to clap along. Once she'd sung through a final verse, she let the audience finish it out.

She clapped, her mic in one hand. "That was awesome, y'all." She kept on clapping. "What do you think? I think these guys are planning to sing now," she teased.

"We've been talking about that." Leon Greene walked across the stage. "We have a surprise for you."

"You do?" She waited, taking care not to look at Brock any more than the other players gathered on the stage.

"We didn't want you to miss out on all the fun." Leon grinned. "So RJ, Bear, me, and Brock *are* going to play you a little song. Then you can show us your throwing arm."

Her throwing arm? Her aim was...bad. Brock knew it, too. One time—*one time*—she'd managed to hit Brock in the face with a soda can, and that was it. Yes, she'd been aiming at her brother—who was a good five feet away from Brock—so it had been an accident. From then on, he and Travis had made a huge production of ducking or covering their head if she ever tossed them keys or an apple...or *anything*. Hands on hips, pride smarting, she asked the audience, "I don't know, guys. What do you think? I know I can throw, but can they make music?"

There was an audible "no" from the kids.

"Not me." Clay held up his hands. "But I'm sure gonna watch." He pulled his phone from his back pocket. "And take video."

"Don't be like that." Leon chuckled. "You just watch and see. You ready?"

Emmy perched on the stool a stagehand had placed on the stage and watched them take their spots. Leon had a brightly painted maraca in each hand, Demetrius carried a tambourine, the one name named RJ held a recorder, and Bear—all six feet six inches of him—raised a triangle. She would have laughed if Brock hadn't carried the same, old, beat-up wood Yamaha that Travis had given him all those years ago. A guitar she'd helped teach him to play. She'd sat between his legs to place his fingers on the right strings while he'd dropped kisses on the side of her neck...

Something thick and rough settled, hard, in her throat. She took a second to look down at her hands, pretending to be fascinated by her fingernails until she could ask, "Did y'all start your own band?"

Leon shrugged. "Sort of. We have been working on a little something."

Bear tapped the triangle, and everyone laughed.

"Bear's the best one," RJ said, looking serious.

Bear tapped the triangle again and grinned.

"We tried to work a solo in for him but..." RJ shrugged.

Emmy had to laugh then. These giant, next-to-no-body-fat men ready to play their brightly colored children's instruments were both hysterical and endearing.

Bear winked her way. "They're worried I'll steal the show."

It was kind of hard to miss the smile on Brock's face. That smile was one of the things she'd missed most about him—when she was still missing him. His smile all but disappeared when his gaze collided with hers. His lips pressed tight, the muscles of his jaw tight, as he turned his attention to his guitar.

Was he angry? With *her*?

The knot in her throat turned jagged. When he'd been drafted into the AFL, they knew things would change between them. But deep down, she'd believed him when he said he'd write to her. He'd promised nothing would change between them—that he'd love her forever.

He'd lied. Not her.

"One, two, three." Leon tapped his foot.

At first it was a bunch of notes and noise, but then it became more recognizable. "Twinkle, Twinkle, Little Star" on the recorder, maracas, and triangle was something else. But the kids gathered at the front of the stage, singing and laughing. She joined in, too. Then the song was over and only Brock was playing.

Emmy Lou sat up, surprised at the first notes. He was playing what she'd just performed, "I Got Your Back." It was one of those songs that stuck at the top of the charts for almost a year. Afterward, the catchy anthem about teamwork and friendship had been used by numerous organizations—including the football league.

Brock might have given her up, but he hadn't given up the guitar. Wrong or not, it hurt. Which made things that much worse. For all her big talk, it—he, their past—still affected her. She didn't want him to have the power to hurt her anymore. *Why am I giving it to him?* She didn't want to be the nun of country music. She wanted to love someone; she wanted someone to love her. One thing was certain: that someone wasn't, and never would be, Brock Watson.

———

His fingers slid along the strings, each note adding to his mounting regret. What the hell was he thinking? The answer was obvious.

Right or wrong, pathetic or not, it was a test. Would she react? Would there be even the slightest reaction to his playing? Or the guitar? Did she ever think about those days, the two of them, so wrapped up in each other—so confident in the illusion of a future together? Maybe it had never been real to her. Maybe he'd been too blind to see that. There was a mile-long list of questions he'd never get answered. But one bothered him more than the rest. Why the hell does any of this still matter so damn much?

When the song was over, the dull roar of the stadium rose. The audience, three-hundred-plus elementary- and middle-school-aged kids, were clapping and screaming like he was a rock star.

"Freight train and music legend," Clay Reese said, still holding up his phone. "Not too bad, but how about we leave the music to the professional? Emmy Lou?"

He watched as she slid off the stool, her ponytail swinging and her shiny, pink lips smiling.

"I might have one or two songs." Emmy Lou nodded, the mic clasped in both hands. "But before that, how about another hand for them? That was some performance, wasn't it?" She tilted her head in their direction, her green gaze bouncing from one to the next—stopping just shy of him. With a little skip in her step, she stared out over the kids and started clapping. "Let's keep this party going."

When Emmy started singing and his friends and teammates started dancing, he carried his guitar off the stage. He crouched, opening the beaten-up case and placing the guitar inside with care.

"Brock." Hank King was there, standing in the shadows just out of sight of the stage. There was a warm smile on his face. "Good to see you, son." He took Brock's hand and shook it, his other hand clapping Brock on the shoulder.

"Mr. King." He was at a loss. He'd looked up to Hank King—thought he was a good man. To Brock, he'd seemed like this genuinely hardworking, talented family man with one hell of a knack for business. He'd welcomed Brock, taken an interest in his future, and supported his dream of playing pro ball. If the man had concerns about the relationship between him and Emmy Lou, he'd never said so. But when Brock had shown up on that long-ago, miserable, rainy morning, Hank King hadn't stepped in or tried to stop his wife from severing the last threads of hope Brock had been clinging to.

"You kept up with it." Hank nodded at the guitar case. "You sounded real good out there."

Brock shook his head. "I'll stick to football."

"Glad to hear it." Hank laughed. "How's the leg? We've been waiting, hoping you'd be back on the field this season."

Brock didn't speculate about who the "we" was. "Doc thinks I should be good soon." He shrugged. *Just not soon enough.* Every damn time he went in for a checkup, the doctor pushed his release back. Brock didn't want to take chances—his body was his career and he needed to be in peak condition—but that was before Ricky Ames had shown up.

"Glad to hear it." Hank shook his head. "The rhythm is off on the field. Without you, there's a hole in the defensive line."

He kept his opinions to himself. His loyalty was with his team, so he'd never agree with Hank—even if the man was right. After his injury, the Roughnecks had struggled through the remainder of the season. And even though he'd been recovering from an injury and nowhere near the field, he'd gotten all kinds of shit for the team's less-than-impressive season.

"Shows the kind of leader you are on the field," Hank continued. He peered onto the stage before adding, "Glad things worked out for you, son. I always knew you'd get what you wanted."

Brock studied the older man's profile. It had been years since he'd seen him, aside from his new music videos and album covers; there was always plenty of Hank King and his family in the media. At times, it seemed like every detail of the Kings' lives was tracked and reported on. To Brock, Hank King had aged with every new picture. In person, Hank King's deeply lined forehead, graying temples, and overall weariness were telling. "I just wanted to say how sorry I am for what your family has been through the last few months." He meant it.

Hank faced him, a sad smile on his face. "That means a lot, son. It's been hell." Hank paused. "You haven't had it all that easy yourself. You doing okay?"

Brock's nod was stiff. Day by day. That's all he could do. The last four years of his life had been one trial after another. Every day, he reminded himself of the reasons he had to stay clean, stay strong, and keep going. Namely, his father—and Aunt Mo.

"Glad to hear it." Hank nodded. "This life will either make you or break you. It's finding the good—good people, good causes—that make it worth it."

Brock didn't disagree. But good people were harder to find than good causes. His glance swiveled to the stage. Emmy Lou, her hand up over her head and one foot tapping, belted out the chorus to "Try and Stop Me." She knew how to put on a show. Her voice was only part of it. When she performed, she lost herself in the music—and carried the audience away with her. The kids in the audience were singing, so Emmy Lou held out the mic to them, her smile wide and sweet and beautiful. A different ache, cold and hard, took up residence in the pit of his stomach.

"Brock?" Shalene was hurrying down the ramp to the side of the stage. "Brock, you have a phone call."

The look on Shalene's face triggered instant panic. "From who?" He was down the stairs and jogging to meet her, ignoring the stares and whispers of the staff and volunteers nearby.

"Your aunt?" She held the phone out.

"Aunt Mo?" He took the phone, covering his other ear to hear.

"Brock? Your daddy's taken a spill. He's hit his head, so they're taking him to the hospital."

"Which hospital?" he asked, already heading toward the exit, Shalene Fowler trailing along.

"St. Joseph's Medical Center. I've got Cliff bringing me, so you just head straight there," she said. "He's breathing, headed where he needs to be, so don't you drive like a maniac and wind up in ER yourself, you hear me?"

"Yes, ma'am." He hung up and handed the phone back to Shalene. "Family emergency."

"I hope everything is okay, Brock." She patted his arm. "You take care now."

He jogged to the locker room, grabbed his bag, and ran to his truck. He put the key in the ignition, his phone beeping from the recesses of his gym bag. He pulled it out, fear ticking his pulse up. Missed calls from Aunt Mo. From ten and fifteen minutes ago. Nothing new.

Calm the fuck down. He rolled his head and took a few deep breaths before turning the key in the ignition. Austin highways meant constant construction and traffic. As much as he wanted to avoid I-35, it was still the fastest route. But the fifteen-mile, forty-five-minute drive took every last bit of his patience—and then some.

He parked and ran, cutting across the parking lot and ignoring the shocked stares of people who recognized him. It didn't help that his neon-green DFLM shirt had his name in bold, reflective, black letters across his back.

He headed straight to the ER. Aunt Mo stood, wringing her hands, staring at the television in the corner of the room.

"Aunt Mo?" He gave her a quick hug. "Any word?"

She shook her head. "They're still checking him out. Knowing him, he's being ornery." But her smile wasn't steady, and her eyes were full of tears.

He nodded. "Probably fighting them and giving them an earful." His father was a big man. When he got aggressive, and he had a time or two, it wasn't easy to subdue or calm him.

She laughed then, pulling a faded blue-plaid handkerchief from the pocket of her sweater. "We'll just wait awhile."

"You want to sit?" he asked.

"In those chairs?" Aunt Mo eyed the plastic chairs with concern. "Goodness knows when was the last time they had a good scrubbing. The last thing I need is to leave here with the flu or shingles or some nasty intestinal thing. I don't have time for that sort of nonsense."

"I'm fine standing." He didn't argue. His father and Aunt Mo were both stubborn people. They liked to be in control. If standing made her feel better, he'd stand with her.

"Mr. Watson? Miss Watson? My name is Jackie." A nurse in pale green scrubs approached them. "It might be best if we put you in another room." She glanced around the relatively full waiting room.

That's when Brock noticed a few cell phones out. A little boy with an ice pack to his cheek waved. Poor kid looked like he'd have a black eye. Brock waved back.

"That would be nice," Aunt Mo said.

Brock took his aunt's arm and followed Jackie from the ER waiting room, through some badge-activated doors, and down a short hallway to a small room with a few chairs and a water fountain.

"Do we know what happened?" Aunt Mo asked. "David Watson is my brother."

"I see." Jackie nodded. "Well, it looks like he got up at nap time and headed to the kitchen. The floors had just been mopped so he slipped on the floor and hit his head."

"After a snack most likely." Aunt Mo's hand tightened on his arm. "Is he awake? Can we see him?"

"Not yet." Jackie glanced back and forth between the two of them. "Once the doctor has finished his assessment, he will come see you." She stood. "I'll come back as soon as I have an update." She pulled the door closed behind her.

"You know how fragile his bones are, Brock." Aunt Mo was shaking her head. "If he breaks something…"

"Whoa. Let's not get ahead of ourselves." Brock steered her to one of the chairs. "Dad's tough. And stubborn." He draped his arm along the back of Aunt Mo's seat. "He's strong, too. Stronger than an ox." Since Brock could remember, he'd heard that about his father. *Stronger than an ox*. When his father had played college ball, he'd been known as "Ox" Watson or just "The Ox." "He's not giving up without a fight. He's not done being a pain in the ass yet."

Aunt Mo stared up at him then, sniffing sharply, twisting her handkerchief between her hands. "He better be. Or I...I..." She broke off, pressing her lips together. "And watch your language, Brock Nathaniel Watson."

"Yes, ma'am." He hugged her close. She was only a few years younger than his father. She was just as tough, but beneath his arm, she felt small and fragile. When she was all bluster and snap, it was easy to forget that. Selfish or not, he needed them—they were what kept him focused. Eyes closed, he rubbed his hand up and down Aunt Mo's arm to comfort them both. He was doing his best to swallow down the knot in his throat. He didn't have any say-so and he knew it but, dammit, he wasn't ready to say goodbye to his father. *Please, Dad, fight.*

Chapter 5

"You're all here?" Emmy Lou said, handing her earpiece to Melanie and walking across the grass football field. "Why are you all here?"

"Besides I've been home for less than twenty-four hours and I want to spend more time with you?" Krystal leaned forward, crossed her arms on the rail, and smiled. "I don't know. I guess I was curious about this whole football-cheerleader song thing." She blinked her eyes innocently. Without her signature smoky eye and dark-red lips, she looked young and—almost—innocent. But Emmy knew her twin. "Isn't that right, Clementine?" Krystal cooed to her fan-adored, three-legged Chinese crested dog. The dog's tail went wild. "See? She's so excited to be here."

"O-okay. Thank you for the support, Clementine." She turned to Travis. "And you?"

"I figure there will be another awkward exchange between you and Brock." He shrugged. "I brought popcorn." He pulled a bag of microwave popcorn from under his seat, propped his booted feet on the chair in front of him, and tipped his green-and-yellow tractor cap back on his head.

"At least he's being honest." Emmy pointed at her twin sister.

Krystal leaned back against her seat, Clementine in her lap. "Fine. I'm here because I, too, am curious to see what's *not* going on between the two of you." She was smiling ear to ear.

"Unbelievable." She turned to Jace. "Can you please, please get her to listen to me?"

Jace held his hands up. "I'm no magician, Emmy. I tried. Believe me, I tried." He reached back and grabbed the bag of popcorn from Travis.

"He is the only one who has a reason to be here." She pointed at Sawyer, standing silently at the end of the row. "He's working."

"I thought today was your day off, man?" Travis asked, grabbing the bag back from Jace and holding it out for Sawyer. "Didn't you say something about going to a tractor pull or something?"

"Are you kidding?" Emmy asked, horrified, as she faced Sawyer.

"He *is* kidding." Sawyer sighed.

"Oh." Emmy had a hard time not laughing then. "Sorry, Sawyer." She shook her head. "If today was his day off, I'm sure he'd be somewhere *far* away." She shot her siblings a look. "Instead of here, making things awkward for no reason. Because *he*, unlike *all* of you, probably has a life outside of my excessively dysfunctional—"

"Personal life?" Travis finished.

Krystal sat back and stared at Sawyer. "Do you wish you were far away from us, Sawyer? Here I thought we'd become your family, sort of. I mean, we *are* totally dysfunctional—you know that, but we also have a certain charm…and snacks." It was her turn to steal the popcorn bag. She and Clementine peered inside. "Okay, we had snacks." She glared at Travis and Jace. "When you're not being our big, brooding, strong-and-silent bodyguard, you know, *deep* down, you'd still hang out with us—even if you weren't paid to do so." Her gaze swiveled back to Sawyer, head cocked to one side, eyebrow raised. "You know, like friends. Or family. You might as well be, at this point."

Sawyer's eyes narrowed the tiniest bit.

Emmy wasn't sure what to make of the odd look that passed between Sawyer and her twin. It didn't last long.

"I'm going to…check the exits," Sawyer murmured, already heading up the stairs, his black "King's Guard" T-shirt stretched across his broad back.

"See if there's more popcorn," Travis called after him. "Or a beer. Am I right? A beer would be good." He nudged Jace.

"Pass." Jace rarely drank.

"The concession booths aren't open." Emmy shook her head. "There is no one here." She pointed around the stadium—right as players began running onto the field.

"You were saying?" Krystal sat back, resting her feet on the bar. "Just pretend we're not here. And afterward, we can go talk about everything that doesn't happen...over barbecue. I really *really* want some barbecue."

Emmy did a quick once-over of the players. No Brock. *Thank goodness.* Not yet, anyway. Four days ago, he'd played her daddy's song on his guitar and disappeared. There'd been no way to ask her father why he'd left or what had happened without her father getting suspicious. And since she wasn't going to think about Brock anymore, she had no interest and didn't need to know more information. Instead, she'd spent the rest of the morning enjoying the kids.

"Barbecue? Sounds like a plan. Ribs." Jace nodded. "And brisket."

"And beer. A cold Lone Star Beer sounds good." Travis nodded.

"Nope. Iced tea. Sweet." Krystal scratched Clementine behind the ear. "With lemon."

"A beer, over ice, always beats iced tea." Travis kept on nodding.

"And pecan pie." Jace nodded. "With some vanilla ice cream."

Travis leaned forward to grab the back of Jace's chair. "Don't forget the beer. Maybe a Budweiser instead?"

Jace laughed.

"If you're that hungry, why not *go* eat?" Emmy asked, ignoring her brother's beer fixation. "Sawyer is here somewhere—since you chased him off. He'll take me home after."

"Emmy Lou?" Melanie called out to her. "I think they're ready to do a quick rehearsal and sound check."

"Go, Emmy!" Krystal called out.

"Check that sound!" Travis added, laughing.

Emmy shot her siblings a look and walked back to the spot marked on the field. "I'm ready."

"Nice to see they came out to support you." Melanie nodded toward the stands.

"Is it? Is it, really?" Emmy asked, shaking her head. "As long as Brock doesn't show, it shouldn't be a big deal."

"Oh, well..." Melanie smiled, her gaze shifting to something beyond Emmy. "About that."

"About what?" Emmy turned to see Brock crossing the field—in a sleeveless, skin-tight, white compression shirt and a close-fitting pair of black joggers. He wasn't just physically fit; he was... What? What words could adequately describe just how massive he was. One thing was for certain: his attire only confirmed her his-muscles-have-muscles theory. The whole hanging-upside-down-over-his-shoulder episode had been enough for her to realize just how physically impressive he was. And seeing him now—head down, earbuds in, all muscles and totally unaware of the audience he had—reminded her of the very mixed swell of emotion his touch and presence and scent had stirred. Also, she was staring.

"Oh no." She spun away. Chill. Calm down. It was no big deal. Unless, "They didn't see, did they?" She risked a look over her shoulder at her siblings.

Emmy didn't cuss. It had never come naturally to her. But right now, with her sister and brother and newly returned bodyguard and her sister's boyfriend all staring at her, she almost did.

"He didn't see y—nooo...never mind, he sees." Melanie tried to move her lips as little as possible. "And he's stopping."

Which has nothing to do with me. "Let's do this," she pleaded. "Can we, I don't know, move this along?"

"On it." Melanie pivoted on her heel and marched toward the director. When Melanie made up her mind, there was no stopping her. She might be tiny and soft-spoken, but she had an iron will and a commanding presence that people tended to listen to. And right now, the director was listening.

The walk-through didn't take long. He pointed at the colored spots on the field, showed her the storyboard, and asked her if she had any suggestions or changes.

"No." She shook her head. "Seems pretty straightforward. We'll film it tomorrow?"

He nodded. "We'll do a few shots here, then finish up in a warehouse, get a gritty vibe, and use a green screen—some effects."

She nodded. Did a football intro need effects?

"Watch it." It happened so fast she didn't have time to process. Hands grabbed her shoulders and spun her away, narrowly dodging a football that slammed into the ground where she'd been standing. "You good?"

She nodded. "Thanks."

"No problem." Her savior couldn't have been more than eighteen. Good-looking, clean-cut, well-built—but young.

"Yes." She shook her head. "Guess y'all don't yell 'fore' when you throw?"

"Holy shit, I know you. You are Emmy Lou King." He stepped back and gave her a head-to-toe inspection. "Damn. You *are* something to look at."

"Um...thank you?" She exchanged a look with Melanie. "Are you one of the team trainers? On a college internship?" Was he even old enough for college?

"Are you serious right now?" he asked, hands on hips. "You don't know who I am?" From the smile on his face, he wasn't offended.

Another look at Melanie, who shrugged, before she admitted, "No. Should I?"

He grinned—he had an adorable grin. "You should. I'm Ricky Ames. Soon-to-be defensive end for your favorite team."

Which had to be a mistake. *Brock* was the defensive end for the Houston Roughnecks. He had been for the last six years. "Oh, right." He must be the backup. "Second-string? Until Brock gets clearance to play?"

"Excuse me," Melanie said, staring at her phone. "I've got to take this." She walked away, the phone to her ear.

Ricky kept right on grinning as he leaned forward to whisper, "Pretty sure I'll be staying around. Consider me the new-and-improved version."

Emmy Lou did her best not to react. New and improved? If he hadn't looked so serious, so confident, she would have laughed. Brock *was* their defensive line. A key player. The team's defense had suffered without him, so getting rid of him wasn't a good idea. And petty or not, this Ricky Ames needed to show some respect to someone like Brock.

But it was more than that. The Houston Roughnecks were Brock's dream team. Even in high school, they were his pick. He'd wanted to play for them more than anything. The idea of him playing somewhere else felt...*wrong*.

This wasn't true. It couldn't be.

Ricky Ames wasn't just highly ambitious; he was delusional. Still, his words were cause for concern. Ricky was Brock's replacement? Permanently? Daddy would know. If he didn't, he could find out—his friendship with the team owner went back years.

"Nice shirt." His attention lingered a little too long in the boob area.

She glanced down at her blinged-out, pink "Houston Roughnecks Fangirl" T-shirt. "Thanks."

"You okay taking a selfie?" he asked, pulling out his phone from a pocket in his athletic pants.

At least he was asking. "Sure." They leaned together and smiled.

Holding up his phone, he did the whole pout thing, eyebrow raised, and head cocked. Clearly, he'd taken a selfie or two. "Cool. We look good."

"Ricky," someone called.

Ricky didn't look; he just held up a wait-a-minute finger. "So, why is Emmy Lou King on my football field?"

She laughed, from surprise more than anything. "Working." *His* football field? "Has anyone ever told you that you're pretty sure of yourself?"

"No reason not to be." He shrugged, then snapped his fingers and pointed at her. "Oh, *right*. You're singing the Sunday night football anthem? Making game night even better."

"That's me. We're taping it tomorrow."

"Ricky." Same voice, impatient this time.

"Sounds like you're needed." Emmy was not impressed.

"I am." He grinned but kept his focus on her. "Guess that means you'll be here again tomorrow?"

"Ricky." This time it was louder.

"In a minute," he called out, staring at her. "We should have dinner. Have some fun."

He was interested, she got that. A little too interested. With her hands on her hips, she said, "You know—"

"Ames." Different voice—razor-sharp and biting.

She and Ricky both startled as they turned to see Brock headed their way. He wasn't happy. Not in the least. Jaw rigid, eyes narrowed, and his game day don't-mess-with-me scowl in place. She almost felt sorry for Ricky Ames. *Almost.*

Brock came to a stop an inch, maybe less, from Ricky and stared him down. "Did you hear Russell?" He gritted his teeth. "He shouldn't have to call you more than once."

Ricky's reaction had Emmy Lou holding her breath. Instead of backing down, he bowed up at Brock and smiled. "I heard him. He's not going anywhere." He tilted his head her way. "I'm in the middle of something here."

She frowned, beyond uncomfortable by Ricky's proprietary stare—and Brock's complete lack of acknowledgment of her existence. She mumbled, "I'm going—"

Brock cut her off, his every syllable edged with hostility. "When it's time to train, you train. Russell expects one hundred percent of your attention and energy."

"As long as she's here, that's not going to happen." Ricky winked at her.

She stared, shocked by his cavalier attitude.

That's when Brock looked at her. Emmy had never seen him angry like this. His hands fisted at his sides, his posture so rigid he was close to snapping. He was barely holding on to control. The problem was, she understood. He wasn't mad at her. He was mad at Ricky. And from their short exchange, she could see why.

———————

Yes, Brock was pissed.

Pissed that Ames didn't get how life-changing this opportunity was—or maybe he just didn't care? Pissed he didn't show one iota of appreciation. Pissed that Ames was wasting Russell's time making an ass out of himself for Emmy Lou. Pissed as hell that Ames was looking at Emmy like she was a piece of meat.

Pissed that this little fuck was on his field, period.

And, from the look on Emmy's face, everyone could tell just how pissed he was.

Her green eyes darted back and forth between the two of them while she chewed the inside of her lower lip. The tension was undeniable, but he had it under control. Correction, he'd get himself under control. He'd been mentally preparing himself all morning. Work out. Help Russell run drills with Ames. Try to do some mentoring shit. Generally, be the professional his coaches wanted him to be.

He'd even made peace with missing the first few games. He'd have Ames up to speed, ready to play, until Brock was released.

All that went out the window the minute he saw Russell's face.

Russell worked his ass off to make their defensive line impenetrable. He knew his shit and he took no shit. He pushed until he got the best out of his player and then pushed some more. And *he* was waiting on Ricky fucking Ames?

Brock closed his eyes, rolled his neck, and shook some of the tension out of his hands. *Get it together.* The kid was trying to assert his dominance, control the dynamics, and get in Brock's head. *And it was working.* He sucked in a deep breath and blew it out, slowly. No way he was going to give Ames the upper hand.

"What's your problem?" Ricky kept going. "I get that it sucks to be replaced, but that's the game, man."

Every muscle in his body clenched.

"This is, what?" Ricky shook his head. "Your third injury?"

A dull roar started, growing louder and louder each second Ames kept staring at him.

"I could be wrong, but isn't there some saying about three strikes?" Ricky's smile grew, the dig unmistakable.

"In baseball. This is football. You should know that." Brock's smile was tight. "I get that you feel the need to prove yourself." Brock kept his voice low and steady. "But the only thing you're proving is that you have a lot to learn."

Ricky's jaw muscle bulged, but then he laughed. "And, what, you think *you're* going to teach me?"

"I wouldn't know where to start." He shook his head. "Football or respect? As far as I can tell, you need a lesson in both, kid." It took effort to turn and walk away. But Brock managed, even though the roaring in his head kept going. The little shit wanted to get a rise out of him. To make him break in front of the team? The coaches? No way he was going to give Ricky Ames what he wanted.

"What did you call me?" Ricky Ames stepped in his path, cutting him off.

"*Kid?*" Brock wasn't sure if the kid had an overdeveloped sense of pride or if he was just stupid. "If 'kid' bothers you, you don't want to know what I'm thinking."

"Talk about trying to prove something. Can't play so you're trying to put me in my place. Trying to make sure people don't forget who you are." Ames bowed up, chest-bumping Brock. "That's sad, man."

From the corner of his eye, he saw Emmy Lou. The wide-eyed terror on her face was enough to make him pause, step back, and issue a warning: "I wouldn't."

"You're not me." Ames's eyes narrowed.

"Believe me, I know." *You're some kid playing second-string hoping to have a career with a record half as good as mine.* He paused long enough to maintain his calm. "You take a swing, you better be ready for what happens next."

Seconds before Ames moved, Brock knew it was coming. Ames's fist, a sledgehammer blow to his jaw. He had to give it to him, it was a solid punch. Busting his lip, whipping his head around, and making him see stars. *Don't do it. Do not lose it.* He moved his jaw slowly, spit out a mouthful of blood, smiled, and took a step closer to Ames.

For the first time, Ricky Ames stepped back.

"What the hell is going on?" Coach McCoy was red-faced and mad as hell. "What the shit was that?"

Brock didn't say a word.

"He's got a problem with me." Ricky Ames pointed at him.

"He has a problem with you?" McCoy asked, running a hand over his face.

"Yeah. He does. Knowing I'm faster and younger and better, maybe? Guess the competition's too much for him?" Ames had no idea what was about to happen.

Brock did. Had he goaded the kid? Maybe. Did he regret it? Not so much.

"Go home." McCoy's eyes were laser focused on Ames. "I don't tolerate this sort of thing on my field or on my team." He shook his head. "Go home."

"Are you serious?" The shock on Ricky Ames's face was almost comical. If he wasn't spitting blood, Brock might have laughed.

"Are *you* seriously asking me that?" Coach McCoy pulled his cap off his head, bent forward, and threw it across the field. "Get off my field! I don't want to see you until Monday."

"Monday?" Ricky echoed. "That's a week—"

"Wanna make it two?" McCoy asked, so red Brock feared he might have his third heart attack right here on the field.

That shut Ricky up and sent him running off the field.

"Is this a problem?" McCoy asked, reaching up to tilt Brock's face.

"Ricky Ames? Or my jaw?" Brock asked. "I'm the one bleeding here."

"Yeah. I saw that." McCoy smiled. "I admire your restraint. I was hoping you'd knock him on his ass." McCoy shook his head. "Get some ice." He headed back to the middle of the field, clapping his hands and telling everyone to get back to work.

"Are you okay?" Emmy Lou's hand—on his forearm.

He nodded, all too aware of her touch.

"Your mouth." She reached up, winced, then pressed her hands together. "You're bleeding."

He was bleeding and standing there, staring, like a fool.

"That was restraint," Travis King said, shaking his head. "That was the single most badass thing you have ever done on this field." He blew out a harsh breath. "Fuck, that was intense."

That's when it registered that all three of the King siblings were there, on the field—while he kept right on staring at Emmy Lou.

"I was hoping you'd put the little shit in his place before your coach showed up." Krystal was still glaring after Ricky Ames. "No one looks at my sister that way," Krystal added. "No one."

Krystal's words kicked up the ebbing fire of his temper, but he managed to nod.

Which earned him an odd look from Krystal. "So, that was *something*. How's life?" she asked. "Haven't seen you in the tabloids recently, so I'm guessing nothing new."

"Good to see you haven't changed." Brock took the handkerchief Emmy handed him. "Thank you."

Emmy smiled. Damn but that smile. Sweetness and concern, all rolled into one. He almost believed it. He stared at the turf at his feet, pressing her handkerchief to his lip. It smelled like her.

Krystal wasn't done giving him a thorough head-to-toe inspection. "I'm surprised to say it, but it's good to see you, Brock Watson."

He hadn't expected her to hug him. From the look on her face, she hadn't expected to give him one, either—but she did.

"That was weird," she said, stepping back. "I don't even like you."

Where the hell had that come from? He hadn't done a thing to Krystal—to any of them. Emmy included. His hand tightened around the handkerchief.

"Jace." Jace Black stepped forward to shake his hand. "Big fan. Hope you'll be able to play this season."

"Me, too." It had become his standard answer.

"So, that was Ricky Ames?" Travis asked. "He's a lot smaller in person."

"That's him," he ground out.

"He's a shit. One in need of a good ass-kicking." Brock didn't disagree with Travis's take on things.

"Good thing you didn't give it to him. You would have broken him with, like, one hit. *Broken* broken." Krystal bent to scoop up a three-legged dog with a puff of fur on its head.

"I'm not the violent sort." Not that Brock hadn't been tempted. But Emmy...she'd been standing there, looking so damn panicked, he'd managed to control himself. For her?

Travis snorted. "Your face said differently."

"He was *thinking* about it," Krystal said. "Thinking about doing something is *not* the same thing as doing it. He can think all he wants. You should take a lesson from him, big brother."

Travis rolled his eyes. "Wait a sec. Now you're defending Brock? I thought you just said you don't like him?"

"He went all knight-in-shining-armor over our sister because the little shit wouldn't leave her alone. I can't hate on him too much right now." Krystal pointed at Ricky Ames, the dog staring in the direction she pointed. "Besides, I don't like *Ames* even more. He is a *total* dick."

Brock didn't correct Krystal. Their confrontation had nothing to do with Emmy... No, dammit, that wasn't true. Was he pissed that Ames was making Russell wait? Hell yes. But would he have confronted the shit if Ames hadn't been outright leering down at Emmy? Best not answer that.

"He's just a...a kid. An egocentric, living-in-his-own-fantasy-land, totally rude..." But then Emmy sputtered to a stop. "You know what? He is *that. Exactly* what you said Krystal." Her gaze met Brock's. She was upset—cheeks stained red, green eyes flashing, and lips pressed tight.

Hell, Emmy Lou was *angry*.

He could count all the times he'd ever seen her truly angry on one hand. Sure, Travis had made a habit out of frustrating her, but that wasn't the same thing. Agreeing with Krystal's curse was probably the closest he'd ever heard her come to out-and-out insulting someone.

Which made him wonder what the hell Ricky Ames had done or said to her before he got there. From what he'd seen, Ames had done most of the talking. "What did he say to you?" The words were out before he could stop them.

She opened her mouth, then stopped. A slight crease formed between her brows.

"Emmy?" He tried again, softer this time.

"Nothing." She glanced at her siblings, reminding him of the attentive audience gathered around them. "So, barbecue? Are you still hungry, Jace? Krystal?"

"I could eat." Jace tugged on Krystal's hand. "Sweet tea?"

Krystal smiled, leaning into him. "Sounds good. Don't you think so, Clem?" The dog's tail was wagging frantically.

"I'm done. Food it is," Emmy Lou said, all forced enthusiasm. "Ready?"

She didn't want to talk to him. *Message received.* He swallowed hard.

"Wanna join us?" Travis asked, knowing exactly what he was doing.

Hell no. Like it or not, Emmy Lou King was his kryptonite. The less time they spent together, the better. So even if Emmy Lou wasn't so anxious to leave or Krystal wasn't shooting daggers at Travis or Jace didn't look so damned uncomfortable, he still wouldn't go. "Practice," he muttered. "Good to see you all." Surprisingly, it was.

"Next time?" Travis was getting under his sisters' skin and enjoying every minute of it. "We'll meet you and Sawyer there, Em?"

Brock didn't wait for her answer or goodbyes as he headed back across the field. Whatever this was, it was over. Time to get his head in the game. He had work to do. Even though Stan was going to give him an earful for running late, he was feeling pretty damn good. Ames might have given him a bloody lip, but it had earned him a week without the kid talking shit and baiting him. Brock could handle that.

Emmy Lou brushed past him, running through the speakers, lighting equipment, and backdrop for tomorrow's filming. Her ponytail swayed and there was an extra skip in her steps—she'd always had a certain energy, positive and enthusiastic and contagious. Even as she stooped to grab something from the ground, she sort of bounced on the balls of her feet. But when she stood, she took one step, teetered, and started to fall. She caught herself on one of the large speakers but her wince, her soft "ow," had him changing direction. Before he figured out why he felt compelled to make sure she was okay when most of her family was here to take care of her, he was standing beside her.

"My ankle." Her nose was wrinkled. "I tripped. It popped."

Considering the web of cords on the turf, he wasn't surprised. "Bad?" he asked.

"Um…it hurts." And yet she attempted to smile—with tears in her eyes.

For some reason, her wobbling smile gutted him. Probably because it made him think of one of the worst mornings of his life. While he'd been rain-soaked and devastated standing on the porch of the Kings' house, CiCi had bragged about Emmy Lou's ability to smile through anything, her gift at performing—on the stage and off. CiCi hadn't just broken his heart; she'd made him doubt every second he and Emmy Lou had spent together. That was probably the thing he hated most—all those memories tainted.

Now, here she was. Hurt and still forcing a smile. "You don't have to smile." He hadn't meant to snap.

She blinked, sniffing hard, and stared down at her ankle.

Yes, he was a dick. For both of their sakes, he needed to let her family handle this. But one look told him the Kings were leaving the stadium—out of earshot. There was no sign of her looming bodyguard. *Some bodyguard.* Or the woman with the tablet.

Dammit. He sighed, running a hand along the back of his neck. "Can you walk?"

She nodded, still staring at the ground—sniffing harder now.

He held his hand out.

"I can manage." Her voice was soft but lined with steel.

Stubborn. He kept his hand out and his mouth shut. From

where he stood, he could see that her ankle was already ballooning up. She needed ice and some anti-inflammatories—and his help.

Emmy pushed off the speaker to stand, hissed sharply, and immediately sat. Because she was stubborn. *And I'm a dick.* He stepped closer, too close for her to ignore his hand. She did—refusing to take his help or look at him. But his frustration faded when a wet spot formed on her shirt, then another.

Tears.

I am a fucking asshole. He'd rather feel irritated than the sudden hard tug in his chest. He didn't have room for softness when it came to Emmy Lou. Then again, when it came to her, he'd never had a choice. "Emmy."

Her head popped up, and she furiously wiped her cheeks with the back of her hand. The tip of her nose was red. And, dammit, she was still trying to smile.

He crouched beside her, ignoring the sensory overload she triggered. "Let me help you."

"You need ice for your face. I don't want to be a bother—"

"Duly noted." He stood, reached for her, and swung her up into his arms.

"Brock, I can walk." Her hands pressed against his shoulder.

"I know." He nodded at her ankle. "If you want to make that worse, you can. Don't you have a video to make tomorrow?" That was pretty much all the guys could talk about—Emmy Lou King, her legs, her voice, and wondering what sort of getup she'd be wearing for the video.

She was going to argue, he could tell. Instead she said, "I need my purse."

He stooped and let her grab her purse.

"Thank you." She stared at her purse.

With his focus fixed on the door to the locker room, he carried her across the field. He didn't think about the brush of her ponytail against his bare arms or the hitch in her breath or the way she relaxed into his hold, her slight frame too fragile. She'd always done this—brought out his protective side. Little did he know, he'd been the one who needed protecting from her.

"What about your leg?" She sniffed.

"What about it?" He frowned.

"Should you be carrying me?"

No, definitely not. But that had nothing to do with his leg and everything to do with the effect she had on him. "I'm fine, Emmy Lou." He would be—once her scent wasn't filling his nostrils.

"I wasn't angry about Ricky Ames," she said suddenly. "I mean, I was. But not about anything he said to me. Guys are like that sometimes."

I bet they are. Men tended to notice beautiful women. But noticing and acting like a complete prick weren't the same thing.

"I was upset because of what he said…about you." Her words ended on a hiccup.

Why the hell did she care what Ricky Ames said about him? He risked a look at her.

"I get that the team has to bring in someone until you're released to play. But…it's like he doesn't know who you are." Her cheeks were going red again. "Doesn't he know your record? Does he have four hundred and sixty-nine tackles? Ninety-one sacks? Does he watch Reggie White footage to be a better defensive end? Does he even know who Reggie White is? Or that *this* is your team? And *you* carry this defensive line? He really thinks he can replace you?"

She was talking about football. His stats, but football. And he liked what he was hearing a hell of a lot. "Never pegged you as a football fan." He waved Todd Flynn, one of the trainers, over and carried her into the game-day emergency clinic. Gently, he set her on an exam table and started unlacing her tennis shoes.

"Thank you." Her gaze shifted, meeting his.

He nodded, carefully sliding the pink sequined shoe off her foot. Her hands fisted at her sides. "Sorry."

She nodded. "It's fine."

He inspected her now apple-sized swollen ankle. Her sock was stretched tight. Pink socks. Pink shoes. It had always been her favorite color. Hell, he'd worn a pink tie to prom for her.

He nodded as Todd came in. "Her ankle."

"I can see that." Todd bent, his fingers moving over the inflamed joint. "Tell me if this hurts."

Brock crossed his arms and watched her face. She scrunched up her features and closed her eyes as Todd slowly moved her foot one way, then the other.

"That." Her hands pressed, flat, against the exam table.

"Probably a sprain. Ice and elevate. I'll go get some. Might call your doctor, get an X-ray to make sure." Todd nodded and glanced his way. "Um, looks like you could use some ice, too?" He shook his head and left the room, saying, "Be back."

"I'm not." She swallowed, staring down at her ankle and wiggling her toes. "A football fan, I mean."

"No?" He leaned against the counter. "I thought only die-hard fans cared about stats?"

"I guess." She shrugged. "I only know yours."

For a split second, he was frozen.

Don't. Don't do this. He wasn't eighteen years old anymore; he knew better.

He pushed off the counter, fully intending to leave but closing the distance between them instead. Standing there, staring at her, was hard. He knew her face like the back of his hand. The tiny mole on her cheek. The dot of blue in the iris of her right eye. The fullness of her lips—he could still taste her mouth beneath his, clinging, gasping for breath, and wanting more.

What was she after? Why was she laying it on thick, acting like she'd kept up with him—acting like she cared? There was no audience. Her green eyes locked with his. *All wide-eyed innocence.* Bullshit. To her, he'd been temporary. To him, she'd been everything. She'd made a fool out of him once. No way he was going to let her do it again.

"Brock—" Her soft voice wavered.

"Em…" *No, dammit all to hell.* He pulled up CiCi's words, played them on repeat until he'd grounded himself in reality. *She is not my problem. She is not, and never was, mine.* "Your bodyguard." The burn of anger made it easier to put distance between them. "Call him." He tore his gaze from hers and waited, pacing, until Todd came back. He took the ice pack for his jaw and walked out, ignoring the curious stares and questions from his teammates…and the sharp twist of his heart.

Chapter 6

"Are we clear?" The director, Chad, held his hand up. "Can we turn up the fog and wind, please? I want her hair blowing."

Emmy tilted her head as her stylist, Andrea, swept a fine dusting of powder along her nose and cheeks. The thrum of the bass was playing already. Even though the music and sound would be added after the fact, she liked to sing during the shoot—it kept her in full performance mode. And since the goal was to wrap this shoot in a couple of takes, she needed to give one of her best performances ever.

"Not too much," Momma said, waving aside Andrea. "You don't want her to look...too made up."

Andrea stepped back, tucking the brush into her apron, and forced a smile. "Yes, ma'am, Mrs. King."

"Stop fidgeting." Momma shook her head. "You look fine."

Emmy Lou wasn't about to disagree. Still, her low-cut, painted-on, gold-covered jumpsuit hugged every curve of her body. The original outfit, a mini-minidress, had been discarded in favor of something that would cover her ankle brace. And it did cover the brace. The rest of her? Well, it didn't matter.

"Don't listen to her, baby girl." Her daddy patted her cheek. "You look beautiful. All lit up." He nodded, his gaze sweeping over her gold-sequin-covered jumpsuit. "That's some outfit."

Momma shot him a look. She wasn't happy. At all. She'd done her best to make sure every single person knew it, too. But even the great CiCi King didn't have the power to remove Brock from the video. She had tried. As soon as she'd found out, she'd started making calls—using her "aw sugar" voice, then moving on to far less cajoling tones. Nothing worked. Brock was in the video.

Since Momma couldn't stop that from happening, she was bound and determined to be there to make sure he didn't bother her. Emmy had done her best to assure her he had no interest in talking to her, let alone bothering her. But she'd pulled out the promotional stills from the DFLM shoot, slid them across the counter, and sighed.

"After all he's put you through, Emmy Lou," Momma had said. "I think it's best if you have someone with you who will look out for *your* best interests." She'd taken her hand. "And since no one else in this household seems to understand what those are, I'm not leaving your side."

That was why Krystal had bailed on her. It was hard enough to have her mother and sister in the same room when Momma wasn't on the warpath. Poor Daddy was bearing the brunt of it. From her razor-sharp tone to the daggers she kept shooting at Daddy, it was going to be a long day—and they hadn't even started the shoot yet.

Five minutes later, Chad waved her forward. "We're ready for you, Emmy."

"That's my cue." Emmy smiled, relieved to put some distance between herself and the storm brewing between her parents. She stood on the green X taped to the field. After three walk-throughs, she knew where to hit each mark. The only difference this time? The players would be on the field with her.

Everything was timed to perfection.

The beat started thumping, Chad pointed her way, and the stadium went mostly dark. When the beat dropped, the lights pivoted up, casting her in a foggy spotlight. As the beat continued, she started walking—the next beat drop raining a shower of sparks from overhead. She stopped, dead center, and started singing.

> *Standing on the field, beneath the floodlights.*
> *I hear the roar of the crowd, wanna make them all proud.*
> *Standing strong and proud, ready for the fight.*
> *My heart's beating in my chest, know my team is the best.*

Each line, a new spotlight would come on and illuminate a player. She'd high-step her way over, toss her hair, pose at their side, and move on. It was easy enough. Some players smiled, others wore their game face; it didn't matter. These were the players people loved seeing. She only teetered once, the burn in her ankle making one step less deliberate than the rest. But she kept going, hoping only she noticed.

Once the chorus came up, another shower of sparks exploded, a backlight cast her in a blinging halo and the fan had her hair swirling around her shoulders.

She belted out the chorus.

Because I'm a warrior.
This game is a battle.
Because I'm a warrior.
And I fight for you.

Since the Kings were well-known Houston Roughnecks fans, it made sense that she'd end her performance next to a Roughnecks player. Meaning Brock.

Maybe it was knowing her mother was there, watching every little detail, that kept her focused. Maybe it was his chilly behavior in the first-aid station yesterday. Maybe, just maybe, she was finally getting over Brock Watson. Whatever the reason, she strutted into the spotlight with purpose. She planted her feet, stopping directly in front of Brock, and threw her head back as she rounded out the final chorus.

"Because I'm a warrior. Warrior…" She drew in a deep breath, ignoring the throb in her ankle. "And I fight for you." She pointed at the camera, smiling brightly into the lens.

"And…cut." Chad was clapping. "That was amazing." He waved her over. "Come check it. I don't want to jinx anything, but we might not need to—"

"I don't want to tell you what to do, of course, but you might want another take." Momma was using her "aw sugar" voice, all Southern charm. "Poor Emmy Lou did a little biddy, teeny-weeny offbeat step. I'm sure it's fine as is. But you might want to consider another take?"

Chad slid his earphones onto the top of his head. "Oh?" He frowned, leaning forward to stare at the screen. "Where?"

"Let me show you." Momma was all smiles as she traipsed across the field in her platform heels, white linen pants, and bright-pink silk shirt.

Emmy deflated, doing her best not to put any weight on her injured ankle—or acknowledge the very warm, very solid presence at her back.

"You okay?" Brock's voice was pitched low, setting the hair on the back of her neck on end.

She barely nodded, not trusting herself to look at him. Especially not now that Momma was watching them, eyes narrowed, over the camera.

"Emmy?" he repeated, his tone far too warm—far too gentle.

She made a show out of pushing her hair from her shoulder, whispering, "Fine," and hoping he'd heard.

His large hand was warm at her waist. "You need a hand?"

She hadn't meant to jerk away from him. The last thing she wanted to do was draw attention their way. But if Momma saw... She held her breath, risking a look at the camera, her mother, and Chad. Whatever they were looking at held Momma's undivided attention. Not that it stopped her heart from pounding.

The harshness of Brock's sudden laugh startled her enough to draw her gaze. And then…she couldn't look away. His face. In all her life, she'd never been on the receiving end of such hostility. It rolled off of him. Crashed into her. Knocked every ounce of air from her lungs… Just when she thought he couldn't hurt her anymore, he did.

"Emmy Lou, your water." Melanie was there, water bottle in hand. "You need anything?"

She needed to stop staring, to stop wanting to explain why she'd just pulled away from him. Stop wanting to explain anything to him. And, more than anything, she needed to stop trying to understand what had happened and how they'd wound up here. But the words were too tangled up to do anything more than clog her throat.

Brock's features hardened. There was nothing gentle or concerned about him now. He swallowed, the muscles in his throat working as his gaze fell from hers. With another bitter laugh, he shook his head. "She needs to sit down—her ankle." He was walking away before his words sunk in.

"Did I interrupt something?" Melanie was blinking rapidly. "I am so sorry, Emmy."

"No." Emmy found her voice. Unsteady but audible. "No, you didn't. Thank you for the water." She took a long swig.

Melanie was watching her. "You should take a break, put that ankle up."

"Emmy?" Chad called out. "You good to do it again? I feel certain we'll get this done in one more take."

One more take. One more and she could go home. "Yes."

"You sure, baby girl?" Her father stood on the other side of the field, far enough away from Momma that he could pretend he didn't see the glare she'd leveled in his direction.

"Let's get this over with," she whispered to Melanie. She ratcheted up her smile and gave her father a thumbs-up.

Daddy grinned. "Well, all right then."

"We need ten minutes or so to reset everything anyway," Chad said, slipping from his chair. "Damn pyrotechnics."

———

Brock stood in the dark on the football field. Watching Emmy Lou King in her element was impressive. No, *she* was…she was mesmerizing. Every head pop had her hair swaying. Every step set the bangles on her sexy-as-hell, skintight outfit swinging. With her dusty-rose lips smiling, singing her heart out, and one arm rising over her head, she grabbed hold and held on tight to every single person's attention. It wasn't just him; it couldn't be.

If he ever needed a reminder that CiCi King knew her daughter best, here it was. This was where Emmy Lou belonged. Front and center, the spotlight fixed on her. He didn't need to be here. Hell, none of the players needed to be here. Who the fuck would be looking at anything other than her? The fog and wind machine and sparks were overkill.

With every practiced step, every rehearsed tilt of her head, and her blindingly beautiful smile, the closer she got to him, the harder it got to breathe.

He flexed his fingers, the warmth of her skin lingering on his fingertips. Why had he touched her? He was no better than a moth flying directly into an open flame. So why was she the one who jolted away from him? Fast and quick—like *he'd* burned *her*.

No, that wasn't it at all. More like she couldn't stand his touch.

His hands fisted. No more of this shit. No more letting her get in his head.

Emmy took another high step, her smile wavering as she planted her foot. Her ankle was hurting. She was hurting. So why was she pushing this? It was obvious every single person in the building was at her beck and call. The Kings ruled—that was clear. CiCi King was there to make sure of it.

The moment the beam of the spotlight illuminated him, he stared down at the turf. He heard the rasp of her breath as she stepped around him. The dangling strands of sequins brushed and bounced against his arm and chest as she planted her feet. She stood—too close to ignore her scent, her warmth, the energy coming off her in waves. His gaze traveled up slowly, lingering on the swell of her hip. With a toss of her head and a sweep of her silky hair across his arm, she belted out the last of the song.

"Because I'm a warrior. Warrior…" Her voice was pure—a stark contrast to the sparkling temptation of a getup she was wearing. "And I fight for you." Five words, five beats, and another shower of sparks poured down over them and the lights went out.

It was over. He'd go his way. She'd go hers. Considering how easily she got under his skin, it couldn't happen soon enough.

The director yelled, "Cut." But the lights didn't come up. "Can we get the lights?" The director, Brock didn't know who he was, sighed loud and exasperated. "Lights?"

It was too dark to see much, so the press of Emmy's hand against his thigh was unexpected. Even more so was the way she swayed into him, more propped up against him than anything. "Sorry…" she whispered, her voice high and thin. "Need to get…my boot… off." She fell more heavily against him.

"Your ankle?" He steadied her, torn between sympathy and irritation.

"Yeah." He could hear her pain.

He'd known full well she was pushing too hard. Why had no one else spoken up? Like him, her body was her business. Her unsteady breathing tipped the scale in favor of sympathy.

Fuck it.

"Hold up." He knelt, tugging the clinging fabric of her pantsuit up and blindly fumbling for her foot. She couldn't have been wearing heels. That would have been easy. Boots. Boots that kept on going—higher… Like his hand. He was holding his breath as his hand slid from her calf to the side of her knee. Another two inches and he was cursing at the dark and her soft skin and the football league for this shoot and whoever'd decided to put her in boots that went halfway up her silky-smooth thigh.

He was at the end of his rope when his fingers finally grasped the elusive metal tab at the top of the zipper. With one angry tug, he yanked it down—pulling a sharp hiss from Emmy. "Dammit. Sorry." He sighed. "Try now." He held the sole of the boot and she slid her foot free.

"Thank you." Her hand, searching, rested briefly against his cheek. "Oh, sorry. Sorry." She moved, her hands landing on his shoulder for leverage.

It was a good damn thing it was dark, or everyone would have seen him lean into her hand. Everyone would know just how screwed he was. One touch was all it took to shake his resolve when it came to this woman. It wasn't fair or right. But, hell, that was life.

"Emmy?" Melanie asked, the beam of a flashlight was moving slowly closer. "Am I close?"

Brock stood, the zap of Emmy's hands sliding from his shoulders to his chest a live wire across each and every nerve. He hated that she could still do that to him. And hated how he'd missed it. The longer he stood this way, the more lost in Emmy he became. With her scent wrapping around him, her soft breathing going unsteady, and her fingers plucking at the front of his jersey…he had to stop this. Whatever *this* was.

Why didn't she answer whoever the hell was coming, armed with a flashlight? Why hadn't he?

"Emmy?" The flashlight beam swung to the right.

"If someone doesn't get the lights back on in the next two minutes, I swear there will be hell to pay." CiCi King's voice was so brittle it sliced through the fragile threads holding the two of them together—frozen. "Do you hear me?"

I hear you.

His brain was spinning, images flipping faster and faster, like a possessed slideshow with no off switch.

Kissing Emmy.

Sweet promises and painful goodbyes.

Letters sent and returned and sheer desperation.

CiCi King.

That morning. That fucking morning…

And now. Emmy Lou prancing across the damn field, all smiles and head tosses.

Maybe he *was* hell-bent on his own destruction. It was a question he'd been asked in rehab: Was he capable of making healthy choices? It'd been a long time before Brock had been able to say yes to that question. And now? There was nothing healthy about this. Whatever empire the Kings had built, he didn't want to be a part of it.

His hands clasped hers, ignoring the cling of her fingers, to purposefully remove her hands. If the lights came on… No. He held her hands away and stepped back, sucking in deep lungfuls of air.

"Over here," he ground out before letting her go and taking one step back, then another—and another—until he was heading in what he hoped was the direction of the locker rooms.

Brock didn't pause when the lights came on, blindingly white, or when he heard the director yell out, "We're good here. We'll do the warehouse shoot tomorrow." Meaning he was done.

He checked his phone, ignored Connie's "How'd it go?" text, grabbed his wallet and keys, and headed out of the stadium. He didn't have time for this. With Dad in the hospital, Aunt Mo would need a break. After that…well, he could use a few hours of work on the ranch.

It wasn't uncommon for there to be a few fans waiting outside—football fans. But there were more than a few fans today. Word must have leaked on the commercial shoot because most of the folk gathered outside held Three Kings posters and were calling for Emmy Lou. He couldn't get away from her.

"Brock." Hank King. "You got a quick second?"

He'd never been so ready to leave a place in all his life. Right now, the promise of sitting on the wide porch of his childhood home, to breathe the clean air and soak up the silence of the countryside, was the only thing keeping him steady. "Sure," he managed. He was pretty sure his expression said the exact opposite.

From Hank's chuckle, he guessed right. "Won't take long. Your guitar." Hank waved him over. "Emmy reminded me. Figured you'd want it back, since you've held on to it this long." Hank King didn't bother looking his way; he'd made his point.

He followed Hank back into the stadium without saying a word. From this angle, higher in the stands, the production value was more obvious. A small army of cameras, lights on top of lights, wheels of cords, and what felt like enough people to fill half the damn stadium covered the field. Hank led him into the seats along the low rail where Brock's battered guitar case sat.

The bodyguard was there, watching every damn move Brock made with narrowed eyes and a clenched jaw. Like Brock was a problem? He stooped, grabbing the handle before Hank could reach for it. "Thanks."

"Of course." Hank nodded.

"Hank—" CiCi King came around the corner and the world seemed to shift into slow motion. "Oh." Her head-to-toe inspection was all contempt. "Emmy Lou says her ankle is hurting her." She held up Emmy's boot. "I don't know how she managed it, but the zipper broke. Guess she was trying to get out of it in the dark."

Why the fuck she was in those boots in the first place, with a hurt ankle, didn't seem to be a concern. Not that it was his business. He stared down at his guitar case and kept his mouth shut. If CiCi hadn't been blocking his way out, he'd have left. As it was, he'd have to ask her to move. He didn't want to say a thing to the woman.

"Must be hurting her something fierce then, I'd think." Hank frowned. "Where is she?"

"Sitting over there." CiCi used the boot to point. "Melanie has her ankle up, icing it. That girl has a dramatic streak a mile wide. Emmy's still smiling—how bad can she be hurting?"

Was she serious? Emmy would smile through anything for the sake of appearances or to make her fans or family proud. CiCi King had been the one to drive that point home for him.

"I'll go check," Hank said, looking none too pleased with his wife. "We ready to go?"

"Yes." CiCi nodded. "If she can walk." She watched her husband and the bodyguard as they left the stands and headed across the field.

Emmy Lou sat, all sparkles and gold, with her leg up. She looked red cheeked and flustered. Or pained. *She's fine. Taken care of. Not my problem.* He needed to get out of here. Now.

"You know, I was pretty sure I'd seen the last of you. Other than game day, that is." CiCi sighed. "I'd like to think you being here now isn't some sort of pathetic attempt to, *what*, remind Emmy Lou that you still exist?" Brock was too stunned to react to the vitriol she continued to unload on him. "I know your manager, Connie Jacobs. Right? She's...tenacious. And clearly, more connected than I gave her credit for." She smiled at him, those eyes narrowing. "She had to have pulled some big strings to get you here. Was it her idea? Or yours?"

Brock wasn't capable of answering her—not without losing his shit.

CiCi smoothed a hand over her hair. "I know Emmy Lou is this bright, shining star that everyone wants a piece of. Having her love and losing it? How do you move on from that? How can anyone else compare? For that, I *am* sorry." She carefully navigated two steps in her ridiculously high heels, then turned back his way. "But this video? And the two of you working on the same charity? Finding ways to get close to her? That ends *now*. You being here now? Someone might think you're trying to use her to get back on top, help with your career 'makeover.'" She used air quotes. "But that's not going to happen. Press, fans, they're fickle. You want to be real careful about whose bad side you wind up on."

Brock stared after the woman. He'd never met anyone so capable of verbally eviscerating another human being. It was, in its own twisted way, a gift. She'd left him tongue-tied and reeling while throwing his motivation and decency into significant doubt. No, she'd let him know how easy it would be to do that to him publicly—and walked away smiling.

He stormed out of the stadium, his grip on the guitar case white-knuckled and shaking. What would happen if he went back in there and set CiCi straight? Hell, he'd set them all straight. None of this had to do with Emmy Lou.

Which was a lie.

Maybe not Drug Free Like Me. That was special to him—way before Emmy. But today, this shoot... Connie hadn't pushed him to do this. It had been his choice, she'd said. He'd known exactly what today would be like and saying no had never once crossed his mind. *Because you're a damn fool.*

He slid his guitar into the back seat of his truck, slammed the door shut, and pulled himself up into the driver's seat. *Fuck it.* He'd made a mistake. All of this—today—one big mistake. But it was over and done and he'd make damn sure not to put himself in this situation again.

Chapter 7

EMMY STOOD OUTSIDE THE HOSPITAL DOORS, SERIOUSLY regretting her spur-of-the-moment outing. It had been over six years since she'd seen David Watson, but that didn't mean she'd stopped thinking about the man. Or caring. Still, why had she thought bringing him a cookie bouquet and gift bag full of sports magazines and puzzle books was a good idea?

In the days since all the video shoot and weirdness with Brock, she'd stayed as busy as her ankle allowed. With the tour coming up, she needed to be in tip-top shape. She'd filmed the rest of the AFL opening—propped up to hide her brace—then kept her ankle elevated and read every piece of news she could get her hands on. From politics to fashion, best book lists and must-see movies, to horoscopes and sports. The tabloids never failed to disappoint. She had to laugh over Jace and Krystal's *secret* wedding, Jace and Krystal's *secret* breakup, and Jace and Krystal's *secret* baby. The King family had a hell of a lot of secrets—but these weren't them.

That's how she'd found out about Mr. Watson. A video of Brock waving to a kid in the ER waiting room made *Tabloid News Media*. The video had *TNM* reporters digging around to discover that his father had been admitted. For what and why had not been released.

"Maybe this was a bad idea," she said, tugging Sawyer's arm. Her ankle brace helped, a lot, but Sawyer had been pretty insistent about her using a cane or crutches…or him. He'd been pissed as hell to learn of her fall, since she was on his watch, and had been even more overprotective than usual. "Coming here?"

His noncommittal eyebrow bob did nothing to calm her anxiety.

"Gosh, thanks." But she didn't move.

After several minutes, Sawyer said, "You can leave your gifts at the nurses' station."

Which was probably for the best. If she'd thought this through, she could have ordered flowers or cookies or something and had it delivered by someone other than herself. Someone Brock wouldn't object to. After their last run-in, there was no denying Brock had serious objections about her.

"That's probably best." *What was I thinking?* "This was really selfish of me." She shook her head, letting Sawyer lead her across the parking lot. "I mean, Mr. Watson is in the hospital. Why would he want his son's long-forgotten ex-girlfriend to suddenly show up with…random, silly things?"

"Are you asking me?" Sawyer's brow rose.

"I'm not sure." She smiled.

And so did he—for a handful of seconds. Once he realized he was smiling, realized *she* saw *him* smiling, it disappeared. Was smiling against some bodyguard protocol? Or was it just a Sawyer thing?

"Yes, Sawyer, I guess I am asking you." She braced herself.

"This isn't selfish. You're the most selfless person I've ever met." No inflection. Almost like he was reading the ingredients off a cereal box or a street sign. He took the gift bag and cookie bouquet from her.

"Oh, well." It was the last thing she'd expected him to say. "Nurses' station?"

He led her inside, his don't-mess-with-me expression the only deterrent needed to keep people at arm's length. People recognized her, it was inevitable, and she smiled and waved but kept moving along—as fast as her ankle would allow.

They'd almost reached the nurses' station when a familiar voice called out, "Emmy Lou King? Is that really you?"

It had been years since she'd last seen Molly Watson, but she'd recognize Aunt Mo's voice anywhere. She stopped and peered around Sawyer. "Sawyer, stop. It's a friend." In a lot of ways, Aunt Mo had been her second mother. Molly Watson was the exact opposite of her momma. Where Momma favored pretty things and flash, Aunt Mo was all about practicality and functionality. Being in the Watson home had allowed Emmy a normalcy that didn't exist in her *real* world.

Aunt Mo had taught her how to iron, sew on a button, treat a strain, and how to do a load of laundry. While her mother liked to remind her that they had people for that, Emmy Lou was proud of her, albeit limited, useful skill set.

"What are you doing here?" Aunt Mo wrapped her in a warm hug. "It's been forever since I saw your sweet face. Emmy Lou, if I hug you too hard, you'll snap. You need more meat on you, girl. And who is this handsome fella you're hanging on to?"

Emmy held on, tight, laughing at Aunt Mo's rapid-fire questions. That was Aunt Mo, concern and reprimand, strong opinions and solid hugs all rolled into one. And right now, being wrapped up in Molly Watson's arms was just what Emmy needed.

"Aw, sweet girl." Aunt Mo's arms were firm. "You're too little; it hurts to squeeze on you. I'm making you muffins. You hear me?" She pressed a kiss to her temple. "Better yet, you and your fella come and we'll make them together. And stay for dinner? I'll make enough for you to take home."

"I do miss your cooking." She finally let go. "But I've missed you even more."

Aunt Mo cradled her cheeks, taking a thorough inventory of Emmy Lou's face. "You've always been welcome, Emmy. You hear me? Always. I'm not too far down the road." There was a flash of concern on her face before she straightened and faced Sawyer. "Now, introduce me."

"Sawyer, this is Molly Watson. Molly, this is my bodyguard, Sawyer." As she expected, Sawyer only nodded.

"Bodyguard?" Aunt Mo nodded. "Well, that explains it. Guess a bodyguard can't go around smiling and making friends now, can he?"

"No, ma'am," Sawyer said.

"Well, good. That's good. You best make sure you take care of this one, too. You hear me? She's a special little bird." She took Emmy's hand, smiling.

"Yes, ma'am." Sawyer nodded.

"I wanted to bring this to Mr. Watson." She pointed at the gifts Sawyer was holding. "We were dropping them here, at the nurses' station."

"You should come up." Aunt Mo patted her hand. "I don't know his mind today but, if he's in a good place, I know he'd like to see you. Brock would, too, I'm sure."

Brock would *not* like to see her. "No." The word sort of erupted. "I don't think that's a good idea, Aunt Mo. I just…I wanted Mr. Watson to know I was thinking of him."

"He'd rather hear it from you." Aunt Mo was frowning now. "It won't take five minutes. David tuckers out real fast. Don't mind him if he rambles; he gets confused easily but he does try. I have no doubt seeing you will lift his spirits."

And just like that, Emmy Lou was leaning on Sawyer, heading into the elevator with Aunt Mo. Her lungs were rapidly deflating but her smile firmly in place.

"Brock said you took a fall?" Aunt Mo eyed her ankle brace.

He had? *Did he tell you he scowled at me and stormed out? Did he tell you how pathetic I was before he scowled at me and stormed out?* "Just a sprain." She shrugged. "You'd think I'd be better at dodging cords by now." Ricky Ames had made her angry—really angry. It wasn't an emotion she regularly dealt with.

Neither was arousal. But Brock, angry and defensive and gorgeous, had detonated the box containing all her wants and needs and desires. While he'd carried her across the field, she'd been grappling with the overwhelming need to touch him. Better yet, for him to touch her. And the video shoot… He'd stooped to help her, cared for her. She didn't care that her boot was broken—he'd broken it to help her. In the dark, close enough to breathe him in and rest her hands against his chest. His heart had been thumping hard under her palm.

But then he'd grabbed her hands and held her away from him. First the locker room, then the football field… She had to accept that whatever she was feeling wasn't reciprocated. More than that, he didn't like her.

"Here we are." Aunt Mo waited for the elevator doors to open, then stood aside for her and Sawyer. "We're straight down the hall, then right."

"What happened, Aunt Mo?" she asked, walking just behind the older woman. "All I read was he'd fallen?"

She nodded. "David's not as steady on his feet as you probably remember. He's been ill now for, oh let me see, four years or so? Like I said, he gets confused so we try to keep things plain and simple."

Four years? "I'm so sorry. I didn't know."

"Brock keeps it hush-hush. You know how he is." Aunt Mo laughed. "He doesn't like people in his business. I keep telling him he went into the wrong line of work for that, but the game is in his blood. Like singing is for you, I imagine." She paused in front of door five hundred and four. "Give me a quick second?"

Emmy nodded. "Of course."

Aunt Mo gave her cheek a pat and slipped inside the hospital room. "Well, how is my favorite brother?" Mo's volume was higher, her words more carefully enunciated—easier to understand.

Emmy heard an answering mumble.

"You have a visitor, David. Emmy Lou is here to see you. She brought a little something for you, too," Aunt Mo said, then paused. "Yes, yes, Brock's Emmy Lou."

"Dad." Brock's voice. "Aunt Mo, is this a good idea?" Of course, he didn't want her here. Not a surprise.

More mumbles. Aunt Mo laughed. Brock did not. But she wasn't here for Brock; she was here for Mr. Watson. Was it a bad idea? Yes. But she was here now and she wouldn't stay long.

"Emmy, honey, you can come on in." Aunt Mo opened the door.

"Give me five minutes, Sawyer." Emmy let go of his arm. "Five minutes." Without waiting for an argument, she took the cookie bouquet and gift bag and braced her hand on the wall for support as she moved into David Watson's hospital room. "Hi, Mr. Watson." She paused, doing her best to keep smiling. Seeing David Watson propped up, barely recognizable as the robust, athletic man she'd known, was going to take extra work. "I figured you could use some cookies." She set the cookie bouquet and the gift bag on the bedside table. "And I brought some puzzle books and magazines, too, in case you get bored."

He reached out a hand. "You know I like cookies."

She took his hand in both of hers. "Yes, sir. Snickerdoodles."

"You're a good girl." He nodded. "Always been a good girl. Molly and I were watching you on television." His words sort of faded off, but he kept smiling up at her.

"I try." She patted his hand. "It's not always easy."

"Now I don't believe that for a minute. If there's one thing I know to be true, Emmy Lou King, it's that you are good, through and through." Aunt Mo shook her head. "You need to sit? For your ankle?"

"No, I'm fine—"

But Brock pushed a chair behind her—without saying a word.

"Okay. Thank you." She let go of David Watson's hand and sat. "My daddy sent a book all about the history of football, the important players, and how the rules have changed. He thought you'd like it." She pulled the book from the gift sack and held it out. "If it's boring, it's Daddy's fault. Not mine."

David Watson glanced at Aunt Mo, then back at her. "You stopped by the house? It's been a long time since you've stopped by the house."

"Dad, we're still in the hospital." Brock stood at the end of the hospital bed, one hand resting on his father's foot. "You fell and hit your head and you're at the hospital."

Emmy hurt to see the older man's struggle with this information.

"Hospital." Mr. Watson nodded. "That's right. Hit my head." He chuckled.

"Good thing you're hardheaded." Aunt Mo sat on one of the plastic hospital chairs in the opposite corner. She pulled a mountain of yarn into her lap and collected her knitting needles from an upholstered bag on the ground next to the chair. "You're doing really well now, David. Doctor said you're healing up fine."

Mr. Watson patted the book cover, frowned, staring off for a long moment before he looked at her. "Brock said you two are getting married after he gets drafted into the AFL? I told him not to wait."

It took her seconds to recover, but she did. "Oh, he did, did he? That's the first I've heard of it." Her smile didn't waver. "He's a little full of himself."

David Watson laughed, hard. It might have been her imagination, but it sounded like Brock chuckled, too. But then Mr. Watson started coughing and the laughter stopped.

"You want some water, Dad?" Brock asked, pouring water into a plastic cup. "Have a sip." He held the cup out for his father.

Mr. Watson took a long drink and leaned back into the pillows with a sigh. "My boy has all sorts of big dreams, Emmy Lou. One of them is you."

She'd believed that once, too. "Dreams are good."

"They are," Mr. Watson agreed. "Glad you stopped by the house. Molly might have some cookies."

"We're at the hospital, Dad." Brock placed a hand on his father's shoulder. "You, me, Aunt Mo, and Denise. Denise will be here soon. You like your nurse Denise."

"Denise?" Mr. Watson smiled. "I do like Denise. She's sassy."

Brock chuckled then, drawing Emmy's gaze. He looked worn out. Dark bags under his eyes and a heavy stubble along his jaw. A quick glance around the room suggested he, or Aunt Mo, was sleeping in the recliner. A blanket was folded over the back and a small suitcase was wedged between the chair and the wall.

She noticed other things, too—little things that would make a difference for someone with memory issues. A sign that said "Bathroom" had been taped to a door—presumably the bathroom. The day of the week written in big, clear letters. The name of the nurse, also oversized and easy to read.

"Emmy Lou." David Watson leaned forward. "You remember that song you used to sing to me? The Patsy Cline song? It's my favorite."

"I do. 'Sweet Dreams.' It's one of my favorite songs, too." She swallowed, awash in memories of a better time and place.

"I miss you singing that." His brow furrowed. "Been a while. Hasn't it?"

Her heart hurt. "You want me to sing it to you?"

Mr. Watson nodded.

"Dad, Emmy—"

"Would be happy to sing to you." She cut Brock off, focusing only to David Watson. If he wanted her to sing, she was going to sing. "But I'm warning you, I'm a little rusty."

"Little bird," Mr. Watson said, closing his eyes. "Sing sweet." Brock's father had always called her "little bird." He remembered that. And it almost broke her.

"Yes, sir." She leaned forward and rested her elbows on his mattress. "Sweet dreams of you…" She sang, as softly as possible, and watched as Mr. Watson's features relaxed into sleep. "Why can't I forget the past, start loving someone new…" Her voice faded.

"You should finish," Aunt Mo said, knitting needles clicking away. "If you don't, I'll try. And no one wants to hear that."

Emmy repeated the last line, then finished. "Instead of having sweet dreams about you." She sat back, nodding at Aunt Mo's smile. She didn't look at Brock—she was too close to tears. But from the corner of her eye, she saw him. Arms crossed, jaw locked, as he walked to the large window and stared outside.

"Thank you, Emmy Lou. He normally fights sleep." Aunt Mo stopped knitting, regarding her brother with love. "Good to see him peaceful."

Emmy stood, swallowing against the lump in her throat, and stared down at David Watson. She couldn't imagine. Being in and out of time and place? It had to take a toll on a person. It had to be terrifying. For him and those who loved him.

"Glad I talked you into coming up." Aunt Mo used her knitting needle to point at her. "But I'm not letting you out of here until you give me your word you're coming to dinner sometime soon. You have my number, now, that hasn't changed. Brock said you were rail thin." She shook her head. "Now that I see you, though... A strong breeze could carry you away."

"It's windy today and I'm still standing." She went around the bed to hug Aunt Mo. "But that doesn't mean I wouldn't love to come to dinner." Another hug and she was on her way to the door, a throb in her ankle forcing her to place a hand on the wall for support. "You tell me when and I'll be there."

While Aunt Mo rattled off dates, Brock remained statue stiff, staring out the window.

"I'll get back to you, okay? And I'll go get food now, Aunt Mo, promise." She paused in the door, but Brock didn't move. *Okay then.* "Take care."

"You take care, Emmy." Aunt Mo's tone would brook no argument. "Have an extra piece of pie or cake, too."

"Maybe a cupcake." Emmy Lou walked into the brightly lit

white hospital wing and took a deep breath. "Thanks." She took the arm Sawyer offered.

"Still think it was a bad idea to come?" He set a slow pace for her.

"No. Not for Mr. Watson. Not for me. I'm glad I was able to spend time with him."

"You sang?" He pressed the elevator button.

"He asked me to." She frowned. "You heard? Why?"

"I did. And some nurses. A few of them stopped to listen." He sighed. "And recorded it."

"Oh no." She pressed against her temples and closed her eyes. Well, that clinched it. She'd waltzed in with cookies and good intentions and wound up putting a media target on Brock and his family. If he'd been mad at her before, he'd be furious now. "Of course, they did. That's the whole reason I came. To keep my family front and center in the papers. Always. Momma would be so proud of me."

Brock stared out the window, the clicking of Aunt Mo's knitting needles sounding just like the second hand of a stopwatch. Each click, each second, a countdown—until Emmy Lou was gone.

Off this floor.

Out of the hospital.

Gone.

Why she'd come didn't matter. She had come. She brought gifts, held his father's hand, and sang him to sleep. She remembered that his father's favorite cookie was a snickerdoodle. She remembered how much he loved Patsy Cline's "Sweet Dreams." She'd made his father happy. She'd done all that.

Why?

Did it matter? *Shit.* He could be too late—she might already be gone. *Shit.*

"Be back." He pulled the door open and headed toward the bank of elevators at the end of the hall.

Emmy Lou was waiting at the elevator, leaning heavily against her bodyguard. Another reminder. Even with a sprained ankle, she'd come to see his father. He hadn't said one word to her. Not that he had any idea what he would say. He reached them just in time to hear her say, "That's the whole reason I came. To keep my family front and center in the papers. Always. Momma would be so proud of me."

Brock came to a complete stop. Her words echoed in his head. The papers? To make her mother proud? *Are you fucking kidding me?*

Ice seeped into his veins, easing the hollowness eating away at his insides. What was wrong with him? One out-of-the-blue visit and he was ready to give her the benefit of the doubt. Why was he so willing to believe she'd changed? That she would *ever* change? What was it about her that turned him into such a fucking idiot?

He wasn't hurt; he wasn't giving her that sort of power. And he sure as hell wasn't giving her one more minute of his time. Before he could turn around, Emmy turned and saw him, her green eyes wide. "Brock?"

Walk away. Don't talk to her.

How could she look him in the eye? How could she visit her father, say and do all those sweet things, for publicity? *What the hell is wrong with* her? It felt good to get angry. Not just angry— furious. *Keep your shit together.* Now that they were surrounded by a group of curious bystanders, there would be no walking away. "Emmy." His voice was thick and low.

She noticed the interest they were causing. "Can we talk for a minute?" They had an audience, which was probably why she wanted to talk.

No. It was one word. But he couldn't say it. Pissed or not, he wasn't going to come off as the asshole here. "'There's a family room down the hall." Whatever happened next would be between the two of them—no one else.

"Okay." Her voice was soft and uncertain. She was so damn convincing.

"Alone," he added, giving her bodyguard a meaningful look.

"Okay." A dip formed between her brows.

"You sure?" The bodyguard didn't acknowledge his existence. He was too busy giving Emmy Lou a very disapproving look.

"I'm sure, Sawyer." She didn't look sure. Probably because the only reason she'd had anything to say was because of their audience. Reluctant or not, she took an unsteady step forward. "Lead the way."

He didn't want to help her, he didn't want to touch her, but—like it or not—manners had been too ingrained in his upbringing not to hook her arm through his. The stroke of her fingers along the inside of his forearm set his hair on edge. Which pissed him off even more. He relived every second of her visit, every smile, every touch… Hearing her intentions firsthand had cut him to the core. Her momma would be proud.

By the time they'd reached the empty family room, he'd managed to rein in his temper—somewhat. He turned on the light and closed the door as she asked, "It's Alzheimer's, isn't it?"

Maybe part of her did care. How else could she sound so concerned and look so damn heartsick? But he'd heard her; he knew her affection for his father wasn't why she was here.

To look at her, he'd never believe her callous and unfeeling. Standing there in her cream lacy skirt and silky pink top, with her hair tied back and sparkly studs in her ears and those ever-steady green eyes, it was no wonder she had everyone fooled. Everyone but him.

"You can sit." He nodded at one of the standard waiting room chairs lining the far wall.

"I wasn't going to come up." She ignored the chairs, her eyes fixed on his face. "I didn't want to intrude, but Aunt Mo saw me in the lobby and hugged me and then I was...here." Her expression was downright sorrowful.

It sounded plausible. Especially the way she delivered it. Too bad he knew she was lying. He stared up at the overhead lights. This was a bad idea. "I need you to stop."

"Stop?" She repeated. "Stop talking?"

He took a deep breath and met her stare. "Stop this. Whatever you're doing. Stop." He was moving toward her.

Her brow creased. "I don't understand." The front of her silky shirt trembled from her unsteady breathing.

How did she do that? Why? There was no one else here. "My family deserves privacy and respect." He sounded detached. He wasn't. If he were, he wouldn't be this close. But somehow, he'd backed her against the wall. "We are not the Kings. None of us *want* the spotlight." She winced, and he hated himself a little.

"I...I shouldn't have come." Her voice wavered.

That waver was a gut punch. Had she ever been the person he remembered? Or had she always been this manipulative? He braced himself, one hand against the wall by her head. "Why did you?" The words were hard and biting; he couldn't help it. He wanted her to admit it—all of it. "Why are you here, Em?"

She swallowed, her gaze searching his face. "I read that your dad was in the hospital and I wanted to check on him."

Once she admitted this whole thing was an act, he could smother out the last bit of hope he had that Emmy wasn't a bad person—that CiCi was wrong. "And?" His pulse hammered away, his lungs deflating as he asked, "Tell me." Another step, both hands pressed flat against the wall, framing her. "What else, Emmy Lou?"

"You." Her brow creased as she reached out, carefully laying her hand against his arm. "I was worried about you. Are you okay?" She was shaking.

He stared at her hand, battling to keep his mind clear. He should hate her. He had every right. He shook his head, angry with himself. With her. Her family. Life. "No. I'm not." If he were, he wouldn't ache for her this way.

"Oh, Brock." One minute she was against the wall, the next her arms were wrapped around his neck. "I'm so sorry."

He pressed his eyes shut, willing himself to push her away. Instead he stood, rigid, in her arms. Her breath was warm against his neck. Her sweet citrus scent teased, making it a struggle not to turn his face into her soft hair. She was soft, so soft, pressing herself closer. The swell of her breasts against his chest emptied his lungs. All of him yearned for comfort—for touch. It had been a long time.

That was why the urge to hold on to her was so strong.

Bullshit.

He wanted Emmy Lou more than he'd ever wanted any woman. He could still feel her lips, the taste of her skin, the curve of her breast filling his hand... But right now, he wanted more than memories. He wanted the real thing. This. Emmy, pressed up against him, all sweet softness and lies, *felt* real enough.

He knew better. As long as he didn't touch her, he stood a chance.

"Brock, I..." The moment their gazes locked, her words trailed off and her mouth formed a startled O.

He should look away—step back, say something, do something. But he couldn't move. The shift on her face was electric. A spark in her emerald eyes flamed to life. Her breathing picked up. Hitched. Color bloomed in her cheeks and she sank her teeth into her lower lip while her fingers dug into the back of his neck. When her gaze fell to his mouth, he almost groaned out loud.

The longer she stared at his mouth, the harder it was not to touch her.

Fuck it. At least this wasn't a lie.

He leaned closer. Close enough for their breath to mingle, close enough to see her pulse—racing—along the curve her neck. When their eyes met, there was heat and want and raw hunger. She was staring at him with wild eyes, a frantic sound slipping between her lips as she tugged him against her.

There was nothing hesitant about her kiss. Her lips touched his and she came to life. Arms tightening around his neck. Fingernails biting his scalp. She arched into him. When her lips parted beneath his and her tongue touched his, her moan obliterated all thoughts of self-control.

He cradled her face, running his thumbs along the line of her jaw, before sliding his fingers into her thick hair. He wanted to touch her, all of her, to make her remember this—make sure she'd never forget how she responded to him. He cupped the back of her head, sealing their mouths as his tongue slid between her lips. Her full-body shudder had him deepening his kiss, tightening his hold, and longing for more.

She was tugging at the back of his shirt, arching into him, clinging to him with the sort of desperate need he understood.

He'd give her what she wanted. He'd show her what she'd lost—what he still ached for.

His hands skimmed down her arms, along her sides, and gripped her hips. She was tiny, petite, easy to lift… With another throb-inducing moan, she hooked her leg around his waist and knocked the air from his lungs. Her skirt slid up, and his hand slid beneath, giving him the satisfaction of skin-to-skin contact. And damn but it was satisfying. The feel of her thigh, her hip… While she tugged his shirt free from his jeans and her fingers raked along his back, he braced them against the wall.

He couldn't stop kissing her, the corner of her mouth and the soft fullness of her lower lip. He could spend hours relearning the shape and taste of her.

She wrapped both legs around him and ground against the

rock-hard evidence of just how badly he wanted her. His fingers ran along the hem of her silk panties as he held her hips tighter, holding her against him—molding her to him. Her head fell back against the wall, eyes closed, breathing shaky, ragged breaths.

Her response was the final snare. He was stuck, trapped, and he didn't care. He'd stay lost in her. Her shudders and gasps, the thrusts of her hips, and the taste of her were all that mattered.

Knocking. On the door. As effective as an ice-cold shower.

Her eyes popped open.

"Fuck," he growled, blindsided by the raw hunger clouding her green gaze.

She was still holding on to him, breathing hard and dazed, when the door opened.

"Emmy Lou." Sawyer. The bodyguard. Of course.

She went rigid, her panicked attempt to untangle herself almost sending her to the floor—but he steadied her. When she was on her feet, with her skirt in place, he stepped away, putting several feet between them. He ran a hand along the back of his neck. *Shake it off.*

But she was still shell-shocked, staring at him with wide eyes. Rapid-fire emotions crossed her face. Disappointment, frustration—then embarrassment. She covered her face with her hands, shaking her head.

"There are some people who need to use the room." Sawyer cleared his throat.

"Of course," Emmy Lou mumbled from behind her hands. A deep breath and she repeated, "Of course." Her hair was messy, and she still looked pretty wild-eyed. Then again, she'd had her head thrown back, grinding against him, breathing heavy, and clinging to him less than a minute ago.

He shoved his hands into the pockets of his jeans.

The bodyguard was staring at him. Hard. The man didn't say much, but his body language said it all. If this Sawyer had a problem with him, fine. But finding Emmy Lou with her legs around Brock's waist didn't exactly make Brock the aggressor here. So, what the hell was the stare-down all about? How far did the man's protective instincts go?

"Here." The man took Emmy's arm.

"Thank you, Sawyer." She squeezed past Brock, avoiding his gaze and stepping carefully around him. Was she embarrassed about what had happened? Or because they'd been caught? If she hadn't touched him, kissed him, wrapped her leg around his waist, nothing would have happened. When her green eyes darted his way, he realized what was troubling her.

He'd kept control.

She hadn't.

For all her practiced charm and calculated maneuvers, Emmy Lou King wasn't as in control as she wanted to be. She wanted him. Bad. It was empowering as hell.

Chapter 8

EMMY LOU STOOD IN THE SPOTLIGHT, A MIC IN HER HANDS. SHE patted her left hand against her thigh, the champagne sequins of her minidress bouncing to the beat. When the guitar kicked in, she took a deep breath and started singing.

You think you're something special, staring my way.
You think I feel so lucky, like you've made my day.
But here's the truth, listen closely, cuz there ain't no way.
I'm looking for Mr. Forever, not you—Mr. For Today.

You're smiling like you've got a secret that I want to know.
But, honey, we've been down this road and that just ain't so.
Let's not waste each other's time putting on a flirty show.
You're just fun and games so, darlin', time for you to go.

But go on, keep on smiling. Feel free to keep on trying.
I know what I want. Nothing you can do.
Sad but true, boy, it isn't you. Oo-hoo-hoo, boy, it isn't you.

The second verse was just as catchy. More than a handful of audience members clapped and sang along with her. She smiled, clapping with the beat and rounding out the number with the final chorus.

But go on, keep on smiling. Feel free to keep on trying.
I know what I want. Nothing you can do.
Sad but true, boy, it isn't you. Oo-hoo-hoo, boy, it isn't you.

"Emmy Lou King, everyone." Late-night television host Guy James stood at the end of the stage, clapping.

Emmy bowed, blew a few kisses, and waved. With the help of a stagehand, she walked across the stage to Guy. He hugged her and helped her to her seat, opposite his large desk.

Brock, Guy's first guest, stood to greet her while she did her best to act normal, even though this was the first time she'd seen him since she'd tried to rip his clothes off. Now he was here, blue eyes shining, watching her. And what did she do? She held her hand out for a perfectly acceptable handshake. But somehow, he pulled her close and they ended up hugging.

Not a big deal. Yes, he smelled like heaven and his arm was rock hard around her waist, and the press of his hand at the base of her spine caused head-to-toe tingles, but...she would pull it together. Starting now. She would definitely not let these four, maybe five, seconds of being wrapped up in his arms remind her of the stroke of his hands or his fingers gripping her hips as he'd pressed her against the hospital wall.

She'd never experienced anything like it. Ever.

And now, here she was, thinking about it. Here. In front of an audience, late-night television host Guy James, *and* Brock. Brock, whose eyes pinned hers long enough to leave her rattled before he let her go and they could all take their seats.

"Well done," Guy said, still clapping. "We are so glad to have you here tonight." He tapped the desk with his pen and stared out over the audience, waiting for their applause to die down. "Really. It's been a while."

"It has." She nodded. "I think I was here as part of a package deal last time."

"That sounds right." He chuckled. "I'm sorry about your ankle. Is it quite painful? Side note, you've somehow managed to make an ankle brace look fashionable, Emmy."

She held her ankle out so the brace could sparkle in the lights.

"Thank you. You can thank my sister for the excessive bling." She'd left Krystal alone with a glue gun and a bag of crystals. Her rhinestones-and-sequins-covered brace was the result. Krystal thought it was hilarious.

"Your twin writes songs *and* decorates medical devices." Guy chuckled, the look he gave her brace causing a round of laughter from the audience. "Will you be wearing that when you kick off your new tour?"

"Our tour kicks off in six days." She'd never been so ready to get back on the road. "Three Kings and a Jace—since Jace is joining us. It's a play on poker. I'm not sure if Jace is the Jack or the Ace, but there you have it." She smiled at the ripple of laughter from the guest audience. "I think it will be our best tour ever. New music, new costumes, and a whole lot of flash and excitement." Some of the new choreography was wreaking havoc on her ankle.

Guy glanced at one of the notecards on his desk. "More good news I see. You're now the voice of Sunday night football? Are you a football fan?"

"Well, I have spent many a Sunday and Monday night beside my daddy, watching a game." Probably best if she kept her Brock fangirl status to herself.

"Don't let her fool you. She rattled off some stats the other day—I'd say she's a fan." Brock shifted so he could face her, his expression all business.

Emmy Lou blinked, momentarily caught off guard. He was teasing her? Here? Two could play that game. "Did I? Are you sure? Guess I forgot." She ran her hands over her thighs.

Brock smiled then, his gaze following the path of her hands and knocking the air from her lungs.

"You're from Austin, too, aren't you, Brock?" Guy asked.

Brock cleared his throat. "Yes, sir. Born and bred."

"And you two are both volunteers for the AFL Drug Free Like

Me campaign. How did you get involved with this project, Brock? This is very personal for you, isn't it?"

It was a loaded question. Everyone in the room knew the answer—Brock Watson's fall from grace had been well-documented. She'd been heartbroken over his troubles and the possible end of his career. He'd always been so single-minded, so driven. For him to have lost his way... It was hard for her to imagine what that was like.

"Short version? My tibial fracture four years ago led to a pain pill addiction and a string of bad choices." Brock shrugged. "I was damn lucky..." He paused, frowning. "Can I say damn?"

Guy nodded. "Damn is fine."

She and the audience laughed.

"It was the wake-up call I needed. Working with DFLM and the kids in this program helps keep me focused. I want to help in any way I can. It's the least I can do." Brock looked acutely uncomfortable at the audience's applause.

"Hear, hear. Well said, Brock." Guy glanced at his notecard. "And you, Emmy? It was your mother's addiction that made you want to participate. How is her treatment going?"

Emmy Lou nodded, doing her best to keep her smile in place. "Momma is a fighter. She's giving it her all." The extent of her addiction and her treatment was all very hush-hush. The little they did know had Travis saying Momma's once-a-week half-day rehabilitation sessions sounded more like high-end spa treatments. Still, Emmy clung to the hope that their mother would do whatever it took to get better. "And a lot of support, of course. We Kings stick together." And that was as much as she wanted to disclose about her mother. "I feel honored to be the first nonplayer on the AFL-sponsored DFLM team."

"You have your own jersey, don't you? Wait, let's look." Guy pointed at the screen. "These promotional photos are for schools, public transportation, libraries, that sort of thing. What is happening here?" Guy's brow rose high.

Brock laughed at the picture, shaking his head.

"Oh." She covered her face. "I'm making the same face as Demetrius, can't you tell?" She laughed.

"And this one?" Guy pointed at a new picture. "I didn't know you two have a history. The two of you were high school sweethearts?"

"Prom. Get it?" She pointed at the picture. "They thought using a football instead of flowers was cute."

"Not as cute as this one." Guy changed the picture. There she was, draped over Brock's shoulder. Both of them midlaugh.

"Aw, yes." She smiled. They both looked so happy—even if seconds later he had stormed off.

"I assume there's a story here?" Guy sat back in his chair.

"It was our senior year." She glanced at Brock, that day forever etched in her treasured memories.

"Our team made state playoffs," Brock added.

She nodded. "It was a close game. The kind where you hold your breath and sit on the edge of your seat."

Brock was staring at her. "You get that way when you watch football?"

People laughed.

"Not always." She tore her gaze from his and looked back at the picture. "When we won, everyone rushed the field. Very exhilarating stuff."

"She was running, I was running." Brock shrugged. "She jumped and this is how she landed."

"I was excited." She smiled, shrugging. "About the game *and* that he caught me."

Everyone laughed.

"We have the original." Guy smiled as the original picture appeared. "From your yearbook."

She tilted her head, studying the wide-eyed teens. "We were such babies."

"You haven't changed." Brock was rewarded with some "awws" from the audience.

"Nice to be reunited, I'm sure." Guy smiled, looking back and forth between the two of them. "For the charity, of course."

"For the *charity*." She had to work at laughter. "I see what you're trying to do there, Guy."

"That obvious, huh?" Guy laughed. "Fine. Before we say good night I have some very interesting information—courtesy of Demetrius Mansfield. He's a good friend of yours, isn't he, Brock?"

"I guess that depends on what information you have." Brock smiled, but his eyes narrowed.

Emmy Lou knew he was only partly joking, but the audience thought it was hilarious.

"He says you play the guitar." Guy paused, watching Brock.

Brock groaned and ran a hand over his face. "I don't play well."

"You do, too," she argued. "He's really good." The look Brock shot her made her wish she could rewind the last ten seconds and keep her mouth shut.

"I have a proposition for you both. You two play something for us?" Guy asked. "I'll donate to the Drug Free Like Me program *and* post the info on our show's website."

Which would give the program a huge boost in visibility.

She risked a look Brock's way. He was sitting forward, elbows resting on knees, looking intent and focused at the floor. She'd seen that face many times—when he was waiting to run out on the field and tackle someone. Was he imagining tackling Demetrius for telling Guy he played guitar? Or was it her, because she'd said he was good? The idea of him tackling her wasn't as unpleasant as it should have been. *Do not go there.* "Brock?" she asked.

He clapped his hands together and stood. "Let's do this."

The audience went wild.

She and Brock were ushered back to the performance area. He helped her onto one of the waiting stools and took the guitar he

116 SASHA SUMMERS

was offered. "Don't blame me if I mess up." He moved his stool next to her and sat, strumming over the guitar strings. A loud "We love you Brock!" from a row of women clad in Houston Roughnecks gear had Brock shaking his head, a dimple peeking out of his right cheek.

Emmy Lou smiled. She had to admit, he looked good holding a guitar. Who was she kidding? He looked good, period. Starched, white, button-down shirt with sleeves rolled up to reveal that even his forearms were pure muscle. Fitted black jeans that hugged and clung and teased at the strength beneath. And cowboy boots. Emmy Lou loved him in boots. He looked even better in a cowboy hat. She cleared her throat. "What am I singing?"

"Something easy." He paused, then added. "And short."

More laughter from the crowd.

The muscle in his jaw tightened. That's when she noticed he wasn't making eye contact or looking at the audience. This big, muscled-up, beautiful man was nervous.

"You pick." She leaned closer to him.

He ran his fingers along the neck of the guitar. "'Sweet Dreams'?" he asked, his eyes glued to hers. "He'll be watching." It was a whisper—for her alone. If Brock wanted her to sing to his daddy, she would sing all night long. Even though the flicker of affection and concern in his gaze had nothing to do with her, it touched her.

She nodded. "Definitely." It took everything she had not to reach for him.

———

Brock kept playing. He'd messed up a handful of times, but no one noticed with Emmy Lou beside him. She had the voice of an angel—always had. The tiny beads and sparkles covering her short dress made her glow. She sang with her eyes closed, head back, long hair swaying as she rocked side to side. Watching her sing—she was something.

According to Connie, Emmy Lou was the sort of PR influencer that automatically gave a bump to whatever product, person, or program she mentioned. Teens looked at her as a role model. Moms appreciated her positive influence. Men, it seemed, either wanted to screw her or protect her. But everyone, *everyone*, had an opinion when it came to Emmy Lou King. That was why Connie was so gung ho about the two of them doing spots like this together.

After their run-in at the hospital, Brock wasn't so sure it was a good idea. But Connie had brought him around pretty quick. "I'm not going to sugarcoat it. Bringing in Russell Ames isn't a good sign. He's not a second-string player," Connie had said on their last phone conversation. "You need options. Having your gorgeous face all over, next to America's sweetheart, will help with that. Trust me."

He trusted her. Otherwise, he wouldn't be sitting here, playing a guitar, on national television.

The song ended and he could breathe easy. Amid all the clapping and enthusiasm, Emmy Lou slid from her stool. She wobbled, reaching back for her stool, but he steadied her. Tucking her hand into the crook of his arm was instinctual.

Her fingers squeezed his arm. "You did good."

"Nah. But you did." It was a whisper, but she heard him, those big green eyes looking his way.

"Ladies and gentlemen, Emmy Lou King and Brock Watson." Guy joined them on the stage. "It's been a real pleasure visiting with you both. Thank you for the song."

"Thank you for the support," Emmy Lou answered, that oh-so-sweet smile in place. "One favor before we go? A picture?"

"I was going to be offended if we didn't take one." Guy nodded.

Brock didn't understand people's fascination with every little

.thing she did, but they were. Social media wasn't his thing, something else Connie wanted him to work on.

Emmy Lou held up the camera, her back to the audience. "Y'all wave," she said, tugging his arm and pulling him closer. "Come on, Brock, squeeze in here so I can get us all."

He shut out the soft brush of her hair beneath his chin and the curve of her hip pressed against his. More like, tried to shut out. But his body had other ideas. The whole night, he'd been distracted by her every movement, every breath, every flutter of her eyelashes, and her glossy grin. Why would that stop now, when he was posing for a selfie with her and a couple of hundred others?

"Smile. A little? You look…" Her eyes met his on her phone screen. She swallowed, her gaze widening. "N-not happy."

He wasn't unhappy. Because, right or wrong, there was something gratifying about knowing he could rattle Emmy Lou King. A whole hell of a lot. He was smiling now.

"Good." Emmy nodded, her voice a little higher, a little breathless.

After they said their goodbyes to Guy, Brock led her from the stage to the green room.

"That was awesome." Emmy's assistant caught up to them, handing Emmy Lou a water bottle. "You two should see the pings on the DFLM site." She handed him a water bottle, too.

"Thanks. Already?" he asked.

The woman nodded, taking Emmy's phone. "I'll post this. Hold on." She stepped in front of them. "Smile. Or act tired. Something cute I can post later."

"Cute?" Brock took a long swig off his water bottle.

"Perfect." The woman snapped a picture. "See?" She held the phone out. He and Emmy Lou were both guzzling water, her arm still hooked with his. "Cute. I'll tag it synchronized hydration. Or hashtag #waterbreak…or something." She shrugged. "Now, *food.*"

He didn't miss the emphasis on the word food. Beautiful or not, Emmy was too skinny. He'd noticed it. Aunt Mo had noticed it.

And now her assistant was bringing it up. "There's a steak place the team goes to every time we have an away game here, Remington's. You want to come?" *What the hell am I doing?*

"Melanie is a vegetarian." Emmy Lou shook her head. "But thank you."

As far as excuses went, it wasn't much of one. "This is LA; it's not like there won't be a vegetarian option." He glanced at Melanie. "You eat salad, don't you?" *Why the hell am I pushing this?*

"I love salad." Melanie hugged her iPad close and held the green room door open. "And you love steak, Emmy Lou. Sawyer and I can sit at another table—you won't even know we're there." She waited for Emmy to sit, then moved one of the stuffed ottomans under her injured ankle. "Beats ordering room service and eating in the hotel room alone."

He didn't give a shit about Sawyer. But he did care about Emmy...about Emmy Lou *eating*, that is. Besides, Aunt Mo would never forgive him if he didn't try.

"That sounds good," Emmy Lou said. "Not you sitting at another table with Sawyer. Room service. In my pajamas. Watching old reruns of *I Love Lucy* or that British baking show."

Melanie stopped working on her phone and looked at Emmy. She didn't say anything, just regarded her employer with a steady gaze. It was clear she was struggling not to say something. The longer she stared at Emmy, the tighter she pressed her lips together.

"No," Emmy Lou said, looking his way. "But thank you." He didn't miss the emphasis on the "no."

Message received. She wasn't interested. Fooling around with him in private was fine. Sharing a meal together wasn't.

"Okay. I'll go see if Sawyer has the car ready." Melanie hurried off, pulling the door closed behind her.

Once the door clicked shut, the air in the room thinned. He was staring at her. She was staring at him. The longer they stared, the more electrified the space between them became.

She swallowed. "Can we talk for a minute?"

"This time I think I'll stay over here." He crossed his arms, doing his best to act casual.

Her green gaze slammed into his, her cheeks going pink. "I guess I deserved that. It wasn't planned. Obviously. I don't know what happened. I just sort of…lost my head?" She seemed sincerely flustered.

He knew the feeling.

She blinked, her cheeks going darker. "I didn't go to the hospital to cause problems."

No, she'd come to get her picture in the paper with a flattering headline. Both of which had been accomplished. Emmy Lou's sweet goodness, singing to Brock's ailing father, had been touted as another example of her selflessness.

"Aunt Mo and your father always made me feel like I was part of the family." She stopped. "Things didn't work out between us, but I still think of you all—"

"You wanted to check up on him." Did she realize she was lying? Or had it become so second nature that it was instinctual? Either way, it pissed him off. Not just at her, but at himself. Even though he knew she was lying, he wanted her. Maybe that's why he pushed back. "You coming to the hospital had nothing to do with publicity? Or this?"

"This?" She swallowed, her gaze darting to his mouth then away.

"This, Emmy. You. Me." He broke off, but the words wouldn't stop. "I know you want me. You know I want you. And flattering news coverage is always a good thing for you Kings." He waited for her to deny it—waited for more lies. "Tell me I'm wrong."

She was staring at him. Frozen. Was she breathing?

"What would have happened if your bodyguard hadn't come in?" He stepped forward, looking down at her.

But she stayed quiet, those green eyes fixed on him.

Shit. Even now, he was giving her the upper hand. He'd just admitted he wanted her. And she hadn't said a thing. *Shit.* He should have kept his mouth shut. Instead he added, "You look me in the eye and tell me I'm wrong. Don't act like you were just there to visit my father."

He heard her sharp intake of breath, but it was the shock and anger on her face that held his attention. "Are you serious? You think..." She broke off. "Travis is right. You are a complete a-ass." She pushed herself onto her feet, pushing his hand away when he would have helped her up.

"For telling the truth?" There was an edge to his voice now. "The truth can be hard to hear. Hell, sometimes it hurts." He could attest to that fact.

She recoiled then, shaking her head, one hand pressed to her chest. "Is that what you want? To hurt me?" The red drained from her cheeks. "What have I ever done to you?"

It took everything he had not to laugh. Was she serious? Making fun of him? Or did she just not have the capacity to understand what love—love and trust—was? Or the hell that followed when that love and trust was broken?

Did he want to hurt her? *Yes. Dammit all to hell.* He wanted to hurt her. He wanted to hurt her like she'd hurt him. He wanted the lying to stop... But then he'd have to stop lying, too. He'd have to admit that every time he heard her sing, saw her face on a magazine or billboard, or touched her, the hole she'd left in his heart ached for her to come back and make him whole again.

Fuck no. He'd never give her that power over him, not again. Maybe the lies were easier.

The sooner he got out of there—away from her—the better.

She drew in a deep breath. "I—"

"Maybe we shouldn't talk anymore." Nothing good could come from this conversation.

"Fine," she agreed, walking to the other side of the room to lean against the wall. "You don't have to stay on my account."

None of this was fine. Not the anger, regret, and longing. Not the hurt she stirred, again. Not the wide-eyed, wounded look she was giving him as he pushed out of the green room and left the studio. He left knowing the last thing he needed to do was go back to his hotel and the minibar. Not right now, not this worked up.

He called his sponsor, went to a local gym, and worked out until he was sweat drenched and shaking. But after he'd showered and eaten his dietitian-approved dinner, he was still too worked up to sleep. He called Milton Thomas, a friend and LA Charger. Milton rounded up some friends and they hit a few clubs. Clubbing sober? Not much fun.

He slept for shit and woke up irritable and ready to get home. He hated leaving his father right now. Aunt Mo kept saying she had things under control, but that didn't make him feel any better. He should be there. Instead, he was heading toward some high-end men's clothing company to talk about a new endorsement deal.

"You were on fire last night." Connie sat across from him in their town car, the tinted window keeping the interior cooler than the triple-digit temperatures outside. "Who knew you could play the guitar?"

"I told you," he murmured, adjusting his sunglasses.

"I didn't think you could *play* play." She had one of those dramatic haircuts—black and supershort, with a long sweep of bright-white hair that fell at an angle across her forehead. With red-tipped fingers, she tucked the white strands behind her ear and grinned. "You should be thrilled. Guy James donated ten thousand dollars—and convinced his network to match it." She paused. "What's got you so uptight?"

Not what. Who. He wasn't going to talk about Emmy. He didn't want to think about her. He shrugged. "Who said I'm uptight?"

She arched a well-defined, black brow and shot him a pointed look. "Okay." The rest of the drive consisted of her filling him in on the latest pertinent player injuries and backroom chatter leading into this weekend's game. The first game of the season, and he wouldn't be playing. Ricky Ames's name came up and Brock had nothing nice to say about the kid.

"Everyone, and I mean *everyone*, knows he's a shit. But everyone knows he is a hell of a player." Connie leaned forward. "One thing he is not? You. *You* are Brock Watson. Don't let some cocky little asshole get in your head." She sighed. "Today is all you. Not the team or the game—just you. Options, Brock. Income streams off the field. Security. Responsible shit."

Standing in the foyer of Alpha Menswear's ultramodern foyer, he read the slogan, in bold, red, block letters, covering most of the far wall. "Be the alpha in the room."

Connie grinned. "I'm seriously psyched about this."

Fifteen minutes later, Brock was feeling pretty damn psyched, too. He did his best to keep a straight face. But it wasn't easy. They were willing to pay him seven figures to launch their new line. It wasn't a men's line so much as a men's underwear line. While he'd never imagined strutting around in underwear for a camera, he was willing to give it a go.

"We feel like Brock is the best fit. Our polling numbers confirm he is one of the most recognizable athletes out there and, frankly, a lot of fans find him attractive. Added appeal means added dollars when consumers are thinking about buying products for their family or significant other." Nolan Young, head of Alpha's marketing, kept going. "Our name is synonymous with quality. Brock Watson is, too."

Connie nodded, then asked Brock, "So?" He gave her the thumbs-up she'd been waiting on. "Then we have a deal," Connie said. "We'll be waiting for the final contract."

There was a collective sigh from the room, followed by a lot of handshaking and congratulations. But Connie had saved the best for last. As their driver took them to the airport and his waiting Cessna, she said, "I thought I'd share a little something with you."

"That's some smile." He waited.

"You wouldn't believe who was campaigning for this." Her smile grew. "I didn't want to tell you before the meeting because I thought it might stress you out." She clapped her hands. "But now... If you thought Ricky Ames didn't like you before, get ready. He wanted this, begged for this. And you got it."

That did it all right. That, right there, was the pickup he needed. It felt good. Maybe a little too good. "Well, damn." He ran his fingers over his jaw, fighting the urge to laugh. "Poor kid." But then he was laughing, hard. Ricky Ames might play hard, but Brock Watson wasn't a quitter. "Game on."

Chapter 9

"WHO WENT TO THE STORE LAST?" KRYSTAL WAS STARING INTO the pantry. "Why do we have nine boxes of kids' cereal?"

"I think Travis did one of those online orders." Emmy Lou sat at the scrubbed plank kitchen table and propped herself up on her elbow. "Probably while drunk. Or getting drunk. Or…" She stopped talking as Krystal emerged, balancing three huge boxes of cereal. "You're not planning to eat that, are you?"

"Yep." She retrieved a bowl and spoon and milk, then sat opposite her sister. "And if you keep up the judgy stare, I will build a protective fort with the boxes."

Emmy Lou laughed. "No judgment."

Krystal poured a large bowl of brightly colored, sugarcoated rings. "Whatever." She glanced at her bowl, then Emmy. "Still doing the self-imposed hunger-strike thing?"

"Hunger strike?" She tried not to think about how yummy the cereal looked. They'd been her favorite as a child—until the day Momma had shown her a diagram about the glue-like effects of sugar at the cellular level. She'd been twelve or thirteen. Krystal had fallen asleep, but Emmy Lou had listened as Momma had rattled off the horrible things sugar would do to her body. Momma drove home how important it was for them to look their best for their fans, how selfish it was to overindulge in sweets, and how anything that tastes really good is probably bad for you. After that, her love of food got complicated. Stress made it worse. A whole cookie or piece of cake—her body rejected it. Now? She was stressed. The Guy James visit. Brock. He'd sounded mad that he wanted her. He certainly didn't *want* to want her. And accusations that she was using his father for press… "Maybe I'm just not hungry right now."

"Or *ever*." Krystal spooned up a huge bite of cereal. "Not since you were like…eighteen?" Krystal could eat her weight in Red Vines without a care in the world. "Oh, this is *so* good." She scooped up another bite.

The kitchen door swung open and Travis came in, yawning and rubbing a hand over his face. He took one bleary-eyed look at the table and advanced. "Whoa, whoa, whoa." He reached for the cereal boxes on the table, but Krystal grabbed the Fruity-o's box. "You can't just raid a man's stash, Krystal. Come on now."

"I can if the *stash* is in my kitchen." She cradled the box against her chest, took another bite of cereal, and smiled up at Travis. But Travis kept standing there, staring, until Krystal eventually snapped. "What? What is your deal, Trav?" she asked, tapping her spoon against the bowl.

"That's my favorite kind." He pointed at the box Krystal held.

Emmy Lou stood up, got a large bowl from the cabinet, grabbed a spoon, and put them on the table. "Give me the box." She held her hand out, laughing now. "The box."

Krystal sighed but handed over the box.

Emmy poured a heaping amount into the bowl, poured milk, and looked at her still-frowning brother. "Eat." She pushed the bowl toward him. "All yours, Big Brother."

Travis ran a hand over his face. "I didn't want it right *now*."

"You are such a child." Krystal threw a fruity cereal O at him.

"Really?" Emmy Lou shook her head. "Just *eat*."

"You eat it," Travis argued. "I just want coffee." Another yawn. "You need it more than I do, anyway."

Emmy Lou shook her head and took a sip of her tea. "Would you both stop? I came down here for peace and quiet and tea."

"Peace? In this house?" Krystal shot her a look of pure disbelief. "Might as well get over that and, you know, *eat* something with your tea. If I were you, I'd eat Trav's. The whole box."

"No thanks. I'm *not* hungry." Emmy Lou picked up her cup and turned to leave.

"Wait, Em, I'm sorry." Krystal pleaded. "I'll stop. Please stay. Please. We haven't had breakfast together in so long—"

"Because you've shacked up with your boy toy." Travis sat, picked up the spoon, and started eating. "Why are you even here eating my cereal…? Right, Momma's got that retreat thing today." He kept right on munching. "Still, you and Jace need to get your own cereal. Keep your mitts off mine."

Krystal was ready to launch another O at their brother but caught Emmy watching her and held her hands up. "See? I'm being good."

How long would that last? Her twin's smile was so mischievous that Emmy had no choice but to smile back.

Travis scooped up a bite. "So…I've been looking at apartments. To keep my cereal safe."

Emmy Lou stared at him. This was news to her. Not necessarily good news. She'd still see her siblings on the road, but she missed this. Lazy mornings full of laughter and teasing and cereal throwing without the time constraints and exhaustion of a touring schedule.

"You can't do that." Krystal threw a piece of cereal at him. "Spill."

Emmy grabbed a piece of Krystal's cereal and threw it at him, too. The bright purple O veered sharply and bounced off the table onto the floor.

"Pathetic." Travis glanced at the cereal on the floor. "I need a reason? Like you two don't know? Freedom. Escape. Breathing room. You pick. Besides, you already moved out."

"Not *officially*." Krystal frowned. "My mail still comes here."

Travis shook his head. "I can't stay here. Momma is like a time bomb. The home studio? The costume approval? She's not happy about you and Jace. She's not happy about Emmy Lou working with the AFL. She's not happy about the direction of our music…"

"The underlying thread in all of that is her lack of control," Krystal murmured.

As far as Emmy was concerned, Momma was just acting like Momma. Travis was just more clued in now. But she might be a little more intense now that Krystal wasn't around.

"Whatever. It's only a matter of time before she explodes, and I don't want to be in the blast radius. Damn, when did we get so fucked up?" He used his spoon to point at each of them.

"We are not..." Emmy Lou started to argue, but it was halfhearted.

"Mm, Em, I hate to disagree but...we *are*." Krystal wrinkled up her nose. "We *so* are."

"I feel like I live on some reality television show. A really *bad* one. 'Tonight, on *The King Family Crap* we explore lingering questions.'" Travis was using his spoon as a microphone now. "'After deserting them in their time of need, will Hank King ever be able to look his children in the eye? Is CiCi King truly a recovering addict? Or is she simply using her possible addiction as an excuse to get away with her evil and manipulating ways? Will Krystal and Jace stop boning enough to make music? Will Travis's parts actually fall off from a horrible sexually transmitted disease? And will Emmy Lou retire her nun's habit and eat a donut or twelve?'" He stopped, his gaze bouncing back and forth.

Laughter filled the kitchen. On and on, until Krystal managed, "You *so* do *not* need coffee."

"I do." He stood, spoon hanging from the side of his mouth, and headed to the coffeepot on the marble-topped counter.

"Okay, fine. But can you not make it strong enough to cause heart palpitations?" Krystal asked.

"I like it how I like it." He kept heaping coffee into the machine.

Emmy Lou smiled. They all had a laundry list of worries. Most of which Travis had ticked off in his faux reality TV voiceover. She'd never dared admit her suspicions about her mother, but apparently, she wasn't the only one. While her brother and sister were angry, Emmy Lou was sad. For her mother and father, Travis and Krystal—and herself.

Krystal pulled her bowl back and poured more cereal. "So you're moving out? What about Daddy?"

Emmy Lou held her breath. The friction between her father and brother was so thick, it made being in the same room as them unbearable.

"What about him? He is not my responsibility." Travis frowned. "It's past time we live our own lives—by our own rules. That includes having my own roof over my head."

"What about Emmy?" Krystal asked.

And then Travis and Krystal were both staring at her, waiting for her to say something. "What about me?" She sipped her now-cold tea.

"If we're not living here to pester the shit out you, you'll starve to death." Travis frowned.

"Ha ha, you're hilarious." Emmy glared at him.

But Krystal and Travis weren't smiling; they were both staring over her shoulder at the kitchen door. From the look on her brother's face, she knew without having to look that their father was there. Travis's defensive posture hurt her. She could only imagine how it made Daddy feel.

"Daddy." Emmy stood, forcing a smile even though anguish tightened her throat. "Want some coffee?"

"I'll get it. You eat." He looked tired—beaten down. "It's been a while since I've seen you all in the same room." He glanced around the table. "Mighty fine sight."

"Emmy Lou wants some real food." Krystal stood. "Since I'm already cooking, I'll make you something, too. Sound good?"

"I won't say no to that." Daddy even sounded beaten down. "No way."

Emmy Lou ignored the victorious flash in her sister's eyes.

She'd choke down bacon and eggs and biscuits if it made Daddy happy. "I do love your biscuits. With lots of butter and jam."

Their father sat at the opposite end of the table from Travis, stretching his legs out in front of him and letting out a long, slow sigh that seemed to deflate him from the inside.

She placed a hand on his arm. "Still coming to the game tomorrow?"

He nodded, sipping his coffee and wincing again. "Damn shame Brock is still on the bench. He mention anything about when he'd be released to play?"

She shook her head. "We really haven't...talked." *About football.*

"No?" Daddy slowly turned the coffee mug between his hands. "I always figured he'd be part of the family someday." He patted her hand. "I never saw a boy so sweet on anyone the way he was on you."

Daddy's words stirred up a tangle of memories full of love and loss and bone-wrenching grief. "That was a long time ago, Daddy. Things change."

"Most times, your first love isn't your only love." Krystal piped up, banging around the kitchen, assembling ingredients. "Besides, Daddy, Emmy Lou deserves someone better. Someone true-blue. A rock."

"I thought Brock was all those things?" He sighed. "Guess I'm not the best judge of character."

Travis snorted. It didn't slip out, either. It was loud and hard and intentional.

Emmy Lou watched the narrow-eyed, unspoken exchange between her father and brother. It wasn't right. None of this was right. Maybe the family counseling wasn't a bad idea. At this point, they could probably all use someone objective to talk to.

"What about you, Daddy?" Krystal asked. "I know you were Momma's first love. But you were young and handsome and on the road long before she came along. Was there anyone special?" Her sister was watching their father like a hawk—all while whisking eggs in a big ceramic bowl.

Where was this coming from? Emmy Lou took a sip of tea, staring at her sister over the cup's edge.

"That *was* a long time ago." Their father shook his head.

"Still, you never forget a first love." Krystal pushed. "Not if it was the real thing."

Daddy nodded, turning his mug again, slowly. "No, you don't." He cleared his throat. "But you do move on."

Emmy shot her sister a what-are-you-doing look about the same time Travis went to pour himself another cup of coffee—and elbowed the bag of flour to the floor. A huge cloud of white billowed up to cover her brother and sister from head to toe. Krystal turned toward Travis, fuming, flour coated, with eggs dripping from her flour-covered whisk.

"Krystal, now, it was an accident." Daddy chuckled. "How about you two get cleaned up and we'll go have brunch before heading out? Emmy Lou and I will clean up the kitchen."

Her daddy was laughing. For a split second, the tension and stress and drama were gone.

———

Emmy Lou King singing the national anthem for the Roughnecks' first game of the season should have tipped Brock off that things were going to fall apart. Since he'd left LA, thinking of her left a bitter taste in his mouth. Now, here she was, like lemon juice in a paper cut. And things just kept going downhill. The Green Bay Bears weren't projected to do well, so going into halftime tied was a serious blow to the team attitude.

Listening to Coach McCoy's halftime pep talk only made him hate being benched that much more. The man was a good coach.

He knew this game, knew how to read the plays…so watching Ricky Ames roll his eyes, looking bored as hell, had Brock seeing red.

Third quarter, Ricky Ames fucked it up. Not some accident; that shit happens. No, he'd been showboating—and lost the ball. Then Ames bowed up and chest bumped an opposing teammate. Flags were thrown, whistles were blown, and the Roughnecks suffered penalties.

Brock was up and on his feet, pacing—willing himself to calm the fuck down.

The Roughnecks had been projected to win by two touchdowns. In the end they won by a field goal.

He headed back into the locker room, more than eager to head home, and yanked open his locker. An avalanche of underwear came pouring out onto the floor. Not just men's underwear. Kids' underwear. Women's underwear. Action heroes, unicorns, lacy panties, and a bag of adult diapers.

"We heard someone scored a big-ass endorsement deal." Gene Byrd had been the Roughnecks' running back since before Brock joined the team. "Congrats."

Brock laughed. "Dicks."

"I'm not sure the world is ready to see you in tighty-whities." Quarterback Jacob Oliver slapped Brock on the shoulder. He leaned forward to tease. "When you're not making money showing off your ass, maybe you could get it out there on the field, with the rest of us?"

Brock shook his head. "I'm trying."

"Try harder. We need you on the field," Russell Ewen murmured as he walked by.

Ricky Ames brushed past him, back stiff, chin stuck out. He was on the defensive; Brock got that. And even though the kid was a pain in the ass, it was his first game and he'd wanted to prove himself. Hopefully, he'd learn from today's mistake and move on. It was the way the game worked. But that didn't mean it was easy.

"It happens," he said.

"What?" Ricky asked, wiping off his face with a towel.

"Mistakes." He started shoving the packages of underwear into his extra gym bag. Throwing them away was wasteful—Aunt Mo frowned upon that sort of thing. Maybe he could donate them—or something. He'd leave that up to Connie.

"Mistakes?" Ricky faced him. It was clear from the fuck-you posture and scowl on Ames's face he didn't think he'd made a mistake.

Should have kept my mouth shut. "Forget it." He finished shoving the last underwear pack into his bag, slung it over his shoulder, and closed his locker.

"I get that you think you have some sort of role to play here. Like it's your job to teach me shit or something." Ricky threw his towel on the ground and crossed the room. "But I'm not sure why I'd listen to a recovering drug addict who spent just as much time on the bench as he has on the field in the last two and a half years."

"Everything you just said is true." Brock was done letting Ames in his head. "Just so we're clear: I don't give a shit about your career or your ego. I care about my team." He shrugged. "If you want to take another swing, go for it. You know what Coach will do."

Ricky Ames didn't budge. He didn't back down—but he didn't open his mouth.

And while Brock didn't relish the idea of walking away first, he had no interest in having a pissing match with the kid. His father was being discharged from the hospital and Brock needed to be there for that. With a shrug, he grabbed his stuff and headed toward the exit.

Outside the locker room, a few fans had gathered for autographs. He paused, signing programs and posing for pictures, then hurried toward the parking lot. His phone started ringing as he unlocked the door. He opened it...another avalanche of underwear came spilling out onto the hot concrete parking lot. "Shit."

He pulled open the back door of his four-door truck and started throwing the packages inside. If he got pulled over, he'd have a hard time explaining this. He answered the phone. "Brock here."

"Brock?" He knew the husky voice. "Hey, do you have second?"

"Vanessa?" He slammed the back door and climbed into his truck. It had been a couple of months since he'd seen his ex-wife. He'd been leaving his Narcotics Anonymous meeting and she'd been going in. She'd looked good. Clean. Healthy. He hoped she was.

"Hi." Her voice wavered.

"You okay?" If she was, would she have called?

"I'm just having a hard day and, I don't know, I wanted to hear a friendly voice."

He started the truck, waited for his phone to sync before answering. "How hard?" he asked, moving slowly through the parking lot and onto the highway.

"Hard." She paused. "Really hard."

"Don't take this the wrong way, V, but you need to call Janine." He ran a hand along the back of his neck. "She's your sponsor."

"No. I know. And I called her. I did. But she didn't answer." She sniffed. "I just, well, I called you."

Because he was one of the few people who knew the true scope of Vanessa's addiction. She'd always dabbled—it helped her stay thin—a job requirement for a model. But when he'd been injured and taking pain pills, Vanessa had introduced him to a new world of things to inject, snort, or smoke. It hadn't ended well. "I'm going to an NA meeting in the morning. You need a ride?"

"Sure." She paused. "I'll call in the morning, though, just to make sure."

"V? You've worked hard to get clean." He didn't know what else to say. Their divorce had been a mutual agreement, so they'd managed to stay friendly—but not close.

"I know. I know." She sniffed. "I heard about your dad. How is he?"

"He's being discharged to his assisted living facility. It's good. At least there will be familiar faces." Or would they be? His dad's memory was continuing to slip.

"I'm glad to hear it. Give him my best, please." Her phone beeped. "It's Janine." The relief in her voice was instantaneous. "Okay. I'll let you go. Take care, Brock. Bye." She hung up.

Talking to Janine would help. He didn't know how he'd make it without his sponsor, Randy. Hopefully, with her new fiancé and her career on the upswing, Vanessa would have the motivation she needed to stay clean.

The Three Kings were playing on the radio. Their number one hit "Your Loss" was the ultimate breakup song. He didn't know who or what inspired it, but after Emmy Lou had started sending back his letters and his heart had been shredded, the angry lyrics hit close to home. It was like Krystal had stolen his thoughts and feelings and put them to music.

He blasted the music, humming along, fingers tapping out the beat on the steering wheel.

> *You tell yourself you never loved me.*
> *You tell yourself you never cared.*
> *But every kiss makes you miss me*
> *And every touch leaves you scared.*
>
> *Now your heart, your soul, your bed is empty*
> *And you know, you see, there's no replacing me.*
> *But, baby, all I can say is: it's your loss.*
> *Oh, baby, baby, baby, it's your loss.*

His phone buzzed as he was parking. A message from Aunt Mo. He's not himself, Brock. They had to restrain him for his own safety. His discharge has been delayed. You don't have to come.

He sat in his truck, clearing his mind of Emmy Lou and Vanessa and Ricky and the pile of underwear he had in the back seat of his car. Aunt Mo meant well, but he did have to be there. When he hit rock bottom, it had been his father who had helped drag him back. Even struggling with the beginning stages of this horrible disease, his father had taken care of him—showed him how to fight, took him to meetings and doctor's appointments, never gave up on his son or stopped reminding Brock what was worth fighting for. His father might not remember any of that now. But Brock would never forget.

Chapter 10

"WAVE," EMMY SAID, POINTING AT THE IMAGE ON ONE OF THE jumbotron screens.

All eleven kids waved, some made silly faces, others had shy, little smiles—one little boy burst into tears and hid behind Shalene. They sat, each in their Houston Roughnecks T-shirt, on a bench along the sideline while the players warmed up.

"Who's your favorite?" Emmy asked the quiet little girl sitting beside her. Anna was adorable, with a lopsided ponytail and massive tortoiseshell glasses that covered most of her face.

Anna shrugged. "I don't know. My daddy likes Gene Byrd so I guess I do, too."

"My daddy does, too." Emmy nodded. "He's a good player."

Shalene had called her this morning, frantic, after one of their ambassadors canceled. So here she was, playing guide to eleven lucky elementary students who'd all signed a Drug Free Like Me Agreement. It was halftime, and the kids were on the field and ready to play catch with the teams when they showed up...

Bear—Emmy always thought of him as the triangle player— had taken a bad hit at the end of the second quarter. While there'd been no official statement on his condition, Emmy suspected he wouldn't be joining them after all. Hopefully, he was okay.

"Is Bear dead?" one of the little boys asked, his teeth and lips dyed purple from his frozen slushie.

"No," Emmy assured him. "He'll be just fine."

"He looked dead," another little boy agreed. "He fell over." The little boy stood up and fell on the ground, flat. "Boom. Just like that."

For the next five minutes, all eleven kids did their own imitation of Bear's fall. Emmy wasn't sure whether she should laugh or not. But when one of the boys shared a story about his goldfish dying and how it did not fall over—it floated upside down—before proceeding to demonstrate how it looked, fish face and all, Emmy had to laugh.

That was why she didn't notice Brock until he was kneeling by Anna saying, "Don't let Emmy Lou throw the ball."

"Why?" Anna asked.

"Trust me." Brock shook his head, looking serious. "She needs to work on her aim." But he was looking at her ankle brace.

"Maybe she needs lessons?" Anna said, pushing her glasses up. "My daddy says lessons make you better."

"Maybe that's it." He nodded, looking up at Emmy. "You want some lessons?"

"Only if RJ has time." *Don't look at him. Don't look at him.* Her gaze bounced his way.

Brock's blue eyes locked with hers a second longer before he turned to Anna. What did that look mean? *I don't care.* Why would she care about someone who thought she'd use a hospital visit for promotion? *I don't.*

The two of them, side by side, were quite a picture. He was a mountain. Next to him, Anna looked like a tiny doll.

"Go easy on me, okay, Anna?" He stood, hands on his hips, staring down at the little girl.

"My daddy says you should always give a hundred percent." Anna shrugged.

Emmy had to smile at that. "Always," she agreed.

"Sounds like your daddy and my daddy would get along." He shook his head, winked at Anna, and ran across the field.

Between RJ acting like one of the young kids was throwing too hard and Gene's acrobatics on the field, the kids were having a great time. Emmy, too. She snapped a few pics on her phone and laughed as five little boys tried to tackle Brock.

But then Ricky Ames came onto the field and headed straight

for her, his eager smile a little too eager. "I was hoping you'd show up again, Miss Emmy Lou King. Looking even prettier than last time I saw you." He smiled. "Been playing my heart out, just for you."

Emmy tucked a strand of hair behind her ear. "Really?" Was he for real?

"Yes, really." He stepped closer, closer than he needed to. "You need to know now, when I set my sights on a woman, I'm all in. Just like I am on the field."

"Ricky." She paused, making sure he was paying attention so there was no misunderstanding her when she told him it was never ever going to happen.

He wasn't listening. He was so focused on her boobs that he jumped when the whistle blew. "Kiss for good luck?" he asked, sticking his cheek out.

"No." She walked past him, following the kids and Shalene back to the sidelines. They waited as the parents came, one by one, to escort their children back to their seats.

By then, the players where back on the field, helmets on, in the zone and ready to go. The air was charged, expectant—kind of like it was for the Three Kings before a show. She blinked, a movement catching her eye. It was so fast she wasn't sure what it was... Something small, moving quickly. But then the ball of black fluff stopped, midfield, tiny ears poking up and fluffy tail barely visible. No. It couldn't be. A kitten?

It was so small. Too small. Would the players see it? The refs? Someone?

Move. Please move.

It didn't. The tiny, black puffball hunkered down in the middle of the twenty-yard line. Terrified and frozen and in harm's way. She looked around for someone, anyone, but no one could hear her over the pure chaos on the sideline. Standing here doing nothing wasn't an option.

"This is a bad idea." Then she took off, running as fast as she could. Everything was a blur. The crowd roared. A solid thunk and crack echoed behind her. Then another—louder. Closer? Her speed picked up, her lungs bursting, her ankle throbbing…but she was so close. All that mattered was getting the tiny thing away from thundering cleats, two-hundred-pound-plus players, and missile-force footballs flying through the air. The kitten took one look at her and mewed. It mewed again when she scooped it up and held it close. "It's okay. We're okay."

That was when she noticed the cheers. The stands were going wild, some booing, some cheering—the overall noise was deafening. And when she turned around, she saw why. Two Dallas Bronco players, on their butts, staring back and forth between her and Brock in disbelief.

Brock, who was breathing hard, the human wall standing between her and them.

"I'm sorry," she said, glancing back and forth between the players and Brock, the enormity of what she'd just done sinking in. "I am so…*so* sorry." She cradled the kitten close and limped/ran off the field, mumbling apologies to the wide-eyed staff along the sideline. But they weren't looking at her. They were looking up.

At the jumbotron. The instant replay… It wasn't pretty.

There she was, racing across the field. And Brock jumping up, putting on his helmet as he charged after her onto the field. He flattened the two unsuspecting Dallas Bronco players headed down the field to score—all while Emmy was scooping up the kitten. Finally, Brock, breathing hard and nodding at the shower of yellow flags flying onto the field before he helped the two Bronco players back on their feet.

This was bad.

"Miss King." A referee was headed her way, two uniformed security guards with him. "We need you to leave the playing area."

One of the security guards stepped forward. "We'll escort you to your seats."

"Oh, that's not necessary." *This was* so *much more than bad.*

"Actually, it is, ma'am." The security guard cleared his throat. "Normally, we'd escort you from the building, but you being you…"

"Oh." She nodded. "Yes. Of course." But guilt made her stop. "This is all my fault. If there's a penalty for disrupting a game… What can I do?"

"Miss King." The referee sighed, tapping his watch. "We will discuss this after the game."

"Right." She nodded, glancing beyond the referee, beyond the players laughing over the slow-motion replay of her kitten rescue, searching for Brock. He was getting an earful from their coach. And it was her fault. The last thing he needed was trouble with his team. He'd been benched for his injury. *His leg.* She stopped again, but one look from her security-guard escorts got her moving.

He hadn't been cleared to play. He shouldn't have been chasing after her—protecting her.

She stared down at the wide-eyed kitten. Which was worse? That her actions could land him with a substantial penalty and prevent him from playing once he'd been cleared to come back? Or that he might have reinjured himself protecting her?

She was all smiles and waves en route to her family's box. But once she was inside and there were no prying eyes or cameras, she sat, kitten held close, and slumped down in her seat. For all the kitten's fluff, the little thing felt fragile in her hold. "Melanie?" Emmy asked. "Can you get the kitten some milk or cream or something?"

"I'm on it." Melanie nodded and hurried from the box.

"Little thing all right?" Daddy took one look at her and patted her knee. "Ankle okay?"

The kitten curled up in her lap and began purring. "I think so." She hadn't given a thought to her ankle. She ran a hand over its silky fur, shaking her head. *What was I thinking?*

"Can't deny it didn't liven things up a bit." Daddy winked and turned around, leaning forward on his elbows to watch the game.

Travis was sitting behind her. As soon as their father was preoccupied with the game, he leaned in and whispered, "That *was* interesting. Brock going all Hulk protecting you."

Yes. No. He was in trouble. Because of her. Not that she'd made him run after her...but he had. "Not now." She frowned at her brother, shooting a silent plea at her sister and Jace.

Krystal rolled her eyes. "Give it a rest, Trav."

"What?" Travis's gaze narrowed. "She should know how many people ran after her."

"*How* many?" *This wasn't bad—this was a nightmare.* "I didn't mean to get anyone in trouble." The kitten was asleep on its back, paws in the air, fluffy tummy exposed.

"It's okay, Em." Krystal pushed Travis's shoulder. "Can you please be nice? She's upset."

"I didn't do anything." Travis sighed. "Don't sweat it. Brock was the only one. You'd barely put one foot on that field and he was already covering you. Pure *instinct.*"

Brock had fast reflexes. He was acting on instinct. It didn't mean anything.

"I noticed that." Jace nodded, looking her way. "Not exactly a tool move. More like a good, decent guy thing to do."

"Exactly." Travis nodded. "Decent. Unless he's after something." He was smiling from ear to ear. "You'll have to talk to him to figure out what that might be." He winked. "Or you can let a different *instinct* kick in. Sex can diffuse a lot of tension. I agree with Jace, you've got options."

"No." Jace shook, looking downright horrified. "I didn't say that at all."

Emmy could only shake her head. Just when she thought her brother couldn't do or say something to shock her, he did. "You're going to bring *that* up now?"

"That? You mean sex? Yes. Jace and I are both guys. Might want to listen to us." Travis nodded, on the verge of laughter.

Jace opened his mouth but Krystal cut him off. "There's no point, Jace. He thinks he's hilarious."

"Stop worrying." Travis was laughing now. "You know what's good for stress? Se—"

"Travis, if you say or hint about…sex one more time…" Emmy's words ended when their father glanced back at them.

"You'll what?" Travis asked, smiling.

"I don't know." She stroked the kitten's tummy. "I hope his leg is okay…" And just like that, she'd said too much.

Krystal gave her a long look. "Nobody made him, Em." She sighed. "I mean, I don't like him. But…what he did didn't suck, okay? Let's leave it at that." She paused, shrugged, and looked at the kitten. "It's so cute. Think Clementine will eat it?"

Emmy looked down at the tiny scrap of fur. "I hope not."

"Em?" Krystal groaned. "I can't believe I'm going to say this but *maybe* Travis is right."

Travis whispered. "Sex will fix everything." He burst into laughter.

"No," Krystal snapped. "About Brock keeping an eye on you. Not all stalker-y—just aware. Of you. He always was that way with you."

"Who knows? Some good press might keep him from getting fired." Travis shrugged, then winced as Krystal smacked him in the back of the head.

Emmy felt downright sick. *Fired?*

"Don't listen to him." Krystal hugged her. "Everything will be fine."

Emmy wanted to believe that. But what if it wasn't? What if her spur-of-the-moment act cost Brock the one dream he had left? Even though his accusation still stung and it would be awkward, she had to talk to him. She had to know and, if possible, find a way to make amends.

Brock kept his head down. The team was still on a high from their win—fourteen points up. It was too much to hope that his team would forget what had happened in the first five minutes of the game. It was damn lucky they'd won the game—everyone was in a good mood.

Everyone but him. Watching Emmy run onto that field had triggered something. He didn't think or question or have any sort of plan beyond protecting her. He wasn't willing to risk one or both of the huge Broncos going through Emmy Lou to make a touchdown. It wasn't like either of them would have been on the lookout for a woman, or a kitten, on the field. Going after her, protecting her, was what he had to do—no matter what the consequences.

Once Coach McCoy was done with the postgame press conference, he expected Brock in his office. After the stunt he'd pulled today, he didn't know what to expect. The whole country had witnessed his antics. Between the sports commentators' comedic narration and the challenge that this year's championship halftime show wouldn't be able to compare to this, it wasn't going anywhere anytime soon. His teammates would make the most of it. If he thought all the underwear was bad...

"Brock?" Russell leaned into the locker room.

Brock nodded, grabbed his bag, and followed Russell to Coach's office—knowing every player, trainer, and staff member watched him go. Michelle gave him a sympathetic wave and a wink before she closed McCoy's office and he braced himself for what came next.

"Sit," Coach said.

He and Russell sat.

Dale McCoy sat behind his desk and stared at Brock for a solid five minutes before he said, "That little stunt you pulled? It's a twenty-five-thousand-dollar fine." He leaned back, his hands behind his head. "Hell, the league could pursue legal action if they wanted to."

Brock didn't argue. He knew better. And in any other situation, he wouldn't have set foot on the field. It hadn't been a conscious decision—it was Emmy. "I'll pay the fine."

"No, hell no." Coach McCoy laughed. "Hank King already paid it. If he hadn't, I have a handful of people who would." He leaned forward, pushing a stack of notes around. "Michelle says the phone calls keep coming in. American Feline Association, Black Cat Rescue Group, cat food companies. There's more." He pushed the notes aside. "I'm pretty sure the league won't pursue anything. It was a damn kitten. Emmy Lou King. And you."

Hank had paid the fine? He didn't know how to feel about that.

"Can't buy that sort of publicity," Russell Ewen added. "It's the feel-good story of the season."

"I don't give a shit about the fines or the publicity. Do you know what I *do* give a shit about?" Coach McCoy pulled off his cap, ran a hand over his head, and put it back on. "Getting your ass off the bench and back on the damn field. Your appointment is tomorrow. Let me know what Dr. Provencher says." Coach McCoy sat forward. "And I mean as soon as you know."

Brock left soon after. His phone kept vibrating the entire walk to his truck.

Connie sent a screenshot. Emmy Lou King, holding up the smallest black kitten Brock had ever seen. She had captioned it "Meet Watson," with the hashtags #mommasboy, #loveatfirstsight, and #fearlessfeline. She tagged Brock and added the hashtag #myhero.

He stared at the image, saved the picture, and stuck his phone back in his pocket.

His phone vibrated again. Connie's enthusiasm was a good thing, but right now, he needed a hot bath and a long sleep. He waited until he was in his truck to answer it.

It's Emmy. Aunt Mo gave me your number. He stared at the screen. I'm so sorry about today.

Don't be sorry, he typed, then deleted, then retyped another text, but instantly regretted hitting send. It read, Watson, huh?

She sent back a laughing emoji. It fits. And it's a way to say thank you. Another text popped up. Krystal and I are also leaving a thank-you apple pie for you at Aunt Mo's.

He put the truck in gear, his heartbeat picking up. You there now?

Headed that way.

He made the trip to the ranch in forty minutes. When he got there, no one else was parked out front of the ranch house.

"Surprise, surprise. I should have called you to get ice cream." Aunt Mo offered her cheek for his kiss. "I figured you'd come running for the apple pie the King girls dropped off. Figured it'd be tomorrow."

Dropped off. Meaning she was gone. He swallowed down his disappointment. He didn't need to see her to know she was okay. She was. That was all that mattered. "You know I love apple pie." Emmy Lou knew it, too.

"Go on and help yourself." She smiled. "Plan on staying?"

"Sounds good." The idea of driving back to Austin wore him out. Out here, he could get his head on straight and face whatever backlash tomorrow brought. For now, pie and bed sounded good. He headed for the kitchen and a monster slice of pie. Maybe he'd eat the whole damn thing.

"We're back." The front door opening. Emmy Lou. "I bought Old-Fashioned Vanilla. It goes best with apple pie. Want another piece?"

Damn his fool heart for speeding up at the sound of her voice.

"Oh, maybe just a sliver." Aunt Mo was smiling, he could tell.

Aunt Mo and Krystal were talking, but he didn't hear a word once Emmy walked into the kitchen.

"Hi." She stopped, a recyclable shopping bag hanging off her arm and sliding to the floor. "Brock, I'm so sorry."

All the panic and fear he'd bottled up since she'd run onto the field flooded his veins. *Don't do it. Don't. Fuck it.* He was walking toward her—aching to pull her against him—to wrap her up, hold her close, and breathe her in. Somehow, he managed to slam on the brakes before he reached for her.

Her gaze locked with his, an unmistakable spark in her emerald eyes. "I am sorry. I keep causing problems…"

She wasn't wrong. Every damn time he saw her—she caused all sorts of problems. Like this. Right now. Pulling her into his arms when he knew better. This was a *big* damn problem. But she felt so good in his arms. Safe. Warm. Her head on his chest. She fit. She always had.

"Put on a pot of decaf coffee, too, won't you, Brock?" Aunt Mo's voice echoed down the hall. "Goes good with pie."

He called out, "Yes, ma'am." *Enough now.* She was fine. This was over. It hurt like hell to let her go. He managed, but it wasn't easy.

She wrapped her arms around her waist. "I wasn't sure you'd come."

"You said apple pie." That was his excuse and he was sticking to it.

"I wasn't sure how else to get you here," she whispered, nibbling on the inside of her lip.

And just like that, his heart was hammering away.

"I can't wait for some pie," Krystal announced, stepping extra hard on the wooden floor. "Almost to the kitchen. For my pie." She peered into the room, her eyes narrowing as they landed on him. "Brock."

"Krystal. Nice to see you," he said, heading toward the coffeepot.

"Is that the same coffeepot?" Emmy Lou smiled. "She's had that for years. I learned to make coffee in that."

He remembered. There were so many good memories between them. He swallowed hard. "You know Aunt Mo." No matter how many times he'd offered to buy things for Aunt Mo, she refused. Eventually, he'd let it go. If she wanted to keep the vinyl wallpaper in the bathrooms and her ancient icebox—it was too old to be called a refrigerator—he'd let her. Her happiness was a priority. Of all the women in his life, she was the only one who stayed.

"Good coffee," Aunt Mo said, sipping the freshly brewed cup.

He heard it then—a high-pitched squeal of a meow. There, among the bundles of multicolored yarn by Mo's chair, was the fluffy, black kitten. Brock picked up it up and gave it a quick once-over. "For something so little, you sure caused a big ruckus today. You know she saved you, don't you?" The kitten stared at him, reaching out a paw to swat at him before yawning. "Good to see you're appreciative."

Emmy moved over on the couch, reaching for the kitten. "He's had a big day." She laughed, placing her pie plate on the table and patting the couch beside her.

He smiled. The plate was scraped clean. It was one piece of pie, but it was a start.

As soon as he sat beside Emmy, the kitten jumped into her lap, purring. "He sounds like a motorboat." Brock laughed.

"Aw, you guys have a Beauty and the Beast thing going on over there." Krystal pulled out her phone. "Hold up your baby. This will make a great Christmas card."

"Aunt Krystal is sarcastic, Watson. You'll get used to it." Emmy leaned in close and held up the kitten. "Smile," she said, shooting Brock a look. "Both of you."

Krystal blinked, giving them a long look before she took a few pics.

"I can't wait. I'd turned off the television, so I missed all the excitement," Aunt Mo said, sipping her coffee. "Can't watch the game with that Ames boy playing; my blood pressure can't take it."

"I'm not a fan," Emmy agreed.

"He's definitely your fan," he grumbled.

Emmy's gaze met his—sweeping over his face to linger on his mouth. Was she thinking about kissing him? Now? Considering the varying degree of hostility Krystal was sending him, she might use one of Aunt Mo's knitting needles on him.

"News should be on." Aunt Mo was clicking through the channels. "Found it. Oh my. Well, goodness. You look good, Brock. They never saw you coming." She chuckled.

"The clip has people speculating," the newscaster said. "Take a closer look."

Brock glanced up to see video of himself—followed by video of Emmy. Once he'd been back on the sideline, he'd been looking for her. From the video, she'd done the same.

"I'm not the only one that thinks something is going on with these two." The newscaster grinned.

"No, you're not." Krystal's whisper wasn't really a whisper.

"It's got people talking. Hashtag #BrockplusEmmy is trending. We've come up with a survey, so you be sure to let us know. Are you pro-Brock and Emmy or anti-Brock and Emmy? We'll say good night with another look at today's excitement." The clip played again, in slow motion, with dramatic music added.

Krystal had her hands pressed to her mouth, trying not to laugh. "A survey? Seriously?"

Emmy Lou glanced Brock's way, not nearly as amused. If anything, she looked panicked. Really panicked. "We should go." She stood, cradling the kitten.

Krystal caught sight of Emmy then. "Right, we should."

"You girls come back real soon and stay awhile." Aunt Mo clicked off the television.

"We will, Aunt Mo. We'll clean up real quick." Emmy nodded, heading down the hall, Krystal on her heels.

"You listen to me, Brock." Aunt Mo pushed out of her chair,

whispering. "I'm not sure you've been right since the two of you went south, but I'm telling you now, leave those past hurts alone. Seems a shame to let a second chance at happiness slip away." She hugged him, giving his back a solid pat. "I'll mind my own business now."

He chuckled. "We'll see about that."

Once Emmy Lou and Krystal came back, they gave Aunt Mo hugs, exchanged quick goodbyes, and headed to the door. Whatever had set her off, Emmy looked on the verge of flight.

"You two have everything?" he asked, following them onto the front porch.

Krystal rolled her eyes. "Yes." She mouthed *Hurry* at Emmy and ran to the waiting black Mustang with sparkling silver racing stripes.

"Everything okay?" They were in such a hurry, it seemed like a valid question.

"I just… Momma… You don't know Momma." She shrugged, tension bracketing her mouth. "We need to get home."

He knew CiCi King well enough to know that she and Emmy Lou were close. CiCi had made damn sure he understood that. His gaze raked over her face. Or were they?

"Thank you for…everything." She opened her mouth, then stopped.

"Let's go, Em," Krystal called from the driver's side window, then looked his way. "I'll be sure to send you the survey results." With a sassy wave, she rolled up the window and headed down the dirt road back to the highway.

Brock stared after the red taillights with a million questions running through his mind. Aunt Mo had said to forget the past and start fresh. If he did that, only one question was left. Was Emmy willing to give them a second chance? Hell, did she even want to?

Chapter 11

EMMY LOU SAT ON THE VELVET-COVERED STOOL IN HER HOTEL bathroom. The illuminated mirror highlighted the shadows beneath her eyes. Watson sat on the vanity, batting her powder puff across the white marble countertop. "Sure, go ahead. I was done with that." She smiled as the kitten swatted the puff onto the floor.

Watson meowed, looking at her, then the puff, then her again.

"You want your toy back?" She asked, tapping his nose and earning the beginnings of a rumbling growl.

"I thought that was for makeup?" Krystal ran her fingertip along the edge of her ruby-red lined lips.

Watson meowed, leaning forward so Emmy would give his little head a rub. She did. "What? You're just as gaga over Clem as I am over Watson," Emmy said.

"Whatever." But her twin was smiling. "Clem is way cuter."

Emmy laughed, returning the powder puff to the counter.

Watson trotted across the counter, spied Clementine on the ground, and swatted the powder puff back onto the ground. Clementine barked, grabbed the powder puff, and ran from the bathroom. Watson was a flash of black fur, chasing after Clementine.

"Run, Clementine." Krystal laughed. "Hopefully they'll stay out of Momma's way."

Emmy peered around the door. "Travis, can you—"

"Door's shut," Travis interrupted.

"Thank you." She smiled. Since Watson had arrived, Emmy Lou had spent more than her fair share keeping Momma and her beloved kitten apart. Momma wasn't an animal lover. Watson had done his best to win her over—following Momma around, purring, meowing, and being adorable. But then he'd stolen one of Momma's silk Hermes scarves and found another way to get attention. Momma had run after her scarf, but after three unsuccessful attempts to get the scarf away from Watson, she'd shrieked until Daddy had managed to step in.

Daddy had returned the scarf to Momma, saying to Emmy, "Best keep this little guy out of her way."

Emmy Lou had only brought Watson with them to New York because Momma had said she wasn't coming. But Watson's rescue video and the will-they-or-won't-they Emmy and Brock memes were still a hot topic. When they knew hashtag #Bremmy started trending, Momma announced she would be going to New York for the AFL Charity Ball.

"I thought that dress was nixed?" Krystal pointed at the Grecian-style seafoam-green dress Emmy was wearing.

"Momma wasn't coming." Emmy turned sideways. Momma favored dressing them in formfitting outfits. Not only did it strike a confident chord, it also made sure she and Krystal kept in shape. But this dress… She felt pretty. And even though there was no guarantee Brock would be there tonight, she wanted to feel pretty. "I like it. I don't think I look pregnant." Momma insisted empire waistlines were a surefire way to get pregnancy gossip started.

"You don't. You look beautiful." Krystal peeked around the door, then whispered, "Have you talked to Brock?"

"Not since we visited Aunt Mo." When he'd stared at her without hostility…like he liked what he saw. "Why are we whispering?"

"Travis." Krystal pointed. "Unless you're enjoying the teasing?"

"No. Nope." Emmy stood, lowering her voice. "I'm sort of hoping Brock won't be here. Momma's worked up over the Bremmy thing—even though there is nothing going on."

"No? Maybe. Not yet. Momma's freaking out because there's

not much she can do about it." Krystal laughed. "Bremmy. What would that make Jace and me? Jystal? Yuck. Or Kace? Nope. Never mind."

"I'm serious. After all he's been through. And his dad now? Nothing is going to happen." No matter how much she wished otherwise. "I won't put a target on his back for Momma."

"Oh, Em, you're too good, you know that?" Krystal hugged her. "Come on. Let's get this show on the road."

They'd rented out the entire penthouse, and where had Travis and Jace picked to set up? Her bedroom. The two of them were poring over a song, pages of sheet music spread out all over the table and floor in front of them. Sawyer stood behind the couch, stoic as ever but reading over the music. It was a familiar sight—a comforting one. Soon enough, this would be the norm. Tour bus living, live shows, hotel rooms, and mobs of devoted, screaming fans. *And no Brock.*

Travis looked at them and nodded. "Gotta say, Em, you look good. Maybe you'll get lucky tonight." He plucked out notes on his banjo.

"Hey, Travis, here's an idea. Let's not start this tonight." Emmy Lou scooped up Watson before he could launch himself at her layers of gauzy skirts. "Or ever? I like that idea."

"I can't help but worry." He shrugged. "It's been decades since you dated."

"Yeah, I had so many dates when I was seven years old." Emmy rolled her eyes at her brother. "Six years. Six. That's all."

"No dates. No kisses. No touching." Travis shrugged. "You're twenty-seven years old, Em. Six years is a long time. The whole nun thing isn't all that farfetched. Am I right, Jace?"

Jace stopped scribbling. "I'm staying out of this." He kept his eyes on the sheet music.

If Travis only knew. She'd had been kissing and touching and hugging—and grabbing and thrusting… She wanted more. Soon.

The familiar ache twisted in the pit of her stomach and made her cheeks hot. She buried her face against Watson, a feline shield.

"Are you blushing?" Travis set his banjo down. "This is getting good. Come on, Sawyer, spill the beans. She says it's not Brock. Who's the special someone who's making my little sister's cheeks go red?"

Sawyer's blue-green eyes met hers, his face as unreadable as ever. "No one." He stretched his neck, glanced at his watch, and left the room. "I'll call for the car."

"Seriously? Maybe she's blushing because you keep embarrassing the shit out of her?" Krystal threw a pillow at Travis. "You are such a dick. Apologize now. To both of them."

"It's fine." Emmy was in shock. Sawyer hadn't ratted her out. "I'm going to get some water. Krystal?" After her sister nodded, Emmy Lou slipped from her room and took a deep breath. She hadn't asked Sawyer to cover for her, but he'd done it anyway. And she felt guilty. "I'm sorry about that."

"About what?" As usual, his face was blank.

"Asking you to lie." She shrugged.

"You didn't ask. I didn't lie." His gaze met hers. "They asked me if there was someone special."

She blinked. "But you saw—"

"Brock?" His eyes narrowed. "Off the field, he's not all that special. How well do you know him, Emmy Lou? He's divorced from a supermodel with a rap sheet that includes shoplifting and possession."

She knew about the divorce. The rest? No. "Um…"

"Did you know he's recovering from a serious drug problem?" He crossed his arms over his chest. "That his addiction was so bad his team had to stage an intervention?"

The drug problem, yes. The intervention, no.

"Did you know he ran his car into a median, and he was so high he didn't even realize he'd dislocated his arm until two days later?"

He'd dislocated his arm? She remembered the pictures of his Ferrari wrapped around that concrete median all too clearly.

"Drug Free Like Me was his court-appointed community service."

At this point, she felt the need to defend Brock. "In the beginning, maybe—"

"He's a good football player. But I'm not so sure he's a good person." He shook his head, the barest traces of frustration evident. "Not good enough for you."

Emmy Lou was terrible at reading people—men especially. Travis thought it was hysterical. Krystal found it annoying. But right now, she was getting some definite non-bodyguard vibes from Sawyer. The way he was looking at her, how intense he was... Why did this matter so much to him?

Unless... No... Did Sawyer have *feelings* for her? No. No way.

"I care about you, Emmy Lou. I don't want to see you get hurt. I've never met anyone so willing to trust and give." He stared up at the ceiling. "People take advantage of that. Especially people needing a comeback—people like Brock."

She was so stunned her words all ran together. "Sawyer, it means a lot that you care. It does. I care about you, too. You're more like...like a grumpy big brother. Someone who always has my back. Or tells me the truth. Or lets me use them as a human crutch." She sucked in a deep breath. "But if you're trying to say you have *feelings* for me...I should let you know I *don't* feel *that* way about you. I'm sorry."

Sawyer stared at her, his blue-green gaze fixed on her. "No, Emmy Lou." A short laugh escaped. "Let me make myself perfectly clear. I have no romantic feelings for you. At all." He opened his mouth, then shut it. With another shake of his head, he walked away, and Emmy headed back into her bedroom.

"I thought you were getting me water?" Krystal asked.

"Oh, sorry." She was still nibbling on the inside of her lip. What was that? What did Sawyer have against Brock? Why was he being so protective?

"What?" Krystal asked.

She glanced at Jace and Travis, completely tuned out and invested in the song they were working on. "I think...I think Sawyer might like me."

Krystal nodded. "Of course, he likes you. *Everyone* likes you."

"No, I mean *like* me," she whispered. "You know?"

"Oh." Krystal shook her head. "Let's go play with your hair."

"We just did my hair," she argued.

Krystal tugged her back into the bathroom and closed the door. "I need you to not freak out over what I'm about to tell you, okay?" Krystal took her hands, waiting just long enough for Emmy to nod. "I've hinted at it. A lot. Maybe it won't be too big a shock. It's not hard to see, really. Give Trav Daddy's hair and eye color and a ton more muscles and you get...Sawyer."

She stared at Krystal, stunned. "Wait..." The weird tics and postures that Travis, their father, and Sawyer shared. It all crowded in on her, clicking into place. "Are you saying Sawyer is our brother?" She paused. "That's why you were asking Daddy about his first love...Sawyer's mother?"

"I'm guessing so." Krystal nodded. "Sawyer and I have *talked*. I told him I knew but I'd keep his secret. For whatever reason, he hasn't owned up to who he is or tried to talk to me or you or anyone about it. Daddy has no idea."

Their father wasn't perfect, but family was his everything. If he'd known he had another son, he'd have moved heaven and earth to make sure he was part of the family. "How? Why would Sawyer's mother not reach out and let Daddy know? Sawyer's a few years older than Travis—it was before Momma. Before us." Emmy paused. "Momma... if Momma finds out... " A painful lump lodged in her throat.

"She can't find out. That's partly why I've kept his secret. He found us for a reason."

Emmy groaned and covered her face with her hands. "I am

such an idiot. You should have seen Sawyer's face when I told him I didn't have romantic feelings for him."

Krystal laughed. "Oh, I so wish I had."

"Either come out, or we're coming in," Travis yelled.

"You good?" Krystal asked.

"I think so." She nodded, shook her head, then shrugged. "I will be. Let's go."

Travis and Jace stood outside the door, guitar and banjo at the ready. Travis waved them close, so they could all see the lyrics.

"A one, a two, a one-two-three-four," Travis counted down.

Jace and Travis played through the melody once, then they took turns singing the lyrics. It was a dance-hall song, made for dancing to. It was the sort of song that would be a hit.

"Hold on." Emmy ran across the room, grabbed her phone—ignoring their groans—and ran back. "Smile. I'm happy—really happy—and I want a keepsake." She snapped a few pics. "Thank you."

"Yeah, yeah." Travis waved her along. "We need to go or you'll be late."

She followed, looking at the picture on her phone. Only one thing was missing: Sawyer.

Her brother. And now that she knew who he was, what he was to her, she wanted to really *know* him. Why hadn't he told them who he was? Who was his mother? The questions kept coming—some leaving a bitter taste in her mouth and doubt whispering in her ear. He'd come here to find his family and he had. So why was he keeping his identity a secret? What could he gain from that? What did he want?

———

Brock stepped inside the ballroom and tugged at the collar of his custom-cut dress shirt. It wasn't the fit; it was the surroundings. He tended to avoid events with free-flowing alcohol. Knowing he could get his hands on pretty much anything else—legal or otherwise—from at least three of the people already present didn't help. It wasn't that he was tempted; it was that he was aware. That shit was evil, and he didn't want it near him or the people he cared about.

But the annual American Football League Charity Ball raised a ton of money to be divided among the AFL-sponsored charities, and the players were expected to attend. The AFL flew them all the way to the Big Apple, put them up in hotels, and provided them with goodie bags full of vendor donations, tickets to Broadway shows, and a variety of other perks. He glanced at his watch. He could do this. He'd shake the right hands, take the necessary pictures, then get the hell out of there and take the goodie bag back to Aunt Mo in Texas.

"Where's your date?" Demetrius shook his hand. "I told Molly we were dancing."

"I'm sure she'll hold you to it next time. She's staying with my dad." And she'd been adamant that he go without her. She'd doled out a big serving of guilt, saying his father wouldn't want him shirking his job to sit by his hospital bed. Then she'd gone on to claim the goodie bag was not something she looked forward to every year. If he hadn't seen a couple of them stacked in the back closet, he might have believed her.

"Gotcha." Demetrius nodded. "How's he doing?"

Not good. His release had been delayed due to a tear in his rotator cuff—something he earned from fighting off a med tech who'd been trying to take some blood. "Hanging in." He glanced at the watch again.

"Planning your escape? I get it. You timed it perfectly. Dinner's about to start. Until then, we're up front. Got us grouped by charity this year." Demetrius pointed, then clapped him on the back.

Brock made his way through the tables, pausing along the way to make the requisite small talk. He caught sight of Leon Greene and smiled—until he saw who else was at the table.

"Brock." Hank King stood, shaking his hand.

"Sir." If Hank was here...

"Brock." CiCi King sat at Hank's side, her smile triggering all sort of warning bells. "Don't you clean up nicely."

"This is a surprise." *This sucked.*

"How's the leg?" Hank asked.

Brock smiled. Damn good now that he'd been released to play. "Getting there." Coach had told him to keep his mouth shut. He said he'd rather let the Miami Raiders sweat it out until they saw him run onto the field.

"You listen to your doctors, son." Hank clapped him on the shoulder, then sat.

The lights dimmed as Brock sat, a smattering of applause going up as AFL Commissioner Shane Thorpe walked onstage. "Ladies and gentlemen, thank you all for coming..." Commissioner Thorpe thanked a long list of important people who had made the event possible.

Brock took a long sip of his glass of sparkling water and scanned the room. CiCi's gaze met his over the rim of her champagne glass. There was nothing warm or welcoming about the smile on the woman's bright-red lips.

He didn't know where he and Emmy stood, but he was going to do his damnedest to follow Aunt Mo's advice. The past was the past. The only way forward for them was a start fresh. That wasn't going to happen tonight. CiCi King being here was going to make that damn near impossible. It clicked then. *That* was why she was here. CiCi King was going on the offensive. But why CiCi thought Emmy Lou needed protection from him was the mystery.

Commissioner Thorpe had paused for the applause. "And tonight, with your help, we've raised close to a million dollars." He clapped, nodding. "Before dinner, we have a special treat."

Commissioner Thorpe kept clapping.

Emmy Lou seemed to glide onto the stage, her long dress a

swirl of blue and green. Green like her eyes. Damn, but she was beautiful.

"Commissioner Thorpe, I appreciate the invitation tonight. And I hope you like my little song." She paused, pressing her hand to her ear.

From the corner of his eye, he saw Hank lean back in his chair and smile.

"Oh, wait." Emmy pulled out her earpiece, looked at it, then slipped it back on. "Hold on. A little technical difficulty."

"Is that better?" A voice from backstage.

"No." Emmy Lou pressed her hand over her ear. "It's still not working."

Travis King came onstage, holding a banjo. "Is it on?"

Clapping broke out.

He took it, listened to it, and shook his head. "I don't think it's working."

"Really?" Emmy Lou asked, hands on hips—almost sassy. "You don't say?"

Brock had to smile then.

"Hold up." Jace Black and Krystal King came onstage. "Try this one."

The clapping and whistles reached a near-deafening decibel.

Brock shot Hank a look. Hank was staring back at him, smiling. "What can I say? This was their idea. Wanted to test out a new song."

"They know how to work a crowd." Brock was clapping, too.

"I think we're good now." Krystal nodded.

Travis started tapping his foot, his fingers flying along the banjo strings. "A one, a two, a one-two-three-four."

Jace on his guitar and Travis, on his banjo, started singing together.

Saturday night and the moon is full,
I see you standing there and can't fight this pull.

Smiling at me from across the dance floor,
Girl, you call my name and I'm coming for more.
Dancing in my arms and it feels so right.
No need to hurry cuz we got all night.

Emmy Lou and Krystal sang.

Saturday night and the stars shine bright,
You're staring at me and holding me tight.
In your cowboy hat looking so fine,
Boy, you smile at me, make me wish you were mine.
Dancing in your arms and it feels so right.
No need to hurry cuz we got all night.

The chorus was a big explosion of music and harmony and pure energy.

Now, baby, when you kiss me, ooh-hoo
Oh, I like the way you kiss me.
Once we start, don't want to stop. Ooh-hoo-hoo
And all I know is here we go. Ooh-hoo.
Back to the start, straight to my heart. Ooh-hoo-hoo.
No fighting this. No stopping fate.
Third time's a charm. My heart can't wait.

They sang through the second verse, alternating lines and, from the looks of it, enjoying themselves. When they hit the final notes and the last line of the chorus, everyone—Brock included—was on their feet.

Hank King looked ready to burst with pride. Surprisingly, so did CiCi.

Emmy Lou hugged her sister. "I guess y'all can stay for one more song."

Four songs later, the Three Kings and Jace left the stage and the big band took over. Brock did his best not to stare as she made her way toward their table. But the minute Emmy Lou saw him, she lit up. That smile was for him? How the hell was he supposed to resist that?

But then CiCi stepped in, sliding an arm around Emmy's waist and whispering in her ear. Whatever she said was enough to snuff out the light in Emmy's gaze. In the minutes it took to find more chairs, it was clear Emmy was giving him the cold shoulder. Even wedged between him and her father, Emmy barely acknowledged his presence.

No one else seemed to mind the tight quarters. Being over six feet meant he took up a lot of space. Space he didn't have with Emmy Lou so close. He was caught up in a battle of sensation. Her silky hair. Her sweet scent. The brush of her hand as she reached for her glass. And when she leaned back, pushing her hair from her neck, the curve of her shoulder and the arch of her neck had him finishing his ice water. He shrugged out of his coat, wishing he could yank off his damn tie and roll up his sleeves.

CiCi King kept right on watching. She was subtle about it, talking and smiling the whole time. But she was watching. What the hell was she looking for?

By the time dinner was cleared and the big band started to play, he knew leaving was the best for all concerned. Emmy Lou was putting on a fine show, but he felt the tension rolling off her. Since he was somehow the cause of the stress, he'd go. He was making his excuses when Shalene Fowler showed up with a photographer. "Brock, you're leaving already?"

"Yes, ma'am." He was forty-five minutes behind schedule.

"Can we get a few pics first?" She paused.

He posed while they snapped pictures of the crowded table, but the whole time he felt the push and pull between himself and Emmy. As soon as they finished, he was up.

"Can we get one or two of you on the dance floor? The Bremmy fans will love it." Shalene smiled. "I know you're in a hurry, so we'll make it fast. Emmy, do you mind?"

If she did mind, she hid it well. "No, of course not."

CiCi King chose that moment speak up. "She needs to stay off her ankle. You can't afford to push it, with the tour about to start—"

"One dance won't hurt a thing," Hank argued "Go on and get your pictures."

"I'll ask the band to slow things down." Shalene headed off, moving rapidly toward the bandstand.

A slow dance with Emmy Lou sounded like the perfect way to wind out the evening. It gave him the excuse he needed to touch her. CiCi King would have to grin and bear it. He slid his coat on and offered her his hand. "If you're ready, Miss King?"

She stared up at him, a hesitant smile on her face. Her hand was ice-cold in his grasp. "Thank you." She was up, hooking her arm through his.

He was acutely aware of the sudden lack of conversation at their table. If he looked—which he didn't—he'd probably find every single one of them watching. When the strains of "When I Fall in Love" began, Brock accepted the fact that the next five minutes were going to be painfully awkward—but well worth it.

He led Emmy onto the dance floor, flexing his hand before placing it on her back. "I'm better at swaying anyway." He glanced down to find her staring straight at his chest.

"I know," she murmured, the ghost of a smile on her lips.

In order to put her hand on his shoulder, she had to stand closer—close enough that he could hear her breathe. But since they were both attempting to keep space between them, it wasn't the most natural pose.

"Great, great," Shalene said. "Let's get some smiles."

Emmy, he knew, would have the smile thing down—no

problem. For him, it was a problem. He wasn't wired that way. And something about this whole evening made him begin to worry about what would happen when this was over. Not to him, but to Emmy Lou.

"You look like you're in pain." Krystal was up, standing beside the photographer, a cell phone in her hand. "Emmy, stop kicking him."

"What?" Emmy was horrified. "I'm not."

"So, you're, what, stomping on his toes?" Krystal asked, watching them.

Emmy laughed. "I'm *way* up on my tiptoes. I can't stomp or kick him."

Dammit. With a sigh, he pulled her closer. "Better?"

They were so close now she had to look up at him. "Yes."

He nodded. Could she feel his heart clipping along? He sure as hell hoped not.

She slowly relaxed against him.

It felt good having her hand in his, his arm holding her close; the rest of the room seemed to fade away. He didn't mind.

"I know you prefer keeping personal life private." She nibbled on the inside of her lip—a dead giveaway that she was worrying. "This Bremmy thing is out of control. I—"

He shook his head. "I made a choice to go after you."

Her throat tightened. "But…are you okay with it? Are Aunt Mo and your father okay?"

"They don't mind. Not that they're big on Twitter." He cleared his throat, smiling broadly.

"Great smiles. Hold it." Shalene nodded as the photographer clicked away. "All right. You enjoy yourselves."

"Do you?" she whispered. "Mind, I mean?"

"I'm not really on Twitter either, but I'm a fan." He was staring down at her now. Sometimes he forgot just how green her eyes were. "Pro-Bremmy."

Her voice was a whisper. "Really?"

He nodded. Privacy was important, but this was different. Primarily because she was involved. Plus, Connie was over-the-moon excited about the positive attention he was getting.

Emmy was studying him, eyes wide and still nibbling away.

"What about you?" He turned slowly, concealing their conversation.

Her breath wavered. "I…I'm a fan, too." Her fingers slid above the collar of his shirt.

"I was hoping you'd say that." He shook his head, the final strains of the song putting an end to the highlight of his day. He didn't want to say goodbye. He sure as hell didn't want to let her go. "I was thinking about coming to a concert."

"I might be able to get you a backstage pass. Watson will be glad to see you."

"That's nice, but I'm not coming to see Watson." It was hard to escort her off the floor and back to her family. Everyone knew he'd been trying to leave for the last hour, so he couldn't decide to stay now. But he paused, waiting long enough for her to give him one more lit-up-from-the-inside smile before heading out—carrying her warmth with him.

Chapter 12

Emmy Lou held the mic closer to Krystal, watching her sister's fingers slide along the strings in time with Jace. With four shows under their belt, the two of them had turned the guitar solo into a guitar duel—and the fans loved it. As the roar of the crowd climbed higher, she and Travis exchanged a smile. Touring was exhausting, sure. And no matter how many hours of rehearsals and performances they put in, glitches happened. But as long as they kept the music going and their energy high, the fans were game for anything.

When Krystal and Jace paused, Travis said, "Finally," and a ripple of laughter joined in the steady clapping. A smile passed among them as they started singing the chorus together.

> *Now, baby, when you kiss me, ooh-hoo.*
> *Oh, I like the way you kiss me.*
> *Once we start, don't want to stop. Ooh-hoo-hoo.*
> *And all I know is here we go. Ooh-hoo.*
> *Back to the start, straight to my heart. Ooh-hoo-hoo.*
> *No fighting this. No stopping fate.*
> *Third time's a charm. My heart can't wait.*

Even though this was their second encore of the night, the energy in the Coastal Shoals Civic Center hadn't waned. Emmy, on the other hand, was wiped out. "Thank you, Raleigh, North Carolina," Emmy Lou said, waving. "Y'all be safe going home tonight."

The four of them took a bow and waved. But instead of leaving the stage with her siblings, Emmy Lou paused at a little girl who was waving a bright-pink guitar at her. She was sitting on her mother's shoulders, smiling and hopeful. Emmy Lou made a beeline in their direction. As resistant as she'd been to her rhinestone-covered silver jumpsuit, it did take the fear out of crouching down on the edge of the stage.

"Hi, sweetie," she said to the little girl. "What do you have there?"

The little girl was holding an inflatable pink guitar over her head. "It's a guitar. Like Krystal's." She held it up, her smile revealing two missing front teeth. "It's for you."

Emmy Lou stared at the little girl, truly touched. "For me? Are you sure?"

The little girl's mother nodded. "It was her idea. She wanted it because it was pink, and pink is your favorite color."

Emmy Lou's eyes were stinging. "I love surprise presents. And this one is extra special. What's your name?"

"Valencia." She smiled.

"Well, Valencia, I'd really love a picture with you, if that's okay?" Emmy Lou asked Valencia's mother.

Sawyer came out to help, lifting Valencia onto the stage with ease. He stood by, stony faced, until the pictures were done and carefully lowered her back to the concrete floor.

"Thank you." Valencia's mom smiled. "I know you hear this a lot but it's real nice for young girls to have a role model like you. They're hard to come by these days."

"I appreciate that." Emmy Lou waved goodbye. "And thank you, Valencia. It was nice meeting you." But when she stood, the stage seemed to tilt, and her head was spinning so fast she wound up grabbing on to Sawyer's arm.

"You good?" Sawyer asked, taking the inflatable guitar and leading her swiftly from the stage. "Em? You okay?"

It wasn't the first time. "I just stood up too fast." It wasn't a big deal.

"You normally get dizzy from standing up too fast?" He wasn't amused. "Come on."

"Sometimes, yes. I'm a little dehydrated." She patted his arm.

He paused outside the dressing room. "I'm probably overstepping here, but I know this isn't dehydration." He sighed. "When did you eat last?"

She was too wobbly to argue. At the moment, all she wanted was a chair and some water or juice. "Sawyer—"

"You spend all your time worrying about looking and acting perfect, keeping the peace, and being a good role model. What do you do for yourself?"

It was hard to make eye contact with him. "Sawyer, you're worrying over nothing."

"That's bullshit." He was scowling now, dropping the inflatable guitar and gently grasping her upper arms. "You're making yourself sick for the approval of a woman you'll never make happy."

All she could do was stare now. "Momma's never—"

"I shouldn't have said that." His jaw muscle tightened. "You are harming yourself, Emmy Lou. I can't stand by and do nothing. I won't." There was surprising tenderness in his blue-green eyes. "My...*job* is to protect you from harm."

"Emmy Lou?" Her daddy was headed their way. He didn't look happy. "What's going on?"

Sawyer's hands slid free of her arms and he stepped back, all traces of emotion wiped away.

"One of you better start talking." Daddy's voice was razor-sharp. "Now."

"I got dizzy." That was true. But the rest of it stuck in her throat. Old habits die hard. Denying she had a problem, hiding the truth, was an old habit. She knew lying wouldn't make this better. Then again, neither would telling the truth. "He helped me off the stage."

By now, Jace, Krystal, and Travis had almost reached them, but their pace slowed when they heard their father. Daddy's anger was a rare occurrence.

"That's what the two of you were talking about? I don't buy it."

Daddy's voice rose. "I don't want to lose you, son. I appreciate how hard you work and your loyalty; you know that. But I can't have lines getting blurred here."

The muscle in Sawyer's jaw tightened. For anyone else, it wouldn't have been noticeable. But for Sawyer and his stoicism, that muscle twitch said more than words.

"I need to know what the hell is going on, Emmy Lou. I won't have any more secrets in my house." Daddy met Sawyer's gaze. "Otherwise, you'll have to find yourself a new job."

Sawyer's gaze dropped.

"Daddy." She wouldn't lose her brother over this. She'd lost too much already. "He was doing his job. He noticed I… I'm not… I don't eat. He told me to take care of myself." She spit the words out. "I try, I do, but…he didn't do a thing wrong. I did."

Daddy was staring at her, confusion and sadness creasing his forehead and tugging down the corners of his mouth. "What are you saying, baby girl?"

"Oh, Daddy." She shook her head, sucking in a wavering breath. "I know you're upset, but this isn't the right time or place for this." Another breath. "It's probably best to talk this through tomorrow. When we've had some sleep and no one's waiting on us. Please."

Daddy shook his head. "I don't give a damn about the people waiting. You and your brother and sister —nothing matters more to me. You hear me, Emmy Lou? Nothing. You three are my pride and joy." He cleared his throat, his gaze searching hers. "Your whole life, you've never broken a promise. So I'm asking you to promise me we'll work this out together. Whatever it takes to get you help, get you eating. Promise me?"

Emmy Lou had big, fat tears rolling down her cheeks. "I promise." It was a whisper. "But I do care about the people waiting. You know I can't let them down."

He pulled her in again, holding her and patting her back. "I know. I know. All right. Tomorrow, then." He sighed, his hold tightening. "It's going to be fine. We'll figure this out."

She clung to him. "I know, Daddy."

Daddy cleared his throat. "Sawyer." He eased his hold on Emmy Lou and stepped forward, holding out his hand. "I'm sorry, son. All you've ever done was take care of my family and I jumped down your throat for it."

"She's your daughter." Sawyer's gaze met Daddy's. "This is my job. Protecting her."

Daddy nodded, shaking Sawyer's hand, then pulling him in for a quick one-armed hug that ended just as soon as it began. It only lasted a second, but Emmy Lou saw the flash of longing on Sawyer's face. She ached for him—for them both.

"I'll find Melanie so she can get you what you need." Sawyer headed down the hall.

"I'll stall them a minute. You go sit, take your time, and come on down when you're ready." Daddy patted her cheek. "You good?"

She nodded.

That was when her father realized they had an audience.

Krystal hugged him, pressed a kiss to his cheek, and said, "I'll go with you. Jace, too. We're so damn charming, they might not even miss Emmy Lou." She winked at Emmy.

"I'll stay with Emmy," Travis said. For the first time in months, Travis looked at Daddy without hostility.

"You hear all that?" Daddy's voice was thick.

Travis nodded.

Daddy nodded, took Krystal's hand, and headed to the meet-and-greet around the corner.

"You don't have to stay." Emmy Lou pushed open her dressing room door. "I'm fine." She took the pink guitar he handed her and cradled it against her chest. "Thank you. Present. It was a great show."

"Yeah, sure." He nodded, pure condescension. "Does that mean you think I'm going to pretend what just happened didn't happen?"

Emmy Lou shook her head. "Trav—" She hadn't expected him to wrap her up in his arms. Travis's hugs lasted five seconds and were followed by lots of dismissive teasing. But he wasn't letting her go. He didn't let go until Sawyer came in with Melanie in tow.

"Gatorade and a banana." Melanie waited for Travis to step aside before putting the half-peeled banana in her hand.

"All of it," Travis said, crossing his arms and leaning against the vanity counter.

Sawyer stood beside Travis in exactly the same pose, opening the bottle of Gatorade. Side by side, it was hard to miss the resemblance. Then again, the idea of some secret half brother somewhere out there had never crossed her mind. She smiled, taking a bite of banana.

"What?" Travis asked, frowning.

Sawyer frowned, too.

"You two… Never mind." She laughed, taking another bite.

"If you're still hungry, these arrived for you." Melanie nodded at the two boxes sitting on the vanity counter. "I didn't read the card, but I think we can all guess who it's from."

"Who?" Travis asked, then winked, elbowing Sawyer in the side. Sawyer glared back at him.

In the week since the charity ball, they'd exchanged a handful of texts. She sent Brock pics of her and Watson. Brock sent her updates on his dad, Aunt Mo, and the Bremmy updates his agent sent him for clarification. It felt like the start of something. She picked up the boxes, opening the card first. "'I'll bring the tags with me to tomorrow's show. Please put your ankle up and eat something. But maybe save me one of these, too. Brock.'"

She finished the banana and opened the box. Inside was a pale green kitten collar covered in sparkly metallic music notes. "Look. It's so cute." She held it out for their inspection. "For Watson."

"Really? It's not for you?" But Travis was smiling.

She shot him a look and opened the other box. A dozen carrot cake cupcakes.

"Your favorite." Melanie smiled. "That's so thoughtful of him."

"Maybe." Travis nodded, eyeing the cupcakes. "Or maybe he's just buying her gifts and buttering her up so she'll lose the nun's habit for a night of s—"

She launched the cupcake without thought. But the look on Travis's face when it smacked him square in the middle of his forehead was more than worth it. Sawyer's laughter was the cherry on top.

———

Brock wasn't sure where Emmy's energy came from. He'd been mingling and shaking hands for over an hour now, and the constant chatter was wearing on him. He couldn't imagine how Emmy Lou did it. Yes, he worked out for hours a day, but he didn't have to do it wearing a smile and shoes that couldn't be good for her ankle—after singing and dancing for two hours straight. There were over fifty thousand people in attendance, and somehow, they'd made the audience part of the show.

As they'd sung their last song, all he could think about was getting to Emmy Lou. Now she was in the same room, her gaze searching him out again and again, and it was hell not doing what he wanted to. But kissing her breathless couldn't happen. Not yet, anyway.

"You keep staring at my sister that way and the whole Bremmy thing will never go away." Krystal's brows rose, her eyes assessing.

That obvious? He didn't bother denying it. "I thought hashtags and Twitter and crap were good?"

Krystal laughed, then shrugged. "Crap, huh? Yeah, I don't get it, either. But it's the measuring stick for stardom these days." Her eyes narrowed. In all the time he'd known the Kings, he'd never once thought Krystal and Emmy Lou looked like identical twins. The difference was in the way they moved, their posture, and their facial expressions. Krystal had the "fuck you" thing down. She was only as approachable as her smile. Emmy Lou had her own gravitational pull, welcoming everyone with one look. With one smile, she'd steal your heart.

"Now you're staring." He wasn't sure if he wanted to know what she was thinking. But he had a feeling he was going to find out soon enough, whether he liked it or not.

Her gaze sharpened as her smile faded. "I'm also trying to figure out why you're here."

"You could ask." He shrugged. "Straight talk, straight answers."

Her sigh was all exasperation. "You broke her once in a way that made me hate you. Now I see her light up over you again and I can't help but remember that." She glanced at Emmy. "I want you to leave her alone, Brock. I want you to go away and stay gone." A deep V formed between her brows as her gaze searched his. "But Emmy's cared more about making other people happy than being happy herself for too long. She deserves to be happy. And if you'll *stay* and make her happy, that's what I want for her... How's that for straight talk?"

Every one of Krystal's words made an impact. Was she saying Emmy Lou was unhappy? But this, all of this, was the life she'd wanted. All she wanted. And how the hell had he broken her? That was a punch to the throat. "You might want to check your facts. Most of what you just said isn't true." He didn't want to open old wounds, but he had to set Krystal straight. His gaze met hers. "Krystal, you have to know I would never—"

"You two look far too serious." Emmy Lou's gaze bounced between the two of them, lingering on his mouth just long enough to make him smile. Her gaze fell away, her cheeks flushed pink.

All he could do was stare.

"What sort of reunion is this?" Krystal asked, nudging her

sister. "You know everyone in the room is expecting more. Like you, Brock, say, 'Hi, Emmy, you're beautiful.' Then Emmy, you'd say, 'Thanks, Brock, hug me in your tree-trunk arms.'"

Brock had to laugh. Emmy did, too.

"She has a point," Emmy said, breathless.

"My arms are tree trunks?" He teased.

She laughed. "Maybe we should...hug." She swallowed, her cheeks more red than pink now. "If people are expecting—"

"Don't want to let the fans down." He took her hand. But once he'd pulled her into his arms, he almost groaned from the feel of her against him. He got lost in the slide of her arms around his neck, the way she rested her head against his chest...and the sweetest sigh he'd ever heard slipping from her mouth. Like maybe this was what she'd been waiting for, too.

"That should cover it," Krystal said. "Really. Probably good now. Anytime."

His arms fell away and Emmy stepped back, but her green eyes had a hold on him, so he stood there staring for the whole damn room to see.

"Well, shit." Krystal was focused on something over Emmy's shoulder. "Momma's headed this way." She grabbed Emmy's hand. "That's my cue to leave. Sorry, but you'll have to face her alone." She squeezed her sister's arm and walked off.

Even though they walked past one another, close enough to touch, Krystal and CiCi avoided making eye contact. "Problem?" he asked, glancing Emmy's way.

"Family stuff." Emmy's smile wavered. "What did you think?" She'd gone back to nibbling the inside of her lip, staring at his arm—his chest.

"Of the concert? Or the reunion?" He chuckled. "You need to ask?"

She glanced his way. "I'm glad you came." There was the smile he loved.

His pulse picked up. "Me, too." There was no place else he'd rather be.

Until CiCi King joined them. "You two lovebirds over here telling secrets?" Her voice was high enough to be heard by anyone listening. From where he stood, a good portion of the room did seem to be listening. Not that he cared. He did care about the warning bells that CiCi King's grin triggered. "Do I want to know what the two of you are talking about?"

"The concert." He nodded. "It was something."

"Something?" CiCi's brows rose. "I'm glad you think so." She draped an arm around Emmy's waist, lowering her voice. "After we get a few pictures of you two, go mingle, Emmy. You know how this works. If we're going to keep this #Bremmy hashtag trending, we need to keep everyone guessing about you two."

How this works? He swallowed. *We?* He risked a look Emmy's way, but she was staring at a basketball photo on the far wall, her smile flat. Something hard and cold settled in the pit of his stomach.

"Your agent is sharp as a tack and full of ideas," CiCi kept going. "You'd almost think that whole kitten business was a setup from it working out so well," she whispered, patting his arm. "Don't worry, Connie told me all about your big plans, Brock. On and off the field. And if all of this will fast-track your comeback, you know we're happy to help." She hugged Emmy. "Hank and Emmy have always had a soft spot for you."

A buzzing started in his ears. *What the fuck is she saying?* That she and *Connie* had cooked up this whole Bremmy thing? That this was all for PR? For headlines? *That's bullshit.* Connie would never reach out to this woman. For one thing, his agent was a control freak. Trying to imagine her and CiCi working together... No way. The rest of it? Was all of this a media stunt? Emmy's smile? That was real... The cold was bone deep now. At least it helped numb the painful throb of his heart.

"Hank, sugar." CiCi waved Hank over about the same time a photographer showed up. "Big smiles, y'all."

He was pretty sure he didn't smile. Not with CiCi's words cycling through, over and over. She was a liar. But was it all a lie? He and Emmy... The only truth between them was attraction. Him hoping for anything more was only setting himself up for hurt—like this right here. After everything he'd been through, he *knew* better. He knew to keep Emmy Lou and the rest of the Kings at arm's distance. But all it took was one look from her, one damn smile, and he willingly headed into a guaranteed clusterfuck of heartache.

Aunt Mo's *start fresh* advice? A joke. Worse? *He* was the joke.

"Weren't there some people Emmy needed to talk to, Hank?" CiCi was all softness and smiles for her husband. "Guitar people?"

"Fender." Hank King nodded, smiling with excitement. "What do you think about a King Limited Edition Fender, baby girl?"

"Wow." Emmy's monotone delivery was off. She was white as a sheet, hands shaking, and green eyes huge in her pale face. Something was wrong.

"Em?" He reached for her hand.

She recoiled, startling all of them. "I mean it." She blinked, turning to her father. "Really, Daddy, that's amazing." But her excitement was forced.

"Emmy?" Hank tilted her face back. "You feeling okay? You... eat the dinner the nutritionist recommended for you?"

Her parents knew about Emmy's eating disorder? That was a relief. Or was it? If they'd known about it, shouldn't they be doing more to help? As beautiful as she was, she'd lost more weight since the last time he'd seen her—weight she couldn't afford to lose.

"Hank." CiCi's voice was a hiss. "People might hear you."

"I don't give a damn." Hank hooked his arm through Emmy's.

The snap in Hank's voice was a shock. So was the resentment on CiCi's face. And Krystal earlier... Was the Kings' close-knit family just one more illusion?

Emmy leaned into her father and nodded. "I ate it, Daddy. Every bite." Her smile returned, but it didn't reach her eyes. "A promise is a promise. Now, let's go see what this King Limited Edition guitar will look like. Better hurry before Krystal has it covered in crystals." Emmy was already trying to tug her father away.

Hank chuckled. "After, how about we go get ice cream?"

"What's wrong with carrot sticks?" CiCi sighed.

And just like that, Emmy seemed to withdraw. "Carrots sound good."

"Not to me." Hank ignored his wife's frustrated sigh. "Brock, glad you came to the show." Hank shook his hand. "Join us for ice cream?"

For ice cream? Or more publicity? He and Emmy sharing an ice cream sundae would be Bremmy gold. It took effort, but he managed to swallow his bitterness and disappointment.

"I'm sure he has more important things to do, Hank." CiCi regarded her husband with what appeared to be genuine affection. "Though you are welcome to stay, of course."

"But thanks for coming, Brock." Emmy's gaze looked right through him. "Take care."

Her quick dismissal emptied his lungs—a balloon with a slow leak. "You too."

With a parting nod, Hank led Emmy Lou back into the crowd of fans.

"Well, Bremmy lives to trend another day. Job well done." CiCi waved at someone walking by. "You've learned how to play the game."

A game. It made sense. Everything about CiCi King was calculated. Like tonight. Everything she'd said, true or not, was deliberate. This wasn't about Emmy, what she felt or wanted. This was about CiCi keeping all *her* pieces on *her* chessboard, making the moves *she* wanted them to make.

"This isn't a game to me, CiCi. It never was." He searched the room for Emmy but wound up locking eyes with Krystal. She was watching him, watching her mother, like a hawk. "I'd never use Emmy to boost my career." Just saying it stuck in his throat.

"You can't say that anymore, Brock. You're here, aren't you? Why else would you be here?" Her eyes went wide, shocked. It was the first authentic reaction she'd given since she'd come crashing in on his evening. "Oh, honey, *no*. Not again. Now you know— *none* of this is real." She patted his arm. "It's done with anyway. After tonight. It's not like the two of you will be seeing each other much now. You take care of yourself, Brock." With a toss of platinum hair and the shimmer of red beads, she crossed the room to join her family.

She wanted him gone, he got that. And soon. For reasons he didn't understand, she was determined to keep him and Emmy apart. She was right about one thing, none of tonight was real. Something was off. More than that. He couldn't shake the feeling that she was hiding something. Nothing else made sense. Something about him. And Emmy. Something that might threaten the hold CiCi had on her daughter. He just wished he knew what it was.

Chapter 13

"MAYBE A CUP OF TEA WILL HELP?" EMMY ASKED WATSON, WHO meowed in response. After tossing and turning most of the night, she'd need more than one cup of tea to get through the day. But she'd manage it; she always did. While Watson scampered off, Emmy cradled her teacup and slipped into the leather-upholstered café booth, custom designed for the Kings' Coach II. Her and Krystal's tour bus had all the bells and whistles, a fact Travis reminded everyone of whenever he had the chance. Chances were, he'd show up soon so she'd laid out all the makings for coffee—complete with his favorite *USA Good Morning* anchor Molly Harper coffee mug.

Watson came running across the room, leapt high, and pounced on her slippered feet. "Are you defeating the evil pom-poms?" She turned her phone over, ignoring the constant alerts. Hashtag #Bremmy was still going strong. She'd turned it off last night, hoping a little peace and quiet would let her sleep. Since she'd turned it on, it hadn't stopped pinging and vibrating. Instagram. Snapchat. TikTok. She and Brock. Last night had only added to the speculation. Their hug. Her staring at his chest. His face when he hugged her. Them smiling at each other. Momma was right. "About everything?" she asked Watson, blowing out a shaky breath.

Watson jumped onto the table, sniffing her cup.

"That's mine." She smiled, tapping Watson's nose. His instant purr made her smile. "At least you love me. Don't you?" Watson meowed, then leapt off the table and darted beneath a couch.

Was she too trusting? *Stupid might be more appropriate.*

She'd written, deleted, and rewritten more than a dozen texts to him but hadn't been able to hit send.

Brock had always protected his privacy. Aunt Mo had said as much at the hospital.

But that was before his ACL tear and Ricky Ames.

For all of Krystal's and Travis's teasing, she respected the power of social media—of a devoted fandom. Momma said his agent had big plans for him. *Plans on and off the field*, Momma had said.

It wasn't that long ago that her family had watched the rise of Mickey Graham. He had no talent or class or creativity, but he'd dated Krystal for one hot minute. Mickey Graham and his manager had milked his heartbreak long and hard enough to earn him a platinum album.

Was she really just a part of his career plan? It hurt to think that was what this was about.

"Morning," Travis said. "Food?"

"Tea." She held up her mug. "And coffee. Help yourself to food."

He flopped down onto one of the leather couches and sighed. "My head is killing me."

"Sorry, Trav." Her phone vibrated.

He peered at her with bloodshot eyes. "What's wrong with you?" He held up a finger. "Wait." He pushed himself up, made a cup of coffee, shuffled to the table, and collapsed onto the bench again. "You look like shit."

"If you're trying to cheer me up, it's working." She blew on her tea.

"Was that sarcasm?" He rubbed his eyes. "*You?* You are Emmy, right?"

"Good morning?" Krystal came down the hall, holding hands with Jace.

Clementine trailed behind, looking all over until she spied Watson. Watson ran to her, meowed once, and the two of them began their morning ritual of racing back and forth down the hallway.

"That's not helping my hangover." Travis groaned.

"Go back to your own bus." Krystal rolled her eyes. "Want some coffee, babe?"

Jace nodded, kissing her cheek.

"Babe?" Travis rested his head on the seat. "Krys, come on. Knock that shit off. Focus. We have a problem. Look at Emmy. Just look at her."

Jace and Krystal both turned to look at her.

"What's up, Em?" Krystal asked, her brow furrowing. "You're all...frowny?"

Emmy shook her head, ignoring yet another ping from her phone. "Tired."

Travis grabbed it, turned it over, and swiped through the screen. "Does it have something to do with this?" He handed the phone to Krystal. "I'd be upset over having Bremmy as my hashtag, too." He shuddered. "As a man, that's painful to say."

"I didn't start it. Why would I?" Emmy Lou hadn't meant to snap, but she did.

And everyone noticed.

"Whoa, so—" Travis was interrupted by Clementine and Watson's circuit around the seating area before thundering back down the hallway. "*That's* gotta stop." Travis pressed his fingers to his temple.

"Shush." Krystal slid into the booth beside him, dismissing Travis with a wave of her hand. "Now, spill." She finished scrolling through the pictures. "Who took all of these? Was someone wearing a spy camera or something?" She handed off Emmy's phone to Jace.

Jace held the phone out to her, the only one to look remotely apologetic over her phone being snatched.

"Go ahead." Emmy smiled. "I think Momma was the one who had the pictures taken. Or maybe Brock's agent?"

All three of them looked at her.

"Like…an orchestrated sort of thing?" Travis scratched his head.

The bus door opened and Sawyer joined them, a large brown paper bag in hand. "Food."

"I love you, man." Travis smiled, reaching for the bag.

Sawyer opened the bag and handed Emmy a clear plastic to-go box.

In the span of four hours, Daddy had located an anorexia nervosa therapist willing to do video sessions and a dietitian who specialized in developing individual meal plans for people with eating disorders. "Thanks, Sawyer." She managed a smile for him.

The corner of Sawyer's mouth twitched down. "What's happening?"

"Not sure, but it sounds like Momma is up to something." Travis shrugged. "So, the norm."

Sawyer nodded, taking the phone from Jace. His blue-green gaze shifted from the phone to Emmy.

"Go ahead. Everyone else already looked." Emmy took a bite of yogurt and granola.

"Last night. Start from the beginning." Krystal pulled Jace into the booth beside her. "Scoot over, Trav."

"Hold on, let me take off my left arm and leg to make more room." Travis shot Krystal a look.

"Okay." Emmy took a deep breath. "He was there. We were happy to see each other. At least, I was happy to see him. Then Momma was there—"

"Hold up." Travis held up his pointer finger. "We're now admitting you have a thing for Brock? We're now allowed to openly tease you and talk about it?"

Krystal covered Travis's mouth. "What makes you think she had something to do with this?"

"She said so. She said *we* were happy to help Brock out, but *we* needed to keep our relationship mysterious for the Bremmy thing.

How they couldn't have planned something as perfect as Watson's rescue." She shook her head. "Some big plans for Brock's career and future and how this is good for him."

"So she implied Brock is using you...which I'm guessing hurt." Krystal frowned. "And then implied you, *we*, were helping out because he *needed* help. Which would have hurt him."

"She's trying to keep them apart?" Jace asked, sitting back in the booth.

"Don't you think that's a little drastic?" Travis yawned. "A lot drastic?"

"Yes, it is. But have you met our mother?" Krystal asked. "Maybe she really believes she's protecting Emmy. I mean, to give her the benefit of the doubt, Emmy was crushed by the way it ended last time."

"Can I ask a question? If she's just doing this to help Brock, what does she get out of it?" Sawyer asked, leaning against the kitchen counter. "Or what does he have on her?"

She blinked, staring at Sawyer. "Brock?"

"He's got a point, Sis." Krystal took her hand. "I know it sounds harsh and I know you and Momma have a better relationship then Momma and me. But bottom line, Momma would never do something for nothing. This isn't adding up to me."

An extended silence settled. She didn't know what was more upsetting: her momma manipulating things to keep her from the only man she'd ever loved, that they were all considering this as a possibility, or that Brock was doing everything Momma said.

The bus doors opened again. Only this time, it was her father... and Momma, too. Momma, who looked less than her perfect self.

"That looks good, baby girl." Daddy eyed her plate. "Strawberries."

"Want one?" Emmy Lou held it up.

"That's all yours." He smiled. "I don't know whether to be happy you're all together or worry over what you're all up to."

Travis sat forward. "Funny you should say that, Dad—"

Emmy stomped on his toe, hard, under the table. Sharing things with her siblings was one thing. But dragging Daddy into this, when there was nothing but speculation, felt wrong. She was still struggling with misplaced guilt—according to her first session with her therapist—for burdening her family with her eating disorder. "There are bagels if you're hungry."

"That's an awful lot of carbs to start the day." Momma sighed.

"I love me some carbs in the morning." Travis stood, stretched, and carried his cup to the counter. "Are we up for a King family meeting? War council? World domination? What? After I have two or three bagels, with a side of extra carbs." He was all smiles.

"Poke all you want, Travis. You're not getting a rise out of me." Momma stood, her arms crossed over her waist. "Daddy and I figured we'd check on you all before we started driving."

"Well now, that's…" Travis paused, taking a massive bite out of his bagel. "Mighty unusual." He grinned.

Emmy turned all her attention on Watson. If she didn't, she'd laugh. Momma might tolerate all sorts of teasing and shenanigans from Travis, but one thing she would not tolerate was laughter at her expense. Watson was all too happy to roll over for a belly rub.

"Everything okay?" Krystal asked, her gaze fixed on Daddy.

"Everything is fine." Daddy nodded, looking at Emmy's breakfast. "Just checking in."

Emmy swallowed another bite. "On me?" Once the carton was empty, she held it up. "All good?"

Daddy nodded but Momma stood, placing a hand on Daddy's arm. "I need a minute, Emmy." She glanced pointedly around the room. "It won't take long. I know we need to get back on the road."

Emmy held her breath until they were in her room, bracing herself for who knows what.

"I owe you an apology." Momma cleared her throat. "I acted poorly."

Emmy pushed her brush aside to sit on the edge of her bed. "Why, Momma?"

Momma picked up her brush. "Let me?" Emmy nodded, turning so Momma could brush her hair. "I used to do this for hours when you were little. You remember? You'd let me braid and clip and give you fancy twists. You've always had the softest hair." She kept brushing Emmy's hair. "A sweet smile and a big heart, too. You give people the benefit of the doubt, even when they don't deserve it." There was a sheen in Momma's eyes. "But not *him*—not again. I talked to him at the field and again last night, did you know that? He's so jealous of you and your success. It's almost like he's come back wanting to hurt you. And he *has*, leading you on this way." She kept brushing. "If his agent hadn't called to thank me, I'd never have known how important this Bremmy thing is for him. It's already changed his life. He *just* signed a seven-figure deal with Alpha Menswear—after all this went viral. That's why he came to the concert." She stopped brushing Emmy's hair and crouched by her side. "I get upset and I get all momma bear. But I am trying harder. I'm just so worried about you. Daddy, too. We love you so much, baby girl. This not eating thing..." She drew in a deep breath. "That comes first. You being healthy. I can't lose you, too, Emmy." She took her hand. "Yes, I'm trying to protect you. I always will... All I can think about is what happens if he hurts you again. You took it *so* hard last time." Momma burst into tears. "You're not strong enough, Emmy."

Emmy pulled her close, crying, too. "Momma, don't cry." Barbed wire seemed to wrap itself around her lungs.

"Can you forgive me?" Her arms tightened around her. "Can you understand? You're my whole world, Emmy Lou. My baby girl. I have to do what's best for you." She peered up at Emmy, tears rolling down her cheeks. "Even if, sometimes, it hurts."

It was easier to hug Momma again and hold her tight than it was to look her in the eye and lie. As earnest as her mother appeared, a sliver of doubt remained. She needed answers, and the only person who could give them to her was Brock.

Brock pulled off his worn leather gloves and threw them into the cab of the ranch truck. He ran the back of his hand across his forehead, tucked his keys into his pocket, and climbed up the front steps of the ranch house.

"Get it all done?" Aunt Mo asked, sitting on the front porch with a bag of snap peas in her lap and a bowl on the swing beside her.

"Yes, ma'am. If we get an early storm, they can pen the herd in the north shed. Heat lamps are working, and I went ahead and replaced the bottom strand of wire. Didn't like the look of it." He leaned against the porch railing, watching Aunt Mo's quick work.

Brock's phone was ringing from inside the house.

"That phone has been ringing since you left." She shot him a look. "If I knew how to turn it off, I would have. Can hardly hear myself think with all that racket."

"Sorry, Aunt Mo." He smiled, but he didn't move.

"Don't sit there. Answer it or turn it off." Aunt Mo frowned. "But from all the ringing, I'm thinking you should go on and answer it."

He pushed off the railing and headed inside. There was a reason he'd left his phone here. It had been a long time since he'd been this wound up, but he knew he wasn't fit for conversation.

Until he saw who was calling. "Connie." He barked her name.

"Sounds like someone is having a rough day?"

"Well, it hasn't been good." He cleared his throat, the anger he'd been fighting damn near making him shake. "Did you talk to CiCi King?" He paced the length of the family room.

"What?" Connie asked.

"Did you call her?" He paused, staring at the framed collage of family photos over the mantel.

"I returned her phone call." Connie paused. "Which, I'll be honest, was out of nowhere. What the hell is going on? I don't appreciate the tone."

"I don't appreciate having the rug pulled out from under me by a woman who I know has some sort of ax to grind with me." Calm down. Breathe. Deep down, he knew Connie would never do or say any of the things CiCi had hinted at.

"Brock Nathaniel Watson." Aunt Mo chastised him through the screen door. "I taught you manners. Use them."

He sighed. "Sorry, Connie. I'm acting like an ass."

"You are." Connie sighed. "Why don't we start over?"

"Sounds like a good idea." He took a deep breath. "Why did CiCi King call you?"

"At first she was looking for advice. Something about a new musician needing an agent or manager. I gave her a few recommendations, but that's not what I do."

Brock smiled. When it came to sports, Connie was the best. Entertainment? If it wasn't sports, she wasn't interested.

"Then she mentioned you. She'd heard about the Alpha deal and asked if that was a done deal. I didn't answer, since it's none of her business. But she kept talking. It became clear she was trying to get me to say the Bremmy thing was the reason the Alpha deal had gone through. I didn't say a thing. As you know, I don't discuss my clients' endorsements or negotiations."

He sighed. "She made it sound like the two of you had some mastermind plan and Emmy was my fucking golden ticket."

"Brock," Aunt Mo hissed.

He walked down the hallway and into the kitchen. "I don't know why I let it get to me, but it did." He knew why. He didn't want to admit it, but he knew.

"I don't, either. And, honestly, I'm a little pissed off. I've micromanaged the shit out of your career for the last five years to put you in the best position."

"And I appreciate it. I appreciate you." He cleared his throat. "I owe you for sticking with me when no one else would."

"Next time, remember that before you snap at me." She cleared her throat. "*If* I was going to recruit backup—I wouldn't—it sure as hell wouldn't be CiCi King. I've never heard anything good about that woman. Only to watch your back when she's around. It sounds like you might need that advice right about now."

"Sounds like it." He got himself a glass of water and drained it.

"What did you do to CiCi King? Or her family?" Connie chuckled. "Must have been something."

He filled up his glass again. "I've been trying to figure that out since I left."

"The logical conclusion would be you and her daughter. You know, America's sweetheart. The one who makes you grin like a schoolboy—don't deny it, I have the pictures to prove it. Me and anyone on any social media platform. Anywhere."

He didn't deny it.

"Maybe she thinks you're going to break her daughter's heart again—"

"I didn't break her heart. But she damn near totaled mine." He slammed the cup onto the counter.

Aunt Mo's firm touch startled him.

He did his best to smile when he said, "That was a long time ago."

"Not that long ago," Aunt Mo mumbled.

"It's my job to give you advice." Connie paused. "I'm not much of a romantic, Trish will back me up on this, but it sounds like you need to talk to this girl. No audience or distraction or interfering mothers. What's that old saying about a picture?"

"A picture's worth a thousand words," Aunt Mo said.

"This is a private conversation, Mo." He shook his head, but he was smiling.

"You should have thought of that before you came into my kitchen to have it." Aunt Mo started pulling things from the refrigerator. "You'll have to finish your private conversation somewhere else because I need to make *you* dinner."

"Hi, Molly." Connie started laughing. "You better tell her I said hello."

"Connie says hi," Brock repeated.

"I heard her." Aunt Mo's smile was huge. "Still hoping you and Trish will join us for Thanksgiving."

"We would love to," Connie answered. "Tell her we said yes."

"You want the phone?" He held the phone out to his aunt.

"What is the matter with you, son? You're all out of sorts." Aunt Mo shook her head. "Good thing you've got practice tomorrow. You need to tackle some people."

"Have I mentioned how much I adore your aunt?" Connie asked.

"Not recently." But Brock knew firsthand just how easy it was to adore Aunt Mo. Even if she was nosy and bossy. "Want me to tell her?"

Once he'd finished his call with Connie, he went back outside to wrap the pipes on the main house. Since Aunt Mo was too stubborn to make improvements to the hundred-year-old home, Brock made sure to do as much preventative work as he could.

He was crawling out from under the house when his phone started vibrating.

Thanks for the other day.

Vanessa.

I just wanted you to know I did go to a meeting and I'm fine.

He stood, dusting the grass and dirt from his jeans. He typed his response and hit send. Glad you're taking care of yourself. Keep it up.

"You going to wash up?" Aunt Mo called. "Dinner's about ready. After, maybe we could take a ride down to the tank. John Wayne's been out to pasture too long."

"I'm not going to say no to that." He kicked off his boots on the back porch and headed inside, leaving his phone on the counter. "Give me five minutes."

"Five." Aunt Mo nodded, turning the massive chicken fried steak. "Gravy will be done and you'll have a feast fit for a king." She frowned. "I wasn't poking at you."

He frowned. "What?"

"King." She stared at him. "Emmy Lou? Oh, never mind." She shook her head. "Go clean up."

A warm shower, a hearty dinner, and a long horseback ride down to the big tank was a perfect way to round out the evening. For all his complaining, he understood why Mo didn't make any improvements. Being here was like stepping back in time. When he was here, he knew he'd work hard, sweat enough to wring the wet out of his shirt, eat well, and slow down enough to appreciate the little things. Out here, nothing changed.

Not the land or Aunt Mo's horse. John Wayne was twenty years old, slow and steady, but he loved Mo and her pockets full of apples and sugar cubes. The horse looked miniature next to Brock's horse Granite, a Percheron mix. Then again, Aunt Mo looked pretty tiny standing next to Brock.

"Been too long since we did this." Aunt Mo slowed John Wayne when they reached the hill leading down to the tank. "I know you were riled up when you got here, but I'm glad you came. It was nice having you around—spending some time away from the hospital."

"I'll do better, Aunt Mo." He sighed, resting his hands on the pommel of his saddle and letting the sunset ease the last of the stress from his shoulders. "I haven't been there as much as I should—"

"You're doing fine." Aunt Mo cut him off. "You are, aren't you, Brock?"

He looked at her. "Why wouldn't I be?"

"I heard your phone call, Brock." She shook her head.

"I know." He smiled.

"I didn't go snooping, now, so don't get sassy with me. Your phone was pinging again, and I looked that way and I saw Vanessa's name pop up." She frowned, shaking her head again. "I wish the girl well, but I also wish her far from you."

"You don't need to worry about that, Aunt Mo." He nodded.

"I didn't think so. Especially after hearing all the carrying on you did with Connie." Aunt Mo was shaking her head. "You should listen to her. She's all kinds of smart."

"About my career? Or Emmy Lou?" He grinned.

"Both." Aunt Mo nodded, clicking enough to get John Wayne headed down the hill. "I still think starting fresh is best. I've mentioned that before? It's past time for you and Emmy Lou to clear the air between you. Once you know what you want, there's no point waiting on going after it."

It might not be as easy as she made it sound, but she had a point. Connie, too. He knew, deep down, it was fear that held him back. Of CiCi being right. Of having Emmy Lou reject him. Or loving her even now... He'd always faced fear head-on—no point stopping now.

A gentle knee to the side had Granite following Mo and John Wayne down the hill. "Anyone ever tell you you're a genius, Aunt Mo?"

"All the time, but you might as well go on and say it, too. I never get tired of hearing it."

Brock was still laughing when they reached the tank.

Chapter 14

"GOOD MORNING, CHARLOTTE, NORTH CAROLINA. THANKS for tuning in to station WTQR, Today's Country." The DJ, Banjo Bryan, adjusted his headset. "If you're just joining us, we're talking to country royalty. The Three Kings and Jace Black are here, promoting their record-breaking tour—'Three Kings and a Jace'. Looks like we've got time for one, maybe two more questions."

"Wow, time flew by." Emmy Lou nudged Travis. He'd been bleary-eyed and slouched in his chair most of the interview, his to-go coffee cup cradled against his chest.

Banjo took a card from a tech. "How does it feel to be breaking more records?"

"Good." Travis took a long sip of his coffee.

"Good?" Krystal laughed. "Amazing. Fantastic. Ignore Travis, Banjo, he's not much of a morning person. Drink your coffee, Travis."

Travis held up his hand, but Emmy Lou grabbed it before he could flip off their sister. She kept holding his hand as she said, "It's incredibly humbling. Our fans' devotion never fails to surprise me." It was true. Tomorrow would be their eighth performance, but their opening night energy hadn't waned—mostly because of the outpouring of love and enthusiasm from their fans.

"What about you, Jace?" Banjo asked. "Is your second tour with the Three Kings as enjoyable as the first?"

"I think so." Jace paused, his gaze fixed on Krystal. "For me, it gets better every day."

Krystal smiled and leaned into him.

"We're almost out of time, so let's see who we've got on the line." Banjo pressed a blue button and held his headset closer to one ear. "Good morning, you're on WTQR with the Three Kings and Jace Black. What's your name and your question?"

"Hi, Banjo. This is Taylor." The voice was high-pitched and fast-talking. "I am such a huge fan. Huge. I can't wait for the concert tomorrow."

"Oh, thank you," Emmy gushed. "We're excited to be singing for you all."

"Hi, Taylor," Jace and Krystal said it in unison, earning a groan from Travis.

Banjo laughed. "What's your question, Taylor?"

"Emmy, since you've got a concert tomorrow and the Roughnecks are playing the day after, will you and Brock get to see each other while you're in North Carolina? Love Bremmy."

Emmy ignored her brother's eye roll and tried a noncommittal response. "That's sweet, Taylor."

"I guess your schedules make it hard to get together. But him *flying* to see your last show so you could be together... It almost made me cry," Taylor gushed. "All the pictures of you two together make me and my friends super happy. I hope you get to see him."

"But we will definitely see *you* tomorrow night," Emmy said. "I can't wait."

"With that, we'll wrap things up." Banjo smiled. "It's been a fun morning. I know it meant a lot to everyone listening. And to us here at WTQR. Until next time..." He held up his finger until the red LIVE light went dark. "And we're out." He stood, offering his hand. "Thank you all. Looking forward to the show."

Five minutes later, they were out front, signing autographs and taking selfies on their way to the waiting vehicle. Sawyer and one other member of their security detail, Jerome, waited, holding open the car door and scanning the crowd for trouble.

"What's with the Secret Service wannabe look?" Travis asked

when they were pulling away from the curb. "The sunglasses give off a retro *Top Gun* vibe. Was that the goal?" Travis laughed.

Jerome and Sawyer weren't laughing.

"Would you behave?" Emmy sighed, ignoring her phone's pinging from the confines of her purse.

"Have you ever thought about throwing that thing out the window? Or running over it?" Travis frowned at her. "Or turning it off? I'm happy to help if it will make it shut the hell up."

"I'll do it." Krystal dug Emmy's phone from her purse, stared at the screen, then smiled. "When was the last time you checked your messages?"

Emmy Lou shook her head. For the last two days, Melanie had been handling all of her social media. "A while. I need…a break." So far, the only break she was getting was from Momma. Some big *snag* in the bathroom renovations had her flying back to Austin in a fit of temper. "Melanie will let me know if something is really important… Why? Please tell me it's not something bad."

Krystal held out the phone.

Brock. A video message from Brock.

"You're not going to play it?" Krystal asked, all gentle sympathy.

But Travis grabbed it, hit play, and held the phone out of Emmy's reach.

"Em, it's me. I guess you can tell. Right. Practicing here all day and I thought… We should talk." He stared at the phone, frowned, and the video ended.

"Do you know where they're playing, Sawyer? Is it far away?" Krystal asked, studying her face. "It's not like you need another rehearsal."

"Don't worry about it, Sawyer," Emmy called out. Krystal might be ready and willing to talk to Brock, but *she* wasn't. "I can't. Just let it go, please."

They were quiet for two blocks. For those two blocks, Emmy's gaze kept bouncing from the window to her phone screen and Brock's frozen image.

"Well, if you're going to stick your head in the sand and deprive yourself of a chance at happiness, let's get drunk." Travis nodded, hugging her against him. "I've never seen you drunk and I'm thinking it'll be hilarious. Who's with me?"

"Was that an attempt at reverse psychology?" Krystal cocked her head to one side. "Or an attempt to get us day drinking?"

"Either works." Travis peered out the window. "Or we can go back to the hotel, unpack, and Emmy can keep staring at Brock on her phone because that's not at all pathetic."

Emmy didn't argue. This—she—was pathetic. But she still scowled at Travis.

"I figured you'd want to talk to him?" Krystal said, then shook her head. "You know what? This is all you. See him or not, just do what *you* want to do. Not me or Travis or Momma. You. Okay?"

Emmy nodded, turned her phone over on her knee—then shoved it into her purse. She knew what she wanted, but it wasn't just up to her... She was scared, plain and simple. Talking to him meant learning the truth. Was Brock manipulating her? Or was it Momma? Not knowing kept her in limbo, but it also prevented her from the pain either option carried with it.

I am so pathetic. Self-loathing burned the back of her throat. She'd rather not know the truth—that way she didn't have to accept that someone she cared about wasn't a good person. *Enough is enough.* Momma was wrong—she was strong enough. It was time to stop giving everyone else power over her. Right here, right now. "Let's go to the stadium."

"Good for you, Em. You should talk to him." Travis looked at her, his smile growing as he nudged her in the side. "Who knows? Might even wind up losing the nun's habit—"

"Are you really going to start that? Now? I am going to *talk* to him." She stared at her brother. "I have *never* said anything about having sex with Brock." Her thoughts and fantasies were for her alone. "You keep bringing it up. Over and over. *You* won't shut up about sex."

"She has a point," Sawyer said, his gaze meeting hers in the rearview mirror.

"Even if I was going to have sex with Brock, that would be my choice and *none* of your business." For the first time in her adult life, Travis was speechless.

The rest of the drive was relatively quiet. Krystal and Jace had a FaceTime call with his sister, Heather, while Travis sat, arms crossed, pouting like a little boy. When they pulled up in front of the stadium doors, Emmy climbed out, Krystal following.

"Hold on." Krystal opened the rear door of the Suburban and dug through her overnight bag. "I'm not judging." She slammed the Suburban doors shut and shoved a box of condoms into Emmy's purse. "Or condoning. I'm keeping you safe."

"Why does everyone keep thinking I'm about to have some… some sex party?" Emmy stared into her purse at the unopened box.

Krystal laughed. "How am I supposed to know if you were just putting Trav in his place or not? If you do decide to have a *sex party*, you're covered." Krystal shook her head and hugged her. "Text me later. He doesn't deserve you." She climbed back into the Suburban—but they didn't drive off until Emmy Lou was inside.

Emmy dodged a few stadium workers, headed up into the stands, and sat down. Practice was underway. Fine, she'd wait. But the words of her ebook didn't hold her interest. After a few minutes on her word game app, she closed it. She was distracted. Brock was…distracting. Running down the field—all rippling muscles and strength. No matter how many drills he ran, he moved with explosive speed and force. He had, without a doubt, the most amazing body she'd ever seen. Which reminded her… *I have a box of condoms.* She glanced around, hugging her purse closer.

When the whistle blew and the team went on break, he grabbed a towel from one of the trainers, glanced her way, and headed toward the tunnel below her seat. He'd known she was there... According to Travis, and Krystal and Jace, Brock was always *aware* of her.

There were times he'd look at her and the pull between them seemed to blot out everything else. But...was that real? Or was she only seeing what she wanted? She'd know soon enough. That's why she was up, heading out of the stands to meet him. By the time she'd made it to the tunnel leading onto the field, her nerves were stretched taut.

She'd barely entered the tunnel when she saw Brock. He was walking toward her, rubbing the towel over his face, sweaty and big and gorgeous. He wasn't smiling, just staring—at her. Almost wary. Then again, she wasn't smiling at him, either. She *was* staring.

The closer they got, the harder it was to ignore the very current drawing her in. When they were steps apart, she said, "I got your message."

"Didn't know if you'd come or not." His blue eyes were searching hers.

"I didn't, either." She blew out a slow breath, trying to calm the tremor in her voice. "What did you want to talk about?"

He ran the towel along the back of his neck, swallowed, and said, "You and me."

"You and me, real life?" It was hard to add, "Or you and me, Bremmy?"

"Em..." His jaw tightened as his gaze met hers. "You know better."

"Do I?" Her words came pouring out. "Or am I so caught up in wanting you that I can't see the truth?"

His eyes were blazing now. "We'll get to the wanting part in a minute." His voice was low and gruff. "I wanted you to hear this from me." He closed the distance between them, his breath unsteady. "If all this media shit disappeared, it wouldn't change what I'm after."

"And what you're after is?" she whispered.

"This, right here. A fresh start…" He cleared his throat. "With you. If that's okay with you?"

A fresh start? The two of them. Her heart was beating so hard and fast, he had to hear it. When he held out his hand to her, there was no holding back. She was wrapping her arms around his waist and holding on tight. Eyes closed, she pressed her ear to his chest. His heart was racing—just as wild and thundering as hers. "It's okay with me."

———

Somehow, even with Emmy Lou in the stands, he managed to focus through the next two hours of practice. It wasn't about proving himself to Emmy or showing off for Ricky Ames. It was about reassuring his team that he'd never stop fighting for them—even when he had the most beautiful girl in the world waiting in the stands.

But when the whistle blew, he was the first one off the field. Not that his team was going to make things easy on him. From jamming his locker to sending him to Coach McCoy's office—McCoy hadn't asked to see him—to hiding his phone to stealing his towel when he was in the shower. He took it in stride.

By the time he was clean and dressed—albeit missing his socks—he was nervous.

"You've got practice tomorrow," RJ reminded him.

Brock brushed aside the onslaught of jokes that followed, shouldered his duffel bag, and headed out of the locker room.

Emmy Lou was standing outside, talking to McCoy.

"I appreciate that," McCoy was saying. "She gets nervous. I know I'm her father, that maybe I don't count, but I think she's a good singer."

"I know she's not taking new clients but tell her I sent you."

Emmy wrote something on a piece of paper. "Maybe I'll get to hear her sing one day." But then she saw Brock. That smile of hers damn near knocked him to his knees.

McCoy read the paper. "I appreciate it." Then coach was looking back and forth between them. "You coming?" He shook his head. "It's rude to keep a lady waiting."

Brock nodded, taking Emmy's hand once it was in reach.

"See you tomorrow." McCoy scowled up at him. "Early."

Brock nodded.

McCoy walked off, tucking the paper into his pocket.

"Good practice?" she asked, tugging on his hand.

"I'd say so." He stared down at her, his chest heavy and his heart full. "You have something you need to do? Rehearsal?" She'd sat through practice; he'd do the same.

"Nope." Her voice was soft. "I'm all yours."

He squeezed her hand and headed to the parking lot. The closer they got to his truck, the tighter her hand became. When he held the truck door open, she stood there, looking at him, then his truck. She bounced up on the balls of her feet and tilted her head back for a kiss.

He kissed her—barely.

She made that adorable sound of want and frustration that set the hair on the back of his neck straight up.

"I'd like to get out of the parking lot." He smiled. Preferably far enough removed from the rest of the world that nothing and no one would interfere.

She took his hand and climbed up into the cab of his truck.

"Where are we going?" she asked when they'd pulled onto the highway.

"Wherever you want." He glanced her way.

She turned to look at him, her eyes zeroing in on his mouth. "I have an idea." Her bright-green gaze met his. "I was thinking we could go to your hotel room and finish what we started. We've waited long enough, don't you think?" She nibbled her lip—damn but he wanted to nibble it, too. "Unless you're too tired?"

"If you're asking, I'm not too tired." He reached across the seat and took her hand into his. After all this time, the last thing he'd expected to feel was nervous. But he did. By the time he handed off his keys to the hotel valet, he was having second thoughts.

Emmy was all shy smiles and flushed cheeks as they made their way to the elevator, her purse held close. When the elevator doors to his floor opened, she grabbed his hand and pulled him down the hall.

Once they were in his hotel suite and the door was shut, Emmy Lou's smile wavered.

"Em, what's this about?" he asked, running his fingers along her cheek. "There's no rush here—"

"Maybe not for you." She cleared her throat, staring up at him. "You have no idea." Her eyes were green fire.

"You could tell me?" He wanted her. Hell, he'd always wanted her.

"I'd rather show you." She turned and headed across the living room area, past the wet bar, into his room.

Her words blotted out all his second thoughts and reservations. He dropped his duffel bag on the floor and his keys on the counter and followed, on fire for her. He hadn't expected her to be so direct—but it was a hell of a turn-on.

Emmy Lou was standing next to his bed, staring around her, unbuttoning her pink-and-white polka-dot shirt with a bow at the neck. "Should I tackle you again?" She was breathing hard, shaking with the force of it.

"Whatever you want, Emmy Lou." *Always.*

She reached up, tugging the band from her hair. "You like—liked—my hair down."

He nodded, the tightness in his chest rivaling the throb of hunger in his blood. She had no idea how beautiful she was to him.

Or how many times he'd imagined this. No span of time had eased the ache he had for this woman.

Her fingers were fumbling with the buttons of her blouse, but her eyes never left his. "I'm not doing a very good job at this."

He was having a hell of a hard time breathing. "What?"

"Seducing you." She glanced down at her button and tugged it free. The button popped off and rolled across the floor. "There should be candles and a bubble bath and strawberries. Aren't there always strawberries?"

He frowned. "In movies, I guess."

"Oh." She untied the bow at her collar. "Movies. So I guess you don't want to sit in a chair and watch? And I don't need to do some sexy dance?"

The more she talked, the more confused he was getting. Not that he wasn't enjoying the view. "Is that what you want?"

Shirt unbuttoned, she paused. "I'm not sure." He could hear her breathing, see the tremor in her hands.

"We have all night, if you want." He closed the distance between them, running his hands along her arms to take her hands.

"And I have a purse full of condoms."

"Not what I expected you to say." He shook his head. "And definitely not what I expected Emmy Lou King to carry around in her purse."

"Oh, no, they're not mine." She frowned. "Of course they're not."

"Of course not." He shook his head, close to laughter. "Anything else I should know?"

"Let's see." Her green eyes traveled over his face, locking on his lips. "Maybe one thing... I don't want to be the nun of country music."

"I have no idea what you're talking about, Em." He tilted her face up, his thumb tracing her mouth. "Damn, you're beautiful. Soft."

"I'm going to tackle you now." She wriggled out of her shirt.

His lungs deflated at the sight of her pink lace bra. The scrap of her pink lace panties—she had no problem getting out of her jeans—just about brought him to his knees. She smiled up at him then pushed with all her might, sending him back onto his bed.

Brock reached up and pulled her down on top of him, his hands sliding up the curve of her back and along her shoulders.

She leaned forward, her lips silky soft against his. He didn't bother holding back his groan. Instead, he tangled one hand in her hair and held her there. He loved the way their lips came together, the slide of her tongue against his, and the rasp of their breath.

Cradling her close, he rolled them.

She was up, untucking his shirt, tugging and pulling the fitted fabric until his shirt was off—and sailing across the room. He reached for her again, pulling her beneath him. Stomach to stomach, chest to chest, he drew her close. His mouth latched on to her neck. The soft spot behind her earlobe. The more he tasted, the more he wanted. The curve of her neck. The blade of her shoulder. The hollow between her breasts.

Her fingers slid through his hair, clinging as his hand slid up her side to cup her breast. Through the lace, his tongue and lips explored, then sucked the pebbled tip into his mouth.

She was arching into him, her fingers biting into his scalp—gasping when he nosed the lace aside. One hand held her close, the other freed her bra. He took his time, learning the swell of one, then the other. He'd missed her. Everything about her. Her broken moan made him shudder. The scrape of her nails on his back made him grip her hip. When her legs parted and she arched against him, he was rolling off of her—smiling when her hands fisted in the satin cover.

He pulled the tie on his athletic pants, kicked them aside, and stooped, pressing kisses along her calf and knee. The tip of his tongue teased the skin behind her knee, his lips clung along the inside of her thigh, sliding her lace panties down and off her legs…but her hands were pulling at his shoulders—pulling him back to her.

He was kissing her then, fueled by her frantic sounds and this all-consuming hunger. It took seconds to pull a condom from her bag, seconds to roll it on—but then he forced himself to slow down. This was what he'd been dreaming about. Loving her this way.

He braced himself over her, his hands framing her face as he kissed her long and slow. Eyes wide, head arched back, she moaned at the feel of him against her.

His breath was a hiss, the first thrust burying him deep. He smoothed the hair from her forehead, watching her face as he moved into her. Her eyes fluttered, lips parted, skin flushed pink, and her hands flexed against his shoulders. He moved slowly, fighting to keep control. But it was too much; she was too much. This was Emmy. Warm and soft, tight around him. She was the one staring up at him, a smile on her lips. She was the one clinging to him and wrapping her legs around his waist.

He did his best to go slow, to hold on until she came first. But there was nothing calm about her. Whatever he gave, she wanted more. Her fingers dug into his back as he moved harder. Faster. Faster and faster until she bowed off the bed beneath him. The sound she made was raw, broken—almost surprised. It gave him the permission he needed to let go.

His gaze held hers, drowning in her eyes, straining against her body. Aching. Closer and closer. His climax slammed into him, on and on, until he was panting and leaning over her.

Her hand pressed against his cheek. "We need to do that again." Her voice was breathy and ragged.

He laughed, rolling off of her to lie by her side.

She turned to see him, breathing hard. "Don't laugh." Wild-eyed and red-cheeked, she was beautiful. "I have a lot of time to make up for." She stared up at the ceiling overhead, smiling. "Who needs bubble baths or strawberries?"

"Not me," he replied, grinning at her.

She rolled up on her side beside him. "I always thought you'd be the first guy I slept with. I just didn't think it would take this long. After that, I think it was worth the wait." She sat up, stretched her arms over her head, and stood. "I'm getting some water. You want some?"

His brain had ground to a screeching halt somewhere between the words "first guy" and "I slept with." He had not heard that. He must have misunderstood. Mainly because what she'd said wasn't possible. "Back up a minute." He sat up. "Repeat that."

Her gaze traveled down his naked body, a soft whoosh of air sliding between her lips. "Do you want water?" She stooped, picking up his shirt.

"Before that." He grabbed her hand, pulled his shirt from her hands, and drew her between his legs. "The other part. The part where you have never slept with anyone before?"

"Right." She nodded, running her fingers through his hair. "Like I said, *so* much time to make up for." Her green eyes met his. "I shouldn't have said anything, huh?" she whispered, her smile fading.

Brock continued to stare at her. "How is that possible?"

"Well…we've already established I don't normally carry around a bag of prophylactics. And for the most part, the men I spend time with are family or employees. I've had opportunities. I just…didn't take them." She shrugged. "It's *possible*."

He nodded, doing his best not to react. "I'd take some water."

"Okay." She kissed his forehead and left the room, giving him an incredible view of her naked ass.

Then she was gone and he could react. There was no reason to lie about this—which meant it had to be true. But how…and why? He ran a hand along the back of his neck. It wasn't a big deal.

Bullshit. It was a *huge* deal.

He shook his head. She'd been the one to initiate everything.

Her whole awkward and sexy-as-hell seduction thing? He'd never have suspected he…this… What the hell?

Well, her orgasm had sounded like a surprise.

He stood up and headed into the bathroom, opening one of the gift baskets the hotel had provided for the room.

"Brock?" Emmy Lou said.

"Bathroom." He leaned over the garden tub, turned on the water, and poured in some Champagne Bubbles Bath Gel.

"What are you doing? All naked with your rippling muscles?" She set the glasses of water on the marble countertop, devouring him with her eyes.

He pointed at the bath.

She blinked, tore her gaze from him, and smiled. "A bubble bath?"

"You wanted one." If she kept looking at him like that, the bath would wait. "No strawberries. Guess I'll have to make up for it in other ways."

"Okay." She perched on the edge of the counter and reached for him. "I'd like to get started on that immediately."

Chapter 15

"ARE YOU SURE?" EMMY ASKED, PROPPED ON HIS PILLOW. SHE wasn't ready to say goodbye. What happened when they left and returned to their respective lives? The question had been bouncing around in her head since he'd slipped from the bed this morning. Maybe that was why she'd enticed him *back* to bed twice already. Not that he'd complained. "Absolutely sure?"

He laughed. "I was *sure* thirty minutes ago." He pulled on a skintight, sleeveless, black compression shirt that hugged his muscles. "Just as sure ten minutes ago." With a sigh, he leaned forward and kissed the tip of her nose. "Now I'm *sure* I'm going to be late to practice."

"Okay." She swallowed her disappointment. "I'll call my ride."

He stood, hands on hips, watching her slide across the bed with the sheet wrapped around her. "You've been naked for the last twelve hours. Now you're shy?"

She glanced over her shoulder, smiling. "I don't want to make you even later."

"Fair point." He studied her bare back, his jaw going rigid.

Staring at him was bad. Instead, she dropped to her knees and reached under the ottoman for her panties. Who knew an ottoman was so useful? She did—now. Thankfully, this one was large enough for Brock to lay back while she enjoyed all the delights of being on top... A now oh-so-familiar throb began between her legs. Images assaulted her. Brock, groaning, the cords in his neck rigid, his hands gripping her hips, while she leaned forward to kiss him. An ottoman should definitely be a required bedroom accessory.

"My bra?" She stood, staring around the room. It had to be there somewhere...

"Here." Her lacy lingerie hung from Brock's finger.

She slid the bra off his finger, doing her best not to think about all the wonderful things he could do with his fingers. And his hands...pretty much every part of him. Everything about last night had been wonderful. Especially when, even in sleep, he'd pulled her close and wrapped her in his arms. "What happens now?"

"That's up to you." He'd been smiling and carefree the entire time they were naked. He wasn't smiling anymore.

She scooped up the extra sheet fabric, held her clothes close, and hurried into the bathroom. She texted Krystal his hotel address.

He leaned against the doorframe, watching her. "You could come back tonight."

Her fingers fumbled with the clasp of her bra, her heart thumping like crazy. "I can't."

"That's up to you." He fastened her bra, his fingers trailing along the edge. "I told you yesterday, whatever you want."

"I thought you meant in bed. In the bath. Or the shower." She teased, sucking in a deep, wavering breath. "My favorite was the ottoman—"

He pressed a finger to her lips, a broken groan leading into his words: "I'm already late."

She pressed a kiss against his fingertip and was instantly rewarded by the flare of his nostrils. "I'm not keeping you." She loved the way he responded to her. Especially the way his jaw muscle locked tight...like it was now.

"You have no idea." His blue eyes locked with hers. "Think about it. Tonight."

"We leave for Virginia after tonight's concert. Besides, you have a game and I'd wear you out with the new list of wants I'm already making."

"I can imagine." He shook his head, swallowing hard. He hesitated, then drew her into his arms. He had a way of kissing her that made her head spin. Holding on tight was her only option. But she didn't want to get him in trouble, so she pulled away from his kiss.

"Good luck Sunday. I'll be there in spirit, cheering you on." She rested her hand on his chest. "Is this where you tell me you'll call me but then I never hear from you again?" It was a joke—but the longer he didn't answer, the harder it was to breathe.

"No. You'll hear from me." For a minute, she thought he had something more to say.

She smiled, her hand slipping from his chest. "Be safe, Brock Watson."

He pulled her close again, pressed a hard kiss to her forehead, then hurried out.

As soon as the door shut, her heart slowed and began to ache. This was real—this had really happened. She could smell him on her skin. Still feel his touch, inside her, exploring her. She blew out a long slow breath, the ache building. He'd asked her what she wanted. The same thing she'd always wanted: *Brock*. It scared her how much she wanted him. More than his body, though the last twelve hours had been incredible. No, she wanted so much more.

Sawyer arrived shortly thereafter, armed with a bag of clothing and coffee.

"Thanks." She peered into the bag. "Nothing like a massive sweatshirt, baseball cap, and…what is this print?" She held the sweatpants up for inspection.

"Cats and thunder." Sawyer shook his head. "Krystal."

"Give me a sec, will you?" She changed in the bathroom, tucked her old clothes into the bag, and laughed at her reflection. "I'm not sure what sort of fashion statement I'm making."

Sawyer's eyebrows rose, but he didn't comment on the outfit. He was all bodyguard on the way out, shielding her from onlookers, guiding her down the back stairs, and sneaking her into the black Suburban waiting at one of the hotel's rear service entrances.

"That exit route was super covert." Emmy paused. "The outfit, not so much."

"Good morning," Krystal said, giving her a once-over. "Someone looks happy."

She smiled, letting Krystal fill her in on a new song Travis and Jace were working on. Once at the hotel, they headed straight to their suite. Emmy put her purse on the counter and dropped the bag of yesterday's clothes onto the floor, hoping there was time for a nap.

"Oh goodness. I thought you'd already headed to the stadium." Momma jumped up and took one look at the papers spread out on the floor, couch, and coffee table. But she paused, giving them a slow head-to-toe inspection. "What are you wearing?"

The likelihood of Krystal answering and actually speaking to Momma were slim. It was up to her to find a reasonable explanation for her un-Emmy getup. "We went for a walk." *Breathe.* "What are you working on?"

"It's just a little project I started when I was in rehabilitation." CiCi smoothed her hand over a page. "Journaling. It helps get all of the things out that you could never say out loud."

"Makes sense." Emmy had kept a diary until high school until Momma had read it. It went missing shortly thereafter. Not long after, Travis had his phone taken away for inappropriate searches and videos. Apparently, Momma didn't just go through their rooms; she monitored their texts and phone calls, too.

Once Brock had been drafted into the AFL, she and Brock decided writing good old-fashioned letters was the only way to ensure their conversations were private. Getting the mail had been Travis's chore and, as long as she'd kept him stocked in candy, he'd gladly kept their secret. Until the letters stopped coming.

"I'll go get food." Krystal left the room without acknowledging Momma.

"Since things are at a standstill with your daddy's career, I thought I'd put it all together. Maybe a memoir?" Momma paused.

Emmy Lou froze. "To publish?"

"Just like Krystal, I've been struggling with something horrible…things beyond my control. Maybe my story can help someone." She nodded. "It's all here. Meeting your father. Being disowned by your granddad. The accident. You kids…and after." Her breath hitched. "None of this is my fault. *You* know that. I'd do anything to protect you kids, anything." She shook her head. "How many times do I need to apologize to her for my addiction?"

Her, meaning Krystal. Had Momma ever apologized? Did an apology count if the "I'm sorry" was followed by a "but"? Emmy Lou didn't think so. And Momma's apologies always came with a "but." If she published this? Aired all their secrets for the world? Emmy felt sick.

"Food," Travis said, carrying a large pastry box. "And coffee."

Krystal followed, handing Emmy Lou her special meal before sitting with Travis at the bar.

"Tell me you're eating something besides donuts?" Momma sighed. "You can't keep your energy up if you're full of sugar. Or keep your waistline under control for that matter."

Even buried in Emmy's purse, there was no missing her ringtone. "Sorry, I meant to silence that," Emmy said. It wasn't Melanie's or Daddy's ringtone; it could wait.

"I'll get it," Travis said, shoving an entire donut into his mouth.

"It's okay, Travis." Emmy waved him away from her purse.

"Want me to answer it? Or see who's calling?" He winked at her. "Might be important."

"No," Emmy said. He was going to bait her about Brock with their mother in the room? She smiled when Krystal reached over and pinched their brother, hard. "It can go to voicemail."

"What if it's Daddy?" Momma said, turning. "Bring it here, Travis."

It happened so quickly, there was no time to react.

One second, Travis was smiling like an idiot with her purse in his hands. The next, he tripped and fell. He caught himself, but her bag upended on the way to the ground, scattering its contents all over the hotel suite floor. Sunglasses. A compact. Two tubes of lipstick. Her phone and a comb. And at least ten red condom wrappers decorated with gold soldiers.

Her mother's shock was one thing, but having Daddy and Sawyer walk in, right then, made it ten times worse. Tension flooded the silence, enough to make Emmy's palms sweat.

"Really?" Travis started laughing. "Come on. Where's your sense of humor? It's a joke."

All heads, including hers, swiveled his way. *What?*

"A joke?" Daddy ran a hand over his face. "You put a bunch of prophylactics in your sister's purse as a joke?"

"Travis Wayne." Momma was not amused. "What were you thinking?"

"What sort of joke is that?" Daddy added.

"Not a very good one, obviously. Since no one is laughing." He pointed at Emmy, looking almost sad. "Condoms. *Emmy.* That's funny. Hell, I think it's hilarious."

Emmy Lou was staring at her brother, dumbfounded. Travis was quick. As wrong as it was, it was also sort of impressive. Were they really buying this?

"You're the only one laughing. Clean that up." Daddy pointed at the ground, sighing. "What is wrong with you?"

Daddy might not see the impact his words had on Travis, but she and Krystal did. Her big brother was covering for her and it had cost him their father's approval. Travis must have seen the worry on her face because he gave her a wink and mouthed, *You owe me.*

She smiled and nodded.

"What's all that?" Daddy asked, pointing at Momma's hastily collected pages.

"Oh, nothing." Momma smiled. "Nothing at all."

Emmy stared at her breakfast, her stomach in knots. This was her family, the people she loved most…and they were all keeping secrets and telling lies. Now she'd added to that. Was it selfish to want to guard the beginning of whatever was happening between her and Brock? Maybe. But her secret could only hurt herself. That was a risk she was willing to take.

―――――――

It had been a long time since Brock had enjoyed watching Monday night football. But tonight, he enjoyed it. The best part of it was hearing his father pick apart plays and argue with the sports commentators—like he used to. He missed his father, missed their shared passion for the game…missed looking in his eyes and knowing his father knew who he was. About midway through the third quarter, his father had dozed off. Brock kept the television on but packed up the snacks, cleaned up their trash, and washed his hands in the sink.

When he came back out, a delivery person was waiting with a massive bouquet of flowers.

"Are you sure you've got the right room?" He eyed the arrangement. "David Watson?"

"Pretty sure."

He paused, staring down at the delivery person's feet. Pink sparkly tennis shoes. Only one person he knew wore shoes with that much pink glitter. He was smiling like a fool as he pushed the door closed, set the arrangement on the floor, and pulled Emmy Lou against him.

"I'm assuming you knew it was me?" She laughed, breathless. Damn but he'd missed that smile. "Or is this the way you tip all the delivery people?"

"Only when I don't have cash on me." He pushed back the hoodie, her hair on end from static.

"That makes sense."

"Hold on," he murmured, bending forward. Her lips were soft beneath his. Soft and clinging, parting enough for their breath to mingle. "What's with the getup?"

"I thought I'd try to be more discreet this time." She smiled up at him, blinking rapidly. "Your dad?"

"He's sleeping." He smiled. "Not that he'd disapprove."

"How is he doing?" She leaned against him. "His color looks better. A lot better."

"He's doing well." And Brock was beyond grateful. "Dehydration was the cause of a lot of it—even some of his memory issues. They've adjusted his meds and he seems more like his old self than I've seen him in a long time." He pressed his nose to the top of her head. "Don't take this the wrong way, but what the hell are you doing here?"

"Daddy flew back for a meeting at the record company, just for tonight, so I tagged along." She frowned up at him. "I missed you and I thought I'd surprise you."

"You did?" He sat, pulling her into his lap.

But she didn't melt into him the way he wanted. "You missed me, too?"

He rested his forehead against hers. "Did I?"

"Don't make me tickle you." Her eyebrow shot up. "I was also curious about the Alpha shoot this morning. How did it go?"

"Everyone was professional. Nice. I'm not used to taking pictures in underwear for four hours in front of a roomful of strangers, but the Alpha people seemed good with it."

"Why wouldn't they? They're getting to use your butt to sell their underwear. It's a nice butt."

"Are you saying you've checked out my rear?" He smiled.

"I have. Many times." She looked up at him. "Underwear is good. Football pants are terrific. But my favorite is uncovered." She lowered her voice. "In bed or in the shower or on that ottoman—"

"Emmy Lou," he groaned, shifting in the chair. "You're not playing fair."

"I'll behave." She sighed but then she went rigid, her green eyes widening. "Oh." She tried to push out of his lap. "Last night."

"What are you doing?" He didn't let her go.

"Your ribs. That hit looked bad." She lifted her hands. "And here I am lying all over you."

"I like it when you lie all over me." He waited, loving the color in her cheeks. "You watched the game?"

"You know I watched the game." She rolled her eyes. "You were playing, weren't you?"

"I was. Played hard, too. Then spent most of the night tossing and turning."

She frowned. "Your ribs were hurting?" She tried to get up again.

He grabbed hold of the front of her hoodie and tugged her against him. "That was only part of it. You weren't there."

Her green eyes searched his face. "You did miss me."

"I missed you." He smoothed her hair back, content to look at her.

"Knock, knock?" The hospital room door opened. "Hello?"

Emmy Lou jumped up before he could stop her. Even wide-eyed and flustered, she was beautiful.

"Brock?"

"Vanessa?" His ex-wife was the last person he'd expected to see here. She'd met his father a total of two times—one of which she was fall-down drunk and probably didn't remember.

"Hi." Vanessa hugged him, pressing a kiss to his cheek. "I'm sorry I didn't come visit before now."

"You didn't have to come." He hugged her back. "I never expected you to."

"No, I know…" She glanced toward the bed and saw Emmy Lou. "Oh. Hi." She looked at him, then Emmy Lou. "I'm Vanessa Trentham—was Watson. Wow. If I'd known I'd be meeting a celebrity, I'd have put myself together."

Brock gave her a quick once-over. Vanessa was a model. It didn't matter what she wore; she always looked like a model. A pair of oversized sunglasses held back her long, black hair. The blue dress she wore looked expensive. The spiky heels on her feet looked even more expensive.

Emmy Lou stood, tugging at her oversized sweatshirt. "Nice to meet you. Emmy Lou King." She smiled. "I was just heading out, actually."

"You don't have to go, Em." Brock shook his head.

"No, not on my account," Vanessa agreed, her dark eyes bouncing between them with unconcealed interest.

"Someone's waiting on me. But it was nice to meet you," Emmy said. Vanessa shook her hand. "I'm glad to see your father's doing better, Brock. Guess I'll see you Thursday for the Drug Free Like Me spot. *The Elaine Show*?" The flash in her green eyes had the same impact as a jolt of electrical current.

He nodded. Connie had called him about it as he was leaving the photo shoot. Another guest's last-minute cancellation had given him exactly what he needed—time with Emmy.

"Good. Great. Looking forward to it." She nodded, pulled her hair back, and tugged up her hoodie. "Bye." With a little wave, she headed to the door.

It took everything he had not to go after her.

But Vanessa was watching him closely. Too closely.

"What?" He asked.

She shook her head. "How's your dad?"

"Better." He glanced at his father. "Being hardheaded is working in his favor."

"I'm so sorry, Brock." She wrapped her arms around herself. "Sometimes life is unfair, isn't it?" Her tone was the first hint that something was up. "I heard about Alpha. That's huge. Congratulations."

"Thank you." He paused, then said, "I appreciate you stopping by to see my father, V; I do. But I'd rather we skip to why you're here."

"Of course." She ran one hand up and down her arm, agitated. "I need help—"

"V, I can't help you." He sat, resting his elbows on his knees. "It's not that I don't want to, but I can't."

"It's not that." She paced the room, then back again. "It's my mom. You know that little artists' community she was all psyched about?"

He nodded. Vanessa's mom had worked three jobs to pay for all of Vanessa's pageants, headshots, and travel. She'd been determined to give her daughter a better life. And she had, for a while.

"She found the perfect place, and she's so happy, and I really want to do this for her, Brock. I do. But I don't have the money... Not right now."

He sat back. "You need money?"

"I can't ask Mark, my fiancé. He's had people use him for money before and I don't want him to think I'm doing the same, you know? He thinks I have money. And I do. But I'm a little short right now. And they need the deposit *now*." She shrugged. "It's my mom. Like your dad, she's never bailed on me."

Brock rolled his neck. "How much are we talking, V?"

"Fifteen thousand dollars."

"Where would I send this money?" He ran a hand over the back of his neck.

"Me." She looked desperate.

He shook his head. "I can't give you fifteen thousand dollars." He pushed out of his chair. "I can pay the property management company, but I can't give it to you."

"Mark would flip if he found out you paid the deposit." She shook her head. "Or that I'm here asking you for money."

"That's all I can do." She could be clean. The money could be for her mother. But if it wasn't... Giving money to a recovering addict was enabling their addiction. He wouldn't do that. "I hope you understand."

"Yep. I do." She nodded. "I really do. You're not the only one who's listened to the whole 'giving money to an addict is like handing someone suicidal a loaded gun' thing. I understand." Her gaze darted to his father. "Take care of him. And yourself."

He felt like an ass. He did. "You, too."

"I am, I will." She gave him a quick hug. "See you around."

He stared at the door a good five minutes after she'd left, second-guessing himself. In the end, there was no way of knowing if she was telling the truth or not. He couldn't own her recovery or take responsibility for her choices. His choices were his own— and he needed to be able to live with them.

"You all right, Son?" his father asked. "You're pacing like a caged bear."

"Hey, Dad." He smiled. "Didn't mean to wake you."

"You didn't." He sat up. "I could go for something to eat."

"Grapes?" Brock asked, carrying the bag to the bed.

"That'll do." He stared up at the television. "Game over?"

"You didn't miss much. At this rate, we'll be going up against the Miami Raiders or the Green Bay Bears in the Championship Bowl." He chuckled. "If we get there."

"You will. You've got a fire in you this season." His father popped a grape into his mouth and leaned his head back against the pillow. "You ever wake up knowing you're forgetting something?" He stared around the room. "People or places or bits of memory on the edge you can't quite see…"

Brock looked at his father. "Sometimes."

"I wonder if I'll ever see the inside of my home again. And if I do, will I know it's my home?" He turned to Brock. "Will I remember raising you there? Watching you grow up? Listening to Molly banging around in the kitchen at all hours of the day and night?"

Brock took the hand he offered, incapable of saying a word.

"While I'm here, I figure I should tell you how proud I am of you." He cradled Brock's hands in his. "You've always gone after what you wanted. Worked hard, fought hard. Never gave up."

"*You* taught me that. I'm the man I am because of you."

"You're a good man, Brock." He squeezed his hand. "I love you. Even when my head's scrambled up, I know I love you. Inside, I know you're my son and I'm proud to be your father."

Brock nodded, too damn close to tears to say a word.

"Enough of that." His father let go of his hands. "How about a donut?"

Chapter 16

EMMY LOU STROKED WATSON'S BACK, HIS LITTLE PURR SOOTHING. And since Momma had insisted on riding with her, talking the whole time, Emmy needed soothing.

"If I didn't have my appointment, I would come with you." Momma had been ecstatic over having her hair done at some exclusive salon. That was the whole reason her mother had accompanied them to San Francisco. "Unless you need me to come with you—because of Brock. Will it be too hard knowing everything?"

Momma was referring to the spin she'd put on things. But Emmy's mind took a detour into the *everything* she'd learned in his hotel room. She glanced out the window of the rented car—to make sure Momma wouldn't see her smile.

"After what he's put you through, it's understandable." There was a razor-sharp edge to Momma's words. "Maybe I should stay. Give that boy a piece of my mind."

No. Oh no. Emmy held her breath.

Sawyer glanced in the rearview mirror.

Melanie, sitting across from them on the rear-facing seat, looked up from her tablet long enough to slide her glasses in place.

"But I feel like that would just give him satisfaction—and more press. He's getting enough as it is." Her gaze narrowed. "Sawyer, you make sure to keep Emmy away from him. You know how sweet she is, and that boy...well, he's up to something." Her blue-green eyes glanced at the back of Sawyer's head. "You hear me, Sawyer? If they're not on camera, he has nothing to say to her."

"Yes, ma'am." Sawyer's voice was flat.

It wasn't the first time Momma had implied Emmy was too helpless or weak to take care of herself, but it still stung.

Momma kept on. "There are a dozen other charities that would have been happy to have you. I don't know what your daddy was thinking, putting you in harm's way like this."

The car seemed to be moving at a snail's pace—probably because of Momma's constant chatter. Emmy turned all of her attention to the traffic-congested street, the crowd of fans lining the sidewalk into the *Elaine* studio already starting to scream.

"Goodness, what a crowd." Momma glanced at her. "I can't believe you brought that cat with you. Really, Emmy Lou. He's not a lapdog."

Emmy smiled at the kitten sitting on her lap. She admired Watson's total lack of fear. Not of riding in cars or Clementine following him everywhere, not of Momma's high heels—he liked swatting at them—or the horrible screams Momma made when she realized her silk hose had been shredded. "He's my lap cat." Emmy picked him up and deposited him in the cat carrier disguised as a purse. "You ready, Watson?"

"Have fun," Momma said. "Try to get them on your left side and sit up straight. Oh, Emmy, Elaine's Book Club picks. Find out how that works for me."

Emmy had never been so desperate for air. She took Sawyer's hand and stepped out onto the sidewalk, breathing deep. Everything her mother said seemed to suck the air out of the car. Brock. Her memoir. The pointed way she'd watched Emmy eat her breakfast this morning. What was wrong with a whole wheat muffin? Everything she ate was approved by the dietitian. It felt like Momma was scrutinizing everything she did or said.

"You good?" Sawyer asked.

"Let's do this." Emmy nodded. She signed posters of herself, posters of the Three Kings, concert shirts, CDs, and one little boy's arm cast. Travis could tease her all he wanted—her fans were the only reason for their success.

"Emmy Lou." Melanie tapped her watch.

"Picture?" she asked the crowd. From the enthusiastic commotion, she assumed they were good with it.

Melanie pulled out her phone. "Here." Emmy handed over Watson and began snapping pictures. "Okay."

With a few more blown kisses and a lot of hand-waving, she made her way inside the studio. "You did great," she said to Watson. "You're going to give Clementine a run for her money."

Sawyer herded them along, following the production assistant who greeted them. He seemed more uptight than ever. Which, for Sawyer, said a lot. While she was getting her makeup and hair touched up, Sawyer seemed to be giving everyone a thorough once-over. He seemed…braced.

"You're making me nervous," she said, staring at his reflection in the mirror.

Melanie nodded. "Me, too."

"Is there something you're not telling me? Some sort of threat alert or something?" She was teasing. Sort of. He was definitely on edge.

"Doing my job," he basically growled.

Melanie glanced his way, then hers.

"You always do, Sawyer." Emmy sipped her water and then asked, "Is this because of my mother?" Emmy Lou frowned and pushed herself out of the makeup chair to face him. "The whole ridiculous overprotective thing—and Brock?"

"I'm not sure it's ridiculous." His gaze stayed fixed on her. "Part of my job is research."

"Research?" Emmy Lou shook her head, stunned. "On Brock? Sawyer…" She wasn't sure whether to be touched or angry. At the moment, she was leaning toward anger. Definitely anger. "This isn't the time for this. I have to go out there, smile, and act like everyone I know sees me as an intelligent, capable woman versus some…some toddler who needs constant supervision and direction about what to eat and wear and think and who to love." She paused, looking at him. "You're with me or you're with her. If you're with me, I expect you to respect my choices—not try to force yours on me."

She brushed past him, pulling away from the hand he put on her shoulder.

"Everything okay?" Brock was waiting for her.

All the irritation and frustration melted away. She was so happy. Maybe a little too happy. But he was here. Finally. Big and beautiful and within touching distance. She couldn't stop herself from smiling—she didn't want to. There was a very real chance of her hugging him, right here and now and in front of everyone.

Until she saw his face.

Brock, scowling at Sawyer.

Sawyer, scowling at Brock.

Without another word, she squeezed between them and went to stand by the edge of the stage. Melanie hovered, holding Watson in his little cat purse. She didn't say anything—something Emmy Lou was grateful for.

"Two minutes," the production assistant said. "Let's get your mic on."

"Am I good?" she asked Melanie, running her hands along the pink-and-white polka-dot dress she wore beneath her rhinestone-studded white denim jacket. Her boots were light tan with the Three Kings logo stitched into the leather.

"You look great. But smile." Melanie handed her the cat purse. "Have fun." She waved.

"Maybe we should go get a spa day? What do you think, Watson? Just me and you?" Watson meowed in answer. "You think so? Me, too."

"Em?" Brock interrupted Emmy and Watson's conversation, the corner of his mouth kicking up. "You look beautiful."

"Thanks. You did, too. Until you went all territorial back there with Sawyer. I have enough people *protecting* me," she said.

His smile faded.

"Ladies and gentlemen, let's welcome country superstar Emmy Lou King and football champion Brock Watson to the stage." Elaine stood, giving them each a hug and kiss on the cheek. "We're happy to have you both here."

Emmy Lou pulled Watson out from his cat purse. "Three of us."

Elaine "awwed" like the rest of the audience.

Conversation started with Drug Free Like Me and the matching program they were running for the rest of November. Elaine said she was going to out-donate Guy James and that she was a huge Bremmy fan.

"Now we'll get to the important stuff. I have a list of general topic questions." Elaine stood up. "Brock, you're playing for this side of the audience. Emmy, this side is yours."

"What are we playing for?" Brock asked, rubbing his hands together.

"It's a surprise." Elaine smiled. "Ready?"

Emmy wasn't competitive by nature, but right now, she was up for it—especially if she beat Brock. "Ready."

"What is the number one color picked as their favorite color?" Elaine asked.

"Blue!" Emmy yelled.

"Correct." Elaine nodded. "Number two—"

"Hey, there's no buzzer or raising your hand?" Brock asked, raising his hand.

"No, but thank you for the demonstration, Brock." Elaine laughed. "Moving on. What is Brock's favorite food?"

"Chicken fried steak." Emmy jumped in again.

He sat back in his seat, pointing at his mouth. "The words were right there."

By the time it was all over, Emmy Lou had won her side of the audience a copy of the Three Kings' latest CD. But then Elaine gave CDs to Brock's side, too—because that's what Elaine did. Still, Emmy Lou had bragging rights.

"That was great." Melanie held out her water bottle as she walked off the stage. "She is so funny." She led the way toward the small studio green room.

Emmy Lou nodded. "What's next on the agenda?"

"Lunch?" It was Brock.

She turned, doing her best not to act like her heart wasn't totally picking up speed over his dimples and smile and blue eyes.

"You are scheduled to have lunch now—with your brother and sister," Melanie announced. "I can call ahead and add another person to the reservation."

Emmy Lou glanced at her assistant in shock. "No."

"Em." Brock's voice lowered.

"I... I have a phone call to make." Melanie left, closing the door behind her.

"You've totally flustered Melanie." Emmy tried not to stare at him. Tried not to picture throwing her arms around him and kissing him senseless.

"She's not the one I'm trying to fluster." He stepped forward. "I am sorry. He put his hand on you—you pulled away. It went all over me the wrong way and I reacted. Actually, I didn't. But I thought about it." He took another step forward. "Mad at me?"

Was she? "No." She shook her head, closing the distance between them in three steps. "No, I'm not." She sighed when he wrapped her up in his arms. "It's been a weird morning."

"It was pretty good for me." She could feel his breath on the top of her head. "I knew I was seeing you."

She tilted her head back and smiled up at him. "Brock Watson. Will you have lunch with me? And my sister, her boyfriend, and my way obnoxious brother?" She paused. "Also, my bodyguard, who has a serious ax to grind with you, and my assistant, who might be crushing on you."

"I can deal with your family." His kiss was soft. "Whatever problem Sawyer has with me is his problem." Another kiss. "Melanie? Nice to know. If things don't work out with us, I have other options."

She pulled away from him. "Us? Is there an us?"

"I'm hoping there is." His brows rose. "If you're willing to try?"

Her pulse was in full gallop now. She was willing. More than willing. This is what she wanted. And exactly what her mother, bodyguard, and sister were worried about. "How do you feel about keeping things in stealth mode for now? I mean the real us—not the Bremmy thing."

"I'm in favor." He smiled, another kiss. "Stealth it is."

She leaned into his hand, against her cheek. "You can keep your hands and lips to yourself?"

"In public?" he asked, pressing a series of kisses along her neck. "Yes. When it's just the two of us?" He cradled her face in his hands. "Hell no."

Brock lit the candles, straightened the large silver bowl full of strawberries he'd ordered from room service, and made sure the bottle of champagne was mostly submerged in the ice. He didn't like strawberries and he couldn't drink champagne, but if it made her happy, he was happy.

He'd enjoyed exploring San Francisco with her. Sawyer continued to scowl like an asshole most of the day, but Travis lightened the mood with his constant teasing and wisecracks.

There was a knock on the door.

Emmy Lou.

He turned off the overhead lights and pulled the door open.

"Brock." CiCi King was the last person he'd expected to see. Ever. "Can I come in? This won't take long." She didn't wait for an answer.

Fucking great.

"Expecting company?" CiCi asked, her smile tight and brittle.

He turned on the overhead lights. "What can I do for you, Mrs. King?"

"I'm so glad you asked." She did a little circle, taking in the room—the room service and the champagne bucket. "I didn't think a recovering addict could drink?"

"I don't."

"Oh, so that bottle is for your company?" CiCi shook her head. "A whole bottle to herself?"

Brock ran a hand over his face, trying not to laugh. Then again, it was hard to imagine Emmy Lou drinking an entire bottle of champagne. Maybe it wasn't the best idea.

"I never thought a football star like you would need to ply a woman with alcohol?" She wrinkled her nose and held up her hand. "Let's get this over with, shall we?"

Hell yes. She'd talk, he'd pretend to listen, then he could get back to important things. Like Emmy.

"I thought we'd agreed to pull the plug on this whole Bremmy media frenzy." Her voice was soft, cajoling.

"I didn't say a damn thing." When the hell would he learn to keep his mouth shut?

"Right, I remember now. You're not playing a game." She took a deep breath. "You've just been pining away for her, all these years, but kept quiet? And now that your position is threatened by some younger, faster player, you've decided to try to win her back publicly?" To listen to her, anyone would agree that he was a self-serving bastard using her daughter for PR.

He knew better. "Is it so hard to imagine that I care about Emmy Lou?"

"Now?" She nodded. "Yes."

Brock shook his head. "Not now. Always."

Silence descended, seeping into every corner of the room. Whatever CiCi was feeling, she masked it well.

Eventually, she looked at the table, the strawberries, the champagne, and the candles. "A deep, abiding love." Her eyes narrowed.

He bit down hard.

The intense vibrating of his phone made them both pause.

"Do you need to get that?" she asked, staring at his phone.

He crossed the room, hit the mute button, and shoved it into his pocket. "Nope."

"There is no one else here. Me and you." She picked up a strawberry. "What will it take to get you to leave Emmy and my family alone?"

"Excuse me?" He didn't like this.

"You heard me. I want you to think about it," she said, searching his face. "I don't know if this is about getting even with Emmy or... Is this to spite me? Because you blame me for your heartbreak all those years ago?"

And that's when he understood why she was here. "You're scared, aren't you?"

"Of what? You? Oh, sugar, you have no idea." CiCi smiled. "You think you got that Roughnecks contract on your own? You think Hank being drinking buddies with Ed Salinas didn't help? Ed Salinas, the owner of your little football team? Wake up, Brock. Hank saw what was happening. The minute someone interferes with his family, his children, he removes the obstacle. Why do you think you were drafted so quickly? Your talent? This family has helped you out more than you deserve. Didn't your father ever tell you it's not smart to bite the hand that feeds you?" She stepped forward. "I'm not scared, Brock. If anyone should be scared, it should be you."

"Leave Emmy Lou alone or face the consequences?" He had

to smile. "You do realize that sounds pretty damn over-the-top, don't you?"

"I do." She nodded, her smile wide. "You're good at knocking people on their asses on the field. I'm excellent at knocking people on their asses in real life. Try me." Her gaze bounced to the room service table. "You enjoy your evening. I'm taking my girls out to this fun little sushi place on the wharf."

He didn't move until the door had closed.

"Fuck." He paced the length of his hotel room, sat on the couch, then stood and paced some more. He pulled his phone out from his pocket and opened it.

The first was a picture of Emmy, pouting, with Watson. Momma has sabotaged our night. Miss me.

I do. He smiled, running his finger along her face.

The second message was another picture. Emmy Lou, lying on the bed, holding her phone over her, with Watson curled and sleeping in her hair. Silly cat.

Smart cat. He saved the pictures to his phone and ran a hand over the back of his head. Have fun.

He blew out the candles, put the room service cart in the hall, and changed into his workout gear. There was a gym around the corner—one of the reasons he stayed here when he was in town. He headed downstairs, earbuds in, and spent the next two hours in the gym. Every time he thought about CiCi King's hateful words, he had to run for another twenty minutes to get the roar in his head to ease.

By the time he was back in his room, standing under the steaming hot water, it was almost one in the morning. He was beat—but at least there was a chance he'd get some sleep now.

He climbed out, running a towel over his hair, when his phone vibrated.

Emmy Lou. Open the door.

He tugged on some clean boxers and sprinted to the door.

"Hi," she whispered, the ever-present navy hoodie hanging to her knees.

He pulled her inside, closed the door, and pressed her against it. "Hi." Kissing her was top priority. Breathing her in. Feeling her melt into him—her hands sliding along his bare back.

"You're all wet," she said against his mouth.

"Went to the gym." He kissed her again. "Just got out of the shower."

"I like it when you're sweaty." She wriggled closer, tugging the hoodie up and over her head.

"We can fix that." He tossed her hoodie aside. "You forgot your bra." He cradled her bare breast, sucking her nipple into his mouth. Nothing tasted like Emmy.

"No." She was panting. "I didn't." She stumbled with him toward the bed, then stopped. "Wait." Emmy gasped as he moved to the other nipple, his thumb tracing the hardened tip. "The hoodie." She gasped, her fingers gripping his hair. "Condoms…"

He smiled, grabbed the hoodie, lifted her into his arms, and leaned forward, depositing her on the bed. Finally, he could touch her. He did—running his hands along her bare sides, teasing her with the lightest of touches. She shuddered beneath him, the tips of her breasts trembling against his chest. The bite of her nails on his back had him arching into her.

One thing he was learning about Emmy Lou. She didn't apologize for one damn thing in bed. She gave in, got carried away, and enjoyed every sensation to the fullest. It was the hottest damn thing he'd ever seen. Watching her, hearing her, was better than any dream he could imagine.

When they were naked, he took his time enjoying the view. From the way her hair spilled over her shoulders to the dusky pink of her nipples, from the flare of her hips to the smile on her lips, there was so much to see and explore.

"Brock?" she whispered again, reaching for him. "Condom.

Please." Her gaze zeroed in on his rock-hard arousal and he stopped breathing. "Or…" She nibbled her lower lip, the slide of her fingers too much.

"Condom." He shook the hoodie until several condoms fell onto the coverlet. "How energetic are you feeling?" he asked, counting eight so far.

"Very." It was a whisper.

He loved the hitch in her breath when he rolled on the condom. Loved how her gaze locked with his as he lay her back on the bed. Lips parted, breathing hard, eyes glazed. "You are so beautiful." He traced her jaw with the tips of his fingers.

"I missed you," she managed, her head falling back as he slid deep.

He didn't close his eyes. He didn't want to miss anything. The way she arched up, wanting more of him, thrusting to meet him. Her fingers tangling in the sheets. Her knees pressing against his hips. The more erratic her rhythm grew, the more broken and frantic her noises became. She was gripping his back, holding on, pressing her lips against his throat to muffle the broken moan of her release. He held her there, one arm anchoring her against his chest as he moved into her. It didn't take long for him to climax. It tore through him in waves, each rising higher until he was free-falling back onto the bed beside her, breathing hard—and damn happy.

She rested her head on his shoulder. "Were those strawberries in the hall for me?"

"Yes." His fingers traced the curve of her hip.

"And the champagne?"

"Yes." He smiled.

"I'm sorry I couldn't get here earlier." She sighed, burrowing closer.

"You're here now." That was what mattered. His fingers kept moving, drawing a lazy pattern along her side. Having her here made everything better.

Something tipped her off because she was looking up at him. "What is it?" She reached up, pressing his forehead. "You're frowning. Did something happen?"

"Your mother stopped by." He sighed, admitting, "She's dead set against us."

"What?" Emmy Lou stared at him, blinking slowly. "I can't...I can't do this anymore." She slipped from the bed, shaking. "I can't."

If that's what she wanted, he'd do his damnedest to let her go. His chest hurt, his heart hurt, but he managed to keep his shit together.

"I keep trying to give her the benefit of the doubt. But her idea of the truth is whatever version best suits herself. Her addiction... I want to believe her. That it's real and she's getting help, but I don't know anymore..." Her gaze darted his way, her lower lip wobbling.

He stood and wrapped his arms around her. "You think she's capable of that?" He was no fan of CiCi King, but it was hard to wrap his head around what she was saying. "Why?"

"If she's a victim, she can't be blamed. I'm not sure she sees it that way or what she's doing, it's just...who she is. An addiction makes all the things she did or didn't do not her fault." She stayed in his arms, stiff. "I can't believe I'm saying this..."

"It's okay." He hugged her closer.

"It's not. She's my mother." There was a long pause before she spoke again. "But I finally understand why there's so much tension between Momma and Krystal." Her green eyes found his. "Krystal sees Momma for who she *is*, not who she pretends to be. And Momma can't deal with that."

He hurt for her, to the core. If there was one thing he could count on, it was his father and Aunt Mo's honesty—even if it was hard to hear. Dealing with CiCi King hadn't been pleasant, but he wasn't her child. He'd assumed all her threats and lies were only for those she considered a threat to her family.

"I can't blame her for keeping such a tight grip on me. If it wasn't for Daddy, Krystal would be lost to her. Travis doesn't put up with her drama, either, but he tends to tease instead of get worked up over it." She stared up at him. "I was the only one who still wanted her approval. But now, I can't help but wonder what she's said and done and lied to me about…"

"What changed?" He stepped closer, smoothing a lock of hair from her shoulder.

She didn't want to answer him. Her long pause told him that. The way her gaze fell to the ground and she was drawing into herself.

"Hey." He took her hand. "You can tell me."

It took a moment for her to look at him, longer for her to whisper, "For the first time in my life I wanted something, even though she was dead set against me having it. The more I wanted it, the more doubts and fears she planted. In *me*, her daughter." She shook her head. "She's my mother. But I don't think she understands what it means to really love someone. If she did, she'd listen to what I wanted—not expect me to replace it with what she thinks is best."

Brock hugged her then, running his hands down her back. Krystal had hinted that Emmy wasn't happy, but he'd never imagined it was this bad. How could the woman look her daughter in the eye and know she was depriving her of happiness? "What can I do?"

Her hand slid up, along his shoulder and around the back of his neck. "You're doing it."

He kissed her until she was swaying into him and any and all thought beyond the feel of one another no longer mattered. Long after she'd fallen asleep, still tangled in his arms, he sorted through everything she'd said. No matter what CiCi King had done or said to him, nothing compared to what the woman had done to her own daughter. Love was a gift, not a tool. Emmy needed reminding of that. There was nothing he wanted more in this world than to be the one to remind her.

Chapter 17

EMMY STARED AT THE GLOSSY WHEELHOUSE RECORDS folder, full of dates, locations, and opening acts. "Wow...just wow. Europe?"

"Wanted to make sure there wasn't a problem with the dates." Daddy sipped his coffee. "Your sister and Jace are fine with it."

"I am, too. In case you wanted to know." Travis winked at her. "You sure you don't want one?" he asked, sliding the bakery box across the table.

"Wouldn't want to deprive you of breakfast." Emmy laughed.

"Oats. Raisins. That's healthy." He shrugged, continuing to chow down on the freshly baked oatmeal cookies he'd had delivered to the Kings Coach II.

The first date was March. In London. Football season would be over. Brock had said "us." She'd liked the way it sounded. Brock and London and March.

"Emmy?" Daddy was watching her. "Do these dates work? I'll be honest, I thought you'd be more excited."

"She might not be, but I am." Travis spun the glossy folder, eating another cookie. "Weeks in Europe. Hot French chicks for me and Sawyer. They dig cowboy hats and boots," he said to Sawyer. "We're going to have a *good* time. Guaranteed." Daddy sighed, shaking his head, but Travis ignored him and glanced her way. "Why the long face, Em?"

"I was just a little caught off guard." She shrugged.

"When have we ever gone more than eighteen months without hitting the road?" Travis pushed. "Or are you worrying about leaving *Watson*?" He was smiling so big, she almost stomped on his foot under the table. He knew she was thinking about Brock. And she knew he was using Watson as code for Brock. "I don't know what sort of papers he's going to need. He eats a lot, too, so that might be hard to keep up with. And he needs exercise... Or you could leave him here with Momma."

She was almost laughing.

"I'm missing something here, I know." Daddy rubbed his eyes, looking confused. "Not sure I want to know what it is, though."

Travis grabbed another cookie, threw it up in the air, and tried to catch it in his mouth. It bounced off his nose, but he caught it before it fell.

"Natural talent," she said. "Daddy, you know what other natural talent Trav has been using? He's been writing songs with Jace. Some good stuff, too." She knew Travis was shooting daggers her way but ignored him. "That *he* could sing."

"Is that so?" Their father looked at Travis. "Might be that we need to have a talk?"

Travis stared at the cover of the tour folder, the Three Kings logo enlarged with metallic touches. "Where do we start? Music? Or our family?"

"Whatever you have to say, Son, I want to hear it." Daddy's voice was gruff.

Emmy Lou heard the plea in their father's voice. He was extending an olive branch to his son; now all Travis had to do was take it.

Instead, Travis pushed the folder across the counter, to their father, and reached for a cookie.

The bus doors opened, and the click of heels was followed by, "I smell cookies. Hank, you better not be eating any more cookies." Momma joined them, the scent of her perfume following her into the bus's compact living and dining space. She tucked a swath of her platinum hair behind her ear, showing off a massive diamond stud, and shifted the oblong box she cradled against the front of her cream linen shift dress. "I won't be too long. We're leaving at one?" She waited for Daddy's nod. "I'll be back by then."

"Where are you going?" Travis asked, giving their mother the once-over. "Pretty fancy duds for a visit with your shrink."

"I am not going to see my *psychiatrist*, Travis." She sighed. "I'm having lunch."

"You look pretty." Their father smiled. "What's in the box?"

"Oh, nothing." Her mother's smile tightened.

Emmy Lou eyed the box, her blood going cold. She knew what was in the box. She'd picked up the pages off the printer before Momma had rushed in to collect them, tucking them into the box she was currently clinging to. Her mother had typed up the journal pages she'd had spread all over the hotel suite a week ago. Now Momma was dressed to the nines, taking her neatly typed pages to lunch? Even though Emmy's hands were shaking and something hard and jagged had lodged itself in her throat, she knew what she had to do. "Is it your book, Momma?" She did it, forced the words out and into the open.

"Book?" Travis repeated, sliding back into the booth with a massive glass of milk. "What book?"

Daddy eyed the box with new interest.

Even Sawyer, who'd been silently drinking coffee on the other side of the bus, reacted—the tiniest eyebrow twitch.

"No, no, not a book." Momma actually blushed. "It's just my thoughts is all. Part of my therapy."

"Why are you taking your therapy notes to lunch?" Travis asked, resting his elbow on the kitchen counter.

"Oh, I forgot." No reason to stop now. Emmy drew in a deep breath and said, "You asked me to find out about Elaine's Book Club picks. I need to check and see if the production assistant sent me that paperwork. Though the assistant said they rarely pick memoirs for Elaine's Book Club, she'd consider it—once it gets published."

"Memoir?" Daddy frowned. "Published?"

"Memoir, as in you?" Travis echoed. "Or memoir as in us?" He pointed at each of them. "And Krystal and Jace?"

"Well…" Momma shrugged. "I'm not an island, sugar. You are my family. And, of course, my family is part of my story."

"Why didn't I know about this, CiCi?" Daddy's tone was sharp.

"What do you need to know?" Her voice rose. "This is something to help me get better."

"Your notes are." Daddy nodded. "Publishing them? How is airing our family's business to the world part of that?"

CiCi's voice was soft. "I thought you'd want this for me? I thought you'd understand how important this is." She was shaking, on the verge of tears.

"What is more important than healing? Your mind and body? Healing our *family*?" He shook his head. "How about we do what we're supposed to do and protect our family?"

Emmy Lou had never seen her daddy like this: red-faced and tight-jawed—his voice raised just enough to make sure there would be no interrupting. Or arguing. Daddy rarely laid down the law, especially when it came to Momma. But the set of his jaw told them all that he wasn't budging.

Her parents' staring contest stretched on until the entire bus felt ready to combust. Eventually, Momma's gaze lowered and she sighed.

"Hank." Momma placed a hand on his shoulder. "You know everything I do is for you and our babies. If it means that much to you, of course I won't publish it."

Emmy Lou was stunned. Travis's jaw dropped, regardless of the amount of cookie he had in his mouth.

What just happened? Did she mean it? It seemed so…so easy. Too easy. Especially since she couldn't remember a time when Momma hadn't won.

Her momma pressed a kiss to their father's cheek and took his hand, catching sight of the folder. "Daddy showed you? What do you think? I'm pretty sure we are the first country music band to have this many locations and dates."

"We're still hammering things out." Her father picked up the folder.

"What things?" Momma frowned, her gaze swiveling to Emmy. "Emmy Lou?" She sighed. "Tell me this isn't about Brock Watson."

"CiCi." Her father sighed. "Let's not start this up again."

"What?" Momma shook her head. "Stepping up? Protecting her? Don't you see that?" She rested her hand on Daddy's arm. "Our baby girl is still pining for the man who broke her all those years ago."

"Momma, what do you have against him?" She pressed her hands on the countertop. "Besides our breakup, years ago?"

"Em, you can't be serious? Let's set aside the fact that this Bremmy spectacle has restored his all-American-boy status. You're not eating. You're wasting away. Your father and I are making sure you get the best therapists and doctors and food, but we're supposed to stand by while you attach yourself to someone who is toxic?"

Daddy frowned, his gaze shifting between the two of them. But he didn't argue.

"What happens when he and his agent decide they don't need us anymore?" Momma paused. "If your daddy hadn't put in a good word with the owner of the Roughnecks, do you think Brock would have been drafted?"

"Now hold on." Daddy shook his head. "That never happened. I was prepared to say something, but Ed had made up his mind about the boy long before I had a chance."

Emmy Lou swallowed. "You mean he was signed on his own? Without using me?"

"Why are you trying to make me the villain, Emmy Lou? Because I'm so worried about this? It took you a year to get over that boy. A year. You didn't sing; you barely smiled or ate. Now he's back…" She shook her head, her eyes narrowing slightly. "You're an adult. You have every right to make your own choices. But you need all the information to do that."

Travis groaned. "Momma—"

Momma held up her hand. "Hear me out and I'll leave it alone."

"Fine," Emmy murmured. Since there were witnesses, maybe she'd keep her word.

Momma risked a look at their father. "I went to see Brock in San Francisco, Emmy."

"You did what?" Travis covered his mouth with his hands.

"CiCi." Their father was just as stunned. "What are you thinking?"

"He was getting ready to entertain a young woman. While you and I and your sister were having sushi." She shook her head, her reproachful tongue click following.

Emmy Lou's gaze fell to the floor, knowing full well who he'd been waiting on. It wasn't her mother's business. None of this was.

Momma sighed. "Did he tell you he gave his ex-wife money? That they took a road trip to Georgetown, just the two of them?"

No, he hadn't said a thing. About the money or the trip. But he would have had a reason. A good reason.

And yet, it was there. Doubt. About Brock. And his ex-wife. If she could just see him—just look in his eyes… All of the ingrained doubt and worry and insecurities resurfaced, twisting things so she wasn't sure what was true.

"I think that's enough." Hank glanced her way, concern lining his face. "Emmy?"

"I'm fine, Daddy." No, she wasn't fine. Her insides were broken. But it wasn't all Brock's fault. Her mother had laid the groundwork long before he'd come into her life. She took a deep breath and met her mother's gaze. "Why is it so hard for you to believe that some-one just wants to love me?" *I'm not going to cry.* Momma thought she was weak enough without her expressing real emotion. "For no reason. No ulterior motive? Just to love *me*?"

Whoever spoke next, she didn't know. She had to get out of there—had to breathe and be strong. She ignored the raised voices of her family, shut out their words, and hurried down the hall to her sleeping quarters. A few more steps and she'd be in her room. If she could hold it together until then… But she was crying by the time she reached the door, crying hard.

"Emmy Lou."

She jumped.

Sawyer's hands rested on her shoulder, turning her slowly to face him. He whispered something that sounded a lot like, "What is wrong with them?" For the first time, he wasn't trying to hide his pain—or sympathy. He hurt. For her. He wasn't looking at her like he was her bodyguard; he was looking at her like he was her brother. "You cry." He pulled her into his arms and held her tight. "I've got you."

———————

Brock glanced at the clock. Emmy Lou was home for one night and he'd made big plans. In a couple of hours, he and Emmy Lou were meeting at Aunt Mo's, then making the drive to Lady Bird Lake. He'd rented out a paddlewheel boat for the evening. First, they'd watch the bats, sail until it was dark, then head to the little honky-tonk that had been one of their favorite spots in high school. And, if things went the way he hoped they did, the night might end with a ring on Emmy's finger. He'd seen it and known it was hers. An emerald, like her eyes, surrounded by diamonds.

He was shaving when his phone started ringing. "Hello?"

"Brock." A sob. "Brock, I'm so sorry to bother you." It was Vanessa.

"V, I can't—"

"He kicked me out, Brock." She sniffed. "Mark found out about the money and my mom and said he couldn't live with someone who lied."

After she'd left, his conscience wouldn't let him rest. If things had been reversed? If it were for Aunt Mo? The only solution was to drive with her to the mortgage lenders, transfer the money to her there, and watch her write the check out. He'd told her not to keep it a secret… But it didn't sound like she'd listened to that part.

"I'm sorry, Vanessa." He meant it. While he understood where her fiancé was coming from, he didn't understand the dynamics of their relationship. *Not my business.*

"All I have is my phone. I don't have my purse or money or any place to go."

He leaned against the bathroom counter. "Did you call Janine?"

"She's on her way back from Dallas. They just left."

Meaning it would be four hours before Vanessa would have help. She needed it now.

"You're the only one I can call." She sniffed. "That doesn't use, I mean. I can't go somewhere where that is an option right now."

She knew her limits. *Good.* "What about your mom?" There had to be an alternative.

"Antiquing in Fredericksburg. I'm not sure sitting in her empty house is a good idea. I can't be alone. I'm sorry, Brock. You've already helped me so much—with everything." She sucked in an unsteady breath. "But…I don't trust myself right now. I've got no one else to call."

He'd been clean and sober for four years. Vanessa had slipped twice. How could he turn his back on her? *Fuck.* He couldn't. He slammed his razor on the counter. "Where are you?"

Once he had directions, he hung up, wiped off his face, grabbed his keys, and climbed into his truck. He called Emmy Lou, but it went straight to voicemail.

"Fuck." He slammed his hand against the steering wheel and waited for the beep. "I hope you haven't left yet, Em. I can't make it. I'm sorry. If it wasn't important, you know I'd be there. See you soon." He ended the call and turned the radio on high, bass thumping.

Vanessa was pacing outside the front of a Super Snak and Corner Gas station. Her makeup was smeared down her face and she was wearing silky pajamas with a suit jacket over the top. Not exactly the safest getup for this part of town. "You should have waited inside, V."

"There's alcohol in there." She climbed into the truck and put on her seat belt.

"I thought you didn't have a purse?" He pulled back onto the highway.

"I don't. It's amazing what a guy will do for a pretty girl who smiles and says thank you." There was bitterness in her voice.

Weird clothing and streaked makeup aside, Vanessa was gorgeous. She'd known her limits and hadn't tested them. "I'm proud of you for not going in."

She looked at him, smiled, then dissolved into tears. "Why am I so stupid?"

He reached over, opened his glove box, and pulled out a napkin. "Here."

"You still do that?" she asked, reaching for a napkin. "You're the only guy I know who hoards drive-through napkins in their glove box."

"Aunt Mo. The woman taught me to be frugal." He tuned the radio to something soothing and left her alone. He wasn't trained for this sort of thing. Until Janine was back in town, he'd keep an eye on her—that's it. After that, it was up to Vanessa's sponsor to help her get things sorted out.

By the time he'd parked in front of his rental house by the stadium, she was sobbing all over again. He went around, opened the passenger door, and helped her out. When she leaned into him, he hugged her. "Hey. You're okay. You're doing okay." He didn't know what else to say. With his arm around her shoulders, he guided her inside.

"Coffee?" he asked. "Tea?" He opened the refrigerator. "A three-pound hamburger?"

Vanessa laughed, wiping the tears. "No. Thank you. As appetizing as that sounds."

He nodded.

"Bathroom? I need to wash this mess." She pointed at her face, then looked down at her shirt. "Great." Drops of mascara covered the silky front of her pajamas.

"I've got something you can wear. Hold up." From his room, he grabbed a T-shirt and some athletic pants with a tie waist and brought them back.

"Is it okay if I take a shower? I feel like shit." She shrugged. "Is that okay?"

"The guest bathroom's down here. Doesn't get used much." He led the way. "The handle sticks, so be careful or you'll end up burning yourself." He leaned into the shower. "Just jiggle it like this."

She peeked around him. "Got it." She sighed. "Brock, thank you. This is my fault, all of it. I'm not mad at Mark; I'm mad at myself. You told me to tell him, but I was too scared he'd think I was a gold digger. Keeping it a secret only made it look like I *am*."

Brock shrugged. "Maybe he'll cool down long enough for you to talk. To *really* talk—about everything."

"You are honestly the most decent man I think I've ever met." She hugged him again.

He gave her a quick pat on the back and pulled the door shut behind him. Luckily, he remembered how Vanessa loved home remodeling shows and there was a whole channel devoted to that sort of thing. Once he'd found it, he headed into the kitchen to make some popcorn.

"That is the cutest picture I have ever seen." Vanessa was smiling at a picture of Emmy and Watson.

He'd printed a couple, stuck one on the refrigerator, and framed another for his bedside table. Whenever he looked at them, he smiled.

"How is that going?" Vanessa asked, sliding onto the kitchen counter. With her face scrubbed clean and her hair twisted into a messy knot on the back of her head, she looked too young and innocent to have injection scars between her toes.

"It's going." He smiled.

"Another good thing about you—you don't kiss and tell." She nodded, glancing around the kitchen. "I appreciate you keeping my secrets. All of them. Tonight included."

While Brock watched game film on his laptop, Vanessa argued with the people on the home renovation shows. She fell asleep after two hours of television. Three hours in, Janine called to say they were running behind.

He didn't hear from Emmy. He thought about calling her. But he wasn't sure what sort of explanation he could offer up, and since lying wasn't an option, he didn't call.

He'd only spent two nights with her, but he missed not having her beside him. It was too early to start thinking long-term, he knew that, but there were times it felt like they were picking up right where they left off. He'd be okay with that. More than okay.

At five in the morning, Janine showed up.

Brock walked Vanessa out. "You've got this, V."

Vanessa gave him a hard hug. "I'm going to be okay." She pressed a kiss to his cheek. "Thank you—for everything."

As they pulled away, Brock ran a hand over his face. He was damn lucky. Vanessa's support network consisted of her sponsor and her ex-husband. She kept her addiction a secret because she was too afraid of what people would think. Dealing with recovery was hard enough. Keeping it a secret while trying to live a normal life? Seemed like it would only add to her burden.

When he got to the stadium, he cleared his head. He'd learned early on that focus was a game changer. Focus—even when his teammates *covered* the locker room with enlarged posters of his brand-new Alpha underwear ads. Ads enlarged and *decorated* with permanent markers.

"Who knew you guys could be so creative?" He pulled a poster off the front of his locker. This one had a crudely sketched smiling snake poking above the waistband of the underwear. "At least it's a friendly snake."

"I'm not sure I'm going to be able to drive in every morning when there's a sixty-foot picture of your ass on the side of the road." RJ shook his head. "Nice or not, that is one *big* ass."

McCoy came in and started yanking down posters. He glared at Brock and called them all onto the field to practice. Brock ignored Ricky's shit-talking, drilled until Russell was happy, and gave one hundred and ten percent until Coach McCoy blew the final whistle.

Coach McCoy told them all to shut up and listen. "Get your gear on the bus. We're leaving in an hour. You miss the bus, your ass is on the bench."

Tonight, they were heading out for this weekend's away game. Emmy would be in New York and he'd be in Oklahoma. It wouldn't be so bad if they'd had their date. Hell, if he'd seen her once in the last week. This was bullshit. Somehow, they needed to make more time for each other. Somehow. Next season would be worse. He'd be back in Houston and she'd be here.

He didn't want to think about next season yet.

The easiest thing to do was go public with their relationship. Knock off the Bremmy teasing and pull out the big guns. Dates and hand-holding and removing any doubt they were together. He didn't relish the idea of being hounded by photographers and reporters. But if it meant he could be with her, whenever and wherever he wanted, he'd deal with the publicity.

He showered, dressed, and ran from the dressing room with his duffel bag in hand. McCoy made a point of checking his watch as he walked around the end of the bus to the passenger door.

Emmy Lou was there—animatedly using her hands as she talked to Russell.

Her hair was up in a ponytail, blowing in the light fall breeze. Looking at her now, wearing her pink plaid top, jeans, and worn-in leather boots—the sense of déjà vu was overwhelming. In high school, Emmy Lou had always come to see him off for away games. Always. Now, here she was. Like it was no big deal. Even though it was. Damn, he was smiling like a damn fool.

As soon as she saw him, her green eyes locked with his. But beneath the smile, he felt her hesitation. Wariness even. If only he could know what she was thinking.

"Hey." He wanted to touch her and hold her so damn bad.

"Hi yourself." She shoved her hands into her pockets, her gaze never wavering. Like she was looking for something. "I wanted to make sure everything was okay."

His gaze darted to his coaches, openly watching. "I'm sorry about last night. Something came up."

"But everything is okay?" she asked, a tightness to her voice.

"Not really." He didn't want to keep secrets from her—she had enough of those in her life. But this wasn't his secret and, dammit, he was in no position to tell Vanessa's story. "I had big plans for us last night. There's never enough time with you."

"If something's important, you make time." She swallowed. "Right?"

He nodded. "Like making time to see me off?"

"How do you know I'm not here for something else?"

"I don't." He shook his head. "But I guess I'm hoping that's why you're here." Something was wrong; he could see it on her face. He spied Coach from the corner of his eye—arms crossed, impatiently shifting from one foot to the other. Worse, every single player on the team was probably watching from the bus. *They can wait.* "What's wrong, Em?" Another step. Too close? *Hell. Not close enough.* "Whatever it is, you can tell me." *Just don't break my heart.*

"I needed to see your face." But she didn't sound happy about it. McCoy made a huge production out of clearing his throat.

"I don't like leaving this way…" He cleared his throat. "When I get back, we need to talk."

Her eyes widened. "Okay." But it sounded like a question. "Be safe. Win." She turned and headed toward the waiting black Suburban—leaving an ache in the middle of his chest.

"You good?" McCoy asked. "Damn shame we are all here getting in the way of your personal life."

He climbed up the steps onto the chartered bus. An explosion of paper balls launched at him by pretty much the entire team.

"That was sad, man." RJ leaned back against the seat, closing his eyes. "Sad."

"I'm with RJ. Talk about a missed opportunity." Gene Byrd shot him a look of pure disappointment.

Brock sat next to a window, scanning the parking lot. Emmy was gone, but the ache in his chest wasn't going anywhere.

Chapter 18

EMMY HELD THE MIC CLOSER, CLAPPING OUT THE RHYTHM against her thigh, as Travis plucked out the final lead in notes.

Krystal leaned in, and they sang the last few lines together.

But here's the truth, listen closely, cuz there ain't no way.
I'm looking for Mr. Forever, not you—Mr. For Today.

The last effect, four cannons full of metallic confetti, exploded with the final drumbeat. As confetti rained down on the audience, the crowd went crazy.

"Thank you and good night, Pennsylvania," Krystal called out. "Be safe going home."

Emmy and her siblings took another bow before waving Jace onstage to join them. The show had been high energy—nothing like a vocal crowd to make them want to give their best performance.

Jace tipped his black hat, the women screamed, and they all bowed again.

"That was incredible." Melanie offered Emmy her water bottle and towel, following along. "More than usual, that is."

Emmy patted her face, still on a high. "I think they enjoyed it."

"They?" Travis shook his head. "The screaming fans? Yeah, I think they might have had an okay time." He draped his arm over her shoulders.

"Gross, you're all sweaty." Krystal dodged when Travis tried to wrap the other arm around her.

"His sweat is better than mine?" he asked, pointing out the way Jace was draped all over Krystal.

"Yes. Way better." Krystal smiled up at Jace.

"How's the meet-and-greet look?" Emmy asked.

"Sold out." Melanie nodded. "There's quite a crowd waiting outside, too."

"Does that make you all warm and fuzzy inside?" Travis asked, hugging her tighter.

She stuck her tongue out at him. "They're here for you, too, you know." She slid out from under his arm. "I'll see you in five?"

They nodded and all headed to freshen up prior to rubbing elbows and taking pictures with the big spenders. She pushed open her dressing room door and smiled.

"Smoothie?" Melanie asked. "And I kicked the AC down, too."

"Perfect, Melanie. Thank y—"

"Emmy Lou?" Sawyer stuck his head in. "Do you have a minute?"

She stopped sipping on her smoothie and waved him inside. "Of course."

He nodded, stepping inside the room. "I thought I'd let you know that Brock is here."

"He is? That's a complete surprise." A good surprise, wasn't it? Maybe? "Where is he?"

Sawyer wasn't smiling. "I had him wait."

Her gaze met his in the mirror about the same time Krystal and Jace came into her dressing room.

"Emmy." Krystal paused, glancing at Jace. "I don't want to do this. I hate him. *Hate* him." Krystal blinked, studying her. "Have you checked your phone?"

"I just sat down." Emmy frowned, looking around. "I don't have my phone."

"I have it." Melanie held it out. "I thought… I'm sorry. I figured you'd need support."

Emmy took the phone but put it facedown in her lap. "Okay. You're all here. Go for it."

"*Entertainment This Week* has breaking news." Jace used air quotes.

"Mark Hammond. The rich tech company guy?" Krystal paused. "The one engaged to Vanessa Trentham? Brock's ex-wife. Well, the engagement was called off."

Emmy sat her phone on the counter, instantly nauseous. "Oh." There was more—there had to be. If there wasn't, Krystal wouldn't be so upset. But she was, so there was. She had to force out the word: "And?"

Krystal sucked in a shaky breath. "What Momma said, about the money? It's true. It looks like Brock and Vanessa put a down payment on a little bungalow outside of Georgetown a few weeks ago."

"Okay." *Keep breathing.* He'd said he wanted to talk to her; now she knew why. "*That's why he's here?*" *To tell her before she saw the news?*

"He's here?" Krystal turned dark red. "What can I do? Tell me, because right now, I just want to hurt him. It's not just that he's hurt you, again, but he proved Momma right."

Emmy Lou's laugh stuck in her throat. About the money. "I was the one who wanted to keep our relationship a secret, not him. Because of Momma—I didn't want her to ruin things."

"I bet he didn't argue with you, did he?" Krystal shook her head.

"Sorry, sorry I'm late." Travis came in, breathless. "Just got the 911 text." He leaned against the wall, frowning. "What's the plan? Sawyer and I can beat the shit out of him?"

Emmy held up her hands. "I can't be mad at him, can I? I mean, we never said anything about not dating other people or...or... I can't be mad at him."

"You can too." Krystal pushed up from the table. "The down payment was made before San Francisco, Em."

San Francisco. When he'd acted like he cared and held her close and she'd believed him enough to bare her soul. *That hurt.*

"We figured you should know before someone asks you about it at tonight's meet-and-greet." Travis sighed. "Better prepared than blindsided, am I right?"

"I am mad," she murmured, carrying her glass to the kitchen counter. She had to move, had to do something. "I'm also confused." He'd said "us," hadn't he? Acted like there was the possibility of them becoming an "us." But he'd been making long-term plans with Vanessa… She wasn't sure what was worse: that the person he was willing to commit to wasn't her or that he was willing to sleep with her when he was making a commitment to someone else. Buying a house was a commitment.

They were all staring at her, waiting.

Thoughts and questions rushed in on her. What was the point? "I know you're always going on about sex, Travis, and now that I've actually had it, I kind of see where you're coming from. But, for me, it was because it was Brock." She tugged her robe together. "It mattered because I love him. I've always loved him." Her throat closed off. "I thought… Well, it doesn't matter what I thought. I was wrong. What is wrong with me?"

"Nothing, Emmy Lou." Jace shook his head.

"What is wrong with him?" There was no hiding Krystal's disgust.

"I'm really trying to be supportive here, I am." Travis ran both hands over his face. "But did I hear you right, Em? You never slept with anyone before?"

"I swear, Travis, now is not the time." Krystal looked ready to jump down Travis's throat. "Can you try to be remotely sensitive to your sister?"

"I am. I don't think I've ever felt like such a bastard. I gave you all sorts of shit about this. Sex is…well, it's sex. To me. I didn't realize how important it was to you." He managed to look her in the eye. "And, Em, I have to admit, I have a whole hell of a lot of respect for you right now."

Emmy Lou turned. "Why? I did it anyway. I caved. And jumped him."

"I'm not prepared to hear you say *those* words ever." Travis closed his eyes and shook his head. "I am, however, fully prepared to go remove his nuts."

Emmy was so startled, she laughed.

Travis crossed the room and tugged her in for a hug. "He's a fucker. A big mountain of shit. An asshole who doesn't deserve you. He's a—"

"I get it." She buried her face against her brother's shirtfront.

"I'm not saying I'll do it. But Sawyer will," Travis murmured against the top of her head. "Am I right, Sawyer?"

"Yeah." It was one word—but it was enough.

"Thank you, Sawyer." She turned her head to see Sawyer. He stood, tense, fully prepared to come to her defense. And she loved him for it.

"Just so you know, Momma made a sound I have never heard before." Travis sighed, his arms easing. "She took one look at that article, saw those pictures, and screamed—basically. Sort of. It was like a scream-groan-cussword thing. Daddy about dropped his cup of coffee."

"Pictures?" Emmy Lou looked up at her brother. "What pictures?"

"Really?" Travis glared at Krystal. "You could have warned me. 'Hey, Travis, we haven't mentioned the pictures yet. So, you know, hold off on that for a sec.'"

"We were getting there." Krystal wrinkled up her nose. "They're all over."

Emmy Lou picked up her phone and scrolled through Twitter, then Instagram.

Pictures of Vanessa and Brock arriving at a house. Pictures of them embracing in a window. Pictures of Vanessa leaving the next morning in what were clearly Brock's clothes. And the parting embrace. But what gutted her most was Brock, standing in his driveway, watching Vanessa drive away. That hurt so much she had to force herself to breathe.

Slow. Deep. Breaths. She wasn't going to fall apart. Not this time. She wasn't going to worry the people who *did* love her.

"Here." Krystal gave her a glass of water.

Emmy sipped, scanning the details. "I feel so bad for Mark Hammond." She shook her head. "I mean, I wasn't engaged to Brock." No promises had been exchanged.

She didn't want to look at or read anything else, but she couldn't stop. That's when she noticed the date. The pictures were taken the night he'd canceled on her.

I wouldn't cancel on you if it wasn't important. Vanessa was important. It would have been kinder just to tell her he wasn't coming, he didn't want to see her anymore, and end it. Why hadn't he? Why had he acted like he was happy to see her at the stadium?

"You said Momma reacted when she saw the pictures?" Krystal asked. "Reacted or overreacted?"

Emmy Lou understood what she was asking. "Does it matter who took them? It wouldn't change what they're of." That was the part that hurt. He'd done this. He'd hurt her. And Momma had tried to warn her about it. Had she handled things well? No. But she'd had the best of intentions, hadn't she?

Or had she?

Her head was reeling enough without adding her momma to the mix.

One thing at a time.

The silence extended until she thought she'd scream. They were all trying to help; she knew that. The truth was there was nothing any of them could do. She'd opened herself up for this. If there was anyone to blame, all she had to do was look in the mirror.

She'd had no idea he was involved with Vanessa. When Vanessa had shown up at the hospital, maybe she should have picked up on something. But he'd been holding her and kissing her…

Why? Why string her along when he had someone else he was planning a future with?

"You don't have to do any more events with him, do you?" Jace asked.

"I can't back out of *Good Morning USA*." She sighed. "After that, you're right." She pushed out of her director's chair. "I'm fine. I'm good. You go on to the meet-and-greet and I'll follow." She swallowed. "Melanie, can you bring Brock to me, please? I need to do this. And I need you all to let me." She deserved closure. Tonight, she'd get it.

———

No matter how many times he saw the Three Kings perform, he was impressed. They'd had years of practice and working together, so it made sense that there was an inherent shift and anticipation among them when they performed. Kind of like him on the field, with his team. He knew the sort of discipline that took. For all Travis's smart-ass comments, his performance showed how invested he was in the group.

Now the wide concrete halls were crowded with fans, the red-roped path leading toward the meet-and-greet space.

His phone vibrated. Connie. He'd call her back.

Tonight, no excuses, he and Emmy Lou were going to have an honest conversation, and he was nervous as hell. It would help if he felt a little more confident about the outcome. But there were risks in life worth taking. She was the one that meant the most.

"Brock?" Emmy's wide-eyed assistant tapped his elbow. "She's in her dressing room. I can take you to her."

"That'd be great, thanks." He followed her from the room, wincing from the volume of the fans lining the hallway waiting for a chance to see one of the Three Kings.

"Is it always like this?" he asked.

"Always." Melanie nodded. They turned two more corners before Melanie said, "Here we are."

Considering Sawyer was leaning against the opposite wall, not even bothering to hide his hostility, he figured this was the place. "Thanks." He nodded, then opened the dressing room door with his heart in his throat and his lungs all but empty.

It was odd that Melanie propped the door open, but he didn't care. As soon as he saw Emmy's face, his pulse faltered.

"Emmy?" He immediately reached for her. "Are you okay?"

She sidestepped his touch, and from the corner of his eye, he saw Sawyer take a couple of steps closer. But she held up her hand—shook her head. And Sawyer went back into statue mode.

An ice-cold current flooded his veins. He froze, his hands falling to his sides. "Just tell me everyone is okay?"

For a split second, her green eyes collided with his. "Eventually." Her gaze fell. "I need to say a few things. I only have a few minutes, so I'll be quick." She cleared her throat. "I'd appreciate it if you'd let me talk without interrupting. Okay?"

He nodded; everything about this was setting off warning bells. *What the fuck is going on?*

"My momma has a lot of flaws. There is no way to deny that. She manipulates people, lies to get her way, and generally messes with people until they don't know which way is up. I know this. It's how I grew up. To be honest, I didn't realize that her tactics were abnormal until this whole thing with Krystal blew up. I've lived my whole life as a puppet, not realizing it, of course. But…" She shook her head. "It doesn't matter."

"Em—"

"Brock." Again, her eyes shifted to him—then at the concrete at her feet. "We have never talked about the future."

"I want to." He swallowed, stepping closer. Her immediate step back made him stop. "We need to."

"Not really." There was a sad smile on her face. "Basically, I wanted to thank you. I've always sort of given everyone the benefit of the doubt. I wanted to believe in the good, even when there was no reason. I honestly believed there was some way you and I could make this work. But between you and my mother, I've finally realized that I need to wake up." She shook her head. "I can count all the people I truly trust on one hand. And you are not one of them." Her breath hitched.

He couldn't breathe—couldn't think.

"I don't know what happened six years ago. You could have told me the truth. It might have been unpleasant, but it would have been over without leaving me to wonder what I did to make you leave. It would have been the decent thing to do. I hope, at least, you burned my letters. If you haven't, please do?" She shook her head. "I loved you too much." Her voice was wavering now. "I guess I always will."

She was talking too fast for him to keep up. One thing was clear, though: she was saying goodbye—and he had to stop her. "Emmy, wait please—"

"No." She shook her head. "I've spent too much time waiting on you. I didn't even realize I was until I saw you in the parking lot. But I'm not going to love you anymore." She wiped her eyes with the back of her hand. "What I don't understand is why you couldn't be straight with me this time. Better yet, just leave me alone. Why? What possible reason could you have for intentionally lying to me again?" Her voice was stronger—angrier. "I'm not going to let anyone else use me, Brock. Not you or my mother. And I'm definitely not going to settle for being someone's second choice...or their backup option." Her gaze met his, flashing with pure fire.

"I wanted to talk to you about all of this." He ran a hand along the back of his neck, searching for the right words. "You should have heard this from me—"

"Yes. I should have." She stared at his chest. "Not from my brothers and sister. Not from the television or the internet."

"What?"

She did look at him then. "You and Vanessa? The pictures." Her gaze traveled over his face. "It doesn't matter. I'm done. We, whatever this was, is done."

He didn't know what she was talking about. Vanessa? What pictures? Emmy was all that mattered. It took everything he had to stay calm. "Will you let me say something?"

She shook her head. "The thing is, when it comes to you, I can't trust myself. I listen to my heart when my head is warning me to walk away." She kept shaking her head. "I'm walking away. Now."

Panic kicked in and he grabbed her hand as she brushed past him. "Emmy, I didn't want you to find out this way." He groaned, beyond frustrated. "There are things I can't tell you."

She nodded. "That's fine. I don't want to hear them anyway." She tugged her hand away and walked, quickly, from the dressing room.

He started to go after her, but Sawyer was blocking his path.

"Leave her alone, man." It was an order—a threat.

"You don't want to do this with me." It wasn't a threat. It was a statement. Sawyer thought he was a badass—he probably was. But now wasn't the time to issue a challenge.

"You're right. I don't." Sawyer frowned. "I don't want to hurt her by hurting you. I think she's suffered enough. You have no idea."

It was enough to stop him.

Sawyer turned and followed Emmy Lou down the hall—out of sight. But the roar of the crowd, the screams of "Emmy Lou" and "I love you," told him she was going on with the show. While he stood there, reeling.

He had to do something. He had to make this right. She was hurting—but she didn't know the truth. If she knew, she'd understand. If he could talk to her, he could explain… What? What could he say?

Not a fucking word.

As much as he loved Emmy Lou, his word meant something to him. When he'd damn near lost everything, his word was all he'd had left. And he'd given his word to Vanessa that her secrets were safe with him.

He was vaguely aware of his phone vibrating, vaguely aware of answering it.

"Brock." Connie. "What is happening? Why didn't you call me? I need to know what's going on and I need to know now. We are talking major damage control here."

Brock ran a hand along the back of his neck. "I don't know what to tell you."

"Well, you better tell me something." She sighed. "Anything. Some rational explanation that assures me, Alpha, and the Roughnecks that you are not and will not get involved with the woman who almost destroyed you."

"V didn't do that." He sighed, walking quickly from the dressing room toward the exits. "I did it. I've never blamed her for the mistakes I made." It didn't seem to matter how far away he got; he could still hear the fans screaming Emmy's name. He needed air. Peace and quiet.

"Brock, this is serious." Her voice was strung tight. "*Serious* serious."

"I get that." He sighed. Considering what had just happened… "What do I need to do?"

"We need a statement. A good one. And soon." Another sigh. "I'll send you a few options shortly. I'll need a quick response. Quick, understand?"

"Yeah." He hung up, his brain working through everything Emmy had said. And she'd said so damn much.

What letters? He'd never received one from her. Not one. He

was the one who wrote one after the other, full of pleas for an explanation—a chance to talk through whatever had happened to change her mind and cut him out of her life. The only letters he'd received were the ones he'd sent to her. Every envelope unopened with "Return to Sender" stamped in big, red letters.

His phone was ringing again. This time it was Coach McCoy.

"Shit." He climbed into his rental car, started the ignition, and answered the phone. "Yes, sir?"

"I'm guessing you know why I'm calling?"

"I'm beginning to figure it out." He sighed. "Haven't seen the details myself, though."

"I'm not sure what that means, Brock?"

"Nothing." He groaned.

"You need to listen to me, you hear? You're one of our best players and I don't want to lose you, so I'm telling it like it is." McCoy cleared his throat. "The owner called. Ed was highly concerned about this."

"Understood." Brock nodded.

"Every player is an investment. The more time and energy invested, the more we expect of a player. I'd like to think you know and appreciate the level of investment this team has shown you—no matter what. Up until a point. And, Brock, you're about to get to that point."

"Yes, sir." He shook his head. "This is my team. My family. My life. I don't know what's floating around out there, but I'm guessing it paints a not-so-pretty picture." He stared out the front windshield. "I wouldn't do anything to jeopardize my career."

There was a long pause. "That's good to hear. Because that little shit Ricky Ames is standing by hoping you'll screw up. And if I have to play him, my next heart attack will be on you."

"Yes, sir."

"I'm counting on you. Counting on your word. You hear me?"

"Yes, sir."

"Get some rest," McCoy said. "Practice. Tomorrow. Early. Chances are, it won't be pretty."

He took a deep breath and opened the internet browser on his phone.

"Fuck." The pictures weren't pretty. Vanessa's breakup didn't help. Neither did the recount of their short-lived marriage and messy divorce.

But the thing that tore him up inside was Emmy Lou's reaction. She'd seen these, believed it, and chosen to walk away. *What else could she do?* If he'd been in her shoes, he'd have done the same thing. But the rest of it? There were so many holes now he had to decide if he was going to try to set her straight or if, like her, he was going to walk away.

But like his dad always told him, he wasn't the quitting type.

Chapter 19

DADDY HUGGED EMMY CLOSE, THE GENTLE SWAY OF THE BUS driving down the interstate almost rocking her against her father's chest. "I'm so sorry, baby girl. For all of this."

"It's not your fault, Daddy." There was nothing as comforting as one of her daddy's hugs.

"I can't believe that anymore. Not with the way things keep shaking out." He let her go. "If that were the case, then none of this would have happened. None of it." He faced Krystal then. "I hope you know, I won't let you down again. Any of you." He didn't shy away from the hard look on Travis's face. "I give you my word."

"Where is Momma?" Travis asked.

Emmy curled up on the leather couch, Watson jumping up to wedge himself in the bend of her knees. "I didn't see her tonight."

"She's taking some time. After the last few days…" He shook his head, his voice low and gruff. "It's what's best for now."

Emmy Lou glanced at her siblings, their shocked expressions mirroring her own.

Emmy Lou captured his hand in hers. "It'll be okay, Daddy."

"There's no point pretending things that aren't true." He sat forward. "Seems to me, we've been doing an awful lot of that. Some I didn't even know about."

"Fuck." Travis's one word said oh so much.

"Pretty much." Daddy nodded. "I brought something." On the table were two large pizza boxes, a shoebox tied with red string, and…

"Is that Momma's book?" Emmy asked.

"Pass?" Travis said, standing up to grab the box of pizza. "On the book. Pretty sure I lived it. But I'll never say no to pizza. Sawyer?"

Sawyer shook his head and stayed in his usual spot, close enough to listen but far enough apart to go unnoticed.

Krystal leaned into Jace, resting her head on his shoulder. "I doubt she'd want us to read that, Daddy."

"You think I'd offer it behind her back?" Daddy took a deep breath, beyond hurt. "We talked about this. Your momma's life wasn't easy. I know you only know your grandpa as a man with a joke to tell and a big laugh. Truth was, he and your momma never got on. I didn't help with that." He shook his head and leaned back against the couch. "All I'm trying to say is, her life hasn't been as easy as it appears. Not that it's an excuse, mind you."

"We all love her, Daddy," Emmy Lou said.

"Even if it's not always easy," Travis replied.

Krystal sat silent—not because she didn't love their mother, but because she didn't want to.

"Are we burning the book or what?" Travis asked.

"I'm going to leave it here." Daddy stared at the box. "In case you want to read it. A lot of things I wish I'd known. And some truths that need to be told and made right." He leaned forward, picked up the shoebox, and gave it to Emmy Lou. "These are yours."

Emmy took the box, sat it beside her on the couch, and opened it. "But…" Just when she thought she'd gotten a handle on her feelings, she had her legs knocked out from under her. There, in the shoebox, were all the letters she'd written to Brock. "I don't understand." And she didn't.

Krystal peered over her shoulder. "What is that?"

"I can't see," Travis pointed out.

Emmy Lou sat the box on the table. "Letters I wrote to Brock." She shook her head. *Letters he never got.*

Travis frowned. "That takes the whole breach-of-privacy thing to a new level of what the hell, doesn't it?"

Krystal sighed, resting her elbow on the table and propping her chin up. "I don't understand, Daddy. How you can live with someone who could hurt her children?"

"I have no excuse for allowing things to go on like this. It might be hard to believe this now, but I hate seeing you hurt." His gaze bounced among the three of them. "At the end of the day, all a man has is his word. My vow to her was my word."

Emmy Lou's attention wandered back to the box of letters. Brock had never received them… It should have been a relief, not a disappointment. But he'd never known that she'd kept up her end of the bargain. Like Daddy, she honored her word.

It didn't change the fact that he'd never reached out to her.

And none of this had anything to do with him and Vanessa.

"She did leave a note for me to read to you all." Daddy pulled out a folded-up piece of paper from his pocket.

"There's something wrong with your making amends on her behalf." Krystal stood up. "Why would I listen to her if she can't be bothered to be here herself? Putting you in the middle of this is wrong," Krystal said. She stood on her tiptoes, kissed her dad's cheek, and headed down the hall to her room.

Daddy didn't try to stop her. "We good?"

Emmy and Travis nodded.

"'I know that you all have problems with me. I am sorry I'm not the mother you kids wanted or needed. I can tell you that everything I have done was an attempt to keep me from losing you. You all are, without a doubt, the most important things in my life. But by doing what I have done, I have lost you kids and your daddy. I promise, I will try to do better. I think, for now, it's best for me to return to the rehabilitation center. I didn't dedicate my whole mind to what they were trying to teach me. That much is clear now. When I'm done, I hope you all will find a place for me in your lives. I love you all so much in my own messed-up way. Momma.'"

There was a lengthy silence, each of them taking the time to work through Momma's note. Travis ate three slices of pizza. Daddy stared into his cup of coffee. And Jace headed down the hall after Krystal.

"So," Travis said.

Sawyer sat beside Travis then, reaching for a piece of pizza.

"I've got a new song I want you to look over, Travis. Maybe tomorrow? After Emmy's *Good Morning USA* spot?" Daddy asked, standing to refill his coffee cup.

"You're not all going, are you?" She wasn't sure which was worse, facing Brock on her own or having her entire family scowling at him throughout their ten-minute interview.

"Well, you know I'm all in favor of front-row drama." Travis smiled. "Hell, I'll make enough popcorn for the whole studio audience."

Emmy Lou laughed in spite of herself.

"We're going, baby girl." Her daddy shook his head. "I'll try to be on my best behavior, but I'll be happy to let Brock Watson know that hurting you is not acceptable, if need be." He stared around the table. "And that goes for all of you."

"Unless it's Jace." Travis shook his head. "I mean, we'd take Jace's side over Krystal's, right? I mean, we need to keep him around."

Emmy shook her head, but she was laughing.

"Then why are you smiling?" Travis was laughing. "Because you know I'm right?"

"I know it's late," Daddy said. "And I'm beat."

"Come on, Watson." Emmy scooped up the kitten. "We're turning in. You'll be comfortable on the couches?"

"Even your couches are more comfortable than the things called mattresses on my bus." Travis used his pizza crust to point at Daddy. "You know I'm right, too."

Daddy chuckled. "Might be time to make some updates."

"Yeah, yeah." Travis glanced her way. "Night, Emmy."

Emmy carried Watson to her room, only to find Krystal sitting on the edge of her bed, Clementine in her lap. "Hi," Emmy said.

"Clementine was missing Watson." Krystal sat Clementine on the ground. "And I figured you could catch me up on anything important I might have missed?"

"Not really." She sat beside her sister. "Momma checked herself back into rehab."

Krystal shot her a look of pure disbelief.

"It could be true, Sis." She sighed, wrapping her arm around Krystal. "I hope it is."

Krystal rested her head on her shoulder and hugged her close. "Emmy Lou? Do you think I'd be a good mother?"

Emmy Lou sat back, staring at her sister. "What?"

Krystal sat back on the bed, pulling one of Emmy's pillows into her lap. "You heard me."

"Where did that question come from?" It's not that Emmy Lou had never pictured Krystal as a mom; she'd expected all of them to have kids eventually. But until now, Krystal had never mentioned kids—or her mothering ability.

Krystal shrugged, running her hands back and forth across the mermaid-scale pillow.

Emmy caught her hand. "Seriously, Krystal, why are you asking me that? It's sort of a really big question. Don't you think?"

"You were sitting at that table, weren't you? If Momma is saying she's a bad mother because of the way she was raised, maybe we shouldn't have kids." The flicker of doubt and fear on her face made Emmy hug her tight.

"You will be the most amazing mother ever. I promise," Emmy whispered, holding her close. "You're not capable of giving anything less than your best. And when you love someone, you love them with your whole heart—just as they are."

Krystal didn't let go. "Are you sure?"

"I'm sure." She pressed a kiss to her cheek. "And I will be an amazing aunt. However, we will have to shield the baby from Uncle Travis. For obvious reasons."

"That is true." Krystal laughed.

Emmy Lou nodded. "That's the only reason you asked? Because of Momma?"

Krystal's green gaze locked with hers. "Partly."

"And the other part?" Emmy Lou did her best not to squeeze her sister's hand too hard. "Like...you are going to have a baby?" she whispered. "You, my beautiful twin sister, and her sweet beau, are going to have a gorgeous and beyond talented little angel baby?"

Krystal smiled. "Maybe."

Emmy Lou was hugging her again. "Really? Really?" She was crying then. "When will you know?"

"Next week. Doctor's appointment." Krystal started crying, too. "I guess I always thought you would go first." She nodded. "I mean, I needed you to go first so I could call you for advice and cry on you and know that you'd have the answers because you always do."

"Looks like you get to do that for me." Emmy hugged her sister again. "It's about time we had something to celebrate, don't you think? I'm so happy for you." She'd hold on to that happiness for as long as she could.

━━━━━━━

Brock kept his gaze focused on the framed print of the Alamo on the set of *Good Morning USA*. His mic was on. The lights were beating down on him. And Emmy Lou had just taken her seat beside him, sitting as far away from him as she possibly could.

He'd been picturing this all morning. Not reacting. Not looking at her. Not wishing she'd give him a chance to explain. Was it frustrating that she believe he was capable of doing this to her? Yes.

But with such damning pictures, he understood. Even if she would talk to him, he could only say so much. And it wasn't enough to make her understand.

The host, Molly Harper, smoothed her red hair over her shoulder and smiled at them both. "It's so good to see you, Emmy Lou. You look great. How's the family?"

"We're good." Emmy smiled. "How about you? I saw that piece you did on insurance scams. That was scary stuff."

"You're telling me." Molly nodded. "The terrible things people are capable of never fails to amaze me."

Brock might have imagined Emmy's glance his way. But he was pretty sure he hadn't.

One of the camera crew pointed at Molly.

"Okay, we're counting down." Molly smiled. "Ready? Five, four, three..." She turned toward the camera. "Good morning, USA. We are right here in Austin, Texas, to talk to country music darling Emmy Lou King and football heartthrob Brock Watson. That's right, we have Bremmy in the house."

The studio audience clapped enthusiastically.

Brock felt sweat running down the middle of his back.

"It's so nice to have you both here with us this morning." Molly paused. "Can I just say, Emmy Lou, you are even more beautiful in person. Just wow."

"Molly, that's very sweet of you." Emmy Lou's voice faltered, drawing Brock's gaze. She was blushing. All pink cheeked and so damn pretty he couldn't look away. "Thank you for having us," Emmy Lou chirped, undeniably cheerful.

He forced his gaze back to the Alamo print. "Good to be here, Molly." He smiled. *I can do this.*

"You two are here today to share the Drug Free Like Me program, is that correct?" Molly asked. "Brock, you've been working with the organization for some time. Can you share what you like best about working with the group?"

If he focused on the charity, the answers were easy enough. He and Emmy Lou had done enough interviews to present an entertaining volley of answers. Emmy was having a hard time looking at him, but she was so damn charming, chances were he was the only one who noticed anything was off between them. Molly did ask about tomorrow's home game and what he thought their chances were.

"Are we going to win?" He smiled. "Yes. Of course. Without a doubt."

"Kind of hard to doubt you with that kind of confidence." Molly laughed. "And, Emmy Lou, you're singing at this halftime?"

She nodded. "The American Football League asked me to, yes. It's to honor the passing of one of their legendary coaches. I'm proud to do it. And as everyone knows, I'm a Roughnecks fan."

Brock glanced her way—about the same time she looked at him.

"I guess we will see how the game goes. Good luck out there, you two. Hopefully there won't be any more kittens getting in the way." Molly smiled. "But if there are, we know the two of you have things covered."

The audience laughed, severing the connection between Brock and Emmy Lou. His chest hurt, the pressure continuing to build as the cameras cut away and a stage tech removed his mic.

If he didn't move, he'd probably make an ass of himself right there.

It didn't help that Emmy Lou had them pose for a selfie. He did it, knowing full well it would be posted and tweeted all over. Hopefully it would draw attention to Drug Free Like Me—and distract from the whole Vanessa and Mark Hammond drama.

Emmy Lou, and the King family, made a point of ignoring him. And since his hands were tied, there was no point sticking around. He stormed down the hall, pushed through the door, and headed for his truck. He was home within ten minutes. He shoved his next meal into the oven and turned on his stationary bike. Burning off steam was a necessity.

He was sitting down to his meal when the doorbell rang.

Sawyer stood there, arms crossed, his emotionless-as-fuck expression irritating the shit out of Brock.

"What the hell are you doing here?" Brock snapped. The front gate guy needed to start looking for a new job.

"Can I come in?" Sawyer asked. "I really don't want to do this on your front porch."

"Sure, why the hell not?" He stepped aside, rolling his neck. "I don't know what this is about, but I can tell you now, for the first time in my life, I'd be okay throwing a few punches."

"Duly noted." Sawyer nodded. "I know who took the pictures."

Brock stared at him. "What?"

"CiCi King's personal bodyguard was fired a few days ago. I feel confident it was over those pictures. I'm not sure if he wanted hush money or what, but it looks like he ended up selling copies to *Entertainment Monthly*." Sawyer stared around him. "If CiCi King isn't careful, he'll sell a whole lot of information, regardless of the NDA we all have to sign."

Brock blew out a slow deep breath. "You're telling me CiCi King sent her bodyguard here to watch me, then fired him over those fucking pictures?"

Sawyer nodded.

"He told you this?"

"He was pretty upset over losing his job. I took him out for a few drinks, asked the right questions, learned what I needed to learn." He stared at Brock. "I don't think she'd ever planned on them going public. She probably was going to send them to you to warn you away or to Emmy Lou."

"For fuck's sake." He ran his hands through his hair. "What the hell does she have against me? No. Forget that. I don't give a damn about CiCi King." He sat, staring at the rug. "But Emmy Lou needs to get out of there. You're supposed to protect her, right? Well, that place isn't safe. I want her safe."

Sawyer nodded, his gaze narrowing. "I figured as much."

"Why are you here?" He sat back.

Sawyer sat, eyeing the mountain of food on the table. "There are a few things I thought you'd want to know."

"More?" He shook his head. "I'm not sure I'm ready for this."

"Emmy never got your letters. She wasn't the one who sent them back." Sawyer was watching him closely. "And her mom kept Emmy's letters so you never got hers."

"Motherfucker." The words were a harsh whisper. It was amazing how quickly those old wounds began to heal.

"When you came over, nobody else knew." Sawyer's jaw stiffened. "That was CiCi making sure she'd cut the last threads between the two of you."

"Which she did." He stood, pacing. "How do you know all of this?"

"It's my job." Sawyer shrugged, his eyes narrowing. "What does Vanessa have on you?"

Brock spun to face him. "What?"

"Why else wouldn't you go after Emmy? Vanessa has something on you. Something bad."

Brock shook his head. "No."

"Then why are you letting this happen again?" Sawyer stood.

"I'm all for employee loyalty, here. But why are you so invested in Emmy Lou's happiness?" He paused. "I see how protective you are of her—but I'm getting that it's not your standard security-guard protocol."

Sawyer's face didn't twitch. "I have my reasons."

"I have mine." Brock sighed, so tired everything hurt. "Are we done here?"

Sawyer pushed out of the chair. "I guess. I was expecting more. I don't think you realize how long she's loved you."

"Probably as long as I've loved her." *My whole damned life.*

"Then you'd be a damn fool not to fight for her. You sit here and say you want her protected—is that my job? Or yours?" Sawyer gave him a head-to-toe once-over. "Good luck tomorrow."

When Sawyer left, Brock felt more unsettled than ever.

Emmy had been pissed when she'd admitted it, but she had admitted she'd never stopped loving him. She had written to him—like he'd written to her. She'd waited, hoping…questioning and doubting and wondering what had gone wrong.

CiCi King had set the perfect trap. The story the pictures told was a lie, but the pictures were real. So was the suspicion and hurt they'd caused.

It was a stark contrast to the memories he had of his time in the King household. He'd always felt welcome. Even with a wall covered in gold and platinum albums, they'd been good people. Hank King had always been supportive and focused.

But thinking back, he realized CiCi had rarely been around. If she had, maybe he wouldn't remember things so fondly.

Sawyer's parting dig had him more than a little riled up. Loving Emmy wasn't a job or a burden; it was a gift. She was a gift. Knowing that the woman who'd brought Emmy into this world, the woman who should put her children above all else, could hurt her so? Yet CiCi had done just that. She'd twisted something good and pure to keep Emmy under her thumb and riddled with self-doubt.

He wasn't one for hating, but CiCi King stirred something powerfully close to it. Still, she was Emmy's mother. Hating the woman wouldn't do any of them any good.

He packed up an overnight bag. Tonight, he'd stay at the hospital with his father. Tomorrow, after the game, he and Aunt Mo would move his dad back into Green Gardens Alzheimer's clinic. Now that his father was on the right meds, there was a chance his mental clarity would last a little longer. With everything else going on in his life, Brock needed his family more than ever.

With any luck, Aunt Mo or his father would have some pearls of wisdom to help him sort out how to win Emmy back.

Chapter 20

"Please, please, please give me tea." Emmy Lou was wiping the sleep from her eyes. "What time is it?" Even Watson looked perturbed by Krystal and Jace's sudden invasion.

"It's nine." Krystal flopped onto the bed beside her. "Open your eyes. You're going to want to see this."

"Tea, please?" She smothered a yawn.

"Jace?" Krystal called out. "Can you make Emmy some—"

Jace came in, a cup of tea in his hands. "I have no idea what I'm doing, so sorry if it's bad."

"Thank you, Jace." Ever since Krystal had shared her possible pregnancy, Emmy couldn't help but see everything he did differently. If Krystal was pregnant, her sister was going to have the best father for her baby. And he'd take such good care of Krystal—he already did.

"Scooch," Krystal said, making room for Clementine on the bed.

Emmy propped herself up on the pillows, took the tea, and smiled as Watson curled back into a little ball on her stomach. "It's not that I don't appreciate the tea in bed, but what's the big development this morning?"

Jace chuckled. "Well, now, funny you should put it that way."

Krystal turned on the television mounted on the wall of Emmy's bedroom. "Jace." Krystal patted the bed beside her.

"Wouldn't want to crowd the four of you." He shook his head.

"Jace, you know she's not going to stop until you do what she says." Emmy took a sip of her very strong tea.

Jace sat beside Krystal, and Krystal pressed a button.

"I appreciate you being here tonight," Guy James was saying.

"This was recorded last night," Krystal whispered.

Vanessa Trentham looked amazing. "I'm assuming there is a reason I'm being tortured this morning?" Long, dark hair. Long legs. Long eyelashes. "She's so gorgeous," Emmy Lou mumbled. With her puffy eyes and bedhead, the last thing she wanted to do was watch the woman she'd lost Brock to.

"Give me the remote." Jace took it and fast-forwarded. "Right here."

"You're saying these were taken out of context?" Guy asked. "I'm not sure how you can take these photos—of you two hugging and you wearing his clothing—out of context."

"That's because people see what they want to see, Guy." Vanessa was shaking her head. "What you don't see is the truth. And because Brock Watson is the sort of man who keeps his word, even when his character is being dragged through the mud, he wasn't going to rat me out. But I can't stand by and let him suffer because of me." She drew in a deep breath. "I've always been too scared to say what I'm about to say out loud, but my problems are hurting good people, so…here we go."

"You've certainly piqued my interest." Guy leaned forward.

"I'm a drug addict. Recovering. I've used on and off since I was sixteen—maybe earlier. You have to keep stick thin to walk the runway. Cocaine and heroin were best for that. Sometimes it was a little; other times, a lot. Brock and I had this whirlwind court-ship; it was a mess of a marriage from the get-go. His injury only added to my little pharmaceutical collection. We both spiraled out of control—"

Emmy was frozen; the image Vanessa's words painted was devastating.

"With the drugs?" Guy asked.

"Yes. With drugs. A lot of them. Anyway, Brock's father and aunt—forgive me for sharing this part, Brock—were the foundation for his recovery. When his father started suffering from Alzheimer's, wandering and getting confused, Brock got clean. Boom, it was like...he needed to be there for the man who's always been there for him." She shook her head. "That was all it took."

Emmy was trying not to cry. Brock would have felt terrible—his father was everything to him. And that Brock might not be there for him or let him down? It would have been enough to get him clean and keep him that way.

"Fast-forward to about three months ago. My sponsor was unavailable, I was in a *bad* place with Mark, and I called Brock. We've talked on and off, more of 'Hey, are you staying out of trouble? Good, bye,' sort of thing. I would call him, he would talk to me until my sponsor was available, and then we'd hang up. But then I took advantage of him, knowing how kind he was. I showed up when I needed money."

"You? Aren't you engaged to the richest man in the universe?"

"Was. Almost. I never wanted Mark to think I was after his money. I've never asked him for money. I had a big shoot coming up, but I didn't have what I needed, and I needed it now. My mom has never asked for anything, ever. The woman is a saint. But she's always wanted to live in this adorable little artist community around Georgetown. A house came open and, if I wanted it, I needed money now."

"But you couldn't ask Mark." Guy nodded.

"And because Brock knows about my addiction problem, he couldn't just hand over money. Because, again, he's this amazing guy who didn't want me to be tempted. So he drove me there, gave me money, and watched me write the check."

"You're not moving in with Brock Watson?" Guy clarified.

"No." She shook her head. "Never was."

"And these pictures?"

"Well, as we have now established, Brock is a saint." She was crying now. "Mark found out about the money. Assumed the worst and kicked me out. My sponsor was in Dallas, so…"

"Ah, you called Brock." Guy nodded. "Yeah, he is turning out to be quite the hero of your story here."

"He is." She nodded. "Okay, the pictures. I was covered in makeup and slobber by the time we got to his place. This picture is him showing me that the shower handle sticks and how to jiggle it here. This one is me hugging and crying on him for coming to get me from downtown in the middle of the night. And that's the next morning. I left in his clothes because mine were gross. Him standing there, like that? It's either relief that he doesn't have to deal with me anymore or, because he's a sweetie, he's hoping I don't do something stupid." She paused. "That's it. There is *nothing* going on with us. His heart is taken, Guy, but not by me. Any woman who gets him, you better hold on tight because he's a rare soul."

Emmy was kicking the blankets back, earning a reproachful meow from Watson and a laugh from her sister. "Sorry, Watson. Mommy has to hurry."

"Well, that takes care of that." Guy nodded. "Let's talk about this new clothing line you're involved in."

Krystal hit the pause button and the screen froze. "I think she's telling the truth. I saw his face that day in the parking lot when you went to see him off. Yeah. She's telling the truth."

"I thought you hated him?" Emmy pulled open the dresser drawer, pulling out pants.

"I don't think I do now." Krystal slipped out of the bed. "Now, get your tush dressed, get your smile on, and go get your man." She clapped her hands. "I mean, you are going to see him today, right? The whole singing at the halftime show during one of the biggest games this season?"

"Right." Emmy nodded, slowing down. "He'll already be at the field." There wasn't much point in hurrying over there. She'd see him at the game. Still, she wanted to see him. The sooner the better. She packed up her makeup and hair supplies and waited for Sawyer to come pick her up. When the black Suburban pulled up, she practically sprinted for the door.

"Guess you saw the show?" Travis asked when Emmy climbed into the Suburban.

"Is that why you're here?" she asked, smiling, as Krystal and Jace climbed in after her.

"We've already established I'm in favor of watching you and Brock's awkward exchanges. They're painful—but highly entertaining." Travis sat back.

"Did you bring popcorn this time?" Krystal rolled her eyes.

"It's game day." Travis shook his head. "We'll buy it there."

The whole ride, Emmy's emotions alternated between pure joy and absolute terror. She hadn't given him the benefit of the doubt. That had to hurt. She should have asked him, straight out, instead of jumping to the same conclusions everyone else had. But Vanessa had said he was keeping her secrets...because he was Brock.

It was hard to stay calm through hair and makeup. She ran through a dozen different scenarios, but none of them felt right. Hopefully, when they were face-to-face, she'd know the right thing to say.

"You look incredible," Krystal said, taking her hand and spinning her around. "Is this the disco-ball dress Travis was talking about?"

Emmy laughed. "Yep."

"I didn't think I'd like it, but I do." Krystal nodded. "You look amazing."

"I have, what, ten minutes?" Emmy glanced at the clock on the wall, then her reflection. "Or I could wait..."

"Go," Krystal said. "Hurry."

Emmy Lou moved as quickly as the formfitting dress allowed, with Sawyer at her side. She smiled and waved, but she tried to keep her head down until she reached the pressroom that fed into the tunnel.

The players were lining up at the tunnel entrance, wearing their game face and getting their minds in the zone. She stood on her tiptoes, looking all over for number eighty-eight.

"Miss King?" Coach McCoy came up behind her. "You know the game is about to start?"

"Yes, sir." Her heart fell. "Sorry..."

He sighed loudly. "He's coming now. Good news?" He waited for her to nod. "Good. Can't have him hearing bad news before a game. Well, from the look on your face, he's going to want to hear this." He glanced at his watch. "One minute. Two tops."

"Yes, sir." She nodded, standing aside while Gene Byrd and RJ trotted through.

Brock was next. Head down, helmet in his hand, he was...the man she loved. *I love you so much.*

Emmy Lou. Sparkling and beautiful and staring at him. He clenched his jaw, holding back all the things he wanted to say. "Emmy."

"I know you have like one minute. That's all I need." She practically ran to him. "I am so sorry."

He frowned. "For what?"

"For thinking the worst. For giving credence to voices other than yours." She shook her head. "If you can forgive me, and I really hope you will, then I want you to know that I...have loved you since the day I met you and I always will." She swallowed. "If you can't forgive me, I understand. But I still want you to know that I did write you—every day. I sent them, but they never reached you. I needed you to know that, too."

He was staring at her, his heart full to bursting. "Anything else?"

She shook her head, nibbling the inside of her lower lip.

"Sawyer told me." He stepped closer, wishing for the time to say all the things that needed to be said. "Everything. Your mother sent mine back without you knowing it."

She was smiling. "You wrote to me?"

"I said I would." He took another step.

"Wait? Sawyer?" She could not have been more stunned.

"Sort of my reaction when he showed up at my place. He has an awful strong attachment for you." Brock shook his head. "I get it, sort of, but he was determined to tell me what a fool I was for not fighting for you."

"He's my brother," she whispered.

That was the last thing he'd expected to hear. "What?" Her brother? "That explains a lot."

She nodded. "And he is getting the biggest hug ever when I see him next. Whether he likes it or not."

"We'll get back to that." He itched to touch her. "As to what you were saying about loving me…"

"Miss King, your time is up." McCoy was red faced, waving Brock forward. "Get your ass out there, Brock. Now."

"Dammit." She winced. "I'm sorry. Go."

"That's some strong language, Emmy Lou King." Brock put on his helmet, grinning like a fool and not caring in the least. "And when I get back, we can talk about that, too." He ran out of the tunnel and onto the field, the roar of the crowd rising up to greet the players.

His focus was crystal clear, holding the opposing team at a standstill and laying those who tried to break through on their back. They were winning at the half. Spirits were high—but none higher than Brock's.

Emmy was here.

She loved him.

She wanted to try again.

What else did he need to know? Nothing. He headed into the locker room, listened to Coach rip apart their offense and point out their near miss in the second quarter, and then turned to the board for a few last-minute strategy points.

While the rest of the team was cooling down, he dug through his gym bag for the ring he'd bought the night Vanessa had called him. All those plans…all the misunderstanding. No more. From here on out, Emmy would always know where she stood with him. He headed out onto the field.

Emmy Lou was on the stage, singing her heart out. She was standing, head thrown back, her long, blond hair swaying as she belted out "Your Loss." The crowd went crazy when she finished.

"Y'all have been a great audience. I've got one more for you. It's new. But you'll probably figure out who I'm singing it to. I'm hoping he'll hear it—but I guess we'll see." She closed her eyes and sang.

One step, what can go wrong? What's left for me to lose?
Each day, a fresh start, stronger, if that's what I choose.
One hope, rising inside me, that you'll hear my song.
Each night, I close my eyes and hope I wasn't wrong.
Cuz losing you, still wanting you, won't leave my mind.
And losing you, yes, loving you has left me color-blind.

All I see is you… All I see is blue.
Blue skies for miles,
Bluebirds flying high,
Bright blue like your eyes.
Don't you know, oo-hoo—I'm blue when you're gone.

One step, I'm going faster. Can't wait to get to you.
Each day, with you here beside me, if that's what you choose.
One hope, rising inside me, that you'll hear my song.
Each night, I close my eyes, beside me where you belong.

Cuz losing you, still wanting you, won't leave my mind.
And losing you, yes, loving you has left me color-blind.

All I see is you… All I see is blue.
Blue skies for miles,
Bluebirds flying high,
Bright blue like your eyes.
Don't you know, oo-hoo—I'm blue when you're gone.

He was moving before she'd finished singing. Jogging across the field with one goal in mind. And the minute people saw him, the crowd was on their feet.

He waited until she was off the stage to approach her; there was only so far he was willing to go. They might be able to see him but what he said was for her ears alone. "Hi."

She was smiling, breathing hard and flushed from her performance. "Hi."

"That song." He didn't stop until they were close enough to touch. "I like it."

"You know blue is my favorite color." She stared up at him, those green eyes blazing. "Always has been."

"You said you loved me." He waited for her to nod. "I'm doing this here and now so that you, and the whole damn world, know where my loyalty and my heart lie." He knelt in front of her. "Because I don't want there to ever be another doubt."

The volume of the crowd was so high, he couldn't hear himself, let alone her. With a sigh, he waved one of the refs over. "Can I borrow that?" he asked, pointing at his mic.

The ref smiled and handed over the mic.

Brock shook his head. "Emmy Lou King, will you marry me?" The question bounced off the stadium walls, so loud he winced. Just when he was certain the crowd couldn't get any louder, they proved him wrong.

"I will marry you, Brock Watson." She was smiling, staring down at him as he slid the ring on her finger. Then she was tugging him up. "We should get off the field before I get you another penalty."

He handed the mic back to the ref and walked off the field, holding her hand. Once they'd reached the sideline, he tilted her chin up. "Family dinners at your house are going to be interesting as hell." His kiss was featherlight. "But I wouldn't have it any other way."

She started laughing.

Until he was kissing her. And once he was kissing her, holding her, everything fell into place. As long as he had her with him, things would be okay.

"I love you, Brock Watson," she said between kisses.

"I love you, Emmy Lou King." He kissed her again. "Always have. Always will."

She pressed another kiss to his lips, then smacked his rear. "Now, go kick some ass."

"Yes, ma'am." But he kissed her again, for good luck.

Don's miss any of Sasha Summers's captivating cowboys! Keep reading for an excerpt from the first book in her Kings of Country series.

JACE

Available now from Sourcebooks Casablanca

Chapter 1

"Are you kidding me?" They could not be serious. Krystal glared at her daddy, country music legend Hank King, in pure disbelief. "Why would this be *great* news? For me, anyway." Blood roared in her ears and a throb took up residence at the base of her neck. She slipped the leather strap of her favorite Taylor spruce acoustic guitar from around her neck and placed the instrument tenderly on its stand. "It's great news for what's his name—"

"Jace Black," her manager, Steve Zamora, said.

"Whatever," she snapped, shooting a lethal gaze at the balding little man. "I'm sure he's ecstatic. He gets to sing my song, my *best* song. With the one and only Emmy Lou King." She downed a water bottle, parched from singing for almost two hours straight.

"Come on now, Krystal. They're singing one of *your* songs," her father soothed. But she wasn't ready to forgive him. Or see any good in this. And when he added "You know Emmy will do it up right. She always does," it stung.

Unlike me. Her spine stiffened and her fists tightened. She and her twin, Emmy, were different as night and day. A point her momma was all too happy to point out at every opportunity.

"Don't get your feathers ruffled, now. You know I didn't mean anything by that." Her daddy tipped his favorite tan cowboy hat back on his forehead, crossed his arms over his chest, and frowned.

Poor Daddy. He said the women in his life were the reason he was getting so grey. It wasn't intentional. She didn't like disappointing him—he was her hero. But, dammit, he couldn't pull the rug out from under her and expect her to smile and thank him. She wasn't a saint. She wasn't Emmy.

Steve tried again. "This is a win all around, Krystal."

"No, it's not. Not for me," she argued. Blowing up wasn't going to change their minds, but maybe reminding her daddy how special this song was. "Daddy, you know this song means something to me, that it's…important. I'm connected to it, deep down in my bones. I can sing it and do it justice." She hated that her voice wavered, that sentiment seeped in. This was business. And while the business loved raw emotion and drama in its music and lyrics, they weren't fans of it from their performers.

"Now, darlin', you know how it works. It's all about timing." Steve used his soft voice, the please-don't-let-her-start-screaming-and-throwing-things voice. Like lemon juice in a paper cut.

"Timing?" she asked. The only thing Steve Zamora cared about was kissing her legendary father's ass and managing Emmy Lou's career. "It's been my sister's time for ten years now."

Not that she begrudged her sister an iota of her fame. It wasn't Emmy Lou's fault that she was the favorite. She had that *thing*, a megastar quality—that universally appealing sweetness that the world adored. Krystal had a real hard time with sweetness.

Why the media, fans, even the record company labeled Krystal the rebel, a black sheep, the wild child of the King family was a mystery. Marketing, maybe? The good twin, bad twin thing? Whatever. She had her days. And her very public breakup with Mickey Graham hadn't helped. To hear him tell it, she was a selfish prima donna who'd broken his heart. It'd hurt like hell that everyone was so willing to believe the worst of her. But her pride had stopped her from telling the truth—the real truth, not Mickey's version of it. His tall tales cemented her bad-girl image, so she'd embraced some of the freedom it gave her.

"I get you're disappointed, Krystal, but there will be other songs." Daddy's hand cupped her cheek, his smile genuine and sympathetic.

He did not just say that. His easy dismissal cut deep. Yes, there would be other songs, but this one *mattered*. People might chalk it up to her breakup with Mickey. She knew better. The song had come from a wound that wouldn't heal. A wound that haunted her dreams and reminded her to guard her heart, to never let anyone in. Every scribbled note, tweaked word, chord change, or key finagle had led her to both love and hate the finished product. But it made her proud.

Her daddy had said he was proud, too. Just not enough. While she'd never asked her father to plead her case at their label, Wheelhouse Records, she realized, deep down, she'd hoped he would—for this song—without her having to ask. But if he had championed her, she'd be cutting the single, not Emmy and some new music reality TV star.

"You good?" her father asked.

No. She glared.

He sighed. "Breathe, baby girl. Don't want you spitting fire at folk for the rest of the night."

She didn't need to be reminded of the Three Kings fans lined up outside. This had been her life for the past ten years. It was more than singing side by side with her twin sister and older brother, playing her guitar until her fingertips hurt, or waking up humming a new melody, new lyrics already taking shape. It was making people *feel*. The only thing that mattered was the fans. Was she upset? Yes. Hurt? Most definitely. But when she left her dressing room, a dazzling smile would be on her face—for them. After the meet and greet would be another story.

Her father let out a long, pained sigh. "Might as well go ahead and send him in."

Send who in? Her dressing room was entirely too crowded already. Not that protesting would make a bit of difference. She flopped into the chair before her illuminated makeup mirror, all but choking on frustration, and rubbed lotion into her fingers and hands. Hands that were shaking.

Steve leaned out her dressing room door, calling, "Come on in, Jace. She's looking forward to meeting you."

Jace. She froze. As in Jace-the-song-stealer Black? She was *not* looking forward to meeting him. Some wannabe singer from a no-count TV talent show. *American Voice*? Or *Next Top Musician*? Or something else gimmicky and stupid?

In the mirror, she shot daggers her father's way. He was pushing it—pushing her. She applied a stroke of bloodred color to her mouth, jammed the lipstick lid back on, and pressed her hands against her thighs before risking a glance in the mirror at the man who'd stolen her dreams.

He was big. *Big* big. He had to stoop to get through the door of her dressing room.

"Mr. King, sir." Jace's voice was deep and smooth and impossible to ignore. But that didn't mean he could sing. "It's a real honor." He extended a hand to her father. Polite. That was something.

"Good to meet you, son," her father answered, shaking his hand and clapping Jace on the shoulder.

Tall *and* broad-shouldered. A weathered black leather jacket hugged the breadth of his shoulders and upper arms. As he pivoted on the heel of his boot, her gaze wandered south, revealing a perfect ass gloved in faded denim. She blew out a long, slow breath. Very nice packaging. *But* a great body didn't mean diddly when you were performing live, in front of an audience of thousands.

He glanced her way then. It was a glance, nothing really, but it was enough.

Oh hell.

Of course he was drop-dead gorgeous. Thick black hair, strong jaw, and a wicked, tempting grin on very nice lips. *Dammit.* He shook hands with her weasel manager, Steve, before giving her his full attention. A jolt of pure appreciation raced down her spine to the tips of her crystal-encrusted boots. *It's not fair. None of this is fair.* She fiddled with her heavy silver Tiffany charm bracelet and tucked a strand of hair behind her ear, too agitated to sit still.

Talented or not, it wouldn't matter. Not when he looked like that. Which was exactly why he was here. That face. That body. Jace Black and Emmy Lou King? His dark, dangerous good looks and her sister's golden sweetness? They'd make quite a pair onstage, singing her song…

Her song.

Her temper flared, quick and hot. She didn't give a damn what he looked like. Or if he had manners. He hadn't earned the right to her words, not by a long shot. And since he was a big boy, she'd take it upon herself to show him how tough this industry could be. Starting right here, right now.

His gaze locked with her reflection. "I can't tell you how… amazing it is to meet you, Miss King." That velvet voice was far too yummy. "I know every word to every song you've written." He needed to stop looking at her so she could stay pissed off and feisty.

But he didn't. And the longer he looked, the harder it was to overlook the way he was looking at her. Admiring her as a singer and songwriter was one thing. But right now, something told her he was appreciating more than her music.

Too bad she couldn't like him. At all.

She ignored her daddy's warning look and stood, turning to face Jace. Her momma raised her daughters with a deep under-standing of female charm and the power it could wield. With a dazzling smile, she shook the hand he offered, fully intending to use her powers for evil. But the brush of his calloused fingers against her palm threw off her concentration. It had been a long time since she'd been even slightly attracted to a man. But this time, there was nothing slight about what she was feeling. *No, no, no. Stay mad.* "Oh, I doubt that, *Chase.*"

"Jace," he said, grinning.

Oh hell, this is bad. That smile. She knew his name, but still… "Right." She bit into her lower lip, drawing his attention to her mouth.

His nostrils flared just enough to make her insides soften. Not the reaction she was hoping for. He cleared his throat and tore his eyes away, that square jaw of his clenched. Tight. That was a weakness of hers—a man's jaw muscle. Only two things made a man's jaw tick like that: anger or desire. And, right now, she was pretty sure Jace Black didn't have a thing in the world to be angry about. But she did. Big-time. The slow, liquid burn taking up residence deep in her stomach was beyond inconvenient.

Steve said something original like, "What did you think of the show?"

"Incredible. Y'all are even better live, I think, if that's possible," Jace said. "I'm a little starstruck—guess you can tell."

Was he? She couldn't tell—his hotness was getting in the way. No way she was going to let a pretty face and tingles lead her astray, not this time. "That's always nice to hear." If it was true.

"I want to thank you," Jace said to her father—of course. Only someone like Hank King could get a nobody reality star this sort of break. "I know how lucky I am to get this opportunity." He had *no* idea. His luck was her loss. Not that he could know or understand how much his words stung. His gaze returned to her when he said, "Your music has always meant a lot to me—a lot of folk, I'm sure. But your new song—"

"*My* song?" She couldn't take it anymore. His reminder lodged a sharp spike in her throat. "From what I hear, it's yours now." She ignored her daddy's disapproving frown and the panic on Steve's face. Like her temper was totally unexpected? They should have thought about that before bringing *him* in here seconds after crushing her hopes and dreams. The sting of tears infuriated her further. None of them would ever see her cry, dammit. Ever.

"It's a good song." From Jace's expression, he knew something wasn't right. But he kept right on talking. "It's one of the best things you've written. When I read it—" He broke off, shaking his head. "I'm still in shock I get to sing it."

"That makes two of us," she whispered. But at least he got it, about the song, anyway.

He hesitated, then stepped closer. If she'd had room, she'd have stepped back. Because Jace Black up close was even better—worse—than Jace Black at a distance. Good skin. Even, white teeth. And a holy-hell amazing scent that had her toes curling in her blinged-out ostrich-skin boots.

"I'm guessing I wasn't your first pick?" His gaze never left her face, waiting for an explanation.

She shrugged, wondering why she'd suddenly lost her ability to fire off something quick and biting.

"And you're not happy about it." He swallowed, the muscles in his throat working.

She heard him—she did. But the air between them was crackling something fierce and it was taking total concentration not to get lost in those light brown eyes. After spending the last two years avoiding men, she wasn't sure what, exactly, was happening. Only that she needed to keep her guard up and as much space as possible between them. Pretty words and even prettier packaging might have made it easier for him to worm his way in with other people, but it wouldn't work on her.

What did he want? Beyond singing her song, of course. She studied him openly, exploring his face and searching his gaze for some nervous flutter or guilty flush. Mickey's eyes tightened when he was hiding something. Just a little, mind you, but when she saw it now, she knew it was a red flag. And Uncle Tig... *No*. She swept thoughts of him aside.

But Jace?

The flash of pure, unfiltered male appreciation in those incredible eyes had her insides fluid and hot. If only they'd met under other circumstances...then it would be okay to get tangled up in bed somewhere—and have one hell of a time wearing each other out.

She swallowed, the images all too tempting. Too bad she had to hate him. "Don't you worry over me, *Jason*. I'm tough."

She wasn't feeling very tough at the moment. The sooner today was over, the sooner she was done with Jace Black. Which was better for his career, anyway. Even though she was pissed he'd taken her song, it wasn't in her to intentionally sink his career just to spite him. No, that was more her momma's MO—and she was nothing, *nothing*, like her momma.

Enough. She was tired and irritable and on the verge of coming undone. Her fans were waiting and they deserved the best her she could muster. She turned, glancing at her reflection and smoothing a wayward strand of long blond hair into place. Crystal chandelier earrings and a beyond-blinding crystal necklace—Momma was all about the bling—accented the plunging neckline of the concert's final costume change. The ultrafine black suede fringed dress felt like silk and was cut to perfection, clinging in all the right places.

From the tightness of Jace Black's jaw, he noticed.

Maybe she could muster up the energy to mess with him a little, for the hell of it. "Time to go meet the fans." A dazzling smile just for him. Yep, that floored him. "You are planning on tagging along, aren't you?"

His gaze narrowed—confused. Maybe even a little nervous.

"We weren't staying—" a man in the corner said.

"Well, that doesn't make any sense." She hooked her arm

through Jace's. A warm, very thickly muscled arm. Not that muscles mattered. "And who are you, anyway?"

"My manager. Luke Samuels," Jace said.

A weasel—like Steve. He had hair and was dressed better, but there was no denying the similarities: too eager to please and dewy with anxious sweat. "Miss King, it's an honor, a real honor—"

"Sure. But since you're here and all, might as well come meet some fans. Since our fans will be your fans soon enough," She beamed up at Jace again, but this time around, he looked downright suspicious. So he was smart, too?

"If you want—" Luke began.

"I do," she said, tugging Jace along. "Besides, you should meet Emmy, maybe get a few pics of the two of you." She didn't know why she was torturing herself. Seeing her sister and Jace together, paired up to sing her creation, wasn't going to improve her mood. But there was no going back now.

Smile in place, she walked into the hall to the sound of those fans that paid extra money for the backstage passes and meet and greet. "You know how to work the crowd, *Jake*?" she asked, emphasizing the name. His delicious grin told her he hadn't missed it. "Now's a good time to get some practice."

Now that she'd led him into the lion's den, he could fend for himself. With a wink, she let him go—but he followed closely—his scent still teasing her nostrils. Best to ignore him and focus on doing her job.

She enjoyed this part of it. This was what it was about—these people loved their music, loved them. Their enthusiasm was contagious and reassuring. As much as she'd like to deny it, she wanted to be liked, maybe even a little bit adored, the way her sister and brother were.

And Jace Black? Apparently, people knew who he was and, from the way they screamed his name, liked him.

If he wasn't stealing her song, she'd have considered being a fan, too. But he was, so she wasn't. Still, from that wicked grin to those beautiful eyes, there was a whole lot about Jace Black to like.

———————

Don't screw this up. Jace tore his gaze from Krystal King.

If he was smart, he'd hang back and watch the Kings work the room. He could only hope to handle a crowd like this with half their composure. When someone recognized him from *Next Top American Voice*, he got red-faced and tongue-tied. He wasn't sure why he'd gone along with Krystal—he just had. And now? He sure as hell hadn't expected to be recognized. Women were screaming his name, waving their cameras at him—some of them were *crying*. Crying?

It made him uncomfortable as hell. Here he was, blushing and stumbling over what to say, and these people knew his name, thought he was talented, wanted to touch him and get his autograph.

"Smile and wave," his little sister, Heather, had told him. "Pretend like you're having fun. Like you're going fishing." He wished she were here, poking fun at him, keeping him grounded. Since she wasn't, he'd follow her advice. He leaned into the crowd and smiled at the dozens of phones snapping pictures.

He didn't know if he'd ever get used to this. To him, it was overwhelming. Crazy. And "*part of the job*"—the Wheelhouse Records PR department had assured him.

Krystal's husky laughter set the hair on the back of his neck upright. Out of the corner of his eye, he saw her hugging a fan. The tenderness on her face was unexpected—and oh so real. He'd been warned about Krystal King. She was guarded. Check. Had a bit of a temper. Check. The spark in her green eyes confirmed that, too. No one had to tell him she was sexy as hell—he'd always known that. But nothing, *nothing*, had prepared him for how fiercely he'd respond to her.

To say he was attracted to the rebel King was an understatement.

But there was more to Krystal King than what the media, Wheelhouse Records, and his manager had to say. Anyone who could write the lyrics she did or create music that made him ache was more than cold and angry. Her music was her voice—weighted with real passion. The sort of emotion that had him wearing out Three Kings CDs in his old truck and singing along whenever one of their songs was on the radio. His favorite songs? The ones she wrote. Not only did he admire her music, but he admired how she handled the bad-girl persona and public character-bashing she was regularly subjected to. He never believed the tabloid headlines or talk show gossip, but if she was angry and guarded, she had plenty of reasons.

Was he one of them now?

The way she'd looked at him…he hadn't been prepared for that. He couldn't tell if she was all angry fire or sizzling from of a different kind of flame. Wishful thinking. There was no way someone like Krystal King was interested in him. All he knew was looking at her too long had him burning in a way that set warning flares off in his brain. Watching her now, blond hair hanging down her back and the fringes of her black minidress swinging around a pair of long, toned golden legs, had him wishing. Hard.

Bad idea. Don't screw this up.

"Jace." A woman grabbed his hand. "I love you. Your voice is perfect." Her cheeks were flushed. "You're perfect. I voted for you every night."

"I appreciate that. But I'm not perfect," he said, smiling. "I can promise you that."

"You are. You are. And I love you," the woman insisted, her grip tightening.

"And he loves you, too. You have to share him with the rest of us," Travis King, the only male member of the Three Kings, gently pried the woman's hand loose. "But he's real glad you came out to meet him. Got something for him to sign?"

The woman nodded and offered him a poster of the Three Kings. He glanced at Travis and signed the corner, feeling like a fraud. He handed it back, smiled, and moved on. "Thanks," he murmured to Travis.

"Clingers are hard," Travis said, signing and talking and not missing a step. "One woman jumped over the tape and into my arms. She was no lightweight, either. Pulled a muscle in my back and had to get one of them to help her back onto the other side of the tape."

Jace looked in the direction of Travis's nod. Three men and one woman wearing "King's Guard" shirts. *Clever.* "Security?" he asked, smiling in spite of himself.

"Always," he said. "I hear my sister roped you into sticking around?"

"Not sure how it happened," Jace confessed.

"Krystal has a way of getting what she wants." Travis laughed. "Come on, take a break in the greenroom. Then it's time for group pics and hanging with the money." He led Jace down the hall, all the while smiling and waving.

Krystal joined them, no sign of her earlier tension present. She sort of…glowed, happy and excited. "You two stand together too long and we might have a riot on our hands."

Was that a compliment? It sure as hell sounded like one.

"Just own it, man. Own it and enjoy every minute." Travis grinned. "You'll never have to sleep alone again."

"Travis, there are times I'm ashamed to call you my brother." Clearly, she didn't appreciate her brother's attitude. By the time they entered what resembled a small conference room, Krystal was back to being tense and quiet.

One wall was lined with mirrors and floor-to-ceiling folding screens. Jace was blindsided by the photographs hanging on the wall just inside. He wandered, reading autographs and shaking his head at the impressive display of talent that had visited the Chesapeake

Energy Arena before him. Willie Nelson. John Connelly. Loretta Lynn. And a smiling, younger Hank King. Here he was, a west Texas roughneck, surrounded by reminders of everything he wasn't. Sooner or later, the rest of the world would snap out of it and he'd be back on the grasshoppers, drilling for oil from dawn till dusk.

Might as well enjoy it.

On the opposite wall, a long table was covered with trays of pastries, fruit, and cheese. He almost took pictures for Heather— almost. She'd love to see this—the fancy sparkling water bottles in large glass bowls full of ice. Above that, three large televisions played, muted. The room and its occupants seemed to be on fast-forward, while he was stuck in slow motion.

He shook his hands out and did his best not to stand out.

His manager, Luke, was waiting with Mr. Zamora, looking almost as nervous as he felt. Jace had taken a gamble hiring him, but Luke had grown up in the business and knew all the right people. Like CiCi King. He had no idea Luke's mother and Hank King's wife played bunco together, but he suspected that was how he'd ended up here. His voice was only part of it—having the right connections sealed the deal. Still, standing against the wall as the room filled with the chart-breaking, award-winning King family and the entourage that cared for them had his insecurities kicking in. Sure he sang some, for himself—or at the bar in town. But he had nothing, *nothing*, like the talent in this room.

Sure, they talked and laughed just like normal folk—but there was nothing normal about these people. He didn't belong here. This was not his life. This wasn't real; it couldn't be.

It didn't help that Krystal kept glancing his way. Even standing there, talking to her brother, she radiated a sort of defiance that was hard to ignore. Hell, if he was honest with himself, he didn't want to ignore her. He'd prop himself up right here, against the wall, and look his fill if he could. No woman should look this beautiful in real life. But she was.

Her eyes narrowed, the slight tilt of her chin baiting him. Damn it all, he couldn't help it—he winked at her. And saw vibrant color bloom in her cheeks.

"Jace?" Luke waved him over.

Probably a better idea than staring at Krystal. With a sigh, he joined Luke. "What happens now?" His ears were buzzing from the noise of the crowd and the concert earlier.

"Hydrate, snack, relax until the Kings say it's go time," Steve Zamora said, tossing him a water bottle. "Through those doors, the big spenders are waiting. The kids mingle, rub elbows with the power-players or their die-hard fans, take pictures, then make their getaway. Thirty minutes, more if you're having a good time. Just waiting on Emmy."

"As always," Travis sounded off.

"I'm here, Travis, be nice." Emmy Lou King made her entrance. There was no other word for it. She sort of glided into the room, drawing every eye her way.

"You shake everyone's hand, Sis?" Travis asked, making a show of checking his nonexistent watch.

"Course you did, darlin'." Hank King draped an arm around his daughter's shoulders and steered her his way. "Emmy, this is Jace. Jace, Emmy. He'll be singing a duet on the next album."

Just when he thought he was getting a handle on things, he was knocked for another loop. First, he was standing in the room with a man he'd grown up idolizing—he'd stomped around in his daddy's boots and hat singing Hank King songs until his parents had hollered for him to stop. Now he was shaking hands with the man. Meeting Krystal. Then Travis. And now the enormity of what was happening hit him. He was singing a duet with Emmy Lou King.

Hell no, this wasn't his life.

"He's new, so try not to dazzle him too much," Travis said.

Jace chuckled. "Good to meet you, Miss King. Tonight has been…unreal." He broke off, shaking his head. They'd grown up in the public eye, so they had no idea how surreal this all was.

"Daddy has that effect on people." Emmy Lou did have an incredible smile.

Hank King looked at his daughter with true adoration. "I'm pretty sure he was talking about you three."

"Or maybe he's still thinking about the women crying over him. Oh, and the one holding on to him with a death grip. That gets to a man," Travis said, biting into an apple.

He might be a little overwhelmed by all the introductions, but the thing that "got to him" the most tonight had nothing to do with his career and everything to do with a woman. Since he'd walked into Krystal's dressing room and they'd locked eyes, he'd been trying to recover. That wasn't what tonight should have been about. But, damn it all, he had no idea how to make it stop.

"We need to get you some security." Luke frowned. "I'll get on that now." He was already typing something into his phone.

"The first time someone grabbed hold of me, I panicked," Emmy said.

"You were sixteen. Being grabbed by a stranger at sixteen is panic worthy," Krystal said. "Don't let it get to you, Jace. Keep on smiling and, if it gets too intense, flag your guy over."

His name had never sounded husky and sexy as hell until she'd said it. And she'd said it right this time. *Jace.* He cleared his throat and took a swig from his water bottle.

"Looks like you've already got your own fan base." Hank scratched his temple. "I don't know much about the show you won, but people seem to already know and love you. That's a good thing."

"Your sales are only as strong as your fan base," Emmy Lou said. "They won't buy you if they don't love you."

"Guess you all don't have much to worry about," he said. Three Kings were a fixture on the charts. And Emmy Lou King? She had an army of fans dedicated to her.

Emmy Lou shook her head. "I always worry. People are

watching everything I do or say—it's a lot of responsibility. I don't want to mess that up."

"That's why people adore her." Krystal's gaze flicked his way. "She's just as loyal to them as they are to her."

Seeing the sisters side by side was a surprise. The sisters were identical twins, but he had no problem telling them apart. Krystal was in her signature black, tight and seductive. Emmy was in pale pink and white, lacy and flowing. But the attire wasn't what did it. Maybe it was their mannerisms or their voices or the fact that one sister grabbed, and held, his interest.

Travis tossed his apple core into the trash. "And why she doesn't have much of a social life."

"*Social life?*" Krystal's smile hardened. "Like you? I'm pretty sure taking groupies back to your place doesn't count. Besides, they might not be a fan when the *party* is over."

Jace did his best not to laugh, but damn, she was good. Even her father was laughing.

"Beware." Travis leaned closer and pretended to whisper to him. "My sister has a razor-sharp tongue. Don't get on her bad side."

Jace had a sinking feeling he was already on her bad side—for reasons unknown.

"We really appreciate the time you've given us tonight, but we'll be heading out." Luke was shaking Steve Zamora's hand. "We'll wait for your call on the scheduling."

"Monday morning, our Austin studio, nine a.m. Right, Hank?" Steve asked. "Let's get this project in the works."

Krystal missed a step, teetering enough so that she braced one hand on the wall. It wasn't much—but it was enough for Jace. She didn't want him singing her song. The look on her face only confirmed it. She *really* didn't want him singing it. He had one choice: prove he'd do it right.

"Already set up," Hank replied, nodding his goodbye and disappearing through the door.

"Jace?" Luke asked.

Jace nodded. "I'll be there."

Steve nodded and followed Emmy Lou through the door.

Krystal finished off her water bottle and turned to face him. Those eyes of hers were blazing. If he'd had time, he'd have tried to talk to her, to calm her fears. It was one of those songs—important, special. He'd damn well make sure anyone listening to it knew it, too.

The first time he'd read the lyrics, he'd been drawn in. After the soul-crushing loss he'd suffered three years ago, "Ashes of My Heart" said all the things he'd never been able to. While he thought Krystal's soulful rasp was a better fit for the song than Emmy Lou, it wasn't his call. Something told him Krystal wouldn't care about his opinion of the lyrics or her voice. She'd think he was sucking up.

Still he couldn't help himself. "Meeting you…well, tonight's been my lucky night. I hope I'll see you again." And he meant it.

She shook her head. "Do you? Guess we'll see, *Jack*." Without another word, she followed her family into the next room.

Chapter 2

"Aw shit." Krystal heard Travis about the same time she slammed into his back.

"Travis?" she asked, pushing against her brother's back. "What's wrong?"

He turned to face her, his hands on her shoulders. "I need you to keep it together. There are witnesses." He shook his head. "Are you listening to me?"

"Not that you're making a lick of sense." She brushed his hands off her shoulders and walked around him, into the room of waiting VIPs. Now she needed to get her mind off Jace, his light brown eyes, and all the witty comebacks she should have tossed his way before leaving him tonight. Chances were she'd never see him again. She chewed on her lower lip, unexpectedly disappointed. No, it was good. Jace Black was bad news, period. She had no use for him.

Unless it was in the bedroom. She'd give him whatever he wanted there... Her body ached to do just that. Contrary to what the media said, she wasn't the sort of girl to have a fling. Still—she blew out a slow breath—that man had kicked her long-dormant libido into overdrive. Every time his heavy-lidded gaze drifted her way, the temperature seemed a good ten degrees hotter, and it had nothing to do with the anger she'd hoped to hold on to.

Someone bumped into her, their murmured apology a reality check. Here she was, in the middle of a room full of people, imagining Jace Black in her bed? Talk about bad timing. As Emmy pointed out, these were the folks who shelled out a minimum of twenty-five hundred dollars for tickets and deserved their attention. For that low, low price, they got floor seats, *free* drinks and food, an autographed picture, a picture with the band, and a guaranteed thirty minutes of cocktails and socializing. Some were true fans, others were big-spending friends of their family or the record label.

Unfortunately, her mother was also there. Because her momma *never* missed an opportunity to collect information that might benefit her later. Krystal had no illusions when it came to her mother: CiCi King was not a nice person. The only thing her mother cared about was keeping Three Kings on the charts and the front page. If there was a way to get Three Kings more press, she was all for it. Her big eyes, bright smile, and charming laugh might have the rest of the world fooled— Krystal's daddy included—but she knew the truth about the woman who'd birthed her.

That was one of the reasons she and her momma had a... *strained* relationship.

Travis hovered beside her. "You look way too calm. It's freaking me out."

What was wrong with him? Had her mother done something she didn't know about yet? Worse than handing off her song, that is? Somehow, deep down, she knew her mother had had a hand in that.

If she were the one singing the song with Jace, she wouldn't be upset. She paused then. Of course she'd be upset. Jace's talent was unknown. What if he couldn't sing? What if he butchered her song? No one knew what the song meant to her—but she did. Soulful eyes, glorious black hair, and a killer grin could only do so much on the charts.

"You sure you're okay?"

"I'm fine, Travis. Give me some room." But then she saw exactly why Travis was freaking out.

Mickey Graham.

The son of a bitch was here. Laughing with her mother and her friends. Drinking beer and rubbing elbows with *her* VIPs.

"What the hell? Why is he here?" she hissed, grabbing onto her brother's arm.

"There we go." He covered her hand with his. "I don't know why. But he is. And people are watching." He patted her hand.

Krystal stared down at the concrete floor, fighting for composure. Nausea and fury clamped down on her lungs and heart and stomach until it was hard to breathe at all. The last time she'd seen him in person had been at the Awards for Country Music. He'd had the nerve to try to get a picture together. That hadn't ended well—for her. Apparently stomping your heel so hard it punctured his boot and sent him to the ER for a few stitches in his foot was press-worthy.

Of course there was not a single picture of his hand on her ass. Or a sound bite of what he'd said about how he considered her voice her second-best asset and what, exactly, he wanted to do to what he considered her best asset. Not one. Instead, every radio show and entertainment magazine and TV show said Krystal King was out of control with bitterness over their breakup. And she was, but not the way they thought. He'd used her, publicly, mercilessly, and managed to turn her into the bad guy.

But it was her fault. She'd let him in. Believed him. Trusted him. Let her hunger for acceptance, for love, blind her. If she'd kept her guard up, he'd never have been in a position to launch the campaign that made him and almost destroyed her. She knew better. She'd been a fool. Again.

Now he was here, invading her world again. And it made her blood boil. Travis was right to warn her. An audience might just prevent her from totally losing it. But it didn't change the fact that he had no right to be here. How had he even gotten in without an invitation?

An invitation.

She knew. Damn it all, she knew. And the veins in her head began to throb so that she pressed her fingers to her temples. "Momma?" she asked, her throat so tight it hurt to say the word.

"She wouldn't, Krystal." But there was doubt in her brother's voice. "No…she wouldn't. Would she?" He glanced at her.

"She would. And you know it." Krystal cleared her throat. "And we're all going to find out why soon enough." Because her momma knew doing things in public, with an audience of highly connected people, was much harder to undo.

"What are you two talking about?" Her daddy hugged her into his side. "Should I be worried?"

"I would, if I were you," Travis said, nodding at their mother, her friends, and Mickey Graham.

"What the hell is that rat bastard doing here?" Her father's whisper was lined with outrage.

That's right. Her daddy loved her. He'd get offended on his little girl's behalf. But what would he do if he found out his wife was the one who'd invited the rat bastard?

"Keep your distance, Krystal," her daddy warned. "If you can't hear him, he can't say anything to set you off. And we both know the man lives to set you off."

"Fine by me," she replied.

And that's when their mother spotted them. For a split second, her mother looked at her. In that blip of time, there was no doubting her mother's excitement. Or her smug little smile of victory. Whatever CiCi King was up to, Krystal was at the center of it. And since Mickey Graham was smiling her way too, she was pretty sure she wasn't going to like it. Not one teeny tiny bit.

"Hank." Her mother held out one perfectly manicured hand, diamonds sparkling. "You look good, honey." She tipped her face so Daddy could give her the obligatory kiss on the cheek.

He did. "CiCi, ladies." He was all smiles for the women circled around his wife. But he turned his back to Mickey.

And Krystal loved him for it. So, so much.

"Wanna drink?" Travis asked, steering her away from her parents and Mickey.

"No," she said, arm tightening. "And don't you dare leave me."

He sighed. "Can we at least walk to the bar then, maybe talk to some people?"

"Sure." She followed his lead and gave it her all. If Mickey knew she was ready to pounce, he'd love it. And she didn't want to give him any more power over her. She was done with that. With him. At least, she thought she was. Until Momma dragged him back into the mix.

Forget about Mickey. She smiled and turned all her attention to the fans and their questions. No, she'd never been to Alaska, but she was sure it was mighty cold in the winter. Yes, she had seen the new Tom Cruise movie but thought it was overrated. She did still have her three-legged Chinese crested dog, Clementine—an Instagram star with a huge following. And she was excited about the tour and how well tickets were selling.

At the moment, she wished she were back home in the rolling Texas hill Country. She could use a little peace and quiet, a long ride on her blue mare, Maizy, and lots and lots of wide-open space.

"Bad news about Josephine and Frankie." His name badge said John. "Did you see it?"

Krystal had no idea what he was talking about. "Did I see what?"

"The arrest?" name badge Irma added. "Backstage, right before you went on."

She blinked. Arrest? Josephine and Frankie? They were the opening act, a sweet couple who played a unique blend of bluegrass, folk, and classic country. They were low drama, something that was a rarity in the music world. "No…no, I didn't see a thing."

"It was all over the news, livestreaming," John said, launching into the drugs found on their tour bus. Lots of drugs apparently.

"Who will be opening for you now?" Irma asked.

"No idea," she said, but as soon as the words were out, she knew. *No. No. No.* Her momma wouldn't do that to her. Mickey?

She couldn't. She was her mother, for crying out loud. The blood drained from her cheeks. Daddy wouldn't let it happen. Surely. Her gaze flew across the room, searching for him.

Mickey Graham winked at her. He winked. And he smiled that lopsided smile that used to turn her insides to goo. Now it made her want to throw up. Preferably on his favorite pair of calf-skin boots. He loved those damn boots.

"Pictures," Emmy said, leading her to the step and repeat wall. A drape of royal blue fabric, their logo—a cowboy hat with a hat-band covered in crowns—and "The Three Kings" repeating every few feet. She, Emmy Lou, and Travis took at least a dozen pics before she noticed her father. He was angry in his own way. He didn't scowl and yell. No, his cheeks turned red, his blue eyes nar-rowed to slits, and the muscle in his jaw locked tight. Like now.

When the cameras stopped and people started saying their goodbyes, she made her way to her daddy's side. "You okay?" she asked, smiling up at him.

"Krystal," Mickey Graham said, sneaking up from behind. Like the snake he was.

Her daddy squeezed her hand in warning.

She nodded, then sucked in a sharp breath. "Mickey," she said, refusing to look at him.

But her mother pulled him around, into her line of sight. "Oh, sugar, isn't it nice that Mickey stopped by to see the show?" her mother asked, watching her closely.

Krystal didn't say a word.

"I've always been a fan, you all know that." Mickey's aw-shucks twang was too much. How had she ever dated him? *Thought* she cared about him?

"Of course you have." Her mother was still smiling, still watch-ing. "It's been quite a night. First the whole drug bust, then Jace Black, and now, you."

Why was one of her mother's friends taking pictures? Holding up her cell phone. Was she recording this? Whatever. If she ever fully understood the way her mother's mind worked, then she'd have reason to worry.

"You know, that Jace Black is all over the place right now. Have you heard him sing?" her mother asked.

Mickey stiffened at the mention of Jace's name. Maybe she'd find a way to like Jace after all. He was sure as hell easy on the eyes. And, when he'd looked at her, there'd been nothing but warmth in his light brown gaze. Nothing like the way Mickey was looking at her now.

"Never heard of this Jace Black till tonight," Mickey said to her mother, his posture defensive. "My manager didn't mention anything about him when he said you'd called."

"Me call?" Her mother rested her hand on her surgically enhanced chest. "Sugar, I never make phone calls. I have people for that."

"Well, someone called," Mickey said, glancing her way. "I thought it was too good to be true—me opening for you all. Especially after what happened between us, Krystal." He stepped closer, his hand reaching for hers. "But at least I can say what I've wanted to say for a while now."

Krystal stared at her hand, caught in his clammy hold, and fought for control. Mickey couldn't be their opening act. And her mother—what was she thinking? The urge to scream at them, to yank her hands away, almost choked her. But she wouldn't cause a scene—no matter how perfectly her mother had laid her trap. Instead, she bit into her lip so hard she tasted blood.

Everyone was staring at her, waiting. Even Emmy Lou looked nervous. So she managed to say, "There's nothing to be said."

"Maybe not for you, Krystal, but I have a lot to say." His gaze bounced between her, her mother, and the camera.

She had to leave. Now. She gently but firmly withdrew her hand from his. "You'll have to find someone who wants to hear it." And she left the room as quickly and calmly as possible.

Acknowledgments

Anyone who knows me knows football isn't one of my passions. My research for Brock meant pestering friends, family, and countless hours studying JJ Watt's diet, training, and...JJ Watt (Brock's character inspiration). It's a tough job but I stuck with it. So, to those friends and family members who endured my questions, thank you!

Big thanks to my mighty writer tribe. From writer retreats, plotting sessions, Zoom meetings, late-night texts, and frequent pep talks, y'all keep me going when I'm pretty sure I have no business being a writer. Teri Wilson, Makenna Lee, Julia London, Molly Mirren, Jolene Navarro, Patricia W. Fisher, Jodi Thomas, Marcia King Gamble, Storm Navarro, Allison Collins, Frances Trilone, and Candace Havens—you guys are the best!

And, as always, to my cowboy and my kids and my parents: thank you for enduring hours of conversation about fictional people and supporting me while I follow my dreams.

About the Author

Sasha Summers grew up surrounded by books. Her passions have always been storytelling, romance, and travel—passions she's used to write more than twenty romance novels and novellas. Now a bestselling and award-winning author, Sasha continues to fall a little in love with each hero she writes. From easy-on-the-eyes cowboys, to sexy alpha male werewolves, to heroes of truly mythic proportions, she believes that everyone should have their happy ending—in fiction and real life.

Sasha lives in the suburbs of the Texas Hill Country with her amazing and supportive family and her beloved, grumpy cat, Gerard, the Feline Overlord. She looks forward to hearing from fans and hopes you'll visit her online at her Facebook page, Sasha Summers Author; on Twitter, @sashawrites; or at her website, sashasummers.com.

LUCKY CHANCE COWBOY

In Teri Anne Stanley's Big Chance Dog Rescue
series, everyone can find a forever home...

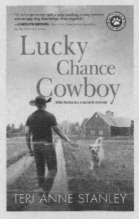

Emma Stern is barely scraping by while working and caring for her elderly
grandfather, but she's running out of options—and hope. The last thing
she has time for is Marcus Talbott and his flirting, sexy as he might be. But
every time Emma thinks she's reached the end of her rope, Marcus is there
to lend a hand. Maybe there's more to the handsome playboy after all...

**"A real page-turner with a sexy cowboy, a sassy
heroine, and a dog that brings them together."**

—Carolyn Brown, *New York Times* bestselling author,
for *Big Chance Cowboy*

more info about Sourcebooks's books and authors, visit:
sourcebooks.com

A COWBOY STATE OF MIND

The good folks of Creedence, Colorado get behind Creedence
Horse Rescue in a brilliant new series from Jennie Marts

Scarred and battered loner Zane Taylor has a gift with animals, partic-
ularly horses, but he's at a total loss when it comes to knowing how to
handle women. Bryn Callahan has a heart for strays, but she is through
trying to save damaged men. But when a chance encounter with a horse
headed for slaughter brings Zane and Bryn together, they find themselves
given a chance to save not just the horse, but maybe each other...

"Full of humor, heart, and hope...deliciously steamy."

—Joanne Kennedy, award-winning
author, *for Wish Upon a Cowboy*

For more info about Sourcebooks's books and authors, visit
sourcebooks.com